DOC SAVAGE

The Wild Adventures of Doc Savage

Please visit www.adventuresinbronze.com for
more information on titles you may have missed.

THE DESERT DEMONS
HORROR IN GOLD
THE INFERNAL BUDDHA
THE WAR MAKERS
THE ICE GENIUS
PHANTOM LAGOON
DEATH'S DOMAIN

(Don't miss another original Doc Savage adventure,
THE INFERNAL BUDDHA, coming soon.)

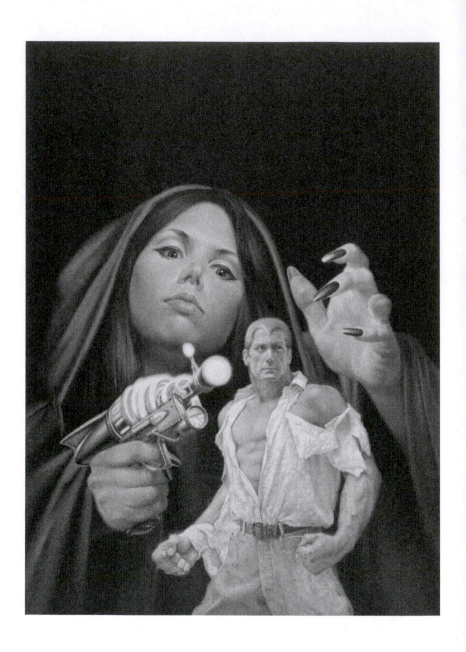

HORROR IN GOLD

A DOC SAVAGE ADVENTURE

BY WILL MURRAY & LESTER DENT
WRITING AS KENNETH ROBESON

COVER BY JOE DeVITO

ALTUS PRESS • 2011

First Edition — December 2011

DESIGNED BY

Matthew Moring/Altus Press

SPECIAL THANKS TO

*James Bama, Jerry Birenz, Condé Nast,
Jeff Deischer, Dafydd Neal Dyar, Jack Juka,
Jill Juka, Richard Kyle, Dave McDonnell, Matthew Moring,
Ray Riethmeier, Art Sippo, Anthony Tollin,
Charles Spain Verral, Jr., Howard Wright,
The State Historical Society of Missouri, and last but not least,
the Heirs of Norma Dent—James Valbracht,
Shirley Dungan and Doris Lime.*

Like us on Facebook: "The Wild Adventures of Doc Savage"

Printed in the United States of America

Set in Caslon.

For John L. Nanovic, who rejected
this premise back in 1935,

so that it could become a reality
in the 21st century!

Horror in Gold

Table of Contents

Chapter I

PASSING STRANGE

COINCIDENCE IS AN intangible thing. Many strange and inexplicable events for which science cannot account are often dismissed as such. If a phenomenon cannot be reproduced in a laboratory, insist some learned men of science, pending a better explanation it must be charged to common coincidence.

The horror that visited Seventh Avenue on a brutally hot August day was no coincidence. It smacked of the uncanny, the unexplainable, the coincidental. But it was not. It was merely the start of a grisly chain of events that would shake a city to its foundations.

It began this way:

The panhandler was going fishing.

He carried a flat length of iron attached to a stout string of twine. The iron slat was smeared with axle grease, surreptitiously purloined from a dead-storage garage, where vehicles are housed for extended periods of time.

The simple contraption was a fishing rod and line of sorts. The axle grease was what passed for a fish hook in the tramp's determined undertaking.

He walked briskly down Seventh Avenue, oblivious to hurried passersby. Passing humanity ignored the tramp in turn, relieved not to be accosted for a handout. Hoboes of this specimen's class freely ranged the island of Manhattan, prowling for nickels.

No one—least of all the indigent one—suspected that he was destined to be at the center of the horror to come.

1

This panhandler—he surely possessed a name but it was never discovered—went off not in search of nickels, but something more valuable.

Coming to a storm drain, the nameless one squatted down, planting the much-patched seat of his pants on the concrete curbstone and his cracked shoes on either side of the sewer grate.

He peered down between the dull steel bars.

There had been a rain the day before, and gutter runoff had poured into the drain. Some leftover rain water stood down below. It glimmered. Other glints shone, as well. One in particular caught the tramp's narrowing eye. Had anyone been paying close attention, they might have deduced that the tramp had earlier in the day spied the interesting glint, was only now returning with suitable equipment for fishing it out of the storm drain.

Into a space between the bars, he lowered the axle-grease-smeared length of iron strapping. It dropped all the way into the standing water below, splashing.

Unshaven face working in lines of comical concentration, the tramp jiggered his rather unwieldy contraption. One eye shut often, as he squint-sighted with the other.

It was evident that the panhandler was attempting to make contact with the interesting glint in hopes that the object that shone so intriguingly would adhere to the sticky slat.

Many times he muttered imprecations of disgust and frustration. Once the tramp hauled up his makeshift arrangement of metal and twine, threw it off to one side, and stamped around in agitated frustration.

"Blankety-blank!" he growled. Or words to that effect.

This caught the notice of pedestrians. One summoned a traffic cop. The cop bustled up, took hold of the nameless individual by the scruff of his greasy collar and demanded, "State your business, bum."

The tramp had had dealings with New York's Finest in the

past. He knew how to behave when confronted by authority. He immediately assumed a docile demeanor.

"I'm only fishing," he bleated.

The cop lost his belligerent tone.

"What's that again?"

"Said I was fishing. Haven't got a nibble so far," explained the homeless one.

The cop noticed the storm drain then. His angular Irish face softened.

"Pal, I know times are tough, but even if you do get a bite off something down there, it won't be fit for eating. You'd get ptomaine poisoning, or worse."

"I'm not trolling for fish," snapped the tramp. "And I'm not touched, either. People sometimes lose coins. They roll into the grate. Fair game, see?"

The cop was young. A probationary patrolman, he had not been on the beat very long, for his heart still retained some soft spots. He relented.

"Scrounging for pennies, huh?" he said, releasing the freeloader. "As long as you don't disturb the peace, I'll let you go about your business."

"Thank you," said the other with injured dignity.

And as the patrolman took a step backward, the tramp applied the seat of his pants once more to the curb and lowered his greasy contrivance into the storm drain anew.

There ensued the same prolonged and frustrating ritual of dropping and maneuvering the axle-grease-smeared bit of iron. From time to time, the strapping clinked against dim objects below, some of which might have been lost pennies. The clink that excited the industrious panhandler sounded too weighty to be a penny, however.

After a while, the cop grew bored and returned to his rounds. He missed what happened next, although he had a ringside seat to the horror which followed.

AFTER fully an hour of stubborn diligence, the tramp grew excited. With extreme care, he raised his device gingerly, taking greater caution when the narrow slat of iron started coming up through the grate.

When it cleared without mischance, the industrious panhandler peeled off an object that clung to the axle grease. It was clotted with a leafy muck. The tramp seized upon it eagerly, wiping it on a sweat-soiled trouser leg.

Late afternoon sunlight made the spaces between his grimy, grasping fingers gleam. It was not the reddish gleam of a penny, however. Nor the silver of a coin of higher denomination. The gleam was warm, yellowish.

He grew very furtive in his actions now. He kept his back to passing pedestrians, his shoulders hunched protectively.

This had the opposite effect than intended.

Spying this, a passing vagrant scuttled up and inquired, "Whatcha got there, pal o' mine?"

"Go away," the nameless one growled.

This only further excited the vagrant's curiosity bump. He reached around to snatch at the unrecognizable object in the other's hand.

The tramp, who had been in the act of cleaning off his prize, now did something only a desperately hungry man would do. He took the unsavory object into his mouth.

Mouth shut, the tramp started off. The other followed for a block or two, hectoring and cajoling.

"Don't you wanna share with a pal?" the vagrant repeated. "I'd share with you, buddy. You know I would."

The panhandler kept his mouth locked up tight and his eyes fixed on the way ahead. He gave his persistent tormentor no acknowledgement whatsoever.

Seeing that he would get no satisfaction, the buttinski vagrant shoved his gesticulating hands into his pockets and went off in search of less troublesome opportunities.

By doing so, he missed the real excitement. He also missed

the horror. Perhaps that was a good thing. Horror is no antidote to curiosity.

Bowling down Seventh Avenue and its fashionable shops, the closed-mouthed panhandler happened to pass his social opposite.

It was a youth of perhaps college age, attired for a night on the town. His lean, well-knit form was encased in a tuxedo of the soup-and-fish variety. It was early in the afternoon for such attire, but the young man's jaunty manner suggested he might be a bit of a show-off.

The well-dressed swell's sartorial ensemble was crowned by an elegant topper. This drew a rather envious glance from the tramp. The one with the topper deigned not to return that glance. And so missed out on the last sight of his brief but privileged existence.

At the exact moment the two men passed, the horror struck.

There was no sound, no feeling in the air that presaged the event that would rule the scareheads of the evening newspapers. Nothing to foreshadow the headlines the newsboys would within the hour be bawling at the tops of their voices.

At the precise moment the two came to pass one another, their heads exploded.

AS phenomena went, this was a simultaneous event. No noticeable interval separated the cranial detonations. The ugly sound registered upon the ear as one sound, not two. This would later prove to be significant.

The panhandler's head simply exploded outward like a watermelon which had harbored a hand grenade.

The other's demise was only slightly less violent.

His face seemed to erupt into a red ruin, after which the fashionable young swell pitched forward in death, his body attempting to continue along in its automatic stride for another two steps. By that time, what remained of his head hinged backward like a puppet whose top string had broken.

Force of the explosion sent his topper sailing into the sky. When it tumbled down again, punctuated with what resembled ragged moth holes, the two chance passersby were heaped on the hot concrete sidewalk, minus their heads. Around them was a profusion of scarlet matter suggestive of the floor of a butcher's shop. It steamed.

In a macabre irony, the topper happened to settle back to earth on the raw stump of the headless tramp, shielding it from the shocked eyes of a gathering crowd.

The suddenness of the event stunned those who witnessed it. For the length of the block, people froze. Shock gave way to horror, and horror turned inward.

Witnesses began running in fear of their lives. An unknown calamity had visited two persons engaged in nothing more unusual than a stroll down Seventh Avenue. They were naturally afraid they were to be the next victims. No one wanted to be next. So they ran.

The pell-mell confusion brought the soft-hearted probationary patrolman running from traffic watch. He skidded to a stop, took one look at the fashionable young man-about-town and the topper-hatted tramp and jumped to an instantaneous if erroneous conclusion.

There had been an altercation between the two. A fight had ensued over the topper. The pair had murdered one another.

When he lifted the high hat and saw the stump, the cop was compelled to revise that opinion drastically.

By that time he was up on his feet, blowing shrilly on his police whistle and going red in the face as a result—and fervently wishing that he had rousted the now-deceased tramp from his beat. He did not understand what had happened, but he fell victim to a common pang, guilt.

"If I'd've only done my job," he moaned between whistle blasts, "none of this might have happened."

He did not know that nothing could have been further from the truth.

Nor did he suspect that this was only the beginning of something that was destined to rock Manhattan and, quite possibly, shake the world.

And it would bring the most remarkable man who ever lived in conflict with one of the most terrible menaces ever to confront humanity.

Chapter II

THE MAIMED WOMAN

THE FIRST TO arrive on the scene was the police sergeant who was the probationary patrolman's immediate superior.

He took one look at the decapitated dead men and blew startled words out of his mouth. "Mother Machree—it's Mulligan Stew!"

"Who? I mean which?" asked the befuddled beat cop.

The sergeant pointed a finger at the dead tramp. "I recognize that one by the scuff of his Brogans. He's Mulligan Stew. They call him that down at the railroad yard hobo camps, on account of that was all he would eat. Nobody knew his real name."

The sergeant knelt beside the other corpse. Gingerly fishing through the man's trouser pockets, he excavated a billfold.

Opening this, the sergeant muttered, "Says here this one's name is Richmond Carter van Delft."

"Sounds important."

"Dressed like that, he is." The sergeant stood up, regarded the two dead men and said, "If this doesn't have all the trimmings of a matter for Doc Savage."

"I've heard of him," the other mused, tugging one ear thoughtfully.

The sergeant favored the beat cop with a bilious eye.

"Heard? You say you've heard of Doc Savage?"

"Sure. Everyone has—haven't they?"

"You make him sound like a rumor."

The cop looked injured. "I've never met him, or seen the boyo."

"I have. Once you get a good look at the Man of Bronze, you never forget it. They call Savage that. And a whole lot of other things besides. They say he's a regular wonder man."

The sergeant regarded the unhappy dead again.

"Yes, sir," he said, rubbing a pugnacious jaw. "This looks like exactly the kind of pie Doc Savage is likely to stick his finger into."

"Are you going to call him, Sarge?"

The sergeant shook his big head. "That'll be up to the commissioner. Doc Savage doesn't get involved in anything small." He gave his gunbelt a resolute hitch. "Come on. Let's collect ourselves some statements."

They began interrogating witnesses.

It was not easy. A good many had scattered in fright. Emboldened perhaps by the shocked lull that followed the dual skull-splitting event, a few had begun creeping back. Curiosity is a powerful instinct.

In his search, the sergeant discovered a woman in distress.

She was trying to hail a taxicab. Her uplifted hand was swathed in a gay kerchief. The kerchief was pale violet, but in spots it was almost a royal purple. Crimson seepage from this ran down her upraised wrist.

Her other arm cradled a cumbersome newsreel camera, whose hardwood tripod legs were neatly folded together.

Gawking, the sergeant started toward the woman.

She caught sight of him, and her head snapped about. Her eyes fell upon his blue uniform. They blazed up, and their color was an unusual and luminous lavender.

Balanced on the curbstone, the woman lifted her injured hand in the direction of traffic.

A prowling cab jerked to the curb and, before the police

officer could do anything further, the violet-eyed woman ducked inside and was whisked away.

The sergeant thought better of following her. A woman with an injured hand in New York was normally worthy of investigation. But he had two grisly corpses on his hands. This could wait. The officer turned his attention to the more pressing matter.

Such witnesses as were found proved not terribly helpful. But they tried. Two persons were discovered who had been in the vicinity at the time the two men met their bizarre fate. They gave statements.

"I heard a sound," volunteered one. "I turned just as they keeled over."

"What else did you observe?" the sergeant demanded.

"I saw them hit the pavement. They were dead." He looked a little sick; then the look went away. "Their heads were... gone."

The other concurred with this testimony. He had nothing to add, other than that he too had detected an unusual noise before the terrible thing transpired.

Both mopped their faces with sodden handkerchiefs. A heat wave had seized Manhattan in its searing grip. The pavement cooked shod feet like hams in an oven. Inhaled air stifled the lungs.

"That sound you heard," the sergeant pressed. "Was it a boom?"

"No."

"Did it sound like a gunshot?"

Both witnesses agreed that the sound was not that of a report produced by a conventional firearm discharging.

"It was soft, not sharp," offered one man.

"Soft, you say?"

"Mushy," the first witness insisted.

"Dull," said the other.

The sergeant had to shake his head to keep perspiration rivulets out of his eyes. The back of his uniform blouse was sticking to his muscular back. He pressed on.

"Did you see anything suspicious? Such as a passing auto?"

Neither man had seen anything suspicious before or after the two men fell dead without their heads. The sergeant took down their names, addresses, and other particulars, then sent them on their way.

The two bluecoats were waiting for the morgue wagon to arrive when something more interesting came along.

A GUNMETAL gray roadster pulled up to the curb. It arrived in such silence it was at first not noticed. Only when the engine died, did the sudden absence of mutter that followed register on the ear that a moment before a powerful engine had filled the air with its quiet vibration.

The sergeant hurried over. He started to say, "Hey, you can't park there!" when the driver of the quietly impressive machine stepped out.

The sergeant's eyes flicked to the license plate. It was a low number tag. Only high officials were issued such.

The tag read: DOC-1.

So it was no great shock when the big bronze man heaved into view.

He was a giant. That much was immediately apparent. Towering over the machine, he looked considerably taller than six feet in height. But when he stepped away from the machine, he seemed to shrink to more reasonable proportions.

"Mr. Savage!" the sergeant gulped.

"That's him? That's Doc Savage?" asked the beat cop in an awestruck tone.

The sergeant nodded firmly. "That," he said, "is Doc Savage."

If metal could be imbued with animation, Doc Savage might have been cast out of some flexible alloy of bronze. Even his hair, which lay close to his skull, seemed to have been hammered out of a substance perhaps a shade darker than his metallic skin. His entire body flowed with a graceful power. Tendons and cords stood out about his neck and the backs of his hands. Due to the symmetry of his physical build, there was the illusion that he seemed nearer the size of an average man. His imposing form was clothed in a tasteful suit whose subdued browns blended with his unusual skin tones.

Doc Savage strode up to the two bodies. His eyes fell upon them. They were perhaps the most remarkable feature about him. Strange orbs, like pools of golden flakes ever stirred by restless eddies and currents, and radiating a compelling force.

When they fell upon the headless dead, they grew animated.

A sound filled the air. An eerie trilling.

It was a tiny sound, that trilling. Low and exotic, yet difficult to describe, it might have been made by a wind coursing through a naked forest, or the cry of some exotic feathered avian of the tropics. Tuneless, inspiring, it was awesome in its undulating cadence. The sound possessed the ventriloquial property of coming from no specific spot.

It died without revealing its source.

The beat cop had the thought that the trilling had emanated from the big bronze man, but there was no indication of that in the latter's metallic features. Doc's parted lips had not moved.

"May I?" Doc asked the sergeant in a voice that was remindful of the now-silent roadster engine. It was deceptively quiet, yet there was a carrying power that arrested the attention.

"Be my guest, sir. We are waiting on the morgue wagon."

The bronze giant knelt, examined the bodies without touching them, and his metallic features became hard. Curiously, he seemed not to perspire.

Reaching his feet, Doc examined the surroundings, paying particular attention to the side of the nearest building. A parked car was also examined. If he found anything out of the ordinary, he did not show it.

"Witnesses say they heard a dull explosion," the sergeant supplied. "And these two keeled over dead. The tramp is called

Mulligan Stew. The high-hat gent is Richmond Carter van Delft. How they got acquainted, we don't know."

"An explosion would produce shrapnel," Doc commented.

"Sure."

"There are no marks of flying metal on the building sides," the bronze man pointed out. "Nor any bullet smears."

The sergeant took a look for himself. "So there aren't, so there aren't," he said, rocking back on his heels. "What do you make of it, Mr. Savage?"

Whatever the big bronze man made of it, he kept his thoughts to himself. He continued his examination of the scene.

The tramp had suffered the worst mutilation. His head was completely gone. Only a raw stump from which neck bone protruded remained.

The other man had the front portion of his head blown off. Normally, this would have been accomplished by firing into the back of the head with a mushrooming soft lead bullet.

With care, the bronze giant lifted the ruined surviving half of the rich man's head and felt around slick scalp hair for a bullet hole.

He found none. This brought into the air the strange trilling sound again. It had a faintly puzzled quality this time.

"I think he's doing that," the beat cop confided to his superior.

The sergeant nudged him in the ribs for silence.

The bronze man now made a circuit of the neighborhood. He circumnavigated the block where the bodies lay. Finding nothing noteworthy, he crossed the street to the next block.

There, he knelt at a dark patch on the pavement.

With a fresh handkerchief, Doc Savage lifted a long object that had lain in a pool of scarlet.

When he brought this back to the two bodies, Doc opened the handkerchief and the sergeant and his beat cop got a good look at what lay in the bronze man's handkerchief.

It was a human finger.

Or rather the top two joints of one. It was a very slim finger, distinctly feminine.

"Where did you find that?" the sergeant blurted.

"Next block," replied the bronze man.

Doc fell to examining the hands of the two dead men. They had retained the customary complement of fingers. None were missing.

This produced a spasm of cap-tilting and head-scratching on the parts of the two police officers. Their sweat-smeared faces assumed baffled expressions.

The sergeant piped up. "Say, I saw a woman hailing a cab up that next block. Had her hand bundled up. Looked to be bleeding to me. Maybe that's her finger you have there."

"Description?" requested Doc.

The sergeant considered. "Average build. Hard to say her age. But she had the strangest eyes—they looked like violets. Only caught a glimpse of her face, and those electric eyes stayed with me. The rest didn't register."

"What make of cab?" asked Doc Savage.

"It was a Blue Eagle. Yeah, a Blue Eagle taxi. I took note of the tag number."

"Endeavor to discover where the woman was taken," the bronze man instructed.

"Right away," said the sergeant, who hurried off to a call box.

The beat cop went in tow, muttering, "He gives orders like he's the commissioner himself."

"Savage has an honorary police commission, rank of inspector."

"Oh."

"When he tells you to jump, you jump."

"The big guy has that much drag?" asked the curious cop.

"The big guy can tell the commissioner where to park his wagon," the sergeant boasted.

"That's a lot of drag," the beat cop agreed fervently.

THE bloody-handed woman, it developed, had been dropped off in Greenwich Village. The street named was a residential one, not far from the placid banks of the Hudson River.

Doc Savage received this datum with no expression. His features might have been cast in solid metal. Only his flaky metallic eyes betrayed a boiling restlessness.

"Thank you," he said. The sergeant beamed proudly. He would have quite a story to tell the missus over supper.

The morgue wagon arrived about that time. The bodies were loaded and conveyed to the office of the medical examiner for the borough of Manhattan.

Doc Savage told the M.E., "I would prefer to perform the autopsies myself."

"Of course," the M.E. said deferentially.

"Expect me shortly."

With that, the bronze man reclaimed the gunmetal gray roadster and took his departure.

His going was as soundless as his coming.

Chapter III

THE INCREDIBLE THING

DOC SAVAGE DROVE south through the Chelsea district of New York, a busy place of brick warehouses, populated by stevedores and dockworkers who toiled at the nearby shipyards, and into picturesque Greenwich Village.

The sidewalks and stoops were packed with sweltering humanity seeking relief from the oppressive heat. Hardly a face was not shiny with flowing perspiration. In the parlance of native New Yorkers, the weather was murder.

The Village is a relatively small section of the metropolis tucked away in lower Manhattan, and the bronze man tooled his machine along its picturesque streets methodically, golden eyes roving alertly.

From time to time, Doc pulled over and knelt at curbs and sidewalks, examining dark stains. None held his attention for very long. The bronze giant seemed to be seeking a definite type of stain.

It might be remarked that Doc Savage's orbs possessed an uncanny visual acuity. Little escaped their eagle-eyed probing. It was as if they were imbued with sight far beyond that of ordinary mortals.

Indeed, this was the case. For Doc Savage was the product of an upbringing unique in human history. He had been raised from the cradle by a remarkable succession of scientists and experts in other practical lines. The goal of this program was to produce a kind of superman, one versed in as many skills as it was possible for the human mind to master. That the scientists and other knowledgeable men had succeeded was evidenced by the myriad accomplishments of Doc, who was still yet a young man.

His Herculean physique and great strength were also the result of his upbringing—although nature had played a hand in that as well.

Long hours did the bronze man expend in sharpening his senses. And it showed now when a brief trilling filled the air about him.

Doc cut the roadster's wheels sharply, braked, and bounded from the driver's seat.

He alighted on a short sleepy street of brownstone homes of the type that were common in Greenwich Village. Tulips were blooming in window boxes. Passersby were few. Somewhere a hydrant, opened by idle children, splashed and bubbled ceaselessly.

A solitary drop of blood, still drying, lay on the sidewalk. Someone had chanced to step on it, blurring its outlines somewhat.

Doc looked around, restive eyes probing.

Another drop lay a few yards away. It led to still another. Doc picked up the seepage trail, followed it.

The person who had left it had evidently quitted the taxi some distance from her intended destination, for Doc walked half a block down and one block over until he spied another crimson splash on the broad step leading to an ancient brownstone building.

There was only one name on the doorbell:

MERLIN

Doc depressed the bell button.

THE result was remarkable.

Perhaps the ringing of the bell and what transpired next were not connected. But in the moment, it seemed even to the normally unsuperstitious Man of Bronze that one action led to the other.

Behind him, Doc Savage's parked roadster gave up a strange sound.

He turned sharply. Doc's reflexes were amazingly swift, but he failed to witness the very beginning of the phenomenon. What he did see caused a flicker of emotion to warp his ordinarily impassive features.

The rear portion of the roadster was no more. It had vanished—evaporated like so much dry ice. The main portion, and most of the back seat, remained intact. But it was if some prowling thing from an adjacent dimension has consumed the rest—tires, wheels fenders, bumpers, and all.

For once, the bronze man stood immobile, too stunned to trill. Even the animated whirling of his aureate orbs stopped cold, arrested as though frozen.

A flicker of shadow caused Doc to look up. A remarkable sight greeted his gaze.

The trunk lid was poised about twenty feet in the air, evidently propelled there by some strange force. Gravity yanked it down again.

It struck the pavement with a disconsolate *clang!*

Doc pitched to the sidewalk, intending to investigate. Then a scream sounded high above.

Keen ears told him the outcry came from high in the brownstone. Wheeling, Doc catapulted up the stoop. This time he did not bother with the bell button. Or even the door.

There was a partly open bay window and Doc got to it, jammed it upward. The bronze man eased into the aperture like a great jungle cat. His soundlessness was uncanny.

Doc found himself in a parlor of thrifty but comfortable furnishings. Lace curtains spiderwebbed the windows. The furnishings were substantial, and upholstered in damask.

Through this and into the central hall, he pitched. A long

staircase led upward. Doc mounted it, taking three stairs at a time, yet hardly making any more noise than a tawny tiger.

On the second-floor landing, the bronze man reconnoitered the rooms at a glance. No sign of habitation. Vague odors reaching his sensitive nostrils told him nothing.

Another scream shrilled. Higher above!

Doc reached the attic regions before the echoes had quite died out. There was only one room. It was a combination study and photography studio of some type. Cameras lay about on worktables. A big motion-picture camera stood on a wooden tripod near the only window.

And although the sound of a woman screaming had been clearly heard, no one occupied the single room. Nor was anyone present in the adjoining darkroom.

Doc checked closets. Nothing. He wrenched up the single window. It yielded after an effort, proving that it had not been opened recently, the sash wood having expanded in the summer heat.

For a moment, the bronze man's trilling pulsed faintly. It sounded faintly baffled.

Doc moved down the stairs and made a thorough search of all rooms. He found no one.

No trace of puzzlement showed on his bronze lineaments. But puzzled he was. It showed in his stealthy careful searching of each room. He discovered no personal effects to mark who dwelled here. There were darker patches on some painted and wallpapered walls, indicating that long-hung pictures had been recently removed, as if the place had been vacated of all but essential furnishings.

Using a first-floor telephone, Doc called a number. Presently, a voice answered.

"Monk, you and Ham meet me at this address in the Village." Doc gave the street number. "Is Long Tom there with you?"

A squeaky voice said, "No. He's off puttering in that gopher hole he calls a laboratory."

"Call him. Have Long Tom join us as well."

"Gotcha, Doc."

LONG TOM was the first to arrive. He drove a Blue Bird racer that belonged on an Indianapolis race track. Few meeting him would have taken him for one of Doc Savage's companions in adventure. Slender, undersized, his complexion none too healthy, he was known worldwide as Major Thomas J. Roberts, an electrical genius of the first rank. The nickname "Long Tom" had been the result of a wartime maneuver wherein he had made extraordinary use of an old "long tom" privateer cannon.

He found the bronze man studying his ruined roadster with inscrutable mien. Long Tom whistled through his big front teeth. They were remarkable. Both were of shiny gold. He had lost the original ivories in a fight long ago. On the rare occasion where a foe knocked them loose, the pallid electrical genius would wrap them in a handkerchief and carry them around, not replacing the metal incisors until he had extracted satisfaction from the offending party. It had been a long time since that had happened. Long Tom was tough.

"Bomb blast?" he asked in a voice that was naturally querulous.

The bronze man shook his head in the negative.

Long Tom Roberts was without question the finest electrical expert since the late Thomas A. Edison. He was without peer in his field, except for one living man. That man was Doc Savage.

Yet the bronze man turned to his aide and asked quietly, "What does this suggest to you?"

Long Tom studied the roadster's ruined rump. There was no sign of melting, or fire, or of any chemical combustion. The roadster might have exploded, but that did not quite account for the way the machine's back end hung low to the heat-softened asphalt.

"Was there an explosion?" Long Tom asked, rubbing his pale

chin.

"Not exactly. There was a noise. One might describe it as a whump, or a whoosh of a sound."

"Damn strange," Long Tom muttered thoughtfully.

"No opinion?" queried Doc.

"One. But it's fantastic."

"Go ahead," prompted Doc. "Let's hear it."

"It suggests atomic disintegration."

"That was my thought. But by what agency? There was no flash of light or other phenomena. No visible ray. No electrical hum, or generator whine."

"And why was only the trunk section affected?"

"That," agreed Doc, "is a question."

ANOTHER machine pulled up presently. This was an elegant town car. The driver who stepped forth was attired in splendid afternoon garb. His impeccable clothes were set off by a slim dark cane of expensive wood. He possessed dark piercing eyes and the wide mobile mouth of a man who made his living by speechifying.

From the rear emerged a squat figure who could pass for the likable caveman from the prehistoric cartoon strip. Rusty bristles furred his apish physique. He grinned so widely his mouth yawned like a cavern of blunt teeth.

They were two more of Doc's assistants. Brigadier General Theodore Marley "Ham" Brooks happened to be one of the sharpest legal minds in the country, and he dressed the part.

His companion had been born Andrew Blodgett Mayfair, but inevitably he was known as Monk. Although built along the lines of a bull gorilla, he was a chemist with a list of discoveries longer than his arms, which nearly reached his knees. Industrial firms on numerous occasions had made him young fortunes for chemical formulas which they found invaluable. Monk maintained a laboratory in a penthouse atop one of the tallest buildings in the Wall Street sector downtown.

"Hiya, Doc," said Monk, his voice a childlike squeak. "Me and my chauffeur got here as fast as we could."

"I am not your chauffeur!" Ham snapped waspishly. "This happens to be my personal town car."

Monk grinned amiably. "Did you drive, my good man?"

"Yes, of course I did!" retorted Ham. "What of it, ape?"

"Well, since I was sittin' in back, that makes you my chauffeur, don't it?"

"A mere detail!" sputtered Ham.

The incongruous pair were as unlikely-looking friends as anyone could imagine. Right now, an onlooker might well predict violence. Monk balled up his furry fists as Ham waved his dark cane around as if picking out a soft spot in the hairy chemist's blunt bullet of a skull. The two glared at one another.

Above all material things, these two loved excitement and adventure. To get into a fight, Monk would run a mile, and Ham would probably be close at his heels. That explained, in part, their membership in Doc Savage's little group of five aides. Those five led an existence more perilous, perhaps, than any other group of men of like number. Around Doc, there was always danger, it seemed.

Too, there was a fascination about Doc Savage, an attraction that drew men to his remarkable personality. Possibly it was the fabulous things he did. No doubt much of it was due to his amazing physique and his undeniably genuine modesty. That helped no little to hold Doc's group of five together.

Abruptly, Monk and Ham noticed that Doc Savage was paying them no heed. They broke off squabbling as if their quarrel were entirely forgotten.

Monk studied the ruin of a roadster. "What done that?"

Ham Brooks unsheathed his sword cane—for the innocent walking stick was precisely that—and poked the tip at a protruding dribble of galvanized steel.

"Acid," he pronounced.

"Stick to your torts, shyster!" Monk scoffed. "And leave the retorts to them that studied 'em. No acid ever found in nature or cooked up by man did *that.*"

"Then what did, Alley Oop?" sneered Ham.

Monk scratched his nubbin head. The expression on his homely features was a picture of simian perplexity.

"Search me," he admitted at last.

A police radio car pulled up at that point. Doc Savage attempted to make explanations to the bluecoat who alighted. It was a futile effort.

"You're saying the minute you turned your back, this happened?" the cop demanded.

"I can offer no other explanation," Doc vouchsafed.

"Well, neither can I! I'll have to impound your vehicle."

"I would like to examine it later," said Doc, not wishing to give argument under the peculiar circumstances.

An elderly man in his shirtsleeves came scuttling from across the street.

"I'm the one that called this in," he volunteered, waving a battered straw hat excitedly. He appeared eager to share something.

"Let's have your story," the cop invited.

The elderly man told it succinctly. He happened to be staring out his window, watching pigeons peck at breadcrumbs left on the windowsill, when Doc Savage had arrived.

"That's when I noticed something peculiar," he stated.

The cop started writing it all down. "You saw what happened to the automobile?"

"Not that part. But when this big fellow went to the door, I saw someone point a big camera of a thing out the top-floor window—point it down to the street."

"Describe this person," Doc directed.

The oldster employed his summer hat to fan his excited features.

"Looked like a woman," he clipped out. "Leastways, I think

so on account a woman screamed around that time. Then I heard the funny sound. And when I looked down, the back end of that fancy car wasn't there anymore."

"A woman did scream," Doc offered. "But after a thorough search, I found no one inside."

The officer decided firmly, "Well, we'd better take another look."

The old man followed them in. No one objected. He seemed harmless enough.

"What type of camera did you see, old-timer?" Monk asked him.

"Looked like one of them big newsreel cameras. You know, like they set up on folding tripods."

"There was such a camera," Doc imparted. "It will be found in the attic."

But when they reached the attic workroom, it was no longer there!

"Secret exit," Doc said quickly.

They looked about. The darkroom was the most likely spot. But they found no false floor, nor any secret doors or panels. The solitary window led to a straight drop down. Escape by that method would have been dangerous, not to mention impossible to achieve without detection.

When they were done searching, no piece of furniture stood in its original spot.

Ham snapped his fingers suddenly.

"Dumbwaiter!" he said. "A lot of these old brownstones still have working dumbwaiters."

"You would know, dumbskull," Monk snorted.

They did find a dumbwaiter. It was concealed behind a large painting of violets. Doc got it open and examined the shaft. It was of old brick, dusty and cobwebbed. He looked up. Then he peered down. The conveying compartment was at rest far below, its cords and pulleys discernible in the dim space.

"Kitchen!" Doc rapped, already in motion.

They worked their way down to the kitchen. Here, the dumb-waiter portal was not concealed. But when they opened it, disappointment registered on their assembled features.

In the gloom of this they spied an unavoidable fact. The dumbwaiter was too small to carry a human being any older than a very small child.

"Blazes!" muttered Monk. "Doc, you say you heard a woman scream and found only a big newsreel camera?"

Doc nodded somberly.

"But now even that ain't here anymore! A regular locked-room mystery, I calls it!"

"Yet someone clearly left this house unobserved, and he or she or another person obviously returned for that camera," Doc related.

"Baffling!" Long Tom muttered. "All of it."

It was. Yet this was only the beginning of the mystery.

Chapter IV

CAVITY

UPON EXITING THE brownstone building, Doc Savage did a strange thing. He pressed the door-bell button. A bell ding-donged dolefully, but nothing else of significance transpired.

That seemed to satisfy the bronze man on one point: no connection existed between the bell mechanism and the uncanny fate that had befallen his ruined roadster.

Doc turned to the elderly man who had reported what he had seen from his apartment window across the street.

"Who lives here?"

With his fingers, the man turned his straw boater in circles nervously. "You got me, Mister. I only know the folks in my own building."

The cop offered, "I can dig up that information for you, Mr. Savage."

It was a mark of the deference shown Doc Savage by the city constabulary that nothing was mentioned about the bronze man's illegal entry of the brownstone, or other technicalities. Doc had more than once assisted the city police in difficult matters. They gave him a very wide latitude.

A wrecker toiled up, chains clanking. The driver took one look at the ruined roadster and complained, "How the heck am I supposed to move this? There's no back bumper to latch onto, or any rear tires to bear the weight if I hook onto the front bumper."

No one had an answer for him.

Doc said, "It might be best to leave it for the time being."

The cop took off his uniform cap and scratched his moist hair. "Do you think this is connected with that weird thing that happened over on Seventh Avenue?"

"What weird thing?" wondered Monk. The other two of Doc's aides looked equally curious.

Doc told them what he knew of the two men who had met such a strange and simultaneous fate by seemingly miraculous beheading.

"Spontaneous combustion?" wondered Monk.

Long Tom scoffed, "Spontaneous combustion doesn't consume people's heads."

"How do we know for certain?" inserted Ham. "Queer things happen in this world."

Monk said, "He has a point."

"Are you taking his side for once?" Long Tom grumbled sourly.

"I'm not agreeing with that fashion plate!" retorted Monk. "I'm disagreeing with you, you animated spark plug."

"What did you call me?" Long Tom exploded wrathfully. He had a fierce temper, and it was in evidence now. Jaw jutting, he squared off against the hairy chemist. Monk stuck out his barrel chest in his best fighting gorilla stance. Ham shook his sword cane.

For a moment, it looked like all three men would fall into a general donnybrook.

Doc Savage's even-toned voice intruded. "The bodies have been taken to the city morgue. You can reach me there. Monk, you and Long Tom perform tests on the roadster. Endeavor to discover what the disintegrating agent might have been. Ham, look into the owner of this house. We have only the name Merlin to go by."

"Merlin," mused the dapper lawyer. "Wasn't he a wizard back

in King Arthur's day?"

Monk snorted loudly. "Well, if some wizard made half of Doc's roadster disappear, why didn't he finish the job while he was at it?"

No one had an answer for that, either.

Doc hailed a cruising taxi and departed for the city morgue, leaving his aides to accomplish their assigned tasks.

The City Morgue of Manhattan is a pile of dignified stone having something of the exterior aspect of a museum. Inside, it was entirely different story. Gloom filled the interior, both spiritual and otherwise. Entering automatically evoked a disquieting feeling. For most of the city's inhabitants, this was a way station to the Great Beyond.

Doc Savage arrived with dusk falling over the city and made his way to the office of the Chief Medical Examiner.

The M.E. knew the bronze man. They had worked together in the past. There was no trouble about Doc donning a white surgical gown and mask and performing an autopsy. A master of many sciences, Doc Savage particularly excelled in the fields of medicine and surgery, hence his nickname.

Soon, Doc was examining the mortal remains of the unfortunate panhandler remembered only as Mulligan Stew.

There was not much to discover. The dead man possessed no remnant of a head. His neck was a raw stump. With a chromium scalpel, Doc probed the torn flesh, seeking any clue as to what had removed the tramp's cranium.

The bronze man found none, and moved on to the other victim.

More remained of Richmond Carter van Delft's head. But not much more. The force of the detonation—if that was the appropriate word—had carried away most of his face. Doc picked through what was left with a fresh scalpel.

"Notice some portions of the upper jaw are intact, but not the lower," Doc indicated.

The M.E. nodded. "What does that suggest to you?"

"Whatever the agency of destruction, it was localized to the lower jaw and largely confined to the front of the head."

"In other words, the blast was smaller?"

"Exactly."

"And therefore there were two blasts, not one."

"That is my opinion," said Doc, drawing a sheet over the inert cadaver of the late Richmond Carter van Delft.

The bronze man was stripping off his surgical gloves when an orderly came bursting in.

"Something just happened over on Fifth!" he said breathlessly. "Not far from where those two got theirs. And it's big!"

Doc Savage moved with unbelievable speed. He pitched out of the autopsy room, shedding his gown like a cast-off cloak. The big front doors seemed to part for him, but in reality steel-thewed bronze arms flung them wide.

Doc was soon riding the running board of a hastily flagged taxi.

The orderly said it was big. It was.

AN entire storefront on Fifth had been reduced to a gaping cavity. That was the only appropriate word for it—a cavity. The floors above were sagging downward, threatening to bury the ruined first floor.

There was no sign of a blast, although it would be difficult to explain the huge hole in the building by any other means. No debris littered the sidewalk before the former establishment.

Stepping from the crawling cab, Doc realized that the incident was only two blocks south of the exact spot where the two unfortunate men had been struck down by an unseen and baffling agency.

A fire engine, bell a-clanging, pulled up. Fireman hauled out canvas hoses, began dragging them along to convenient fire plugs. They quickly realized that their services were not needed in that regard.

There was no sign of fire, nor smoke. Only mute destruction.

Doc Savage moved among them, warning, "It is not safe to enter."

"I can see that," the fire marshal said. "This is a job for a demolition crew. Any sign of victims?"

Doc shook his head slowly, "None. That was the Kromgold jewelry concern. Since it is after hours, it is unlikely that any customers were on the premises."

The fire marshal clapped his helmet to his chest solemnly.

"Well, if anyone was inside, they're done for."

Doc suggested, "You had better evacuate the upper floors of the adjacent buildings."

"Right." He turned his head, hollering over his shoulder, "Men, follow me in."

Bravely, the firemen stormed the stairs and began going floor to floor.

Doc Savage drifted closer to the gaping cavity. He moved with a fluid grace that partook of calculated caution, golden eyes ranging ceaselessly.

The manner in which the metal and granite facade lay exposed suggested nothing the bronze giant had ever seen before. If the clamshell bucket of a steam shovel had swung in to take a bite out of the building, that would fully account for the destruction wrought.

But of course that was impossible. No steam shovel had been constructed capable of wreaking such abrupt havoc.

There were witnesses. Doc questioned them. They described a sound. Huge, yet strangely muffled or smothered.

"One minute there was a jewelry store there," recounted one, "the next minute, *poof!*"

"It was more like a *whoom* of a sound," corrected another.

Neither of which furthered understanding.

The commissioner of police turned up next. He stepped from his official car and, spying the Man of Bronze, made a beeline for him.

"What do you make of it, Doc?"

They were obviously on familiar terms.

Doc Savage said frankly, "It is like nothing ever before seen."

The commissioner heaved a hearty sigh. "I'll give you that."

"Without question," Doc went on, "some utterly mysterious agency killed two unrelated persons, destroyed my car, then decimated this building."

"Devoured it, you mean?"

Doc Savage said nothing. The choice of words was too apt to argue the point.

The commissioner wondered aloud, "Do you think robbery is a motive here?"

Doc Savage did not reply. Instead, he moved deeper into the cavity, a wary eye on the tangle of wire and broken pipes and support beams over his bronze head. It was apparent even from casual inspection that the building would have to be taken down. There was no salvaging it.

Doc picked through the floor—what remained of it. It had been marble. Portions survived. In other spots, bare soil lay exposed. Amid the rubble, Doc detected sharp gleams.

He picked up a few of these, wiped them clean with a handkerchief. Even in the dim shadowy light they were recognizable. Diamonds. Some were of the type that were cut for wedding rings. But they were loose. A few showed signs of fracture. Others were scarred in other ways, made cloudy by some violent upheaval.

There were broaches, necklaces, and other bangles. All were twisted, deformed. And all were of silver or platinum.

Nowhere in the large space that had formerly held one of the most swanky selections of jewelry in Manhattan, was there any sign of gold.

The dust-fine aureate flakes in the bronze man's eyes seemed to have turned to frost. That was the only outward sign of emotion he displayed at this discovery.

Doc eased back to the relative safety of the sidewalk.

"No," he told the commissioner. "Not robbery."

Witnesses supported the bronze man's theory. The window display was clearly visible in the moments leading up to the fantastic event, whatever it was. Diamond rings, brooches, earrings and other baubles worth many thousands of dollars were set in place before the establishment was obliterated.

"It's baffling," the commissioner complained to no one in particular.

"It is just the beginning," predicted Doc.

"Exactly my feeling. But the beginning of what? That is what I want to know."

That was what the entire city wished to know. And before long, the populace got their first disquieting inkling. There would be no comfort in it, either.

Chapter V

THE VAULT ENIGMA

THE DESTRUCTION OF the Kromgold jewelry concern was not the worst of it.

Across town, the Chemical Trust Bank on Broadway was hit. Not quite thirty minutes had elapsed since the earlier incident. This one was equally baffling.

The bank was closed for the day. A muffled sound came from within the repository's polished granite confines. It was followed by a tremendous metallic clangor. This caught the attention of a passing police officer, making his evening rounds.

The reverberant quality of the disturbance excited the cop's imagination in an understandable way. He immediately leapt to the conclusion that a gang of safe crackers was at work, attempting to blow the bank vault with nitroglycerine—nitro being the explosive of first resort among the city's bank-robbing class.

The cop got down on one knee and began hammering the curbstone with his sturdy nightstick. The unmistakable sound was heard and taken up by nearby patrolmen. Soon, a trio of bluecoats congregated before the bank.

One sniffed the air.

"I smell something funny," he said suspiciously.

Since they lacked keys to the bank door, the summoning officer called Headquarters, while the others stationed themselves at the entrance to block any escaping criminal. None came out. It was vaguely disappointing.

A patrol car came grinding along and out stepped no less than a precinct captain, who took command of the situation. A riot squad was called in next. Swiftly and efficiently, the bank was surrounded.

But only smoke and a pungent metallic odor drifted out of the chinks in the bank's otherwise solid windows. The police waited tensely for the arrival of a representative from the bank.

DOC SAVAGE put in an appearance around the time the president of the bank rolled into view via taxicab to unlock the front door. The bronze man pulled up in a nondescript coupé and alighted, seeming to swell in size as he approached.

Doc and the bank president evidently knew each other, for the latter said, "Thank goodness you are here, Mr. Savage. I have no idea what it may mean, but there seems to have been an explosion."

The bank president was no political apple polisher. Doc Savage happened to be one of his largest depositors. It was one of the reasons that the repository—one of the most secure in the city—had weathered the financial panic of a few years previous. He fidgeted with his pince-nez eyeglasses nervously.

"Thieves would have made their exit by now," Doc suggested.

"Indeed, yes," agreed the bank official.

With the permission of the banker, the bronze man sought a quiet entrance to the repository. Once this was obtained, Doc disappeared around a corner.

That was all. He was not seen again until ten minutes later when the front door opened from within and the bronze man stepped out. Doc was wearing a small gas mask over his inscrutable metal countenance. Goggles protected his arresting eyes.

Pulling these off, he said, "The vault door is off its hinges, and the safe-deposit room is in ruins."

The bank president barged in to see for himself. A foul odor forced him back. Wearing regulation gas-protection equipment, the police charged in and opened such windows as permitted ventilation.

When they got the bank sufficiently aired out to allow investigation, all saw that the massive safe door now lay on the cracked marble floor, leaving the vault gaping open. They crowded into what was left of the safe-deposit room.

It was a square chamber with three walls consisting of locked brass drawers. Or had, rather. Now portions of all three walls were blown out in an odd way. Some drawers remained intact, however. These were farthest away from the blown-out drawers. The entire effect was of a pocked patchwork of craters. There was surprisingly little floor litter or debris.

"Looks like bombs went off in some of these drawers," the police captain suggested.

The bank official had to agree that was the look of things. He turned to Doc Savage with a questioning mien.

"No one would attempt to gain entry to individual boxes by explosive means," offered the bronze man, surveying the damage.

The banker gravely agreed. "Yes, typically in robberies such as these, boxes would be pried open and rifled of their contents. Blowing up the drawers would only destroy valuable contents. And there is no sign of forced entry of the room itself."

Indeed, the safe door appeared to have been shot out of its jamb by the force of the deposit-room detonations. Its massive stainless steel hinges were sheared off in an alarming way— alarming because the force required to perform such a feat was prodigious, incalculable.

Without comment, Doc Savage scrutinized the broken hinges and his tuneless trilling was again briefly heard. He employed a tool like a scalpel to scrape some steel filings from the exposed burrs and deposited them into a small glass receptacle, which he capped and stowed on his person.

"What do most people keep in these drawers anyways?" asked a bewildered officer.

"Securities, cash, jewelry and the like," the banker admitted.

"Of course that is entirely the renter's business. We do not pry into their boxes once they are properly rented."

"Would anyone keep explosives here?" the officer persisted.

"Preposterous!" sniffed the bank official. "See for yourself, more than one drawer appears to be at the center of this detonation. Even if some insane person were to store dynamite here, why are so many sections obliterated?"

Obliterated was exactly the proper word, too. On the floor, there were a few papers, or fragments of paper. Bonds. Treasury notes. But no sign of the types of valuables normally stored in safe-deposit vaults. No cash, coins, jewelry or precious metals like silver or gold.

Everyone looked at Doc Savage hopefully.

"A common source will have to be determined to account for all the mystery detonations," was all he offered.

That told the assembled investigators that the bronze man had no more idea than they did of what was plaguing Manhattan. It was a dispiriting realization.

While they were debating the matter, Doc Savage slipped silently away.

HAM BROOKS was ensconced in the reception room of the eighty-sixth floor headquarters in the midtown skyscraper where Doc Savage maintained a suite of offices.

Offices might not be the most appropriate term for the three rooms which comprised virtually the entire floor. One was a vast scientific library, and the other an experimental laboratory, each unmatched in all of the world, save one. Both the library and the laboratory were exceeded by a mysterious place far in the frozen north, which Doc Savage called his Fortress of Solitude. Here, the bronze man sometimes retreated from the outer world, to study and toil on some difficult or perplexing problem of science or medicine, which required intense uninterrupted study. No mortal other than Doc had ever seen the inside of this polar retreat, nor knew location, either. It was Doc

Savage's deepest secret.

Ham was seated behind the exquisitely inlaid table of Oriental design that served as a receiving desk in the smallest of these chambers, the reception room. He was busy at a bank of cradle telephones, making call after call, taking copious notes on a pad of linen paper.

Monk Mayfair and Long Tom Roberts put in an appearance not long after, looking relieved to be out of the insufferable heat and plainly enjoying the refreshingly air-conditioned atmosphere of Doc's headquarters suite.

"I have made progress," Ham announced with pride.

"Toward your wake, I hope," cracked Monk.

Ham looked injured. Rising from his chair, he picked up his sword cane and shook it. The sheath flew off and he used the exposed blade as a pointer, much as a school master would berate a recalcitrant student.

"One of these days I intend to shave those rusty nails off your homely face and use them to re-tack my shoes!" he warned.

"One of these days," Monk shot back, smacking one meaty fist into the other, "I'm gonna brush those pearly whites of yours with a knuckle toothbrush."

"You fuzzy baboon!" Ham gritted, slashing the air before him. "You mistake of nature!"

"*Ow-w-w!*" moaned Long Tom suddenly, feeling of his mouth.

"What's wrong with him?" Ham wondered, restoring his sword cane with a click.

Monk said, "Him? He's got a toothache, that's all."

"Not a toothache," groaned Long Tom.

Monk glowered. "Yeah? Then what've you been complainin' about all the way here, if not a toothache?"

"My teeth hurt, but they don't ache," corrected Long Tom.

"What's the difference?" asked Ham, genuinely puzzled.

Long Tom had to think about that a moment.

"My natural teeth are fine," he explained. "It's my front teeth."

Long Tom was possessed of a naturally sour disposition. So seldom did he smile, few realized his upper front teeth were artificial. These gold incisors were removable, and he removed them now.

"Dat's better," the pallid electrician lisped, sounding surprised. "Dey smarted like the devil."

Monk looked at him dubiously. "What did it feel like?"

Long Tom ruminated over question. "Once, I ran a piece of Christmas tree tinsel between two teef and it created an electrical shock. It stung me clear to my skull bone."

"How is that possible?" Ham demanded.

Long Tom scowled. "The tinsel made contact with a metal filling and created an electrical current. Mouth saliva acts as an electrolyte. What I was feeling just now reminded me of that, only not so painful."

"When did this come on?" asked Ham, his legal mind eager to establish facts and times.

"On the way over here," supplied Long Tom.

"Maybe you need new teeth," Ham suggested.

Monk immediately disagreed. "Maybe this has something to do with all the commotion tonight," he suggested.

"Hogwash!" Ham retorted.

Monk asked, "Well, it ain't ever happened before, has it, Long Tom?"

"Never!" snapped the electrical wizard, staring at the two gold incisors cradled in his palm. His voice sounded odd, and his expression was more sour than normally.

"What the deuce!" Ham squawked suddenly and gave a violent jump.

Monk whirled. Almost at the same instant, something struck his legs, all but upsetting him. The newcomer was a dwarf ape of some unclassifiable type.

This was Chemistry, Ham's pet. The dapper lawyer had come

upon him in a tropical jungle deep in South America. There was considerable question as to what branch of the anthropoid tree Chemistry belonged. He might have been part chimpanzee, part orangutan. He bore a distressing resemblance to Monk Mayfair—which was the main reason that Ham adopted him.

"I thought you sold that blasted what-is-it to a zoologist!" Monk complained.

Chattering excitedly, Chemistry leaped into Ham's waiting arms and grabbed the dapper lawyer's silk cravat. He began untying it.

Ham carefully set him down on the reception desk and fussed with his tie, saying, "Chemistry is being studied by a famous zoologist in an effort to prove what I have been claiming for months. Namely that he is a pure-blooded descendant of pet apes kept by the Inca rulers of South America."

Monk scowled. "So what's he doin' here?"

Ham finished restoring his cravat. "He missed me terribly. So I have temporarily taken custody of him. Later today, the zoologist will reclaim him."

Monk favored Chemistry with a doubtful eye. "If that—that goriboon turns out to be a pure-blooded anything," Monk vowed, "I will eat your hat."

Ham blinked. "My hat. Not yours?"

"I like my hat," Monk said blandly. "Yours ain't fit for a human head. If I were you, I'd turn it upside down, fill it with birdseed and set it in a windowsill."

Ham took great offense at this. He prided himself on two things: The fact that he was a favorite son of Harvard Law School, and his reputation for sartorial splendor. Tailors had been known to break out in fisticuffs over the fine points and correctness of his daily attire.

"I happen to have purchased that hat at the finest haberdasher's shop," the dapper lawyer sniffed.

Monk's deep-set eyes danced toward the silk topper. His wide mouth split into a great grin.

"Maybe you should take it back," he suggested.

"Back! Why?"

"To get a new hatband maybe," said Monk.

Ham's sharp gaze shot to the top of the enormous safe occupying one corner of the reception room, onto which Chemistry had climbed. He was happily unraveling Ham's hatband and winding it about himself.

Ham howled, "Chemistry! You stop that this very instant."

Monk burst out in laughter. "Maybe there's somethin' to that royalty story. Looks like he's tryin' to make an Inca robe for himself!"

Long Tom announced sourly, "You two need to find yourselves wives."

MONK and Ham were still arguing their respective points of view when Doc Savage finally arrived.

"Any progress?" asked the bronze man.

"No," offered Monk. "Long Tom and I went over every inch of that roadster before the cops hauled it off, and all we earned for our trouble was dirty fingernails."

Ham spoke up, "I for one have accomplished something useful. The brownstone is owned by one John Merlin, an electrochemist. Merlin is in the employ of a metallurgical concern called the Elektro-Alchemical Company, and at present he is out of the country, conducting experiments of some kind. I was told this by his employer, S. Charles Amerikanis."

"I've heard of Amerikanis," put in Long Tom. But his words were so distorted by the absence of his front teeth that he was difficult to understand. Long Tom hastily restored them and elaborated on his statement.

"Skelton Charles Amerikanis is known as 'Master Bonesy' for his skinflint chiseling ways. He buys up failing companies for a dime on the dollar and adds them to his empire." Feeling of his front teeth, the pallid electrical wizard added, "Elektro-Alchemical is a legitimate enterprise, though."

Doc Savage regarded the puny electrical genius intently.

"Long Tom's teeth have been bothering him," Monk informed Doc. "He'll get over it though."

Doc nodded. To the others, he said, "Interviewing Amerikanis might be a productive first step in the direction of confronting this mystery."

Ham volunteered, "I will endeavor to ascertain his present whereabouts."

While Ham was engaged with the telephone, Doc turned to Long Tom. "What seems to be the trouble with your teeth?"

"Darned if I know." Long Tom ran his tongue over his gold incisors saying, "They feel O.K. now. But man alive, did they smart!"

"Describe the sensation," requested the bronze man.

"Galvanic shock kind of a feeling."

Doc reached over and pried open Long Tom's jaw. His flake-gold eyes examined the two gold front teeth.

"Are you certain of that?" asked Doc, releasing the puny electrician.

"Of course," Long Tom returned.

"He would know," Monk pointed out. "He's got copper wires for blood vessels."

"These are a gold alloy, are they not?" Doc questioned.

"Electrum—gold, silver and copper," said Long Tom.

Doc Savage appeared thoughtful for a time. His ever-active eyes stirred more briskly. But the bronze man said nothing.

Ham Brooks banged down the telephone receiver. "I have just learned that S. Charles Amerikanis is still at his office. He is refusing to take calls, according to his secretary."

"That ain't stopped us before," Monk pointed out.

"We will interview Amerikanis," Doc Savage decided.

Chapter VI

MORE AMPUTATIONS

THEY TOOK DOC'S private elevator to the sub-basement garage. This lift operated with tremendous speed.
For some sixty stories of the descent, the occupants seemed to
stand in midair.

There was no small shock as the cage braked to a halt at the
sub-basement level. All but Doc Savage were forced to their
knees.

Monk grinned broadly. When the speed lift was originally
installed, the hairy chemist ran it up and down for days, joyrid-
ing.

They entered a basement garage, which held cars ranging
from a limousine to open phaetons and speedsters. The machines
had one thing in common—they were powerfully engined.

Selecting a reserved black sedan which was not expensive
enough to attract attention, the bronze man maneuvered it out
onto the street. The garage, the cars it held, were maintained
by Doc Savage. Few outsiders were aware of its existence.

Doc wheeled the sedan through evening traffic. The afternoon
heat remained oppressive.

City thoroughfares were unusually deserted. Police had evidently called up the reserves because the presence of bluecoats
on every street corner was marked.

Manhattan was uneasy, not knowing when or where the
uncanny menace would next strike.

At a corner stop light, Monk dismounted to purchase a pair

of late editions off a soggy-faced street urchin who was crying the news.

"*Wuxtra!* City in grip of miracle bombings! Authorities flummoxed!"

"It'll be a miracle if anyone ever figures this out," Monk grinned as he climbed back in.

Doc resumed driving. Monk skimmed the front pages for new information.

"It says here that foreign agitators might be back of this."

"Any time the police can't find their man right off," Long Tom grumbled, "they always blame foreign agitators."

"No more places have exploded since that jewelry store and bank," continued Monk. "The commissioner of police is askin' the public not to panic. He thinks it might be a robbery gang workin' in a big way."

"What do you think, Doc?" asked Ham.

The bronze man was silent as he drove. It was Doc Savage's custom not to offer theories far in advance of facts. But in this case, it appeared that the bronze man was as stymied as the lowliest beat cop. In any case, when he did not wish to answer a question, Doc pretended not to hear it.

"The hospital emergency rooms are seein' a lot of people complain' about missing fingers," Monk reported.

Abruptly, Doc Savage pulled over and took the paper from the burly chemist's hands so suddenly that Monk thought it had evaporated into thin air.

Doc scanned the sheets. His trilling piped up, dying to a nebulous tremolo. There was a wondering quality to it.

When he got his machine in gear again, the bronze man made a detour to the city hospital, driving with a studied urgency.

DOC SAVAGE was soon in conference with the resident chief physician in the latter's office. His men remained outside, where a bank of overtaxed standard fans offered relief from the heat.

The chief physician—a distinguished white-haired individual with a distinct black streak on one side—was saying, "The peculiar thing is that in every case, it was the third finger on the right or left hand that was severed."

"In other words, the ring finger," prompted Doc.

The medico nodded soberly. "Precisely. Every one of these amputations was traumatic. Another odd feature was that they were cauterized at the stump, but the patients could not explain how that came to be. They were simply going about their business when they felt a sudden, sharp pain and their finger was no longer there."

"Disintegrated?"

"I am not certain I would use that word," said the physician. "In one case, the patient discovered the lost finger and brought it in. Of course, there was nothing that could be done about it."

Doc asked, "Did a woman seek treatment for the loss of the third finger of one hand?"

"No, none of which I am aware. All the injured have been men."

"Have other hospitals reported similar cases?" demanded Doc.

"Not so far."

"I would like to see one of your patients," Doc requested.

"By all means, Dr. Savage. It has completely baffled the medical staff."

Only one patient was still on the premises. A middle-aged man named Fisk. He was conducted into the bronze man's presence.

"My wife will never understand this," he was moaning. The spouse in question must have been a swell cook, if the size of the man's mid-section was any indication.

The chief physician was considerate. "I am sure that she will. After all, it was not your fault that you lost a finger."

The distraught man looked as if he wished to wring his hands, but his bandaged digit prevented this.

"I wasn't talking about my finger, doctor. I can't find my wedding ring! My wife will be terribly upset when I try to explain this. She's the jealous type, you understand. Wields a mean rolling pin, too."

He took out a linen handkerchief and mopped his brow of excess perspiration.

Removing the bandage, Doc examined the man's maimed hand, the left. The third finger had been severed just below the first joint. The wound had sealed in a way that suggested the flesh and remaining bone had fused in some inexplicable manner.

"Tell me what transpired," Doc requested.

The unhappy man did. It was not much of a story, as stories go. He had been buying a magazine at a news stand when his finger seemed to sever itself. At least, that was how he told it.

"There was a sudden sharp pain and it just dropped off," the man explained. "My finger, I mean."

Doc asked, "No flash of light? No sign of a blade or bomb?"

The man shook his head definitely. "No. My finger just fell to the pavement," he said sheepishly, as if not quite believing his own tale. "There was no blood either."

"Is there anything else?"

The other shrugged helplessly. "I picked up my finger and ran here. I forgot about my wedding ring. It must have fallen off too. But I didn't notice it laying on the ground."

Doc's uncanny trilling seemed to ooze out of him, unprompted.

"Any pain?" he asked.

"It throbs," replied the injured man.

"The others said the same thing," the chief physician enlightened. "The nerves appear to have been deadened by some action."

"What do you make of it?" asked the attending doctor, who had been an interested observer up until this point.

"Nothing remotely like it has ever been witnessed before to-day," confessed Doc.

"Yet we have a rash of them," put in the chief physician.

Doc re-bandaged the man's finger and made a request.

"If a woman is admitted seeking care for a missing left ring finger, I would like to be notified," he directed.

"Of course, Dr. Savage."

"WHAT could have done it, Doc?" asked Ham as they exited to the darkening street. The city air seemed to smother them. No cooling night breeze had been forecast.

Doc Savage said, "In every case, the injured persons were afflicted in the general vicinity of the scenes of carnage this evening. There can be no doubt but that these two phenomena are connected in some way."

They climbed into the waiting sedan. Doc asked, "Long Tom, when your teeth first began acting up, were you in the area of the detonations?"

"Thereabouts," Long Tom admitted.

Thumbing the ignition, Doc Savage said, "Speak up if you feel that sensation again."

"O.K."

Doc's voice became grim. "Do not hesitate one second, Long Tom. Our lives may depend upon it."

"Blazes!" exploded Monk. "You sayin' Long Tom's teeth are sensitive to whatever's causing all this danged carnage?"

"We will see if my supposition is borne out by future developments," said Doc, shooting out into sparse traffic once more.

There were no incidents as they crossed the Brooklyn Bridge into the borough of the same name. Sight of the setting sun created a sense of relief from the blistering heat of day, even if the difference in temperature was negligible.

"I wonder," Ham mused. "Could this infernal heat wave be causing these blasted explosions?"

Riding in the front seat, Monk craned his bullet head around and asked, "Hey, Long Tom. What's the boiling point for lawyers?"

"You're a chemist," the electrical wizard said sourly. "Why don't you look it up?"

"Maybe I will. Because if the one you're sittin' next to blows up, we don't want to be around."

For his quip, the apish chemist received a resounding thwack on the top of his skull. Although the cane was made of hardwood, Monk seemed barely to notice.

THE headquarters of the Elektro-Alchemical Company lay nestled in a wooded section of Brooklyn. It was a two-story brick building, constructed in wings, like a hospital or school. A hurricane fence surrounded it. Oak trees predominated the surrounding grounds, their leaves giving the appearance of wilting in the heat.

Night was falling when Doc Savage brought his sedan to a halt before the locked gate. A night watchman came out of his guard box to greet them. His uniform was surprisingly crisp, given the heat.

Doffing his hat, Ham Brooks stuck his head out a car window, and said, "Doc Savage is here to see S. Charles Amerikanis, my good man."

The guard went to his telephone and spoke for a few minutes.

"Mr. Amerikanis doesn't want to see anyone," he said upon his return.

Ham Brooks turned an exasperated shade of purple. "Don't you know who Doc Savage is!"

"I do," replied the guard. "But I also know who pays me. And orders are orders."

Doc Savage stepped out from behind the wheel. He loomed up, a tower of metallic might in the gathering dark. The guard was not short. But suddenly he felt as small as a child.

The bronze giant produced a billfold which, when opened, revealed his official standing with the police. He had the rank of inspector.

"Police business," Doc said quietly.

That settled the matter. The guard opened the gate, saying, "You'll show that to Mr. Amerikanis, won't you? I have kids to feed."

The sedan rolled in through the opening gate. Ham Brooks said, "Amerikanis sounded extremely agitated over the phone when I questioned him. I wonder what he has to hide?"

Monk started to object to Ham's assumption, thought better of it, and growled, "Whatever it is, I'll wring it out of him if I have to use my bare hands."

The dapper lawyer waggled the gleaming gold knob of his elegant cane in the apish chemist's direction. "Leave the cross examinations to me, you hairy mistake."

"I'll wrap that sword cane around your neck, you interfere with me again, you ambulance chaser," Monk flung back.

"You two," complained Long Tom Roberts, "give me a bigger pain than my front teeth."

Chapter VII

THE LOOMING NOOSE

WHEN DOC SAVAGE and his three aides reached the executive offices of S. Charles Amerikanis, they were informed by his personal secretary that, "I am so sorry, but Mr. Amerikanis has stepped out of the office."

Normally, Monk or Ham would have dealt swiftly with anyone blocking their path, but this particular secretary happened to be a blonde, and a very shapely one at that.

They offered their most forward smiles. Ham tipped his hat. Monk grinned from ear to ear, threatening his earlobes in the process. Their elbows got busy pushing the other aside. Both thought themselves ladies' men.

"Which way did he go, may I ask?" invited Ham.

"He did not say," returned the secretary primly.

"He say when he'd be back?" beamed Monk.

The secretary smiled back. In a contest between Ham's gallant manners and Monk's infectious grin, the homely chemist invariably won.

"I am afraid not," she said sweetly.

Except for the energetic elbowing, it was all very pleasant.

Doc Savage intruded. "We will split up and locate Amerikanis."

Retreating, Monk and Ham all but bowed in farewell.

Long Tom snorted, "Bugs to you both." The puny electrical magician was usually womanproof.

The quartet swiftly separated and got to work. It did not take long to accomplish their task.

Much of the Elektro-Alchemical concern was given over to laboratories and workshops, none currently in operation. Doc found Amerikanis in one of these.

The chamber stank of malodorous chemicals and burnt matter. A great deal of metal fabricating equipment was in evidence. There were electrical furnaces bolted to the wooden flooring. Metal forms, ingots, and blanks lay strewn carelessly about.

Vast ceiling fans were toiling to suck up the smells and heat both.

The nickname of "Master Bonesy" did not quite fit Skelton Charles Amerikanis. He was not really as old-fashioned as the outdated honorific, although he was not very young, either, looking about fifty. He did tend towards a spare leanness which made the bones of his pinched face stand out rather prominently. His colorless eyes were disturbingly deep-set. The entire effect suggested a morose skull clothed in thin, dry flesh.

No doubt the nickname was a play on his seldom-used first name, which was one letter shy of the word "skeleton."

"What is it?" Amerikanis asked when Doc thrust the door open.

Amerikanis swallowed his words when he recognized the big bronze man. Doc Savage was unmistakable in the flesh. No newspaper or magazine photographer ever did him justice, but the photos captured Doc sufficiently to mark him as unique.

"My associate, Ham Brooks, spoke to you earlier," Doc began. "We have questions for your employee, John Merlin."

"He is not here!" snapped Amerikanis.

"Where can Merlin be found?" pressed Doc.

"I would rather not say," came the peevish response. "No, I would not."

"What was he working on?"

"What Merlin was working on, he is still working on!" Master Bonesy retorted. "And it is no concern of yours. It is a private business matter—very private. Now that I've answered your questions, kindly—"

Doc Savage's eyes ranged over the array of test tubes and other delicate equipment. No science, from chemistry to botany, had escaped his study. Doc was well versed in many disciplines. He began categorizing and analyzing the array of apparatus before him. Among the electrical furnaces were vats, smelters—virtually everything needed to work with molten metals.

"An unusual line of experimentation is being conducted here," he ventured.

S. Charles Amerikanis all but hissed like a cat. "Say no more! It is not any of your affair. None!"

Doc offered no comment. Instead, he glided over to a vat from which the stink of hot metal was coming. His flake-gold eyes took in the dull molten matter.

"Lead," he decided.

"Yes!" snapped Amerikanis. "Common lead. Nothing to interest anyone. Now kindly leave these premises before I have you arrested."

Doc showed his police identification. That silenced Amerikanis. "You would do well to cooperate," the bronze man advised.

"You cannot arrest a person for ill manners," sulked Master Bonesy.

"There will be no need to arrest anyone if answers are forthcoming," said Doc, implying that an arrest was not out of the question.

S. Charles Amerikanis's narrow features twitched. "Very well, Merlin is in Alaska, conducting dangerous experiments. What business is it of yours? What, I ask you?"

"There is cause to connect him to the strange deaths that have lately plagued Manhattan," Doc supplied.

"Nonsense! Merlin is a scientist, not a terrorist. These damnable bombings are the work of alien anarchists. The newspapers all say so!"

Doc Savage made no reply to that. His eyes were roaming

the laboratory, as if to divine its purpose. The varied apparatus were not unusual, but the bronze man could see that they were grouped strangely, suggesting an unorthodox approach to some experiment.

At that juncture, Long Tom Roberts came barging in.

"Doc! It's happening again. My teeth are killing me!"

THE bronze man reacted like lightning. He gathered up both Long Tom and Amerikanis and threw them under a heavy work bench behind a massive electrical furnace. Then he slid beneath himself. Holding both men down as if they were weak and helpless children, Doc waited, as if in expectation of something.

It came!

The sound was difficult of description. A smothered commotion of some sort. It arrived and departed in an instant.

In the aftermath, unsettling sounds of breaking plaster and shattering glass came. Another, deeper, sound followed, heavy with finality.

Doc heaved out of the room and into the corridor, shouting, "Monk! Ham!"

The two aides came running from opposite wings, looking startled. Ham had his sword cane out and ready, while Monk brandished one of the supermachine pistols of Doc's invention. These were amazingly compact weapons, resembling oversized automatics, and could emit a wide variety of shells in a stuttering flood.

"It came from back there," said Monk, jerking a hairy thumb behind him.

They set out in that direction, threading a maze of corridors.

The area was not far from Amerikanis's office. It proved to be some kind of storage room, walls crammed with shelves on which stood an assortment of tools and other implements.

At one end was a floor safe, rather substantial. Modern, too. It rivaled in size the commodious one in Doc Savage's office headquarters.

The door to the safe was completely gone. Something had catapulted it from its hinges, and clear through a long factory-type window. The window was in pieces, pebbled glass and chicken wire strewn on the floor in a wild profusion.

The safe door proved to be lying on the grassy grounds beyond the window. Monk discovered it by leaning out the shattered pane and moving his bullet head about.

"Blazes!" he said. "What force!"

Doc peered into the safe. The interior was neither smoking nor burning. But the inner walls—which were quite thick—were pitted and pocked.

The others stuck their heads in.

"Good night!" barked Ham.

Monk sized it up perfectly.

"No ordinary bomb did *that.*"

Long Tom chimed in, "That's sure right. Nitro wouldn't do that. Nor T.N.T."

Monk went to fetch "Master Bonesy" Amerikanis. He brought him back by the scruff of his well-starched shirt collar.

"You know what done that?" demanded Monk.

"No—no," Amerikanis stammered. He looked drawn as a hungry ghost. "I have no idea."

Doc Savage addressed him. "What do you store in that safe?"

"Industrial metals used in the work of the concern," he said. "Where are they?"

"Up in smoke," said Monk.

"But there is no smoke," Amerikanis pointed out. "None."

"Well, they went up in something," said Ham Brooks. "Perhaps they were stolen."

S. Charles Amerikanis looked as baffled as anyone could ever be. He took out an old-fashioned silver pocket watch and consulted it as if it might hold the answer. He snapped it shut.

"I have no idea what has happened here," he gulped at last.

Doc turned to Long Tom.

"How are your teeth?"

Long Tom gulped, "Huh? I forgot all about them. They feel all right now. But they were really hot just before the explosion hit."

"Hot?"

"Like a live wire," explained Long Tom.

"We might search the grounds," suggested Doc.

THE grounds proved unremarkable. Nothing was found that might have explained the mysterious blowing of the big storage safe, or the equally mysterious absence of its metallic contents.

The crisply-attired night guard had come trotting up to the shattered window and fell to examining the safe door lying in the dirt, scratching his round head as he did so.

"That door weighs a quarter ton!" he said. "Easily."

No one contradicted him. It was a fair estimate.

Doc Savage inquired, "Was there any suspicious activity prior to the explosion?"

"I didn't hear any explosion. Only the window flying to pieces."

Monk put in, "What do you think caused all the ruckus?"

"Well, I didn't hear any blast noise," the guard shot back. "Wouldn't a bomb blast big enough to blow off a door that size make a huge racket?"

Monk swallowed his rebuttal. No blast had been heard. But the door had plainly been blown off its hinges, so there must have been a blast.

Doc Savage repeated his question. "Did you see anyone lurking about the premises?"

"No.... Er, yes. There was a fella taking pictures across the way."

"Where?"

The guard pointed beyond the main gate. "He was over yonder, lugging a big camera. He was shooting the plant. I figured it was for a newsreel or some such thing."

His voice becoming charged, Doc demanded, "He was operating a newsreel camera, you say?"

The guard nodded. "It was set up on one of those folding tripods."

"Describe him, please."

"Not too big, nor tall. Dark glasses. Cap. Leather jacket. That's about all. I didn't get a real good gander at him."

"Did you see anything unusual about the camera?" queried Ham.

"No, he just stood there, cranking away at it. Then the window broke and I came running."

"Blazes!" squawled Monk. "What if that guy threw a bomb—"

Doc Savage was suddenly not there. The bronze man could move with blinding speed. But this time it was as if he had dematerialized.

A moment later, the sound of Doc's sedan came. It went roaring off into the hot night.

"Don't that beat all!" the watchman marveled. "He just left you three behind."

"When he gets movin'," Monk grunted, "Doc don't waste any time."

THE access road to the Elektro-Alchemical Company went one way—north. Doc negotiated it with the speedometer crawling toward its highest digits.

That the bronze man did not know what make of vehicle he was pursuing did not matter to him at all. At this time of night, on a road such as this, traffic would be sparse. Any machine encountered could be a possible getaway vehicle for the mysterious operator of the newsreel camera that was not what it seemed to be.

Doc drove with consummate skill and precision. Before long, he spotted a solitary red tail-light far up ahead. He wrested more speed from his machine. The sedan surged forward, motor purring energetically.

The speed at which Doc was traveling did not allow much time for reaction to danger. Still, the bronze man's reflexes, like so many things about him, verged on the uncanny.

Doc Savage spotted the obstacle in his path in the proverbial nick of time. It showed up in the brilliant white funnels of his headlights with all the starkness of a hangman's noose. No time to swerve to safety. Doc did brake, but had that been the limit of his reaction, he would not have survived the encounter.

Braking, Doc threw himself to one side. He kept one foot depressed on the brake, managing simultaneously to slam his big body prone across the front seat. One cabled bronze hand vised the steering wheel, holding it steady.

Amid a jangle of crumpling metal and shattering glass, the sedan slewed to a side-slipping halt.

The radiator grille struck a tree. The radiator split, and scalding water began erupting geyser fashion under the hood. But the motor was not jammed backward into the front seat, as might have been the case had the bronze man not kept control of the hurtling machine.

Doc Savage sat up.

The entire top of the sedan—windshield, side windows and roof and steel support columns—had been swept away. No doubt it lay in a tangle far back in the road.

Doc brushed granular glass from his clothes and lap. The windows were bulletproof, thus they had powdered under impact of the thick steel cable that had been strung between two sturdy oaks on either side of the road.

Exiting, Doc examined the surroundings. He found footprints indicating a recent lurker. The shoe size was very small. He took some time committing these prints to memory.

Nothing else of interest was uncovered. The automobile that had doubtless carried the bronze man's assailant away was not discernible to eye or ear. It was already far distant.

DOC SAVAGE returned to the Elektro-Alchemical Company on foot. He found Monk, Ham, Long Tom and a nervous S. Charles Amerikanis hovering around the damaged office safe.

Amerikanis was saying, "I do not give permission to examine my safe."

"Your permission," Monk growled, "ain't exactly necessary."

"But you are not with the police!" Amerikanis sputtered.

"When he returns," Ham said firmly, "Doc Savage will show you his police credentials, if he has not already done so. In the meanwhile, here is my card."

It was pointedly ignored.

Doc's arrival was so soundless that when he spoke up, Monk and Long Tom both started and nearly bumped their heads on the ceiling of the safe.

"Our quarry managed to elude capture," was all Doc said about his ill-omened encounter.

The three aides took in the bronze man's disheveled appearance, and Ham deduced the rest. "Are you all right, Doc?"

Doc nodded. "We will require a taxi to return." To Monk and Long Tom he inquired, "What have you discovered?"

Long Tom said, "The inside of this box is smeared with all types of different metallic elements, or something."

"Yeah," added Monk. "We're scraping up some samples for chemical analysis later."

Doc turned his attention to Amerikanis. "Do you," he inquired, "ever store radium in that safe?"

The metallurgist's lower lip quivered. "Radium?"

"Yes. A rare element that has the property of radiant emissions."

Amerikanis seemed insulted by the explanation. "I know what radium is!" he snapped. "But no, we never use it in our work. Why do you ask such a pointless and ridiculous question?"

"Radium," explained Doc, "naturally came to mind because

no ordinary explosive created the destruction we have witnessed."

Skelton Charles Amerikanis looked as if he wanted to refute that assertion, but thought better of it.

Instead, he again looked at his silver watch. It was the old-fashioned type once known as a turnip, due to its shape and size. Snapping open the cover, he consulted it, and said sharply, "It is well past the hour this plant closes. If you must, finish your work. The entrance gate will be padlocked in ten minutes sharp."

With that, he took his departure.

"Are we done with him?" wondered Ham Brooks.

"For now," said the bronze man. "Further inquiry must wait. If we are to devise a method of dealing with these inexplicable detonations, it is urgent that we analyze the matter adhering to the interior of that safe."

The gravity of the bronze man's tone impelled Monk and Long Tom to finish up their work with alacrity.

Chapter VIII

SILVER-EYED SIREN

MIDNIGHT FOUND DOC SAVAGE in the white-walled laboratory of his skyscraper sanctum, working among a profusion of complicated apparatus that would have been the envy of many scientists around the globe.

Upon his return to the city, the bronze man had changed to a white smock and immediately set to work on the samples taken from the company safe of S. Charles Amerikanis. Long into the night he toiled, subjecting the metallic smears to numerous chemical tests and other rigorous scientific analyses.

From time to time, Monk Mayfair poked his rusty nubbin of a head in to offer an opinion or observe Doc's progress with a clinical eye. Monk was considered without peer in the field of industrial chemistry. But Doc Savage far surpassed him. It was thus with all of the bronze man's assistants.

Long Tom Roberts and Ham Brooks were busy elsewhere, investigating other angles of the miraculous maimings.

No one slept. But these men had been toughened by the rigors of the work that they did. Going without sleep for long periods did not faze them.

At one point, far into the evening, Doc Savage broke off, not to rest, but to take the two-hour exercise regimen that he had performed daily since he was first placed in the hands of scientists when small.

Monk happened to walk in on this, and watched with interest.

Many of the exercises were familiar portions of the bronze man's routine. For example, Doc produced compact apparatus that tested his faculties of sight and smell. Some of the devices he perfected himself. Not a few of these exercises Doc performed while blindfolded, reading Braille writing and identifying subtle odors captured in stoppered flasks.

The physical routine is what Monk most liked to observe. In addition to regular exercises which pitted Doc's impressive muscles against one another, Doc took a large potato in each hand and gave them a simultaneous squeeze. With a single bursting noise, both potatoes were reduced to pulp. Doc made it look easy.

Monk made a mental note to try that stunt at his next opportunity. He had a hunch he could pull it off with one potato, but not both at once. And Monk could bend horseshoes in his simian hands.

When Doc Savage was done, he seemed more refreshed than before.

"Whatcha discover, Doc?" the homely chemist asked.

"I have subjected the metallic samples adhering to the interior of the Elektro-Alchemical safe to various tests," Doc imparted. "Much of this matter consisted of metals of several recognizable types, but they have combined in ways that do not suggest conventional metallurgy."

"Meanin'?"

"They did not fuse by smelting, or through any recognizable heating process."

Monk made a monkey-like face. "That makes sense, I guess. If there had been that much heat, that steel box woulda turned to slag."

"Which is why the condition of these metals is so baffling," said Doc. "These metals have formed a number of alloys, and even amalgams, including what appears to be silver combined with the steel of the safe itself. High heat did not produce these results. A *force* did."

"*Ye-e-o-w!* What the heck kind of force would mix cold metals?"

Doc Savage paused a long moment before answering. "A force," he said at last, "that is so far beyond present-day science that it can only be called incalculable."

"Whew!" Monk exclaimed. "You sayin' you can't figger it out?"

Doc did not reply to that. It was a habit of his not to comment when he had only theories—and unproven ones at that. But it was clear to the apish chemist that Doc's investigations were pointing in some direction, to which the bronze man was as yet reluctant to commit.

Monk scratched his chin, which was bristling and unshaven. "You know," he said slowly, "people have been claimin' that they're gonna work out how to split the atom any day now. Experts say there's enough energy locked in a lump of ordinary coal to drive one of them big ocean liners for a year without refueling."

Doc Savage made no reply. He placed one eye on a microscope eyepiece, becoming absorbed in one sample.

Monk wandered out, saying, "Think I'll go see how Ham and Long Tom are doin' with their end of things. They've been touring hospital emergency rooms, looking for new victims. But it's been quiet all night. I don't think they had much luck."

DAWN found the bronze man still hard at work. Only one who knew him well would detect the faint lines of fatigue etching his regular features. But he pressed on, as if vitally concerned with the progress he was making.

The vast laboratory possessed windows on three sides and they gave a commanding view of the city spread around the skyscraper—the tallest in Manhattan. On a clear day, one could see New Jersey and Pennsylvania in the far distance. Not for nothing did the press refer to this as the bronze man's aerie.

A sudden flare threw salmon-colored illumination over the

laboratory interior. Seconds later, a boom came through the windows of bulletproof "health" glass. These panes shook momentarily.

Doc Savage glanced up from his study, eyes flickering alertly.

They came to rest on a smoky black blot that hung in the sky several miles distant from the skyscraper headquarters, beyond the Hudson River.

Moving to a window, Doc observed. The black blot began to turn gray and pieces of something started to rain down from it. Many were on fire. Among them, the bronze man made out what appeared to be the broken wing of an airplane. Falling.

Doc whipped to a cabinet and extracted a pair of powerful binoculars. He trained these on the aerial blot, adjusted the focusing screw, saw that it was fast fading.

Flashing to an intercommunicator on a marble-topped work bench, Doc pressed a button. His voice was edged with urgency.

"An airplane has just exploded over New Jersey. Endeavor to discover everything you can about this."

Ham Brooks's voice came back. "Righto, Doc!"

The bronze man returned to his work. So great was his concentration, it was as if the tragedy he had just witnessed had happened long ago.

IT was mid-morning when Doc Savage went into the big scientific library to consult a shelf of tomes from the section of the room given over to metallurgical works. Some few of these Doc himself had authored. But he did not look at those books, whose contents were firmly fixed in his amazingly retentive mind.

Rather, the bronze man selected a specific work from a glass-fronted book case, and carried this into the great laboratory. Consulting it at length, he began a series of experiments.

Long Tom interrupted him. He had returned from canvassing hospital emergency rooms, which had been quiet.

"Someone here to see you, Doc."

"Important?"

"She says it is."

Doc looked up. "She?"

"Says her name is Trixie Peters. Works for S. Charles Ameri-kanis."

Doc Savage was silent for a moment. Then: "I will be out directly."

The bronze man divested himself of his smock and changed into a fresh shirt, but no tie. He entered the reception room where a woman in her early thirties sat waiting.

Doc took his chair behind the great inlaid table that functioned as a desk.

Trixie Peters was dressed all in gray. Her clothes were tasteful and of the latest style. They were set off by white summer gloves. Her hair was a shade of lustrous black so deep it reminded one of a raven's wing. No hat adorned her head.

She regarded Doc Savage through a pair of dark glasses.

"You have the most unsettling eyes, Mr. Savage," she remarked.

Doc did not comment on that. His flake-gold eyes were active, probing. But his voice remained steady and without inflection.

"How may we be of assistance?"

"I am in the employ of the Elektro-Alchemical Corporation," she said crisply. "In fact, I am Mr. Amerikanis's confidential secretary. I fear my life may be in danger for what I am about to tell you."

"Go on," Doc urged.

Trixie Peters tugged at the fingers of her white gloves, as if about to remove them. She began to, then apparently changed her mind, and kept them on. It could be seen that one hand—the left—was carried stiffly.

"I have an utterly fantastic tale to tell you," she declared. "It both staggers the imagination and beggars belief. There are things going on at that company that threaten the existence of the entire world."

Long Tom Roberts was no lover of womankind. He had been listening impatiently, and now grumbled, "Get to the point, please."

Trixie Peters favored him with a withering look of disapproval.

"I have been made aware that you visited the plant last evening," she went on. "I wonder if you gleaned any inkling of the work that is going on there secretly?"

Doc said only, "Certain suspicions have been aroused as to the nature of experiments being performed at the Elektro-Alchemical concern."

Trixie Peters nodded somberly. "Then I need not go too much into details. It might be safer for me that way."

"The point," Long Tom repeated querulously.

The raven-haired woman continued fiddling nervously with her gloves. She transferred this nervous energy to her dark glasses, which she removed. Thus exposed, her features displayed a ripe beauty that suggested that she been quite ravishing a decade or so in the past, and was undeniably striking today.

Trixie Peters eyed Doc Savage steadily. She had large gray eyes which seemed almost silver. With her pale skin, gray ensemble, and richly ebony hair, the entire effect was a bit stark— as if she were a black and white photograph come to life.

"Instead of accusations, perhaps you would like to see proof of what you already suspect," she intoned.

"Proof," allowed Doc Savage, "would go a long way towards explaining many mysteries."

"Excellent," she said, rising. "I shan't take up anymore of your valuable time. Allow me to arrange for a package to be delivered to this office in a very short while. After you have had time to examine it, I will call you to discuss it further. Would that be satisfactory to you, Mr. Savage?"

Doc Savage stood up. "At what number can you be reached?"

"I am in hiding at present. Allow me to call you."

"If you feel that your life is in danger, it would be better if we accompanied you," countered Doc.

Her large silver-gray eyes flared. "No! That would be unwise. Most unwise. You must trust me. I have to go now. Expect a delivery before noon."

Hovering nearby, Long Tom scowled at her. "Listen! You know what this is all about, don't you?"

It was a wild shot, but it seemed to draw results.

"Oh!" The silvery-eyed woman put one white-gloved hand to the front of her frock.

"Settle down, please," Doc Savage advised quietly.

Trixie shook her raven tresses violently. "No!"

Eyes blazing, she hastily replaced her dark glasses.

Then she moved her right hand suddenly—the gesture was just a trifle too quick for the electrical wizard's eye to follow, but she evidently took a small silver derringer from her purse, for Long Tom was suddenly looking into both uninviting barrels.

"You keep away!" she gritted. "I've been tricked, and I'm leaving here!"

She backed for the door.

DOC SAVAGE's hand drifted to the top of the Oriental table at which he was seated, where numerous inlays of ivory and other materials served as hidden controls. The bronze-colored entrance door—it was really forged of tempered steel—was closed. Doc could lock or unlock it by tapping a rosewood inlay. He locked it.

This cautious motion on the bronze man's part did not go unnoticed. The double-barreled derringer shifted in his direction.

"Hands still!" Trixie barked.

Doc Savage said evenly, "You have the advantage."

Taking a step back, Trixie put her back to the door. It refused to budge.

"Unlock this door!" she ordered.

The bronze man did so. The electric locking relay let go with an audible sound. Trixie started to push her way out of the reception room.

Long Tom had been loitering beside a panel carved in the outline of a windjammer. He popped this open, disclosing an insulated black instrument panel. This controlled several defensive devices with which the reception room had been outfitted. His fingers slipped toward this.

Without hesitating, Trixie Peters whirled, sent a slug crashing through the Bakelite control board.

This produced several unfortunate results.

First, the composition panel split, short-circuiting the electrical connections. A long sizzling blue spark snaked out and seared Long Tom's reaching fingers. With a yodel of pain, he snapped his hand back, then danced about, fanning stung fingers and going *"Whooo!"*

Doc Savage was out of his chair by then. He plunged across the room. He would have seized the fleeing woman, but for the fact that before shorting out, an array of defensive traps let go.

The first was a black billow of smoke. It issued from a ceiling vent and almost immediately consumed all light and visibility, as it was formulated to do.

Long Tom began barking expletives. He could be heard fumbling about blindly.

The bronze man had cleared more than half the room in that brief interval. His uncanny senses would normally have carried him to success. But for the fact that a thick sheet of bulletproof glass, designed to protect the occupants from gunmen entering from the corridor, dropped down from above, blocking his way.

Doc slammed into it, recovered, and endeavored to circumnavigate the shield in the close-pressing pall. He succeeded, groped his way out into the corridor, which was filling with black gloom, reaching a stretch of hazy air just in time to duck a fresh bullet sizzling from the direction of the closing elevator doors.

With that parting shot, the raven-haired woman took her departure.

Chapter IX

LEAD INTO GOLD

THERE WAS NO recalling the elevator, which was of the self-service type. Doc Savage raced back to the reception room to place a call to the lobby. He first had to clear the room of impenetrable smoke, which he did by engaging great fans in the ceiling. These drew the murky pall into vents, to be carried outside.

By the time the bronze man completed his call, the elevator had reached the lobby. It was empty!

Macabre touch, a pair of shoes identical to those lately worn by their visitor, stood empty on the floor of the lift. They were still warm.

"It's almost as if she vanished into thin air!" Doc was told by a lobby guard who was in his employ.

Long Tom kicked a waste-paper basket clear across the hazy room in frustration. "Women!" he snarled.

"If Trixie is her true identity," said Doc, "she is well named. As you know, the rubber mat in the corridor is impregnated with a chemical that will adhere to shoe soles, leaving sticky tracks which will fluoresce when subjected to ultra-violet light. By removing her shoes, she has foiled that particular precaution."

A thorough search of the great skyscraper failed to locate the silvery-eyed Trixie Peters. It was puzzling. The lobby guards swore up and down that no female fitting that description, young or old, had exited the building. Nor was there any indication that she had stepped off on any other floor.

Doc Savage replaced the desk telephone at the end of a long and frustrating series of conversations, looking grim.

"No luck," he reported.

"What was that all about?" Long Tom wanted to know.

"Complications," said Doc. "Long Tom, let me know immediately when the package arrives."

"*If* it does."

"Be sure to subject it to the usual precautions," Doc reminded.

"Naturally."

Doc Savage returned to his laboratory. On his way through the library, he paused to remove a fat black book from a wall bookshelf in a far corner of the room. This section was devoted to unusual subjects. Some of these books were very old, their spines cracked with age. The tome selected came equipped with a tiny brass padlock.

THE package arrived a half-hour before noon.

There was a routine for screening all mail coming to the bronze man, who had earned a great number of enemies over the course of a hectic career. Packages addressed to Doc Savage were routed from the building mail room to a special office where they could be subjected to X-rays and other examination designed to certify the safety of any package of questionable origin.

This item passed all tests with flying colors. It was externally ordinary—simply a box enveloped in brown butcher paper and secured by stout twine. It was very heavy. But no infernal device was revealed by the fluoroscope.

Long Tom did the honors. When he was satisfied, he took the private elevator to the eighty-sixth floor laboratory and set the unwrapped package on a glass-topped working table before Doc Savage.

The bronze man undid the twine, stripped off the paper wrapping and opened the box. It proved to be a lady's hatbox.

Inside lay revealed a blob of gleaming, yellowish metal, weighing no more than ten ounces. It lay nestled in a bed of wood shavings.

Doc's uncanny trilling saturated the surroundings, then faded into insignificance. He had throttled it, as if suppressing his own excitement. Often he did not realize that he was making the melodious sound.

A metallic hand removed the misshapen lump and weighed it briefly.

So sensitive were Doc's senses that he unhesitatingly announced, "Ten Troy ounces."

"Gold?" breathed Long Tom.

Doc nodded. "So it would seem."

"It's not iron pyrite," Long Tom said. "I know fool's gold when I see it."

The bronze man placed it on a porcelain tray atop the work bench. He applied a simple steel tool to the mass. The yellow metal took small indentations wherever he pressed. It was not very soft.

"Not pure," Doc said.

Long Tom noticed a note at the bottom of the hatbox. It was typed. It read:

> One week ago, this was an ordinary lump of lead. By an application of the ancient science of alchemistry, it has been converted to purest gold. The dream of the ancients has been realized. If you are the man that I think you are, Mr. Savage, you will realize what a danger to humanity this discovery represents.
>
> Trix

Doc read this in absorbed silence. Swiftly, he subjected the golden lump to a battery of tests to determine its exact nature, chief among them the application of *aqua regia*, an acid employed to determine the purity of gold.

Long Tom watched him immerse a speck of the substance

into a tray filled with *aqua regia*. Reaction set in. The speck bubbled, soon dissolved.

At the end, Doc pronounced, "Gold."

"No question," concurred Long Tom. "But how do we know that this is really gold from lead?"

Before Doc could answer, a telephone buzzed. There were instruments in every room, and owing to its vast size, several were stationed strategically about the laboratory, each with its own distinctive ring.

Long Tom scooped up the nearest handset, saying, "Doc Savage headquarters." He listened a moment.

Clapping a hand over the mouthpiece, he undertoned, "It's that tricky Trixie Peters. She wants to know if you received her package yet."

"Inform her that I am convinced that this is true gold," Doc said.

The puny electrical wizard relayed the information. Then he said, "O.K." Hanging up, he told Doc, "Says that she's on her way up here to explain more."

"Trace the call if possible," Doc directed.

Long Tom made a call to the building's switchboard and hung up. "Call came from one of the pay telephones in the lobby. She never left the building!"

"No doubt she made arrangements for delivery in advance," Doc observed.

Long Tom was already phoning the lobby. But no sign of the elusive Trixie was discovered.

"Bet she slipped out."

"We will shortly see," said Doc.

Doc and Long Tom returned to examining the mysterious lump of gold that might have formerly been mere slag lead.

"Transmutation of lead to gold is theoretically possible," Long Tom mused. "Atomically, both metals are very similar."

"Men have sought this secret for centuries, but it has always eluded them," Doc Savage admitted. But doubt troubled in his voice.

Long Tom noticed one of the books the bronze man had brought in from the adjacent library. Its age caught his attention. Looking at the title page, he read aloud, "*Ye Ancient & Noble Science of Alchemy!*"

Turning to Doc, he said, "You already guessed this!"

"Last night at S. Charles Amerikanis's lab," he explained, "I noticed equipment suggesting experiments along the lines of the transmutation of base metals over to precious ones. There was also a vat of molten lead, supporting that supposition. Also copper, another element which ancient alchemists thought to be convertible to gold, was present in noticeable quantities."

"But what has this to do with all these mystery detonations?"

Doc Savage declined to answer. But his very silence seemed to suggest that such a connection was unavoidable.

Trixie Peters failed to appear. Neither man was surprised. A renewed search of the building failed to turn up any trace of the wily woman.

NOT long after that, Monk and Ham returned from their investigation. They were quarrelling, as usual.

"That pig chewed on my shoe the entire way here," Ham was saying, "and I insist that you pay for a replacement pair!"

The pig in question had been named Habeas Corpus. Habeas was Monk's pet pig. To a scrawny body were attached dog-like legs and ears which, when extended, would have made serviceable wings. The unusual porker was trotting along at the apish chemist's heels. Evidently, Monk had collected the shoat from his penthouse on Wall Street, where Habeas idled away his luxurious days in a perfumed hog wallow.

Monk snorted derisively. "Habeas wasn't chewing. He was just nuzzling."

"What's the difference?" demanded Ham.

"Them kicks of yours look like pigskin to me. Maybe he

recognized a distant relative."

Ham backed into the room and his sword cane was out, flashing. "If you won't make good on the damage, then I may have to skin that ridiculous hog and deliver his hide to my cobbler."

"You touch that hog," Monk warned, "and I'll plant both feet on the seat of your trousers, and make you eat them fancy shoes."

Noticing the gleaming lump over which Doc and Long Tom were hovering, Monk asked, "Is that gold?"

"That's not the question of the hour," Long Tom remarked dryly.

"Then what is?" inquired Ham.

"The real question is: was it lead *before* it was gold?"

Monk started to say, "Was it *what*—?"

Long Tom Roberts' sour features suddenly acquired a twisted expression. He winced, grabbed at his mouth, tried to speak.

"Teeff!" was all he managed.

"What did you say?" Monk demanded.

Long Tom pointed at his gold incisors. "Teeff! Teeff! Teeff!" he repeated excitedly.

Ham howled, "His teeth! There's something wrong with his teeth!"

All eyes turned to their leader.

Doc Savage was already in motion. A bronze blur, he grabbed the lump of slag gold, and leapt for the bomb-disposal chute tucked away in one corner. This functioned exactly like an office mail chute, except that it terminated in a reinforced vault deep in the sub-basement garage constructed to smother any conventional explosive.

Doc grasped the handle of the brass door. The sudden expression coming over his bronze face registered doubt, hesitation. Perhaps he feared for the great building's foundations.

Reversing himself, the bronze giant lunged toward one of the big windows that overlooked the city.

The windows were constructed of bulletproof glass thick enough to stand up to machine-gun lead, if anyone could manage to position one eighty-six stories above the street for the purpose of attack. It was tough stuff. And the windows were locked with an electrical mechanism that could only be unsealed by application of a powerful magnet.

No time to locate the magnetic key. Doc took down a racked fire axe and drove a hole into the pane. Then he began chipping away it, enlarging the fracture in a controlled fury such as his men had never before beheld in the bronze giant.

Monk and Long Tom, understanding the chemical constituents of the glass, would have thought it impossible to shatter the pane so swiftly, if at all. But in short order, Doc Savage had excavated a jagged hole.

Swiftly, he thrust the golden blob through the splintered opening, then he flung himself to the floor.

The others did not need any vocal warning to do the same. They threw themselves under the handiest working tables. Habeas Corpus wisely followed suit. Monk covered him with Ham's fallen hat.

They waited. Not many seconds later, they heard a report—surprisingly modest. It sounded like a basketball had been stepped on violently.

That was all. Still, no one stirred until the bronze man climbed to his feet.

Moving to the shattered window, Doc began picking at the shards of thick glass, creating an opening sufficient for his head. He thrust it out, looked down, then withdrew. His bronze countenance was strange, the way metal is strange when nearing its melting point.

The others took turns doing the same. The skyscraper was constructed on the order of a wedding cake, with setbacks every so many stories. These formed ledges that were wide. An object thrown from any high window would almost certainly land on the ledge immediately beneath. But there was nothing visible down there.

"I don't see it," Ham said, puzzled.

Monk ventured, "Musta bounced off the ledge into the street."

Long Tom said, "We'd better check!" His voice was muffled, for he had removed his front teeth during the uproar.

Monk, Ham and Long Tom charged for the elevators.

STRANGELY, Doc Savage did not follow.

Instead, he busied himself with the hatbox, which was un-damaged. From a cabinet, Doc removed a jar of what a chemist would recognize as common graphite and, taking up a small brush, dipped it in the granular gray powder and began brushing the interior of the hatbox with great care.

When the interior was painted a nearly uniform gray, he removed what looked like an ordinary cigar humidor from a pocket and began to unscrew it. His regular features grew more set with resolve.

Out of this receptacle, Doc removed a grisly object: a human finger. It was slim, the nail tapering to a point after the fashion of a woman's manicured fingernail.

Employing a small set of tongs, the bronze man brushed the pad of the finger with graphite and impressed this upon a sheet of paper, creating a distinct fingerprint.

One glance was all that was required to ascertain that the two fingerprints were similar—although there was no single print that was a precise match. This could be explained by the fact that the person who had touched the hatbox lacked the missing finger. The disorderly array of prints made it impossible to say with certainty.

Doc Savage picked up a telephone and called a number with a midtown exchange.

"Patricia, Inc.," a musical voice said by way of greeting.

Doc did not identify himself except to say, "I would like to speak to my cousin."

"One moment, please."

The voice that came onto the line was bright and very feminine. It was a voice that would have curled the toes of any healthy male.

"Doc! I've been practically in hiding since this thing started."

"A wise course," said the bronze man. "Pat, I need your assistance."

"Have I passed away and gone to Valhalla?" Pat exclaimed. "Or am I dreaming?"

"Neither," said Doc. "I have a crucial piece of evidence in this matter. I need you to convey it to a safe place."

Pat's voice shrank in disappointment. "Oh, is that all?"

"It is very significant, Pat," Doc insisted. "I will send it to your establishment by messenger. Do not open the package under any circumstances. Instead, take it out of the city where it will be safe and can be claimed later."

Pat's voice turned suddenly suspicious. "This isn't a trick to get me out of the city, is it?"

"You have never ceased trying to involve yourself in my affairs," Doc continued, as if not hearing the question. "Here is your golden opportunity to perform a valuable service. Attempts may be made to seize this evidence. You are the only trustworthy person outside of my five aides. Will you do this?"

The line hummed briefly. Then Pat said, "O.K. You talked me into it. Where do I stash the swag?"

"Let me suggest Miami. Take your personal plane and fly there without delay."

"Got it."

"You do not mind?" asked Doc.

"Business is slack," Pat said cheerfully. "I was thinking of taking a vacation anyway. Besides, I have been reading about all these horrible human grenades in the papers. Just imagining myself blowing up has been keeping me up nights."

"I am glad that you are being reasonable," said Doc, replacing the receiver on its bronze pedestal. Faint relief was etched on the metallic lineaments of his face. Patricia Savage was his cousin and only living relative. Ever since coming to the big city, she had campaigned to join the bronze man's group of adventurers. Sometimes she had succeeded in tagging along, but never permanently. Doc usually found excuses to eject her.

So it was unusual, to say the least, that the bronze man was enlisting her aid.

Chapter X

THE FIEND'S WEB

MONK, HAM AND Long Tom conducted an exceedingly thorough search of the block surrounding Doc Savage's skyscraper headquarters.

Taking the speed elevator to the lobby, they reached the ground floor in surprisingly rapid time. Monk ran it down at its swiftest rate of speed, with the result that only the hairy chemist kept his feet, so fast did the cage descend. Ham and Long Tom were thrown to their knees when the cage stopped abruptly.

Picking himself up, Ham Brooks examined the knees of his immaculate trousers. They were discolored.

"You hair-coated missing link!" the dapper lawyer complained, brushing them off with a monogrammed handkerchief. "You did that on purpose!"

"Ain't my fault you can't keep your feet!" Monk flung back. "Next time use your cane, grandpa!"

Long Tom barked, "Pipe down, you two!"

The three piled out into the street and sought the west side of the building, from which the lump of gold had fallen.

They did not expect to see it. Nor were they disappointed. The sidewalk was full of pedestrians who acted as if nothing untoward had transpired. It was the hot shank of the afternoon. Perspiration stood out on every face, made clothing sticky. Men did not seem to know what to do with their hats.

"Back upstairs," Ham suggested, mopping his forehead with

his handkerchief.

This time, they employed the public lift, getting off at different floors, which the express elevator could not do. In this way, the trio covered more territory than if they had acted in a group. They invaded offices, flung up windows, looked out of them—but found exactly nothing.

At the end of the futile search, they reported to Doc Savage.

"No sign of the gold," announced Monk.

"It must have gone somewhere!" Ham insisted.

"Maybe it was transmuted again," suggested Long Tom thoughtfully. He had his gold teeth back in his mouth, and sounded like his usual sour self.

"Why do you say that?" Doc prompted.

Long Tom shrugged deceptively frail shoulders. "What else could have happened to it?"

"What do you mean—transmuted?" demanded Ham.

Long Tom handed Ham the note that had come in the box containing the lump of gold. Monk read it by peering around the dapper lawyer's sharp elbows. His jaw fell open.

"Blazes!" yelled Monk. "Doc, you gotta hear this!"

Interest flickered in Doc Savage's eyes.

"That plane that blew up?" Monk continued. "It was a transport craft. No passengers."

"Cargo?"

"Gold bars, Doc," Ham interjected. "Bullion to strengthen the financial position of a Chicago bank."

"That's not all," added Monk. "The pieces of the plane came down in a Jersey cemetery, so no one was hurt. Me and Ham took a run out there and nosed around the wreckage. There was a big crater, and workers were digging for the pilot's bodies. They found them all right—but there wasn't any trace of the gold ingots they was ferryin' to Chicago."

Doc Savage's trilling emerged from him like a wild thing. It ran up and down the musical scale as if chasing something elusive. In time, it trailed off to nothingness. It left the air quivering afterward.

"This explains why my roadster suffered the weird fate that it did," he said distinctly.

Monk snapped his fingers. "I get it! You always carry extra equipment cases in the trunk."

"Exactly," said Doc. "Among that equipment were experimental devices whose electrical connections included some fashioned of gold."

Ham looked baffled. "Gold?"

Doc Savage nodded. "Not as efficient a conductor of electricity as copper or silver, for example, but gold has the added advantage of not tarnishing. No doubt the gold connections were violently excited by the unknown force we are presently facing, which caused the uncanny destruction of the trunk."

Expressions of understanding roosted on the faces of Doc's three aides.

Long Tom said it first. "Something has been making gold explode!"

"Jove!" breathed Ham, twisting his sword cane absently.

"It is a fact that some metals, upon being exposed to shortwave rays, will heat up," Doc Savage elaborated. "A similar scientific phenomena may be at work here."

"Probably the work of some nut inventor," Monk opined.

The bronze man moved to a telephone and began making a series of calls to high officials in the city. For nearly a half-hour, he made one after the other, in the end hanging up with a look of rare determination on his bronze mask of a face. Casual emotion had been schooled out of him, but if his present expression was any sign, that discipline was not perfect.

WITHIN an hour, the extras were hitting the streets. The scareheads were stark, and set in bold type:

DOC SAVAGE WARNS OF GOLD RISK!

MAYOR CAUTIONS CITIZENS
TO DIVEST OF ALL HOARDED GOLD

The stories were scanty of facts. Doc Savage almost never gave interviews to the press. So this fact alone caused people to sit up and take notice.

In brief, the accounts all ran the same way. The mystery man known as Doc Savage had issued a warning to the effect that the recent violent detonations which had maimed several innocent persons and damaged a jewelry store and a bank, were all connected by a common thread—of gold.

Doc Savage urged every citizen to cease wearing gold rings, cufflinks, bracelets and other auric jewelry. Further, he noted that while the U.S. government had banned private ownership of gold coins and bars, anyone still hoarding such booty was advised to turn it over to the proper authorities. The bronze man stressed how dangerous ownership of metallic gold was, and would continue to be, until the person or persons behind the deadly detonations were apprehended.

These warnings were backed up by statements from the mayor of New York City, its commissioner of police, and the governor of the state, attesting to the good character and reputation of the great humanitarian, Clark Savage, Jr.

In short, this was no hoax.

Response from the citizenry fell into predictable categories, human nature being what it is.

Some thought that, despite assurances to the contrary, it was all some sort of gigantic publicity stunt.

Others derided it as a swindle calculated to confiscate all the yellow metal in New York City. Rumors that Doc Savage himself possessed a secret source of gold received a big play in the yellower tabloids, one of which had dubbed Doc the "Modern Midas of Manhattan." These rumors fed suspicions on the part of the more gossip-hungry citizenry.

There was a run on the banks, but in reverse. People besieged all savings institutions, seeking space in the big vaults for safety deposit boxes to rent for the express purpose of storing their gold valuables.

Mindful of what had happened to the Chemical Trust Bank, bankers were turning these people away. If elemental gold was somehow becoming unstable and explosive, no sane bank official wanted it on their premises.

In fact, the Federal Reserve Bank of New York surreptitiously began shipping their own gold reserves out of the city proper—the only area affected up until that time.

When an armored car fell victim to a mysterious accident, that activity ceased. The armored car was moving over the Queensboro Bridge when the rear doors blew out and went careening into trailing traffic.

One door smacked into a touring car, with the result that the chauffeur found the windscreen, bent but still in its steel frame, sitting in his astonished lap.

The other door caused three cars to swerve wildly. Two collided. The third banged into the bridge's steel rail, shedding a bumper. No one was seriously injured, although all vehicles involved were ruined.

DOC SAVAGE was on the scene as soon as the first report came over the radio. He pulled up in a coupé that, like all of the bronze man's machines, was painted a subdued hue.

The police had cordoned off the damaged armored car and were talking to the bewildered driver and his accompanying guard as vehicular traffic whizzed past, encouraged by short blasts of police whistles.

"You sayin' you heard a noise?" a police officer was asking of the driver.

The latter was swabbing his sweat-smeared face with a handkerchief. "Yeah, I thought a tire got punctured. That was about the sound. Not sharp like a blowout, but dull."

"Then the doors blew clean off," the guard added.

"So where's all the gold you were carrying?" asked the cop.

The pair looked as confused as caged monkeys. Glances were swapped. They had no explanation.

So they were only too happy to let Doc Savage examine the interior of the truck.

Although bank records indicated that no less than one million dollars in brick gold had been loaded into the truck, not a gram remained. The interior of the armored car was scarred and pitted, but in none of these pocks was even the most microscopic bit of auric metal.

"Transmuted!" Long Tom muttered.

"But into what?" countered Monk.

The pale electrical wizard tugged at an earlobe. "Atoms, I guess."

They all looked to Doc Savage, who was stepping from the interior. "Atomized, possibly," he ventured.

"Are you sayin' that someone had finally figgered out how to split the atom?" asked Monk.

"That would be one of the greatest discoveries of the century," Long Tom breathed. For once, the electrical wizard sounded impressed.

"It is vital that we return to headquarters at once," said Doc.

The others exhibited symptoms of being flummoxed. They lived for danger, and excitement. As did their bronze chief. It was the wine of life to them.

"Shouldn't we be canvassing the city for that Trixie Peters?" Ham inquired.

"I provided the police with her description," Doc supplied. "For the moment, they are better equipped to investigate that aspect of things, having patrolmen stationed all over the city."

"Do you think she's in cahoots with that violet-eyed mystery woman you trailed to Greenwich Village?" Long Tom wanted to know.

"Not exactly," said Doc.

"Why the heck not?" Monk demanded.

"Her fingerprints off the box containing the supposedly transmuted gold tell a different story." But that was all the bronze man said, as if this explained more than it did.

THEY drove back to headquarters, where Doc secluded himself in his impressive experimental laboratory for well over an hour.

When he emerged, the bronze giant handed them each a gleaming gold wristwatch.

"Wear these close to your skin," he instructed. "They are made of electrum, the same alloy that comprises Long Tom's front incisors. If they begin to feel warm, it means that the author of these crimes has activated his device."

"What if they explode?" Monk wanted to know.

"There is no risk of that," explained Doc. "Apparently, electrum does not respond to the force as violently as unalloyed gold."

Ever fastidious, Ham examined his. He noted that instead of the usual two hands of the clock, there was only a minute hand. It was not moving.

Doc explained, "The inner mechanism is sensitive to heat. When the watch casing warms up, the minute hand begins to sweep, and the dial face will light up."

"Swell!" Ham said, evidently pleased with the workmanship.

They put the devices on, including Doc Savage. All except Long Tom, who said, "I'll stick with my lucky teeth."

"If they were that lucky," Monk snorted, "you'd show them off more."

"It is time," Doc Savage said, "to pay another visit to S. Charles Amerikanis."

Monk smacked one rusty fist into the opposite paw, saying, "I'm all for that!"

Ham seconded Monk's enthusiastic opinion by unsheathing his sword cane and vowing, "If that pinch-faced penny-pincher gives us any further grief, I will slice off his ears first chance I get."

Suddenly, the dapper lawyer looked strange. "Jove," he said, his voice sounding queer.

"What is it?" Monk muttered. "Acute indigestion?"

Wordlessly, Ham raised his sword cane to display the head, which was formed in the shape of a knob—a golden knob.

"This is sixteen karat gold," he said thickly. "Why did it fail to detonate?"

Doc Savage took the cane, felt its heft. It was heavy enough to be genuine gold, even accounting for the concealed blade of Damascus steel. The bronze man carried the cane into his lab and subjected it to a quick chemical test.

Doc returned, saying, "Not gold. Brass. But painted to resemble gold."

"I know gold when I see it!" Ham insisted. But then he noticed the guilty look on Monk Mayfair's simian features. Ham eyed Monk with narrow suspicion.

"Is this the sword cane you gave me on my last birthday?" he demanded, an edge coming into his voice.

"I dunno," retorted Monk. "Ain't you got a bunch of spares?"

"Yes, but I believe this is the one you presented to me with great ceremony, after accidentally breaking one of my finest canes. I have always been suspicious over that incident."

Monk had never been skilled at keeping his innermost thoughts off his wide, pleasantly homely features. He struggled with keeping a straight face.

"I guess the guy I bought it off musta pulled a fast one on me," he said finally.

"You hairy mistake!" Ham exploded, purpling. "You hoodwinked me! I have been carrying this cane around for many months—and all the time it was a patent fake!"

Long Tom put in dryly, "If he hadn't, you might have been blown apart when that lump of gold was vaporized to smithereens."

Ham looked stricken. The expression on his sharply chiseled features wavered between rage and relief. Relief won.

Monk grinned broadly. "Guess it looks like I saved your life, don't it?"

"*All* of our lives," Doc Savage pointed out.

"What do you mean?" Ham sputtered. "You just told me that you were cheated!"

Monk regarded the ceiling blandly. "Well, if I had noticed it," he said airily, "I'd have taken it back to the crook that sold it to me and had a gold head put on. Then where would you be?"

"A likely story!" fumed the dapper lawyer.

"Better hold onto that cane, Ham," Doc suggested. "Under the circumstances, it would be too dangerous to replace it now."

The bronze man led the way to his private elevator.

As they trailed him, Ham told Monk Mayfair with strangled vehemence, "You have not heard the last of this, you fuzzy gossoon!"

Monk wore an expression balanced between smug satisfaction and genuine concern. For years, Ham had been promising to whack a side off Habeas the pig and fry it up for breakfast bacon. Ham hated pork in all forms, but the apish chemist knew that he might make an exception in this case.

Chapter XI

FEAR OF GOLD

A S DOC SAVAGE and his men pulled into afternoon traffic from the sub-basement garage which housed his fleet of vehicles, they were witness to a metropolis gripped by fear.

City streets were filling with office workers en route to their homes. Evidently, many were leaving their places of employment early. Moreover, an unusual number of newsboys were on the streets.

Practically every peddler of newspapers was surrounded by a crowd. The papers, marked by large black headlines, sold rapidly. Those who bought them stood and read, instead of tucking the sheets under an arm. This itself showed that the day's news was startling, for it was a sweltering day, unfavorable for comfortable outdoor reading.

The headlines were amazing. They conveyed the most fantastic story to appear within the memory space of most readers.

Almost a dozen persons had died in New York City during the previous hour, struck down in their homes, in theaters, riding subways, while driving and otherwise going about their normal routines. Most had suffered head injuries that resulted in the utter obliteration of said heads. A few had bled to death after losing their hands, which had been amputated at the wrist by no visible agency. Remarkably, all of the latter were women. Few men had suffered the loss of a hand, although many people, both men and women, lost fingers through unaccountable violence. This particular phenomenon was ascribed to the fact that woman often wore gold bracelets, but men never did. However, what few men who lost hands had been discovered to possess gold wristwatches. In one ghastly case, a wealthy dowager had had her cranium savagely compressed by the simultaneous detonations of her gold earrings.

The dead were largely ordinary New Yorkers, although some were individuals considered to be respectable citizens of some renown. The attacks appeared to be random, and had occurred at scattered parts of lower Manhattan, but nowhere else. There seemed to be no discoverable purpose to the strange slaughtering of common humanity.

Death in some hideous form was sweeping the city, said the newspapers. One self-proclaimed criminologist expressed the opinion that an epidemic of terroristic sniping had struck. Despite the man's reputation as a dilettante, police were dispatched to prominent city roofs with binoculars to watch for the phantom sniper. The tabloids carried such pictures of the dead as their reporters had been able to snatch. Most proved too grisly for print.

"No sniper could inflict such fearful injuries," sniffed Ham Brooks, after skimming one such account. "Not even with explosive bullets."

"Whoever's back of this," Long Tom assayed, "cares not one whit about human life."

"And he's pickin' up the pace of his reign of horror," growled Monk. "Why do you think that is, Doc?"

"The goal of all this senseless terror," observed Doc Savage, "remains to be discovered."

The bronze man shot through traffic, silent and watchful. He was driving a nondescript coupé. Nothing about it suggested that the hood concealed a powerful motor, nor that it was armored and equipped with other interesting features the manufacturer never considered.

Police radio cars were everywhere. Several times, ambulances scooted past, sirens howling. Once, it was a dead wagon, evidently conveying a recent victim to the busy City Morgue.

"The bodies are sure piling up," Long Tom observed gloomily.

They were on Broadway now. Traffic was thicker than normal. As a consequence, they hit many stop lights and were forced to idle in the heat.

A sanitation truck came trundling along. Persons came out of their apartments and places of work to throw rings and other valuables into the open back.

"Blazes!" said Monk, eyeing bracelets and bangles piling up in the rear of the truck. "People are sure scared if they're dumpin' their valuables like that!"

They were. The city was terrified. No one knew when next the horror would strike. But no one wanted to take a chance that they would be spared.

Not only rings and personal jewelry, but gold in all its myriad forms were being discarded. A bar of gold weighing no less than twelve Troy ounces had been tossed from the upper story of a building. It chanced to strike a passerby on the head, crushing his skull.

As the body was removed to a waiting ambulance, the careless party was clapped in handcuffs.

The police and the medicos stepped gingerly around the gold ingot. When the sanitation truck came along, a cop tossed it in, wearing a strangely stricken expression. No doubt he was calculating how many months' pay that single length of yellow metal equaled.

It was like that all over the embattled city.

A criminal gang who had been stealing from private residences decided that their ill-gotten wealth was not worth the risk involved, and called the police to come pick it up. The swag was found where the crooks said it would be—in a big heap in Central Park.

There was so much of the stuff that the gleaming pile was

cordoned off and the bomb squad was called in to dispose of the potentially-unstable metal.

IT was breathtaking. The city was at a virtual standstill. Doors were locked. Businesses stood shuttered. Commerce had ground to a halt. Few dared to venture out of doors. Many persons fled the summer heat and the cloud of horror hanging over all by taking hasty vacations. The ever-present hum of human activity that marked Manhattan by day was muted to a degree that struck lifelong Gothamites as unnerving.

"Don't this beat all!" Monk breathed.

"What gets me," complained Long Tom, "is what's behind the terror? What I mean, where is the motive?"

"Perhaps," offered Ham Brooks, twisting his cane nervously, "the person behind this devilment seeks to corner the market in gold."

"Or drive up the price of silver," suggested Long Tom.

"How so?" asked Ham.

"Don't you get it? If there's less gold around, silver becomes more valuable."

"In the past, attempts to corner the silver market have resulted in abnormal speculative schemes," Doc Savage reminded, turning in the direction of the Brooklyn Bridge.

"Gold is still gold," Monk pointed out. "Ham, ain't you worried about your digs at the Midas Club?"

"What do you mean?" the dapper lawyer snapped.

"Ain't that where you store your extra canes? What if they all explode at the same time?"

Ham actually turned pale. He gripped his dark cane all the more tightly.

Seeing this, the homely chemist grinned broadly. "Maybe we ought to swing over there and help you contribute them to the gold drive."

The thought of parting with his valued collection of sword canes caused the normally voluble lawyer to lapse into a thin and uncharacteristic silence.

Grim of countenance, Doc Savage left the paralyzed city behind. Soon, he was on the road to the Elektro-Alchemical Company. The afternoon was wearing on. Traffic was more plentiful outside the city, where the sudden scourge had not yet touched.

THEY found the plant closed and padlocked. The guard on duty from the night before met them at the entrance gate.

"Mr. Amerikanis says to tell you that he isn't here, Mr. Savage," offered the man helpfully.

"Where is he?" asked Monk.

"Here," said the guard pleasantly. "I was just telling you what I'm supposed to say. That's all. But Mr. Amerikanis has got the place shut down and I'm not supposed to let anyone in. It will be my job if I do. He thinks someone is trying to kill him."

Doc Savage removed a card from his billfold. Offering it to the gate guard, he said, "Report to this location if you find yourself unemployed. A position with a good salary will be yours."

The guard broke into a happy grin and, all but saluting the bronze man, unlocked the padlocked gate. He said, "Go right in."

There was a different secretary at the reception desk. She was the equal of the other one, except that this specimen was a ravishing redhead.

"Here to see old Bonesy Amerikanis," said Monk, grinning broadly.

"I am instructed not to admit anyone," sniffed the secretary, who appeared immune to the hairy chemist's charms.

Long Tom interrupted querulously. "We've heard that song before. Cough up. Where is he?"

"I am terribly sorry, but—"

Monk shoved into the office, found it to be empty, then wheeled about, saying, "Let's hunt 'im down, brothers."

Doc Savage had already started off. They caught a glimpse of the bronze man rounding a corner, and hastened to follow.

Doc tracked S. Charles Amerikanis to the same work room where he had held forth the night previous. Master Bonesy could be seen through a half-open door, pacing restlessly. He seemed oblivious to his surroundings.

The moment he heard the door open, Amerikanis drew a pistol and began firing wildly.

"Back!" he snarled. "Stay back, I say!"

Gunsound banged off the walls.

DOC SAVAGE seemed to step to one side in a casual way. But three bullets volleyed by him, fanning the front of his coat. The bronze man's reflexes were eye-defyingly swift.

Lunging, Doc pitched into the room.

Another bullet was squeezed from the pistol, and this time Doc took the full brunt of it square in the chest.

He skidded on his feet, recovered, and drove forward as if the slamming slug were but a minor hindrance.

A tendon-wrapped bronze hand surrounded the pistol, twisted. The weapon was suddenly in Doc's hand and Amerikanis was standing there wringing injured fingers with his undamaged hand.

"Bulletproof under-vest," explained the bronze giant.

Ham next popped into the room. "Assault with intent to murder!" he exploded. "That will be the charge lodged against you!"

Amerikanis collapsed into a chair. "I—I did not know that was you!" he stammered. "Believe me." Pain lingered in his sunken eyes.

"*Make* us believe you," suggested Long Tom, the next to arrive.

They surrounded him. Amerikanis seemed to cave inward, like a collapsed toy balloon. There was no more resistance in him.

"I thought you were enemies trying to kill me," he moaned. "Ever since the horrific events of last night, I have lived in fear of my very life."

Doc asked, "Who would wish to kill you?"

"That is the abominable thing. I do not know!" Amerikanis insisted. "I do not have an enemy in the world. None! You must believe me!"

Monk and Long Tom began eying the workroom with professional interest. Monk's deep-set eyes took in the chemical apparatus, while the slender electrical wizard paid close attention to the wiring arrangements.

"What's this setup for?" Monk wanted to know.

Amerikanis stuck out his chest, and looked as if he wanted to tell the gorilla-like chemist off. Words failed him.

Doc Savage regarded S. Charles Amerikanis with steady gaze. The bronze man's eyes were not comfortable to look at, as they were now. The illusion—if that was what it was—of animate life constantly swirling in them was an arresting effect to behold, but under extended scrutiny it could unnerve a susceptible man. It did so now. Perspiration began popping out of Amerikanis's visible pores.

"This area of the plant," Doc Savage said steadily, "is not constructed for ordinary commercial metallurgy."

"I will grant you that," Amerikanis said miserably. "In recent years, my concern has been branching out into experimental endeavours. To that end, I hired a man with the same interest in advancing science as myself."

"John Merlin," supplied Doc.

"Yes. A brilliant man, Merlin. He understood, as did I, that the ancients made certain discoveries that the modern world has yet to rediscover. We were working toward the reclamation of certain lost metals. This work area was constructed to his specifications."

"Which metals?" prompted Doc.

"Have you ever heard of Corinthian bronze?"

Had S. Charles Amerikanis known more about Doc Savage's remarkable upbringing, he would not have bothered to ask that question. There was little knowledge the bronze man had not absorbed, ancient or modern.

"A rare metal that existed in ancient times, but is unknown today," Doc stated. "It is thought to be an alloy of gold, silver and copper."

Amerikanis nodded. "Exactly. It was first created when the city of Corinth was burned to the ground in the year 146 B.C., causing vast stores of copper, silver and gold to melt and run together. But no modern metallurgist has ever been able to duplicate the process. Nor has the forgotten Egyptian secret of annealing bronze so that it retains its ductility ever come to light. Despite decades of research, we simply do not know how these storied metals were fabricated."

"I get it," said Long Tom. "They would be worth a fortune today."

"Not merely the metals!" Amerikanis flung back. "The manufacturing process would be worth a king's ransom! In ancient Rome, Corinthian bronze was more precious than gold itself!"

Doc Savage glanced about the room briefly. "You have not been working with silver or gold here."

"I was coming to that," Amerikanis snapped. "There is another secret. One that has never been discovered, by modern metallurgist or ancient wizard." He paused, seemingly reluctant to part with this information. "The solution to transmuting base metals to precious ones."

"You mean lead to gold!" Ham exclaimed.

"Yes! Yes! Imagine the possibilities!"

Doc Savage said, "We received a package today containing a sample of gold ore that was said to have been extruded from a lead lump."

Amerikanis perked up. His jaw quivered, then sagged. "What is this you say!"

"Within minutes of its receipt," Doc continued, "it exploded into atoms."

"Yeah—just like the stuff in your safe last night," added Monk. "Blooie!"

The expression on S. Charles Amerikanis's graveyard countenance was a kind of hollow-eyed blankness. "I fail to understand," he muttered.

Doc Savage clarified, "The gold was sent to our headquarters for the sole purpose of getting us out of the way. Or, failing that, throwing us off the trail. For tests I conducted proved conclusively that it was not pure gold, but red gold, a common alloy of gold and copper used in costume jewelry."

Amerikanis blinked. "Not pure, you say?"

"Would you agree that if someone were to convert base lead into gold, the result would be a ductile gold of the highest purity?"

"Yes, yes. Very soft, very pure."

"This gold was of a hardness suitable for commercial use," said Doc. "It could not conceivably have once been lead."

"You figgered that out already, Doc," squeaked Monk, grinning.

"Of course, you dish-faced ape," inserted Ham. "It's obvious, isn't it?"

Monk glowered. "Yeah? Then why didn't you—"

"Quiet!" Long Tom inserted. "Doc makes sense. The only question is who is back of all this?"

Doc Savage addressed S. Charles Amerikanis. "All trails converge on the home of John Merlin."

"Impossible! Merlin is—" Amerikanis went pale. The metallurgist hesitated, then gave up on silence. "John is at this time in a secluded laboratory, working on the device we believe will eventually transform lead to gold."

"Explain," prompted Doc.

"He developed an electro-sonic device that exerts a peculiar force, or emanation. When subjected to its influence, common lead reacts violently, altering its chemical constituents. We believed that with further work, an electrical process would lead to making gold."

"What effect did this device have on gold itself?" asked Doc.

Amerikanis rubbed the point of his lean chin. "None that I know. We were not attempting to turn gold into lead, you see, but the other way around. Of what possible use would converting gold to ordinary lead serve? It would be rank foolishness."

Doc Savage said steadily, "We have reason to believe the horrific events now transpiring in Manhattan are the result of this device in operation."

S. CHARLES AMERIKANIS looked ill. A greenish tinge actually collected around his skeletal jawline. He seemed to sag at every knobby joint.

"Impossible!" he blurted. "I recently received a telegram from Merlin. He is definitely in Alaska. Has been working for many weeks now. And the device is with him."

Long Tom demanded, "Why Alaska?"

"Two sound reasons. The need for secrecy, and the risks involved. We had already seen that the device was unstable in its effects on metal."

"Who else knows of this device?" asked Doc.

"No one. Just myself and John Merlin. And my secretary, of course."

"Which one?" asked Ham. "We have met two in as many days."

Amerikanis frowned. "Bah! Mere fill-ins for my regular secretary, Miss Peters."

"Miss Peters," said Doc Savage. The words carried an unexpected charge. "Describe her."

"Black hair. Fetching. Her eyes are a most unusual shade of—" S. Charles Amerikanis suddenly went silent. "She wouldn't. She could not. It's too far-fetched—"

Doc Savage took hold of Amerikanis by his shoulder and

exerted mild pressure. "Out with it," he said.

Amerikanis flinched as if a bear were digging in its claws. "John and Elvira Merlin were having… difficulties," he gasped painfully. "She was upset at his long hours. And when this trip to Alaska came up…well, she threatened to leave him. As far as I know she has not."

"Have you ever met her?" Doc inquired.

"I have not had the pleasure," Amerikanis retorted. "But I have spoken to her by telephone on occasion. For a time, she hounded me for information on her husband."

"The voice on the phone," Doc probed. "Would you recognize it if you heard it again?"

S. Charles Amerikanis was trembling now. "I fear that I would. You see, I am this very minute realizing that Mrs. Merlin's voice is very similar to that of my absent secretary, Miss Peters."

"In your employ how long?" asked Doc.

"Not nearly as long as John Merlin has been absent—but close enough to it that I fear for my business secrets." S. Charles Amerikanis was growing greener by the minute. "And I am just now realizing another uncomfortable fact. Namely, that Miss Peters has been out sick these last two days."

"Since the first detonation," Long Tom pointed out.

"Is there any reason she might wish to see you dead?" Ham demanded.

Amerikanis winced as if from a blow. "That—that is just what I was thinking."

"Gold was stored in your plant safe, was it not?" Doc questioned.

"Yes, of course. Among other metals."

Doc advised, "The killer might have known that and assumed that if it could be made to explode, you might perish in the detonation."

If possible, Amerikanis grew even more mossy of countenance.

"What color did you say were her eyes?" demanded Doc.

"A very striking shade of amethyst."

Ham frowned. "Purple, you mean?"

"Yes, yes, they are quite purple."

"We will add that detail to the description for the police dragnet for Trixie Peters," said Doc Savage.

"Trixie?" asked S. Charles Amerikanis.

"An apparent alias for Elvira Merlin, Mrs. John Merlin," supplied Doc.

"But Miss Peters' first name is Tracy, not Trixie."

"I say, Doc," interjected Ham. "Trixie Peters possesses silver eyes, does she not?"

Monk muttered, "Maybe Trixie and Tracy are sisters."

Doc Savage offered no insights on the theory. As was his custom, he reserved his opinion.

S. Charles Amerikanis squared his sagging shoulders, said abruptly, "I will need police protection. My life is in danger."

"You will come with us," said Doc Savage.

Amerikanis hesitated. "Are you not going into danger?"

"Your part in this matter has yet to be fully cleared up," Doc pointed out.

"I protest. I—"

Monk Mayfair grabbed Amerikanis by the scruff of the neck, while Ham Brooks showed him the point of his unsheathed sword cane.

Amerikanis's eyes fell upon the tip. It appeared to be daubed with a sticky brown substance. "What is that?" he croaked.

"Poison," lied Monk.

"And if you don't want a taste," added Ham emphatically, "you should come along quietly."

S. Charles Amerikanis showed by his rubbery facial expression that all resistance had drained out of him. He submitted meekly, colorless eyes harboring a strange, haunted look.

Chapter XII

MAD ALCHEMIST

DOC SAVAGE DROVE directly to Greenwich Village. If anything, the great city was more like a ghost town than before. But for police officers walking their beats and the ever-present taxis and radio patrol cars, streets and thoroughfares were deserted. The taxi companies seemed to be doing a brisk business, as always. Those hackmen daring to venture out preferred to rush to their destinations, rather than risk being caught up in one of the inexplicably frightful detonations. Speed laws were broken lavishly.

A beat patrolman was waiting for them outside the brownstone residence of the missing electrochemist, John Merlin. The wilted state of his summer uniform suggested that he stood the oppressive heat with difficulty.

"Have you heard the latest, Mr. Savage?" the officer asked as Doc emerged from his machine.

"Latest?"

"The police commissioner and the mayor have received demand letters from some crank. It's in all the papers."

The officer pulled a rolled tabloid from his coat pocket. The paper was among the yellowest of sheets, despite the fact that it was printed on lavender paper.

The headline blared:

EXTORTIONIST DEMANDS
DOC SAVAGE SURRENDER!

Letters were received citywide this afternoon from an extortionist who signed himself "A. Alchemist." The text follows:

I have embarked upon a magnificent undertaking, one fated to reshape the world as we know it. The fact that some have died or lost limbs is of no importance and wholly insignificant in comparison with the main goal, which in the course of years may well represent the saving of millions of lives.

The city of New York has beheld my handiwork. Through the magic of modern alchemistry, I have transmuted gold into something truly fearsome: Sudden death!

I am preparing to reveal this grand scheme. One man stands in my way: Doc Savage. He must surrender to me.

Take heed. You have three days.

—A. Alchemist

"Doc, what are you going to do?" asked Ham, knuckles whitening against the barrel of his elegant cane.

"Investigate this further," said the bronze man, starting up the stairs.

"No one has come or gone since a detail was posted on this block," the perspiration-soaked patrolman assured Doc.

Doc forced the door. He went straight to the kitchen and opened the dumbwaiter hatch. It was evident in his manner that something about it had stayed in his mind, unresolved.

"It is patently impossible for anyone larger than a small child to leave any floor via this dumbwaiter," Ham pointed out.

"Misdirection is a magician's greatest weapon," commented Doc. "All along, it was clear that the home dweller possessed some secret means of exiting the building unobserved."

Grasping the pulley cord, he ran the dumbwaiter upward.

Very quickly, a strange thing became apparent. The dumbwaiter compartment had an attachment bolted to its base. This lifted into view. It was a cage of an affair, of light metal, similar in construction to an old-fashioned open-ironwork elevator. It was exceedingly narrow, but not so narrow that a person of average height might not stand in it. For it was very deep—over five feet in length.

Doc Savage was too large to insert his tremendous physique into it. Further, he doubted that the mechanism would carry a man of average size, or larger. He looked to Long Tom Roberts, the slightest of his men.

"Long Tom, climb in. I will operate the mechanism."

The slender electrical wizard complied. He clambered in and squeezed his undersized frame into the vertical cage.

"Monk, go down into the basement," directed the bronze man. "Listen for sounds of a concealed terminus."

The hairy chemist disappeared in the direction of the back patio. The sound of him exiting through the rear door came distinctly.

Doc Savage then lowered the cage. The dumbwaiter compartment dropped back into view and came to rest where it belonged—on the level of the kitchen. Doc ran it downward.

Monk called up, "I found it!"

Doc and Ham ventured below via a set of chipped brick steps accessed by a bulkhead door in the rear patio. These led down into a low-ceilinged cellar.

The floor consisted of packed dirt and loose stonework. A furnace sat on a crumbling concrete base. Additionally, there was a wooden coal bin, a giant porcelain sink dating from the days before modern washing machines. An open fireplace—another relic of a bygone time—dominated one wall. The massive hearth looked as if it had not seen a blaze in many years. In older days, clothes would be boiled in a massive laundry kettle set therein.

In the gloom of the basement, they congregated around a thick steel pipe which connected floor to ceiling in the fashion of a pillar. Someone had painted it a dull cobalt blue. It looked solid, seamless.

Yet after a series of clickings, a hatch heaved open and Long Tom stepped out, saying, "That is no accommodation for a person suffering from claustrophobia."

Monk brightened. "Talk about a lead-pipe cinch! She hid here while we searched the joint. And after the coast was clear, she snuck out the back way."

"Our opponent has twice demonstrated a gift for misdirection," Doc Savage offered.

"I'll bet this is an old bootleggers' setup," Ham opined, twirling his cane with practiced ease.

Closing the pipe hatch—it pivoted on concealed hinges—Doc returned to the first floor, climbing stairs to the attic story. From an under-vest he wore that was sewn with innumerable pockets, the bronze man removed a small kit for taking fingerprints.

The assortment of cameras stored there appeared to be undisturbed. Doc began dusting these with graphite powder, fine enough to bring out the tiny lines and whorls left by fingertip contact. He applied ordinary adhesive tape to each of these, and examined each sooty example adhering to the sticky side.

His trilling came then, small and sounding satisfied.

Doc joined his men outside, where they had repaired to keep an eye on S. Charles Amerikanis, who had been left in the car under the watchful eye of the attending police officer.

To the bluecoat, Doc said, "Have you observed any party coming in or going out of the adjoining courtyard?"

The policeman considered. "Once or twice I saw a woman leave."

"Description?"

"I didn't get much of a look at her. She wore a veil one time."

"What color eyes?"

"Grayish. Kinda silvery, like a dime. They were spooky looking."

"Black hair?" pressed Doc.

"Hard to say. Head was covered by a lavender kerchief. Thought I saw some streaks of gray, though."

"If you see her again, call me at once," instructed Doc. "Do not accost her. She may be dangerous."

"Right you are, Mr. Savage."

Reclaiming his machine, Doc Savage took the wheel and drove north and then east, toward the towering pinnacle that was his headquarters. The streets and sidewalks seemed unnaturally quiet. Despite the blistering heat, New Yorkers remained huddled indoors. Window fans were busy.

Monk had picked up another paper and was perusing it.

"Says here that the dentists are doin' a land-office business, extracting gold teeth," he reported. "What dentists haven't closed up shop are seein' lines around the block like it was a Broadway show."

"Speaking of teeth," said Ham Brooks. "How are yours, Long Tom?"

The puny electrical wizard glowered. "Quiet—and I hope that they stay that way."

For S. Charles Amerikanis's benefit, Doc Savage explained, "Long Tom's front teeth are of a gold, silver and copper alloy, and react whenever the mysterious device is in operation."

Amerikanis bobbed his narrow head. "Perfectly understandable. Electrum is an excellent conductor of electricity—especially if it also contains copper. In fact, our modern term electron comes from the Greek name for the metal. To the ancient Egyptians, it was white gold, and superior in all ways to yellow gold as a coin metal, since it is far more durable than gold. Yes, far more durable."

"We don't need a lecture," Long Tom grumbled.

NOT long after, they were assembled in Doc Savage's impressive laboratory setup. The place was so up-to-date that S. Charles Amerikanis could not help but wander through its profusion of equipment, inquiring after the nature of this or that complex apparatus. Most of it appeared to be beyond him, and the pinched expression on his funereal face told plainly that this incontestable fact confounded him.

A teletype machine in a corner of the laboratory began

clacking. This fed off one of the wire services. Doc strode to it, began reading the bulletin as it reeled out of the noisy device.

"There has been a fresh spate of slayings," he reported.

Monk warmed up a console radio, twirled the dial until he encountered the staccato voice of a famous radio commentator.

"Flash! Another wave of senseless slaughter struck Brooklyn this afternoon," the radio personality ripped out. *"The scene: the gaiety of Coney Island's amusement park! An unknown force selected innocent citizens at random as they sought relief from the brutal heat. Heads, hands and even ears were obliterated in an instant! There has been victim after victim. The bodies were mutilated, some dismembered. Two of the dead were suicides—young women who had lost hands and could not live with the resulting disfigurement. As one hardboiled wag from the press described the grisly scene, it was a swell mess of butchery."*

Ham Brooks sniffed, "That man seems to revel in tragedy."

Doc Savage got busy with an array of telephones. Calls went in to the mayor, the police commissioner, even the New York office of the Federal Bureau of Investigation. Doc spoke briefly to each.

When he was finished, the bronze man approached S. Charles Amerikanis, saying, "It is imperative that we reach John Merlin as soon as possible."

"Impossible! He has no telephone. He goes into town once a month for supplies and to telegraph any progress to me."

"What town?"

Amerikanis hesitated. He wavered too long.

Doc Savage went to a cabinet and returned with a hypodermic needle, which he charged from a labeled bottle.

Doc Savage seized the trembling man in his iron grip. The needle plunged into Amerikanis's arm without any preamble or warning. The industrialist slumped into the bronze man's waiting arms and was deposited in a comfortable chair, morbid features ghastly.

Soon, Amerikanis was talking in a slurred and rambling

manner.

"That truth serum works mighty fast, don't it, Doc?" beamed Monk proudly. The hairy chemist had whipped up that particular batch himself.

S. Charles Amerikanis began showing signs of inebriation.

Doc Savage said, "Amerikanis, where is John Merlin to be found?"

"Alaska," came the slow reply. It actually sounded like "Alashka."

"Which town?"

"Novosibirsk," managed Amerikanis.

"Sounds Russian," muttered Monk.

"Never heard of it," said Ham, who fancied himself quite the traveler.

Doc directed, "Monk—Renny and Johnny are presently visiting British Columbia. Contact them by shortwave radio. Direct them to fly to Novosibirsk immediately and conduct a search for John Merlin."

"But we don't know for sure he's really there."

"Which is why time is of the essence. If Merlin cannot be found in Alaska, he may be here in New York. Either way, it is imperative that he be located."

"Gotcha, Doc. Right away." The ape-like chemist ambled off to make the radio call.

Doc addressed the dapper lawyer. "Ham, while Renny and Johnny are conducting their search, we will set a trap for Mrs. John Merlin."

"Or Trixie Peters," Ham countered, twisting his sword cane.

"They are one and the same," said Doc. "Fingerprints taken off several cameras at the brownstone residence matched the fingerprints on the hatbox used to convey that volatile lump of gold to us."

"So you *are* making progress! I had been wondering."

"Of course he's making progress," snapped Long Tom peevishly.

"The fingerprints also match that of the severed finger found in the vicinity of the first human detonations on Seventh Avenue," added Doc.

Ham abruptly said, "Say, I'll wager that those two unfortunate victims both had gold teeth! That's what caused their heads to blow apart like they did."

"It is the only reasonable explanation," admitted Doc. "And in that same destructive event, a violet-eyed woman walking nearby lost a finger when her wedding ring vaporized to atoms."

Long Tom looked perplexed. "But how does that tie up with the woman's finger being found? If this Trixie Peters is behind this, wouldn't she know enough not to wear a gold wedding ring when she began her terror campaign?"

"Perhaps," ventured Ham, inspecting his reflection in the shiny knob of his sword cane, "there are two such women, one whose eyes are silvery, and the other the purple-eyed woman seen after the first decapitations. Trixie and Tracy!"

"That," said Doc Savage seriously, "is why it is so important that Renny and Johnny determine if John Merlin is in truth working in Alaska."

Long Tom brightened. "I get it. You think they might be in cahoots. It wouldn't be the first time a wife joined her husband in a life of crime. Look at all the gun molls back in the Prohibition days."

Doc Savage said only, "We have three days to ferret out the truth."

Chapter XIII

THE BAD BREAK

CONTRARY TO DOC SAVAGE, they did not have three days.

Long after night fell, a milk delivery truck rolled up to the ornate entrance to the Manhattan House of Detention, popularly known as the Tombs, situated in the southern part of the city, near Police Headquarters on Centre Street. This was not unusual. Fresh milk is often delivered well before the crack of dawn.

The driver eased out from behind the wheel, wearing a peaked cap and a brown leather jacket of the type favored by truck drivers.

Going to the back, the driver broke open both doors and extracted two burlap sacks. These sagged as if encumbered by heavy burdens. It took some doing to sling first one, then the other, over the driver's back.

Hunched over, the driver laboriously dropped off the sacks and reclaimed the machine. With deliberate speed, the milk truck drove off. This unusual activity attracted attention.

An alarm was given. A searchlight began playing about the vicinity. One fixed upon a burlap sack, which lay open, some of its contents spilling out.

The gleam of gold was unmistakable.

A voice cried out, "Somebody dumped what looks like a sack of gold jewelry at the front gate!"

The deputy warden was summoned. He took one look and

turned pale as a sheeted spook.

"Back! Back from the gate. Everyone!"

There was a general exodus from the front entrance gate, which faced Centre Street. The Tombs was an imposing structure. Erected in the heart of New York City, it was constructed along the lines of a stone chateau transplanted from Europe. Massive gray walls shielded it from the busy streets. A conical stone tower shaped like a witch's hat gave it an unreal quality. Its turrets and battlements looked to have been transported out of the Dark Ages. Some of these served as watch towers.

The milk truck drove a comparatively short distance and the driver again got out.

This time the driver extracted a bulky newsreel camera from the passenger seat and set this up carefully on its wooden tripod.

The camera lens was pointed at the prison entrance several blocks away, and careful adjustments made. A switch was thrown with a distinct *snap!*

No sound attended these operations. But within a very short time an unnerving noise could be heard. A low rumbling, as if something ponderous was toppling.

Shock of some type of an explosion drove air in all directions. It knocked the peaked cap off the driver's head, disclosing long iron-gray hair that fell down in lank profusion.

The driver was a woman! Her eyes flamed with a lavender light.

BACK at the Tombs, the prison was thrown into an uproar. The front doors sagged off their hinges and the inner structures lay open for any escape that might be contemplated. A stone wall had also collapsed.

Fortunately, at this late hour, all prisoners were locked in their cells.

A line of official cars came careening out of a garage and went in search of the fleeing milk truck.

Since the entrance could not be closed again, it was naturally left open. This was unfortunate, as events later proved.

It was then that the source of the low, thunderous crashing sound was discovered. Connecting the Tombs Prison to the Criminal Courts Building across the street was an enclosed stone walkway, called the Bridge of Sighs. Along this, the condemned and the convicted alike were escorted from their lonely cells to the court room and back again to serve their sentences.

It would be a long time before that morose walk was repeated. For the Bridge of Sighs lay athwart the street in several broken sections. A single gray-uniformed keeper lay entangled in the shattered structure, crushed by the punishing fall amid heavy stone and masonry. He was carefully extracted and found to be deceased. A sheet was placed over his broken corpse.

The milk truck was found a short distance away, deserted. In the back lay the body of its driver. The driver had been dead several hours, proving that he had been murdered and his truck stolen by another. The dried blood surrounding the single bullet hole in his temple led to this unmistakable conclusion.

"Must have switched to a getaway car!" the captain of the guards decided. "Split up! We'll find him!"

The improvised search party made an excellent effort. They expended well over an hour in scouring the surrounding area— without concrete result.

By that time, it was too late.

A SHADOWY figure crept up to the Tombs' yawning ruin of an entrance not long after this.

No one spotted the intruder, the assumption being that a prison break would naturally start within the cell blocks themselves. After all, the Tombs was a jail from which prisoners break out. No one breaks *into* a prison.

By that faulty logic was a disaster constructed.

The figure wore something in the nature of a hooded purple cloak. This garment enabled the marauder to slip along the inner walls of the courtyard, in the shadow of the big gray stone walls, under the very noses of the guards in their conical stone towers, virtually unseen.

These tower guards were all tough fellows. Each was equipped with a Thompson sub-machine gun and the will to use it.

Many an attempted escape was quelled by liberal doses of .45 caliber lead. As a result, few escapes were contemplated, much less carried out.

Since no tower guard was attentive to the prospect of someone entering the Tombs, the cloaked intruder was not detected as it scuttled into the courtyard and lurked in the deep shadows of the high stone walls.

The uproar had died down somewhat. But the Tombs was by no means quiet. Noses were being counted in the tiers of cell blocks. The lowermost tier housed the permanent convicts. Those in for minor infractions, or awaiting trial in the attached court house, occupied the upper floors. For the Tombs was a combination temporary jail and penitentiary.

Finally, a guard captain announced that all prisoners were accounted for.

After that, the place settled down.

By that time, the cloaked one had managed to slip into the prison proper, unnoticed. The manner in which it progressed was a spider-like scuttling. It could be seen that a large black velvet hat sat upon the intruder's head. It was a slouch hat, one side pinned to the brim so that it resembled an upright sail. A long white ostrich plume floated above that ebony crown.

In the shadows, the chapeau suggested a woman's summer hat. But a person possessing knowledge of historical headgear would have recognized it as a cavalier's hat, of the type favored by the musketeers of old.

Between the enshrouding hat brim and the face-framing hood, nothing could be discovered of the person's features.

Habitually, this being clung to the shadows, making its way to one cell block in particular, ultimately encountering a lone keeper making his nightly rounds.

The guard had a ring of keys and this jangled as he walked. The jangling covered all sounds, such as a lurker's breathing, or the rustle of a cloak as gloved hands removed weapons from concealment.

The guard possessed good nerves, ordinarily. But he was jumpy after the inexplicable explosion, with its attendant commotion.

When a cloaked thing stepped from a shadow-clotted corner and stuck what appeared to be a fat fountain pen in his face, the keeper gave an uncharacteristic bleat and jumped backward. He lost his footing, attempted to recover it, then lost his life.

A grayish vapor squirted from the fountain pen and caught him in his unprotected face.

He died possibly thirty seconds later from the effects of the vapor.

The cloaked one dropped the protective hem shielding mouth and nose from the vile vapor, and collected the guard's ring of keys, carrying them muffled in vulturine folds so that they did not jingle.

Still clutching shadows, the cloaked one unlocked a door. This led to another area—a block of cells facing a narrow courtyard. Light was gloomy, but two guards wielding hardwood batons were discernible.

The cloaked intruder struck without mercy. The lethal fumes from a fountain-pen device accounted for the death of one inner guard. The other guard was shot with a pistol whose barrel was engulfed by an especially fat silencer. The weapon's report was hardly more distinct than the ticking of an old-fashioned Grandfather's clock.

Since this was an up-to-date cell block, the doors in each tier were all locked from a master lever, which in turned fastened to an alarm circuit. The cloaked one showed a knowledge of electrical circuits in wiring around the alarm swiftly. The locking levers were actuated.

The prowler now moved to the door of a cell which housed one of the most desperate life-termers, opened the door, crept in and shook the inmate awake.

The convict started, blinking his eyes sleepily. Evidently, he had been having a well-deserved nightmare, because the expression on his features suggested horror. At sight of the cloaked intruder—who might well have stood in for the Grim Reaper—he emitted a yelp of surprise.

"Silence!" warned the enshrouded one in a growling tone. "I take it that you are Jake Means?"

"It ain't my time yet!" the convict blurted, thinking that death had come for him.

"You were sentenced to life for knocking over a Federal Depository, making away with nearly a million in gold bullion by plane."

"Y-yes. Almost got way with it, too."

"You discovered that gold bars were harder to dispose of than you ever imagined. You are the type of felon that can be of use to me."

Jake Means gulped, "What of it?"

"I have need of ruthless men," the other hissed. "Are you with me?"

"What's the game? I mean, what am I in for if I join up with you?"

"That is my business," snapped the cloaked figure. "The question is, will you take orders from me if I get you outside of these stone walls?"

"I gotta know more. I'm in for life. But I ain't looking to come back here just to squat on Death Row."

"Without argument," growled the cloaked one. "Make up your mind!"

"O.K. I'm with you—whoever you are."

"Then follow me. *Swiftly!*"

Jake Means said suddenly, "Say, I got a pal here who is as

tough as they make them. He'd be a handy one to have along."

"I know the men I want," the cloaked marauder retorted sharply. "You were chosen because you were a pilot. The others have been picked for various very good reasons. I only want the men I have selected."

Convict Means frowned at his rescuer, "What's the big gag?"

"Shut up and keep moving!" directed the other.

"Hell, what have I got to lose?" muttered Means, following his bizarre recruiter out of the cell.

THE outrageously costumed prowler began to move among the cells, opening barred doors and stirring others to awaken.

Criminals are not the most trusting of souls, by temperament. Most hesitated. Several declined point-blank, fearing unforeseen consequences. Almost all felt there was a catch somewhere.

One demanded, "You want us to crack banks and give you the swag? Is that it?"

The plum-colored apparition hissed, "You are mistaken! I want none of you to steal anything whatever for me. I have far grander plans in mind."

A scarred man grinned. "Just as long as they include escape."

The commotion made by all this nocturnal activity brought other prisoners to their waking senses. Some had left their cells, only to be forced back in by the harsh orders from the cloaked figure of mystery, orders emphasized by the waving of a large pistol which had come from under the purple garment.

In all, six men followed their weird redeemer from the cell block.

"I must be still sleepin'," grumbled one. "This is like a dream come true."

"It'll be a nightmare if we're caught before we go over the wall," mumbled another.

"Nightmare is right! They put you in solitary for a month for tryin' to bust out."

"Solitary, hell!" gulped the first convict. "We'll get the blame for these guard murders and they'll fry us all!"

Yet they made it to a side door opening on the narrow courtyard running around the big gray pile of stone. From there, it was only a short sprint in semi-darkness to the street. All six released convicts could see that the high masonry wall had been demolished. It was an unsettling sight, smacking as it did of strange and powerful forces at work.

"What done *that!*" blurted out Jake Means, eyes popping.

"A power greater than you can comprehend," returned their purple-cloaked rescuer in a dog-like growl.

"Well, I don't doubt that!" grunted Means. "What power could knock down a stone wall like that and not wake up the joint? I'm what you call a light sleeper."

The cloaked one did not enlighten him. This only added to the eerie nature of the situation in which they had found themselves.

They shoved forward in an ominous crowd.

A GUARD named Frank Riley had been on duty in one watchtower when the front entrance was destroyed so mysteriously. It was he who had spotted the glimmer of gold profusion in the scalding illumination of his turret searchlight, and gave the first warning of impending disaster.

Riley was an avid reader of newspapers. He had been following the mysterious detonations in lower Manhattan with deep interest as they unfolded. Hence, he knew the significance of the gold piled before the gate before the virtually soundless detonation came.

With the dying down of the initial alarm, Riley began to relax. He took up the newspaper he had been reading and returned to its pages.

He was reading about the call for Doc Savage to surrender, wondering what it all portended. In that, he was hardly alone. But Riley also liked to read detective story magazines and fancied himself an armchair sleuth of sorts.

A flurry of furtive movement caught his eye.

Penitentiary guard Frank Riley looked up from the newspaper story about Doc Savage, and saw the last of the file of convicts slipping through the ruined wall. One figure stood out among them—a scuttling creature like a human spider with a deformed head.

Dropping his paper, he swung into action.

Guard Riley's tower was thoroughly fitted up for the giving of alarms. Two buttons were at hand, and there was in addition a mouth whistle.

Frank Riley pressed the two buttons. He put the mouth whistle between his teeth, leaned out of the tower battlement and issued one long tweedling blast. He gave only one warning because a bullet smacked him in his stomach.

The bullet came from the knot of prisoners who were in the middle of escaping, and it was fired by the cloaked mystery figure, who then melted into the shadows with the others.

Frank Riley chanced to be leaning far out of the tower, so he fell. The bullet had inflicted a bad wound. And the fall finished the job. The tower was all of eighty feet high.

Alarmed guards surged into the broken courtyard and discovered Frank Riley on the concrete pavement below the guard tower. They turned him over, saw the spreading stain over his midsection.

"Done for!" a keeper exclaimed. "Whoever shot him, fixed him but good."

But Frank Riley was not done for just yet. His lips writhed painfully, began turning scarlet. Words emerged.

What the dying man said with his last breath was vaguely surprising. A psychologist would have probably explained it by saying the man was speaking what was most prominent on his mind; in other words, his incoherent mutters were about the thing that had affected him the most deeply during his last moments. Strangely enough, it was not the escaped prisoners who had disappeared into the night. It was something else.

"Doc Savage!" groaned Frank Riley.

"I don't recollect a con by that name," one guard muttered.

"Don't be so simple-minded," suggested another guard. "He's not talking about who shot him."

"Yeah? And who is Doc Savage?"

"Quite a guy, from what they say. He—"

Frank Riley interrupted by giving a final convulsion, and a long gusty breath expelled red droplets over the surrounding men. With that, he died.

The deputy warden raced up at that point, and began issuing instructions to get organized. The Tombs guards scattered and searched grimly.

The entrance was still agape, but there was nothing to attach suspicion to it, so they did not attempt to scour the surrounding area just yet.

The dead guards in the cell house were the first untoward thing discovered. A head count turned up the unsettling but not surprising fact that six of the most desperate criminals were missing.

In the cell block, several prisoners told about a purple-cloaked shade of a figure who had invaded the place and freed the missing prisoners. The convicts who told the story hoped to curry favor. Contrary to legend, there is no honor among thieves where there is no fear of reprisal.

Stories about the cloaked figure differed as to whether that sinister individual was man or woman. Or even human. In other words, no one had gotten a clear look at the stealthy apparition.

"Reminded me of a scuttling purple spider," was the way one convict had put it. Others agreed wholeheartedly.

By the time the small contingent of guards got themselves organized, it was too late to catch up to the escapees. They were handicapped by a lack of numbers and the fact that every official car had gone off in search of the attacker who so ingeniously brought down the stone facade and walls of the Tombs prison.

No trace of the escaped convicts, or the murderer of Frank Riley, was found. They might as well have vanished in a puff of purple smoke.

The warden arrived just as dawn broke. He had been breakfasting with the governor. Immediately upon reaching the scene, he listened to the story of what happened.

Climbing to the main tower where Frank Riley had been shot, he discovered the newspaper the unfortunate guard had been reading. He scanned the latest headline relating to Doc Savage:

BRONZE MAN REFUSES SURRENDER
TO MAD ALCHEMIST!

SAVAGE PROMISES SOLUTION TO CRISIS

MYSTERY WOMAN SOUGHT IN CASE

"Inform Doc Savage of the breakout," the warden instructed his deputy. "Be certain to emphasize the brutal method by which the entrance was breached. If I know the bronze man, he will waste no time in getting here."

Chapter XIV

SNARE IN BLUE

DOC SAVAGE LISTENED in silence as the warden recounted events of the night. The bronze man had come to the Tombs within minutes of receiving radio notification of the unusual breakout.

He arrived alone. The speed with which he made the trip was explained by the fact that he arrived, not by car, but via a gyroplane of his own devising. A black dragonfly of a craft, it was a breathtaking example of modern aeronautical engineering. It alighted in the street, which had been cordoned off from all vehicular traffic.

The bronze man had been aloft, circling the city as part of his investigation, employing various scientific apparatus in his quest for the perpetrator of the outrages. Use of infra-red and ultra-violet rays, as well as sonic listening devices, failed to disclose much.

Tombs guards escorted Doc to the warden's office, and loitered curiously in the vicinity. Most of them had heard of the Man of Bronze, of his fantastic feats, of the mystery surrounding him. They had learned of Doc Savage's prospective arrival, for news travels swiftly inside stone walls, and they had been wondering what to expect.

Doc Savage interviewed the deputy warden and then those prisoners who had witnessed the "crush-out," as they termed it.

"It was some guy in a purple cloak, wearing a wild black hat," stated one lifer.

Another objected. "You ask me, that was a frail. No guy would wear a feathered hat like that—that was a woman's hat."

A third offered, "Man or woman, it looked like the Angel of Death himself. He took away some rough ones, too."

"Bad actors?" queried Doc.

"The worst," said the deputy warden, "starting with Jake Means."

The files on the missing criminals were presented to the Man of Bronze. He studied them. Then said, "There is no obvious connection between these men, save one."

"What is that?" asked the warden.

"All are experts in their respective illicit lines. Means was a pilot before he went bad. Custer is an expert safecracker. The others are also men of peculiar knowledge."

"What does it add up to?"

The bronze man did not answer right way. "The use of gold as an explosive to breach the penitentiary walls indicates that this could only be the work of the master mind going by the alias, A. Alchemist. No other person would have the means to cause ordinary inert gold jewelry to detonate violently."

"So it's that purple-eyed woman the police are after?" said the captain of the guards.

"The police, the FBI and for all I know the Royal Canadian Mounted Police, and the Texas Rangers," snorted the warden. "She's bucking for Public Enemy No. 1."

"It is not certain that this missing Elvira Merlin was the cloaked invader," asserted Doc. "But it is a reasonable supposition."

"Well, if it is," gritted the warden, "she's a man killer."

Doc Savage did not dispute that point. Instead, he said, "These mug shots will be of inestimable help."

"How so?"

"Before tonight, the dragnet was cast for a woman whose

features were not well known. Now there are seven identifiable suspects."

The warden put out his square jaw. "I would still like to know their aim. According to the other cons, this was not a planned escape. The six who disappeared were recruited by this mystery personage."

"Efforts are underway to flush her out of hiding," Doc Savage supplied.

With that, he strode out of the prison to the street where his gyroplane sat waiting. The bronze man climbed in, gave the starter a whirl, and the windmill machine started revolving its vanes.

Soon, it had lifted off like a kite that had been caught up in a sudden gust of wind—almost straight up. This was an improvement on the conventional autogyro, in that it was capable of nearly vertical takeoffs and landings.

The gyroplane beat its way toward the west like an ungainly pelican.

It finally alighted, not on a landing field but in the Hudson River, near an old brick warehouse squatting on a pier on the Manhattan side of the river.

A faded sign in front read:

HIDALGO TRADING COMPANY

This was Doc Savage's private boathouse and aircraft hanger. Doc taxied the gyroplane to a concrete apron and surged up into the waiting confines. Like all of the bronze man's aircraft, the windmill craft was amphibious.

Inside, an amazing fleet was revealed. They ranged from assorted two- and three-motored seaplanes to a dirigible moored to a platform designed to lift the airship into the cavernous roof area. Exposed machinery evidently functioned to open the roof once the dirigible was hoisted into a position for takeoff.

Over in a concrete trough lay a steel cigar of a thing that could only be a submarine of unusual design. In fact, it had been constructed for polar exploration. It was conceivable that some small nations did not possess a fleet of conveyances so varied and up-to-date.

So vast was the bronze man's wealth that he commanded such machines. The world knew not its source, however.

Deep in remote Central American mountains lay a lost valley, a chasm on the floor of which dwelled descendants of the ancient Mayan civilization, a people shut off from the world. In this valley was a fabulous deposit of gold, the greatest mine of the old Mayan civilization. Doc had befriended these people long ago. There was a radio receiving set in the valley. Doc had but to broadcast a few words in Mayan at a certain hour each seventh day, and a week or so later, a burro train of bullion would appear mysteriously from the mountains with funds to be deposited in his account in the national bank of the Central American republic.

Monk and Ham were waiting for him.

"It's all set, Doc," said Ham.

"Yeah," chimed in Monk. "Everybody's cooperatin'."

Doc nodded. "Then we had best return to headquarters."

Time was of the essence, so Doc ignored the phaeton that had brought his aides to the warehouse establishment and went instead to a corner of the building. There, a concrete blockhouse housed a remarkable pneumatic car. It resembled a big bullet, but with both ends tapering off in blunt noses.

It sat waiting, double hatches open.

All three men clambered in. There was not much space, nor any seats to speak of. The interior was padded with upholstery. Doc closed the hatches, and the sound of compressed air moving with great velocity came.

THE bullet car whirled east a few blocks, turned and shot upward for what seemed a very long interval, but was in reality mere moments.

They came to a stop in a vertical position, the double-ended vehicle hanging downward within the great steel tube which conveyed it, clamped by an arrester mechanism.

Hatches in Doc's big laboratory opened and the three men stepped out, all but the bronze man wobbled-legged. Ham appeared faintly dizzy.

"I will never get used to that contraption," he fumed.

Monk beat his barrel chest in sheer enjoyment. "That go-devil sure gets my blood to pumpin'!" he proclaimed.

"No wonder," sniffed Ham. "You have no brains to be dashed out by the wild gyrations it puts one through."

The elegant attorney regarded his sword cane, inspecting it for damage, suddenly glowered at the shiny head.

"Brass!" he said in disgust. "I have half a mind to—"

"One quarter of a mind," Monk remarked unkindly. "Don't give it anymore credit than it deserves."

Ham purpled, and closed one eye as if to fling the knob for the express purpose of beaning the homely chemist.

Seeing this, Monk bunched up his rusty knuckles belligerently.

"Easy does it," cautioned Doc Savage.

Attracted by the quarrelsome voices, Long Tom sailed into the room.

"It's all set, Doc," he advised.

Doc nodded. "Arrangements all squared away?"

"I was just talking to the commissioner of police. It's scheduled for noon."

"What is?" asked Monk curiously. "I ain't heard the details yet."

Doc Savage explained, "With the threat to detonate more gold in the offing, arrangements have been made for all of the gold reserves stored in the Federal Reserve Bank to be evacuated to another location."

Ham brightened. "Good thinking, but where will they go?"

"The Philadelphia Mint. The gold will be transported by

armored trucks to Philadelphia."

"Why Philly?" wondered Monk.

"Simply because no gold detonation has yet taken place outside of the confines of the Island of Manhattan and Brooklyn," explained Doc. "And to load it on a New York train so conspicuously would invite attack."

"But will not all of those armored cars attract attention?" asked Ham.

"The idea," explained Doc, "is to convey the bullion before the story can break in the newspapers."

"Sounds risky," mused Ham.

"A skeptic to the last," snorted Monk. "It's a swell plan, and it's bound to work."

"It had better," grumbled Long Tom.

"What makes you say that?" demanded Ham.

Doc Savage answered that question.

"The quantity of gold stored at the Federal Reserve Bank, if it were to erupt with proportionate force to the other detonations, might well level a sizable portion of the city."

This was a sobering thought. The room was very quiet after that.

THE bronze man's master plan started off without a hitch.

The contingent of armored cars assembled at different locations in the city. Initially, they drove around lower Manhattan as if merely conveying currency from one to bank to another. There was nothing unusual in the movements of these rounds, and so they attracted no undue attention.

Few knew of the operation, and these men were sworn to secrecy. They also understood it would mean their jobs if any word leaked out.

But no keg is entirely airtight and while the armored cars wended their methodical way through heat-clogged streets, a news tip was called into a reporter on one of the city's least reputable sheets, the *Morning Blade.*

The scribe took the tip to his city editor.

"The word is that Doc Savage himself has ordered this."

"That bronze guy is gettin' too big for his britches," snarled the city editor, tilting back his green eyeshade. "Listen to him, ordering the commissioner about like he's a four-star general talkin' to a lowly corporal."

"Does that mean we run the story?" asked the journalist.

"Run it? We run *with* it! I want it on the streets in an hour. *Less!*"

The reporter raced to his typewriter and began pecking out the letters and words that might spell death for thousands of people. But so absorbed was he with the scent of a hot scoop, he thought only of pleasing his editor.

The extra was on the streets within the hour. It was in fact quarter past eleven—less than sixty minutes until the gold was to be collected and spirited out of town.

A telephone in Doc Savage's headquarters shrilled. The bronze man answered it.

"Yes?"

"The *Blade* just broke the story of the gold shipment," said a grim voice. It was the police commissioner himself. There was no time for pleasantries.

The line was silent a moment.

"Do we go ahead with it?" asked the commissioner of Doc Savage.

"The mere fact that the *Blade* has advertised the existence of all that gold bullion in the Federal Reserve Bank makes it too dangerous not to," declared the bronze man.

"I'll give the word to charge ahead."

"Thank you," said Doc, and then hung up.

AT the designated hour, the armored trucks began congregating. One by one, they slipped into the heavily gated and guarded confines of the Federal Reserve Bank of New York. And one by one, they reemerged into daylight, rolling more heavily on their suspension springs.

The caravan wound west toward the Holland vehicular tunnel, and New Jersey. From there, it would travel south to the so-called City of Brotherly Love, and supposed safety.

Even with all the unwanted publicity—the radio stations had picked up the story the moment it broke in print, and were broadcasting it excitedly—there were few witnesses to the convoy.

Sweltering Manhattan still lay hunkered down as if fearing the worst. Now there was better reason to. For if the convoy were to be attacked en route, the damage would be incalculable— and perhaps all the more terrible because it would be spread out rather than localized to one sector of the city.

Police patrol cars led the way. A second phalanx brought up the rear. Extra officers stood on the running boards, Tommy guns cradled in their arms.

That cleared the way—not that there was very much traffic. In fact, other than some delivery trucks and the ubiquitous taxi cabs, the city streets were remarkably quiet. Such was the abject fear of gold that had seized all of Gotham.

Carefully, as if carrying a cargo of volatile nitroglycerine, the armored truck fleet approached the tunnel. The lead police machines began to slow down. No doubt a single thought was going through the minds of all involved.

What if the gold was made to detonate while they were passing through the tunnel? Death would be certain, if not by explosive blast, then by drowning or being crushed by the collapsing tunnel walls. It was a chilling prospect to contemplate.

After a few minutes pause, the caravan started up again.

If it was possible to drive as gingerly as a man might walk though a mine field, these men did. The procession seemed to crawl along the tunnel like cautious mice. They maintained an orderly space between vehicles.

When at last the other end came into sight, with the blinding sunlight and fresh air it promised, the lead patrol cars picked up speed as if eager to complete the subterranean passage.

Trouble was waiting for them on the other side.

IT was perfectly understandable that the Fourth Estate of Jersey City would want to cover the story of the largest transfer of gold bullion in living memory as it traveled into the Garden State. Since the story had broken into print, it should have been expected.

But what greeted the eyes of the police officials in the lead patrol car caused the living blood to drain from their tense faces.

There were reporters of all kinds waiting for them. Some were news hawks wearing red press cards in their hatbands. Others had bulky flashgun cameras poised to snap photographs of the emerging armored trucks.

This type of journalist was not what caused that sinking feeling in the pits of many stomachs.

It was the liberal sprinkling of newsreel cameras in the group. There were half a dozen of them.

All of those who had been briefed on what to expect were told about the newsreel camera that might not be a newsreel camera, but a housing for the destructive device of A. Alchemist.

Now they found themselves staring at the big lenses that might at any minute begin emitting silent but violent death.

The lead officer cracked his car door open. He faced the line of trucks in back of him.

"Back!" he shouted. "Turn back! Danger!"

This brought instant action, but not of the type expected.

The third radio car in line exploded into action. Both doors burst open and men in blue poured from within, their fists bristling with peculiar looking pistols studded with horns and drums and other protrusions.

Charging forward, they plunged into the rows of close-packed press, firing their guns into the air.

These weapons made a monstrous sound—one unlike any weapon normally utilized by the police. A bullfiddle as large as a bus might emit such a racket. It was deafening. Ears rang. There was surprisingly little powder smoke, however.

"Hands up! All of you!" a man shouted, his voice imperative.

The press, not realizing that they were being addressed, began snapping pictures. Flashbulbs exploded. These impinged upon the advancing officers.

"Dang!" exploded one in a squeaking voice. "Cut that out! Stop takin' pictures!"

That only brought more flashbulbs popping madly.

Return gunfire erupted. This was of the conventional type. Spiteful snapping sounds of ordinary bullets whizzing through the air came sporadically. These shots were coming from the packed press contingent.

The squeaky-voiced officer suddenly slammed backwards, landing on his backside. Complaining, he clambered to his feet and continued his charge.

"Are you injured?" asked a voice that could be recognized as that of Ham Brooks.

"Mind your business, shyster," returned Monk Mayfair, the erstwhile cop. "And get to workin'!"

Long Tom Roberts, blinking the flash-stars out of his pale eyes, leveled his supermachine pistol and with a short burst, cut down a newsreel cameraman.

The man crumpled, his camera toppling over and dislodging from its tripod.

This had a remarkable effect upon the Fourth Estate. They suddenly understood that they were under attack. They failed to comprehend why, but with one mind, they broke, scattering in all directions.

This made it easier for Monk, Ham and Long Tom. The reporters encumbered by heavy cameras could not evacuate so readily. Some kept cranking their cameras. Others endeavored to pick up their equipment and seek shelter.

Dressed in police blue, the attacking trio separated and fell upon such camera men as were convenient.

Monk tore apart one newsreel camera with his bare hands. His huge mouth yawned in surprise. The homely chemist seemed disappointed when ordinary film unspooled like broad black noodles.

Ham Brooks was firing single shots, clipping targets. These fell instantly. Strangely, no blood attached itself to these successes. In fact, the fallen simply lay down and began breathing as if asleep, and not mortally wounded.

Long Tom accounted for two of them. He aimed for their legs. And they went down.

The explanation for all the bloodless conquest was simple. Doc Savage's disguised men were firing so-called "mercy" bullets. These did not penetrate far, and were actually thin metallic shells that broke upon impacting flesh, introducing a stupefying chemical into the bloodstream. Unconsciousness invariably resulted.

By the time the dust and gunsmoke had cleared away, every newsreel camera had been confiscated and was in some stage of dismantlement at the hands of the police.

Doc Savage emerged from the tunnel by that time. He was attired in a quiet brown coat. He had stayed out of the fray in order to be free to pounce upon any outstanding perpetrator. None had been observed.

"Any luck?" Doc asked his men.

The disappointed expressions on their faces told it all.

"No sign of our terrorizer," Monk said glumly.

Doc went among the fallen, raising heads and turning faces to the noon-day sun. He seemed satisfied with what he found until he came to one man, a tow-headed fellow whose face was unusually pale and pasty.

"I recognize this one," he said.

Monk ambled up. "Yeah? Who is he?"

"One of the six missing convicts. Let's remove him to headquarters before he wakes up."

"What about the gold?" asked Monk.

"There is no gold," returned the bronze man. "This entire production was an elaborate ruse."

Ham looked confused. "Ruse?"

"Intended to flush the Alchemist out of hiding."

"Well, it didn't succeed," muttered Monk.

"We are not going back to headquarters empty-handed," reminded Doc Savage, his flake-gold eyes intent on the slack face of the pale man who had been operating a newsreel camera entirely devoid of film.

Chapter XV

DIABOLICAL DECEPTION

THEY ARRIVED AT Doc Savage's skyscraper headquarters full of questions. The speed elevator deposited them on the eighty-sixth floor corridor, and they approached the plain bronze door with the name CLARK SAVAGE, JR. on it.

"I knew it was a trap," insisted Monk.

"You did not!" flared Ham.

"We were all in on it, weren't we?" Monk countered.

"But you didn't know the gold was imaginary."

"Not imaginary," corrected Doc. "Merely copper bricks intended to convey the impression to an observer that the armored cars were heavily laden."

The bronze door opened of its own accord when Doc neared it. This was explained by a radioactive coin the bronze man habitually carried on his person. Emanations from this actuated a sensitive electroscope connected to an electrical relay, which in turn caused the panel—it bore no door knob or handle—to open electrically.

They passed into the reception room. The bronze portal closed behind them.

"Too bad the word got out," continued Ham.

"That was intentional!" snapped Long Tom. "Don't you see? Doc wanted the convoy to be attacked. It was the best way to flush out our quarry."

"And all we caught was this poor fish here," clucked Ham,

indicating with his dark cane the captured convict.

"He may be useful," said the bronze man, carrying the tow-headed prisoner into the laboratory.

Doc deposited him in the same chair where S. Charles Amerikanis had been questioned. Then he took a hypodermic syringe from the cabinet where he had earlier brought out truth serum. Now he charged the needle with an altogether different solution. Long Tom left the room to look after Amerikanis, who had been locked up in the library for his own safety.

"So what happens to the gold in the Federal Reserve Bank?" asked Ham worriedly as Doc rolled up the convict's sleeve and plunged the contents into his arm.

"It was spirited away overnight, at my suggestion," the bronze man offered. "Ordinary delivery trucks accomplished the transfer. The gold is now housed at the Philadelphia Mint, where it is unlikely to be attacked."

"That's a relief," said Monk. "I was sweatin' bullets thinkin' about what would happen if it was all detonated at once. Talk about blooie!"

Within a minute the man in the chair began to stir. His eyes fluttered open. His close-shaven head jerked up and he looked around with the drowsy expression of a possum emerging from its den.

"The Devil his bronze self," he muttered groggily.

Ham said, "He's a fast one with a quip. I'll give him that."

Monk ground one fist into the other and grunted, "Let's see how his brains stand up to a little skull rattlin'."

Doc Savage said, "You are one of the convicts who vanished from the Tombs."

"You're crazy!" the pale man insisted. "I've never been in stir in my life."

"The newspapers published your pictures," Doc reminded him.

The man glared at them. Then all the inner fire went out of him.

"All right," he said resignedly. "You've got me. Send me back—"

He froze. His eyes got round with fear, mouth hanging so slack it seemed that it might drop to the rubber mat at his feet.

A horrible thought had rolled across his brain. He swallowed, once, twice and then again—as if all the juices in him had evaporated.

"That guard what got shot—did he... die?"

"He died," said Doc.

"Maybe I'm a dead man either way," the prisoner said thickly.

"What do you mean?" asked Doc.

"If I go back to the Tombs, I'll have a fat chance of getting any more of that special elixir when I need it," he muttered.

Doc said, "Will you elaborate?"

The man shut his eyes tightly. He stuttered a little when he spoke.

"Th-that purple spider g-gave us some kind of a drug. A p-poison. It's in our systems. Unless we t-take an antidote regularly, it'll kill us."

Doc was silent a moment. "The spider did this to you to keep you under control?"

"You got it." The man moistened his lips again. "That's what we were told, every man jack of us."

"It is possible you were lied to," Doc advised. "It would be very difficult to introduce into the human body a drug which had a lethal effect that would persist and could only be kept in check by regular administration of an antidote."

The prisoner blinked. "Any way to know for sure?"

"An analysis of your blood should tell."

"Hell," gasped the man, offering his arm. "Take all you want! And if you find we've been kidded, you can put the kibosh on this spider's gang mighty simple. Just advertise in the newspapers that the elixir ain't necessary. Darned near all of them other convicts will give themselves up."

Ham said, "It sounds to me like none of the escapees is particularly fond of their benefactor."

"That damn purple-eyed spider," said the other, "is either crazy as a loon, or is the Devil straight from the hot place."

"Why did this strange person get you out of the Tombs?" Ham asked him.

The convict wrung his hands aimlessly. "We hadn't been told yet. My job was to take films of the armored trucks as they came out of the tunnel, for use in the terror campaign to come."

"What campaign?" demanded Ham.

"I don't know that either," the man protested.

Monk said harshly, "Better come clean, guy!"

The cornered convict seemed to want to do just that.

"Listen," he said. "We were led out of the busted front gate and into the back of a milk truck, only there was no milk. It was dark inside the darn thing. The spider told us to stand still, then shoved a hypodermic needle into my arm—and that's the last I knew until I woke up in a basement somewhere and listened to that story about the elixir being necessary at intervals to keep us from dying."

Ham asked, "Didn't this person tell you what it was all about?"

"No. Said she hoped it would remain a mystery."

"*She?*"

"I don't know, but I think the spider is an old woman," said the convict. "Her hair was long and gray, like a Salem crone."

"Bless me!" muttered Monk. "An old lady giving us this run-around. Boy, are we slippin'!"

"What is the spider trying to accomplish?" Doc Savage put in quietly.

"Something crazy," said the convict.

"Crazy—what do you mean?"

"Something that will change the course of entire civilizations," said the other. "At least, that's the trend of the old bat's raving. Claims what is underfoot will go down in history as the great turn in man's progress, as the coming of the great light. And not a word as to what it actually is."

Monk remarked, "Our spidery witch is off her nut."

"You would know," Ham said waspishly. "Being an expert on the condition."

Doc Savage said, "So you gleaned no hint as to what is back of the spider's machinations?"

"No," said the convict.

"What if we told you that your newsreel camera was devoid of film?"

"That don't make any sense," the escapee admitted.

"It does if you were bait for a trap," Doc informed him.

"I don't know about any trap."

Unobserved by the others, Long Tom had escorted S. Charles Amerikanis into the room. They had been listening quietly in the background for some minutes.

Doc indicated Amerikanis. "What is his connection with all this?"

"I don't know," said the man promptly. "He may not have any for all I know."

Monk snorted disgustedly. "If you ask me, I think all this crazy talk about a magic elixir that might keep him alive is so much bushwa. I think he's lyin' through his teeth."

"So help me," said the prisoner, straining his disordered hair through thin fingers, "I can do you guys a good turn. Maybe that'll show I'm on the up and up."

"You might," Monk admitted. "But I doubt it."

"I can tell you where you may be able to get your hands on the she-spider and the rest of the convicts," said the other.

"Eh?"

"I heard her say they were going to the home of a man named Hale Harney Galsworth," the convict announced dramatically.

"The patent attorney?" Doc interposed.

"The same, I guess."

"This may be a trap," Ham warned.

The convict shrugged. "I won't argue it. Either you take my word or you don't. They were going to meet up with this Galsworth gink."

S. Charles Amerikanis began to make strangling noises deep in his throat. He stifled them too late.

Monk eyed him and asked, "What have you got to contribute to the conversation?"

"Nothing! Absolutely nothing," Amerikanis bleated. He fled to the solitude of the adjoining library. Long Tom followed him in, the better to keep an eye on the perpetually nervous industrialist.

DOC SAVAGE now drew blood from the convict. The pale man turned even paler. His recent experience with needles had clearly unnerved him.

The bronze man then busied himself at a microscope. Droplets of crimson were placed on a slide and this was clipped into place beneath the microscope lens. Doc placed one golden eye on the eyepiece and began making adjustments with the knurled focusing knob.

No sound attended this work. The slide came out and the blood sample went into another device, the purpose of which was unclear. The contraption shook vigorously for a time.

Further testing went on for some twenty minutes. Presently, Doc Savage broke off from his work and looked at the anxious crook with absolutely no readable expression on his metallic features.

"What's the good word?" the pale convict demanded anxiously, rising to his feet.

"Remain seated," Doc Savage directed.

The criminal fell back into his chair, plainly expecting the worst.

Before Doc Savage could speak, the connecting door opened and S. Charles Amerikanis burst in.

Amerikanis said wildly, "Mr. Savage! I couldn't keep silent any longer. You must not go to Hale Harney Galsworth's home!"

"Why should we not go to Galsworth's?" Doc demanded.

"I can't tell you!" The skull-faced man kneaded his shaking hands. "But you dare not! It's too dangerous! It is a house of deceit. Maybe even death!"

The convict shot back to his feet and yelled, "I gotta know if I'm going to die if I don't take that special elixir!"

"Pipe down!" Monk shouted.

Doc Savage addressed the convict. "The spider, as you call her, was engaging in a clever bit of deception."

The convict's pale features went slack in sudden relaxation. His mouth broke into a broad grin of relief.

"You were not poisoned, in the sense that you were given a chemical," Doc explained. "Nor were you inoculated with an enormous dosage of a germ which requires another germ to keep it in check. There are germs which fight one another. That much is true."

The man gasped, "So I'm—"

"Were that the case," Doc interposed, "any expert on germ culture would not only equip you to combat the germs, but could completely cure you," Doc added.

The grin widened on the convict's face. "Free! I'm free!" he exulted.

"I wouldn't exactly say that, my good man," drawled Ham. "There is still the matter of your interrupted incarceration."

"Yeah, and those murdered guards," added Monk.

The prisoner seemed not to hear a word of it. He almost danced a jig of happiness. He was the picture of a man over whom an executioner's sword had hung, only to receive a reprieve.

Doc Savage stated, "There are other tests yet to be conducted, to be absolutely certain that you are in no peril."

"Go ahead. I just had a death sentence took off me. I feel like eating again."

Doc asked sharply, "Your appetite has been off?"

"Since I got out of the pen," the prisoner replied.

"This elixir—what did it taste like?"

"Taste? Bitter, like iron pills. Kinda metallic, if you really want to know."

Doc rushed back to his instruments. He began doing things, his hands almost blurring. The microscope came into play once again.

Monk and Ham snapped to attention. They knew that the bronze man's movements indicated great concern. The convict picked up on this and all the relief washed from his face. It drained of blood as well. He became a wan ghost.

"What's goin' on?" he demanded weakly. "I'm O.K., ain't I?"

The trilling that was Doc Savage's sole indicator of emotion pulsed out. It sounded weird, twisted with horror.

When the bronze man spoke at last, his words were clipped.

"Recently," he said carefully, "there have been successful experiments in treating sufferers of rheumatoid arthritis with a new solution."

The convict looked pained. "I ain't got arthritis. Maybe a touch from bein' in that damp cell. But not enough to trouble me."

"This substance is typically administered orally in pill form," Doc continued. "Other times it is injected into the muscles."

"Yeah? So?"

Doc continued, "I suspect that the first injection that knocked out you and your fellow convicts was a combination of a barbiturate and this particular substance in solution. After that initial inoculation, you were given further doses in beverage form."

"So what're you trying to say?"

"You understand that the human body needs specific minerals and metals, such as iron, for good health," Doc imparted.

"Blazes!" said Monk, the truth dawning.

"Jove!" exclaimed Ham, eying the man with ill-disguised horror.

Doc Savage imparted, "You have been given daily doses of gold grains suspended in liquid."

The convict looked blankly curious. "Is gold poison?"

"Ain't you read the papers since you got out?' Monk demanded.

The man flapped his hands helplessly. "No, I've been in hiding. I'm a fugitive."

Doc Savage said with studied calmness. "Suppose I told you that instead of going back to jail, I can have you sent to a place where you can be treated for your condition."

"What condition?"

"Criminality. As well as the foreign gold coursing through your bloodstream, which is no doubt lodged in your muscles by now."

"Sure, sure," the con agreed. "Just because I was willing to go back to the pen doesn't mean it was my first choice."

Doc Savage began writing on a tablet. Much of the writing was in the symbols employed by chemists.

"An ambulance will come for you shortly. This is a prescription that will insure your life."

The convict accepted the offered sheet. "Can't thank you enough," he murmured as if not believing his good fortune. "Guess it was my lucky day when I got busted out, huh?"

No one spoke. Long Tom was on a library telephone, calling instructions to a concern which Doc Savage owned. An ambulance would soon come for the man and he would be transported to a strange institution in the wilderness section of upstate New York.

Crooks who fell into the bronze man's hands were subjected to an unusual form of rehabilitation. Something a little fantastic happened to them. It was something which, should news of it get out, would have been a front-page sensation on every newspaper in the country.

Only Doc, his five men and the specialists who worked at the place knew of its existence. Doc sent his captured criminals here. They underwent a delicate brain operation, which completely wiped out all knowledge of their past. Then they received training in the ideals of upright citizenry, after which they were taught an honest trade.

The former crooks had no knowledge of their pasts once they were released from Doc's strange "college." Not one of them had ever gone back to outlawry.

The call completed, the puny electrical wizard hung up. Suddenly, he let out a painful howl, hands flying to his gold front teeth.

"Doc!" he shouted. "It's starting again!"

All eyes careened in the direction of the uncomprehending convict, standing there oblivious to his own mortal peril. Through his bloodstream flowed unnumbered scintillas of gold—particles that were poised to explode with unimaginable ferocity.

DOC SAVAGE moved as never before.

The pneumatic car was fortunately at rest behind its concealing door only yards away, where it awaited necessity. No greater or more urgent necessity had ever presented itself than now.

Doc scooped up the man with one arm, an incredible feat by itself. The latter cried out a baffled, "Hey!"

As Monk and Ham dived for the safety of the library, the bronze man flung open the hatches and shoved the protesting convict inside.

Bronze fingers punched buttons, causing both hatches to slam shut. The suspended conveyance was now hermetically sealed in its tube.

The muffled sounds of the man's expostulations were abruptly cut off.

Doc depressed another button, then flung himself as far from the departing car as humanly possible.

The muffled *whoosh* of the car dropping eighty-six stories

came to his keen ears.

When no other sound followed, Doc surged to his feet. He pitched through the library, making for the super-speed elevator.

"Did he make it?" Monk wondered, bounding up from the shelter of a heavy book case. "Did he get out of range in time?"

Doc Savage did not reply. The speed at which he was moving defied belief. Monk, Ham and Long Tom found their feet and raced after him, reaching the elevator just as the doors guillotined shut.

They literally fell to the basement level and Doc piled out. He was the only one who did not have to regain his feet from the abrupt shock of descent.

The go-devil car could be set to stop at the sub-basement garage level, or whisk on to the Hudson River warehouse. But there had been no time to set the controls governing this part of its operation.

Once Doc ascertained that the bullet car had not halted at this floor—a glass inspection port in the vast pneumatic tube told him this—Doc seized the handiest machine. The others were climbing in as the coupé shot up the ramp to the street level. Monk, the last to grab on, had to content himself with riding the running board, Ham having closed his door sharply.

Doc Savage broke traffic regulations all the way to the Hidalgo warehouse. The radio-actuated doors rolled open to receive them and the fast-braking machine disgorged them in a frantic flood.

Doc was the first to reach the concrete blockhouse where the bullet car had come to a stop, arrested by automatic braking devices.

There was so sign of damage to the outer hatch, which relieved them somewhat, until Long Tom reminded, "Any detonation would have happened long before the car got here."

Still, the bronze man hesitated to open the hatch, a peculiar expression warping his normally inscrutable face.

Monk shoved in, saying, "Better let me do it, Doc."

Monk was a notoriously bloodthirsty soul, and had no sympathy for criminals. The apish chemist pressed a button and the outer hatch valved open. He saw at once that the inner hatch of the bullet car was dislodged.

Monk tried to open it, but it refused to budge. So he put his considerable might into the task. Finally, with a groan from both man and machine, the hatch surrendered.

An expression of simian curiosity on his homely face, Monk peered within. The others could not resist looking, too.

At sight of the gory, bespattered interior, Ham blanched and turned away. Long Tom let out a moan. "Damn bad," he pronounced.

Doc Savage said nothing, his flake-gold eyes bleak.

Knowing of Doc's pledge never to take human life, not even in self-defense, Monk Mayfair turned to the bronze giant and said, "You did your best, Doc. There was nothin' more you coulda done."

"Yes," chimed in Ham. "Undoubtedly, you saved all our lives in the bargain."

"That's straight," said Long Tom. "Amen."

Silently, Doc Savage turned on his heel to reclaim his automobile. They could sense the steely purpose radiating from him like heat from a furnace. The others followed with subdued alacrity.

Chapter XVI

MURDER IN PURPLE

DOC SAVAGE AND his three aides returned to their
headquarters in a grim and subdued mood. Thus far in
the affair of the miracle murders, they had not made very much
progress in confronting the perpetrator behind the horrific
attacks upon Manhattan citizens. Too, repeated attempts on
their lives had begun to wear on their nerves.

The utter ruthlessness of their foe, combined with the master
mind's uncanny power to reach out and destroy at will, was
something difficult to work against. It got them down.

Even Monk and Ham were without harsh words for one
another as they entered the reception room. Habeas Corpus
trotted up to meet his owner. He ran around Monk's big feet
in excited circles. There was no sign of the freak ape, Chemistry, who evidently had been reclaimed by the zoologist studying
him.

An insistent buzzing was sounding beyond the library.
Hearing this, Doc Savage plunged through the stacks of weighty
tomes and into the laboratory.

The polished brick floor of the great laboratory was freshly
wet, as if from a recent rain. That was preposterous, of course.
The big windows were closed. The damaged pane had been
replaced the previous day.

Monk peered around, "Hey, where's that ghoul-faced Amerikanis?"

"He fled, you dope!" snapped Ham. "Why didn't you handcuff him to something?"

"Why should I?" Monk countered. "We locked all the doors. Without our special keys, it's impossible to open them."

Doc Savage moved to one of the more prominent features of the room—a great glass globe set in an open section of the laboratory which was floored with composition material.

This was an immense tropical fish tank, containing exotic species from all over the world. Normally, they presented a colorful living display. The piscatorial specimens were instead lying inert at the bottom, for the bowl had drained of all water.

Doc removed the fish to other containers in an attempt to revive them. But all had perished.

Ham was examining the glass. "Jove! It has cracked!"

The globe rested on a pedestal. It was not merely ornamentation, but a secret method of exiting the building without recourse to the conventional public elevators.

Climbing in, the dapper lawyer peered down a concealed shaft whose entrance projected above the former water line.

"The secret elevator is no longer on this floor," he announced.

Doc nodded. "Escaped."

Monk worried his bristled head with blunt fingers. "But why would he break the dang aquarium?"

"He did not," Doc supplied. "The destruction of the globe and subsequent release of water no doubt exposed the secret shaft to view. Without any other way out, Amerikanis took advantage of the opportunity presented to him."

"No point in trying to trail him now," Ham mused. "The elevator lets out into the subway tunnels. He could walk the tracks in either direction and lose himself among the subway crowds."

"So what busted the fish bowl?" Monk wondered.

Doc, finishing his examination of the lifeless specimens, came over to scrutinize the glass fish bowl. "Not a bullet pock," he said. "Further, glass splinters have been expelled outward, showing plainly that the disturbance took place within the aquarium itself."

"Then what happened?" asked Long Tom.

Doc said, "It is a scientific fact that particles of gold can be found in solution in the salt water of every ocean. These particles are so minute and so widely scattered that it is not practical to sift out sufficient gold to make the process pay. But virtually every sizable body of salt water doubtless contains some trace of free gold."

"I follow you," said Ham, snapping his fingers. "That infernal device did it."

"Yes. Fortunately, the trace amount of gold was so minuscule, the resulting explosion was only sufficient to damage the glass and kill the fish through violent shock or asphyxiation."

Ham frowned. "So why did it fail to detonate on previous occasions?"

"Don't you get it, shyster?" Monk exploded. "That means the gold-destroyer isn't a force like radium, but a ray. Only when the ray comes into contact with the gold does it go whango!"

"Exactly," said Doc Savage. "The use of a newsreel camera as a housing for the device pointed in that direction."

Long Tom snapped his fingers suddenly. "I just realized something! The reason that Tombs escapee had no film in his camera. He was a sacrificial lamb."

Doc nodded. "Something to keep in mind for the future."

Drains had carried away most of the salt water, so there was nothing more for them to do here.

Doc Savage addressed Ham Brooks.

"What do you know of Hale Harney Galsworth?"

Ham made a prim mouth. "A patent attorney by trade. He has a rather unsavory reputation."

"Hah!" snorted Monk. "Another ambulance-chasing credit to his trade."

"Bite your furry tongue!" Ham snapped. "I belong to a respectable profession."

"We will visit Galsworth at once," decided Doc.

"What about Amerikanis?" Long Tom wanted to know.

Doc said, "The three of you split up. Monk and Ham will seek out Amerikanis. Long Tom, you search the area for any perch from which a ray device might be aimed at our headquarters. Start with the upper floors of nearby skyscrapers."

"Righto, Doc," said Ham.

AFTER ascertaining by telephone that Hale Harney Galsworth was not at his uptown law offices, Doc Savage drove out to Long Island, and the attorney's residence.

The hour was growing late, and dusk was swelling the air. The city appeared nearly deserted, further proof that the horror bombings had all but shut down the great metropolis. The general effect was unsettling, as if a great storm impended. The oppressive heat lingered like a curse.

The residence of attorney Hale Harney Galsworth was a presentable gray edifice in the classy suburb on Long Island's tip known as East Hampton. It was not large as the neighborhood went, but it stood out due to its utter paleness. In the climbing moonlight, the house resembled a great block of soot-soiled snow, or a conglomeration of very old bones.

Doc Savage stopped his sedan behind maple trees some hundreds of yards from the gray estate. He got out, so soundless in his motion that not even the clicking of the closing car door disturbed birds roosting nearby.

A fence of wire so thick that it was almost metal bars separated the bronze man from the building. It was fully a dozen feet high and the top was equipped with a row of sharp spikes.

Doc drifted into the shadow of the fence and began to scout the area. A life of danger had taught him an abundance of caution.

His care was rewarded when he spied a hump of shrubbery twitch in a way that was not natural. There was no wind. The evening was still. The agitated chirping of heat-stimulated crickets masked all other sounds.

Gliding in the direction of the shrub, Doc kept to the shadows. His silence verged on the uncanny. He had learned the art of stealth in many corners of the globe, apprenticing to experts ranging from Apache scouts to Zulu warriors.

Thus it was that the individual lurking within did not know that the big bronze man was present until corded hands reached in and seized him. Doc was prepared for a yelp of surprise. One metallic hand clamped over the lurker's mouth.

Doc bore his captive into the lee of the fence and turned the latter's features to the moonlight.

The face was a familiar one. Skull-eyed S. Charles Amerikanis.

"No noise," Doc warned.

Amerikanis nodded, his startlement subsiding. His hair was damp, his morbid features smeared in summery sweat.

"What happened?" Doc asked in a low-pitched tone.

"Th-the aquarium exploded. I feared for my life. The doors defeated me, but I discovered a secret way out."

Doc nodded. "Why did you come here?"

"To see lawyer Galsworth."

"How does Galsworth fit into this?"

"Galsworth happens to be Mrs. Merlin's attorney," revealed Amerikanis, hooking sweat out of his ghastly eyes with a bony finger.

Doc eyed the trembling man intently. "That does not answer my question."

"That, I would rather not say. No, indeed."

"Are you game to enter?" asked Doc.

Amerikanis eyed the fence and clattered, "We'll have to find a gate. A gate. Yes—"

Amerikanis gasped loudly as Doc Savage, without speaking, calmly picked him up and walked to a nearby tree. It was not the unceremonious act of the bronze man which amazed Amerikanis, as much as it was the utter ease with which the metallic giant handled his weight.

"Want to wait here?" Doc demanded.

"No," Amerikanis insisted, a bit shrilly. "No. Someone tried to kill me. I want to get to the bottom of all this."

Amerikanis gulped as if trying to swallow his tongue as Doc grasped the branch of a tree and swung them both up. Some greenness appeared around the industrialist's gills as they went higher and he saw the sharp spikes of the fence below.

Unexpectedly, he found the gold-colored handkerchief which had been in his coat pocket jammed between his teeth, and he was swung on the bronze giant's back. There was nothing for him to do but hang on. They hurtled through space—across the fence to another tree—a distance Amerikanis would not have believed possible. They were on the ground inside the estate before the industrialist, pale, trembling, got the handkerchief out of his jaws.

"To keep you from yelling," Doc explained.

Amerikanis gulped. "What—why—why the precautions?"

Doc pointed at a spot ahead, slightly to the left. "See that cab?"

Amerikanis had not seen the taxi, but he could discern it now, parked on a lane which ran through high landscaped brush. Its colors were a two-tone blue livery familiar to New Yorkers.

"That is a Manhattan cab," Doc said. "Unusual to see so far out on Long Island, would you not agree?"

They advanced cautiously. Amerikanis stared, eyes apprehensive, as Doc walked slowly around the car. Not fully aware of the keenness of the metallic giant's eyes and ears, Amerikanis did not realize Doc was sure that no enemies lurked near.

On the other side of the hack, Doc stopped and stood very still. He knelt. One bronze hand drifted into a pocket, withdrew something. Doc began performing manipulations about one rear tire. In the absence of street lights, it was impossible to discern what he was doing.

A moment later, Amerikanis also approached. He jumped back, his jaw slackened, then wagged two or three times before he could speak.

"Is h-he dead?" he managed.

"No," Doc replied. "But they used an ingenious method of keeping him from talking coherently for several hours."

A man was sprawled beside the cab. From time to time, his breath fluttered his lips, waggling his long white mustache. His age was well past fifty.

"The taxi driver, unquestionably," said S. Charles Amerikanis. "Yes, the driver, but what ails him?"

Doc picked up a bottle that had escaped Amerikanis's attention. It was of quart capacity, and the label indicated it had held one of the most potent of alcoholic liquors. It was empty.

"They made him drink until he passed out," Doc surmised. "He will have to sober up before we can get information out of him. Come on. Let's try the house."

Amerikanis kept to the rear, at Doc's suggestion, as they went forward. This reflection on his ability as a woodsman seemed to injure the fellow.

"Listen," he said. "I carry my principles of business acumen into each move I make. For instance—"

Just what he was going to say never did come out. From the direction of the gray house came a cry, piercing and charged with terror.

Doc leaped into a position where he could see the house.

THE cry repeated itself. The first outburst had been muffled, but this was much more distinct, as if the author of the cry had reached into himself and pulled out all of his vocal strength. There was desperation in the sound, and more—a distinctly mortal fear.

A bronze tornado, Doc Savage pitched for the house.

There was a bay window high up. This was illuminated. A strange figure was silhouetted against the ornamental small-paned glass. Hunched and shapeless, it looked like something out of a nightmare. It was the color of royal purple as to its loose garment, and the face was shrouded in a hood of the same unsettling hue.

The purple one was stricken with terror. He dug at his garments with a frantic haste, brought a gun out—a revolver of considerable bulk. He lifted it.

Before he could get the gun up, another weapon thundered inside the house. A long tongue of saffron flame was momentarily visible. Shadows leaped.

The weird purple figure half spun, collapsed against the bay window. Glass and frame broke under the sudden weight.

Hanging half out, the figure twitched like a convulsing puppet—evidently impaled on shards of broken glass. Then, the twitching became jerky. Gradually, even that fitful animation subsided.

Long scarlet yarns flowed down the side of the house like a vampire form of ivy creeper.

DOC SAVAGE arrived at the house alone. S. Charles Amerikanis had stayed behind, visibly shocked by the unexpected event.

The side door to which the bronze man came was locked, but a slender pick defeated it in seconds. Doc crossed the threshold and interior darkness absorbed him so utterly that he became virtually invisible.

Upstairs, the light went out in the room off which the bay window opened. Slightly warm murk filled the room and a breeze, filtering in through the shattered window, stirred powder fumes and gradually sucked them away into the night.

Breathing sounded in the room, harsh, stentorian. After a moment, feet shuffled on a rich carpet. A drawer whispered open, then a flashlight, taken from the drawer, spouted light.

The man holding the flash went over steadily to the broken bay window. There was nothing about the man's manner to show that he had just killed a human being, although he did glance down a few seconds at a sprawled figure in purple. Satisfied the latter was dead, he locked the room door, then moved to the hallway and stood listening.

The man was paunchy, greatly overweight—he would balance the scales in the neighborhood of three hundred pounds. Correctly proportioned to his height and bone size, he would have weighed less than two hundred, still a big man, however. He had extra chins, but there was a quality of iron under the fat jaw. His mouth was grim, his nose a predatory hook, and his eyes as emotionless as a pair of glass marbles.

Absently, he juggled a large automatic in his right hand. As an afterthought, he extinguished the flashlight which he held in his left.

The man made his way to a telephone. He did not make as much noise as might have been expected. He lifted the receiver off the hook, placed it on the table, apparently so both his ears would be free to listen to sounds—if any—in the house, and pressed his lips to the mouthpiece.

He did not speak immediately. He seemed to be considering. Absently, he fingered a gold stickpin that decorated his silk tie.

"This is Hale Harney Galsworth speaking," he whispered into the mouthpiece at last. "Send the police to my house. I have just killed a prowler in self-defense. I think there are others around."

Then he lifted the receiver, intending to make sure that the operator understood. But no sound came from the diaphragm. Hale Harney Galsworth snarled and dropped the instrument.

The wire had been cut.

Galsworth seemed to sense another presence. He took a hasty step backward. It was very dark, and he rested a fat thumb on the flashlight button. Light leaped.

The next instant, Galsworth felt pain in his gun hand. Agony leaped to his shoulder. He was conscious of the gun being twisted from his clutch.

Not until he had lost the gun did Galsworth perceive the metallic giant of a man who stood beside him. Galsworth's heavy, grim face registered stunned surprise, bewilderment as to how the bronze man could have approached so silently. Then he pursed his lips and nodded slowly.

"I recognize you. Doc Savage, is it not?"

Doc ejected cartridges from Galsworth's automatic, flipped the shells through a nearby open window, and placed the weapon beside the telephone.

"You might," Doc suggested, "explain yourself."

Galsworth said unsmilingly, "What I have to explain is best reported to the police. Only to them will I speak."

Recognizing the stubborn firmness of the attorney's tone, Doc guided him with ease to the closed door.

The bronze man approached the body hanging out the window so grotesquely, the vital fluid running out of him as if from a crushed spider.

Below, S. Charles Amerikanis was staring up in shocked horror, his thin mouth open and empty of utterance.

Reaching out, Doc Savage stripped the purple hood from the slain figure's limp head.

Below, words were shocked out of Amerikanis.

"My mother in Heaven!" he bleated.

"You recognize him?" Doc called down.

"Yes," croaked Amerikanis. He attempted to name the dead person, but words failed him. Only his lips moved. Breath escaped them, but no distinct vocalizations.

Doc mouthed a single word so that Galsworth could not hear.

"Merlin?"

S. Charles Amerikanis nodded his head miserably. His shoulders shook, then fell in a defeated posture. Fingers became futile fists of despair.

"Come upstairs," ordered Doc.

Footsteps on the staircase increased in loudness until S. Charles Amerikanis presented himself. He seemed incapable of speech.

Galsworth glowered at the nervous metallurgist. "I might have known that you would stoop to an outrage such as this!"

"Me?" Amerikanis gulped. "Me, you say?"

"If John Merlin, or any other of your crowd is around here, they can get out, as well!" ordered Galsworth.

"John Merlin appears to be dead," Doc Savage stated.

Without changing expression, Galsworth growled, "I am personally glad as hell."

"He was murdered," Doc elaborated.

"Probably by some person he had swindled lawfully," rasped Galsworth. "Excuse me, gentleman, if I do not burst into tears."

"You ought to be ashamed of yourself," S. Charles Amerikanis said scathingly. "Yes sir, ashamed of yourself for speaking ill of the dead."

Galsworth glowered at Amerikanis and snarled, "What did you do, send your friend in the purple hood to murder me?"

Amerikanis exploded, "Why you—"

"What reason would he have for desiring your death?" Doc put in quietly, flake-gold eyes resting on Galsworth.

"Revenge, maybe," Galsworth answered.

"Revenge for what?" Doc persisted.

"Possibly he was trying to get even with me for communicating with Mrs. John Merlin over personal legal matters," Galsworth gave Doc Savage and Amerikanis an ugly glower. "Or perhaps you do not know what I am talking about?"

Doc Savage turned to Amerikanis. "What can you contribute to this?"

S. Charles Amerikanis yelled, "You blackguard, you have just shot John Merlin in cold blood!"

Galsworth accepted the news with his predatory features impassive, except for a narrowing of anger in his chilly eyes. He clamped his lips together and took a purposeful step toward the skull-faced industrialist, a fist upraised. Amerikanis jumped back apprehensively, and Doc was forced to move aside to get out of the way. Amerikanis was now between Doc and Galsworth.

Changing his course suddenly, Galsworth leaped for the door. Ordinarily, he would not have reached it. But Amerikanis was in front of Doc, hampering him. Galsworth got though the door, slammed it, rattled a bar fastener on the other side. He doused his flashlight.

Doc hit the door, and all but bounced back. The door was of wood, and stoutly paneled. Doc shucked off his coat, and wrapped it around one bronze block of a fist to protect the knuckles.

Before he got the door open, Doc paused for a time, listening. He gripped Amerikanis's arm to silence him—thus warned, even Amerikanis caught the noise which Doc's sensitive ears had picked up.

It sounded like a struggle in the distant reaches of the house, the sound they were hearing. It lasted for only a moment, then subsided.

"Something has happened," gulped Amerikanis. "Yes, something!"

Doc Savage drove one fabric-wrapped fist into the center of the door. It split. A second blow reduced it to splinters.

They got through the ruined door a moment later and rushed toward the spot where they had heard the struggle. They came to a small study.

Nothing remained of the altercation but ruined furniture—and an open door.

Outside, a car engine started up. Gunshots sounded. This latter racket encouraged caution.

By the time Doc Savage reached the grounds, the taxicab was gone, its driver laying in a welter of gory matter that had formally been the contents of his head.

He would never talk now.

Racing across the lawn, Doc heard more shots. He angled left into sheltering bushes, bending his mighty frame to present a smaller target. His bulletproof vest did not protect the head.

When he reached his sedan, it was to discover that all four of his tires had been removed. The steel wheels sat on concrete. A tire iron lay carelessly discarded nearby. Pursuit was now impossible. By the time Doc could jack up the car and replace the tires, the trail would be cold.

It was patently obvious that one man could not have accomplished all that in the interval of time encompassed by Hale Harney Galsworth's rapid departure. A gang was involved.

As proof, the gold stickpin that had pierced the knot in the large lawyer's elegant tie gleamed on the ground.

Doc Savage went to collect S. Charles Amerikanis, cowering in the house. The industrialist was exceedingly pale. He stared at the purple-shrouded body sprawled on the floor.

"It is," he stuttered, "inconceivable to me that John Merlin is dead. But if what my eyes tell me is true, he has paid for his terrible crimes."

His tone of voice was sad and shaken.

Chapter XVII

QUANDARY

DOC SAVAGE CARRIED on his person a wide variety of gadgets, most of his own invention. These ranged from defensive grenades to ultra-advanced tools of all types. The problem of where to tote these myriad devices so that they could be accessed with efficiency was one that the bronze man had solved early in his remarkable career.

At one period during his unusual upbringing, Doc had spent a considerable period on a working cow ranch in the far West, learning how to ride a horse, rope, read sign and other traditional cowboy skills. Doc noticed that the punchers were required to carry small tools such as bobwire-cutters as part of their work routine. A clever method had been devised to keep them organized. Cowhide vests with many small watch-pockets did the trick.

The special vest Doc Savage designed for this purpose was of leather, lined with chain-mail to make it bulletproof, and literally walled with padded pockets of different sizes for the express purpose of keeping his array of gadgets handy.

Doc reached into his carry-all pocket vest, and removed a flat case only slightly larger than a cigarette case. The bronze man did not smoke, however.

Opening this, Doc exposed dials and a speaker grille. It was a two-way radio, marvelously compact, operating on the short-wave band. Batteries supplied power.

Doc began chanting, "Doc to Monk. Come in, Monk."

Through a burst of static came the homely chemist's squeaking voice, *"Hiya, Doc. Any luck?"*

"Yes. All bad." The bronze man succinctly reported the events of the past hour, omitting nothing, ending with the embarrassing fact that he was marooned in East Hampton without an automobile.

"Be there in a jiffy."

Less than two minutes later, Monk Mayfair pulled up in a jalopy of doubtful character, but which was capable of one hundred and fifty miles an hour on a straightaway.

For once, the bronze man showed a twinkle of surprise in his otherwise unyielding features.

Alighting, the homely chemist examined the scattered tires of the bronze man's disabled sedan, remarking, "Our ground fleet is gettin' kinda thin."

Doc said dryly, "That was quick work."

"Huh? Oh, I was already on my way out here. Ham and me split up to start searchin' at different subway stations. But I had me a hunch. Checking with the taxi starter outside our headquarters, I learned that old Bonesy hailed a cab in front of the building. Looks like when he got to the subway stop, he backtracked to the cab stand."

"A fortunate break," Doc stated.

"I'll say. And I'll bet that shyster Ham is still ridin' the subway lines lookin' for him. Took me a heck of a time to track down the cabby. That ain't him, though," the apish chemist added, gesturing toward the body of the murdered taxi man.

"We had best summon the State Police," Doc advised.

Monk did so on the short-wave set in his car. All of Doc's machines were thus equipped.

When the State Troopers arrived, Doc gave them a description of the fleeing New York taxi along with the tag number, which his retentive mind had memorized. After the troopers had alerted the local barracks, the bronze man led them to the body robed in royal purple, which still hung from the bay window like so much laundry set out to dry.

"You say that this is the missing John Merlin?" a trooper asked Doc.

"That is what his employer asserts," Doc stated.

S. Charles Amerikanis volunteered, "Yes. That is positively John Merlin, late of my employ."

Monk growled, "Didn't you say he was in Alaska?"

"That was my understanding," Amerikanis said nervously. "But as I informed you, I have not heard from Merlin in some weeks. It is obvious that under the stress of solitary scientific work, his mind simply snapped. Look at the poor wretch."

The body was promptly hauled off the impaling glass and laid out on the rug, twisted features exposed to the ceiling light.

The face of the man was neither young nor old, but comfortably middle-aged. The slackness of the features in death told little. The hair of the man was the hue of a mink coat. The open eyes were a glassy gray that verged upon blue.

"Answers the description of the marauder who busted those convicts out of the Tombs," the trooper decided.

"Except for the eye coloration," said Doc Savage.

Without asking, the bronze man knelt and stripped the gloves off either hand. He examined them, held each one up to the light, giving special attention to the blunt fingers.

"This is not the individual who perpetrated the raid on the House of Detention," Doc said flatly.

"No? He's wearing the same purple getup."

Doc said, "The individual who accomplished that daring act also wore gloves, and thus left no fingerprints at the scene. But I examined the markings left by those gloves. Two things were clear to me. One, the gloves left marks of stitching common to women's gloves. These are clearly a man's gloves."

"Anyone could change gloves," Amerikanis inserted.

"Two," continued Doc, "although no fingerprints were left by the robed raider, the glove-tip imprints found at the prison were conspicuously absent the third finger of the left hand. This could only be the case if that finger were missing. As you can see, this man possesses all of his digits."

"It is still Merlin," Amerikanis snapped. "Faces do not lie!"

"No one is questioning your identification," Doc said. "The issue is, what was Merlin's connection with Hale Harney Galsworth?"

"They were enemies!" snapped Amerikanis.

Monk looked at the dead man, and muttered, "Then I'd say Galsworth got the better of the feud."

"Care to add more to your account?" Doc invited.

"Not at this time," Amerikanis asserted. "I am still in shock. John Merlin, my employee, has proven to be one of the most notorious mass murderers of recent memory. I do not wish to besmirch his memory any further than that ridiculous costume has damned him as a fiend."

One of the State Troopers looked at the industrialist and said flatly, "Maybe you'll change your mind once we get you down to the barracks."

Amerikanis paled. "I—I need some air," he quavered.

"Stay handy," a trooper warned.

"Yes. Of course. I, too, have a reputation to uphold," said the departing man.

Doc Savage then conducted a thorough search of the house. Nothing seemed untoward, until they came to the basement. It was a typical winter basement—a cold furnace, a wooden bin half filled with the previous winter's coal supply, and assorted gardening tools in good repair.

Partially smoked cigarettes and empty bottles of various liquid refreshments were littered here and there.

"Looks like Galsworth had visitors he didn't know about," Monk suggested.

Doc studied the refuse. It appeared unremarkable, although the bronze man examined individual cigarette butts carefully.

Then, he noticed a coil of binding twine that had been cut, apparently with a knife. It resembled the twine used to tie the woman's hatbox that had been delivered to Doc Savage's head-quarters.

"A man was held prisoner here," Doc said suddenly. "These were his bindings."

"Yeah... who?" wondered Monk.

Instead of answering, the bronze man returned to the upper floor and again examined the body of the slain intruder. This time, he hauled back the flowing purple sleeves, exposing the dead man's wrists. They were scored and red.

"Tied up!" a trooper burst out. "No doubt about it."

Monk asked, "But how'd he get loose? And why'd he attack Galsworth?"

Doc Savage looked about, eyes at last lighting on a large revolver that had slid under an armoire. It was the weapon the dead man had whipped out in his failed attempt to shoot down Hale Harney Galsworth.

Doc retrieved the gun. Its heft felt curiously light. He broke the action and showed the others what the cylinder contained.

"Empty!" Monk exploded. "What's it mean?"

"Evidently," said Doc, "this man was released, handed this weapon and told to attack Hale Galsworth, possibly in return for sparing his life. But in reality it was a clever plot to trick Galsworth into slaying him in self-defense."

"Then this Merlin fellow had no chance!" a trooper observed.

"None at all," agreed Doc.

Monk scratched his rusty nubbin of a head and said, "Sounds screwy if you ask me."

"Well," a trooper decided abruptly, "it's something we can settle back at the barracks. I hope you won't mind coming along, Mr. Savage," he added.

Doc said nothing. It was plain that he was thinking over the significance of his findings.

Unexpectedly, he asked, "Where is Amerikanis?"

S. CHARLES AMERIKANIS had been loitering in the hallway by the telephone whose cut wires had rendered it useless. Beside him on the telephone stand lay the automatic which Doc Savage had taken forcibly from Hale Harney Galsworth. He picked it up and flipped out the empty magazine. Into it, Amerikanis inserted cartridges.

The industrialist had been outside when Doc threw the cartridges through the open window, and he had collected some of them. Amerikanis eased from the room and through the darkened house, the automatic gripped in his fist, a determined expression on his sunken features.

Creeping down the carpeted staircase to the ground floor, he paused in the well-furnished parlor and cast a glance up the stairs down which he had come. Easing the front door open, Amerikanis wormed his way toward the cars parked outside. He ignored the State Trooper machine as well as Doc's disabled sedan with the missing tires.

Monk's disreputable jalopy car admitted him, and he ground the starter to life.

The resulting engine noise brought consternation within the confines of the residence of the missing Hale Harney Galsworth.

S. Charles Amerikanis wrestled the car around and waited momentarily. When the front door opened, he took careful aim and sent a short volley of shots ripping in the general direction of the entrance.

By accident or design, he managed to plink a door light, but otherwise caused no significant damage.

Still, it was carnage sufficient to cause the party to withdraw in haste. No one walked directly into a storm of lead, no matter how brave or foolhardy they were.

In the aftermath, S. Charles Amerikanis roared away, discovering as he did so that the jalopy concealed a motor of wonderful pickup and power.

By the time Doc Savage, Monk and the two State Troopers reached the waiting car, he was well into the night.

The troopers gave chase, of course, promising, "We'll come back for you!"

Doc Savage turned to Monk and said, "Let's get those tires replaced and be on our way."

"That chiseler stole my car!" Monk fumed.

"It will not be hard to recover. You left the radio transceiver on, of course."

Monk beamed broadly. "Natch."

All of the bronze man's fleet was equipped with radio transceivers which emitted signals that could be traced using a simple loop antenna.

The tires restored, Doc got behind the wheel of his sedan. He sent it hurtling away. Doc soon had the machine rocking along at its top speed.

"Monk, get the ultra-violet projector from the glove compartment," he instructed.

"Sure. But why? It won't help us locate my bus."

"We will leave that to the troopers," said Doc. "Right now, it is more important to track down the taxi that carried off Hale Galsworth."

"How're gonna do that?"

"When I was examining the taxi prior to entering the Galsworth residence," the bronze man explained, "I took the precaution of smearing one rear tire with a sticky substance that will leave a track which can be seen under ultra-violet light."

"I get it!" Monk had the device out. It resembled a folding camera with a purple-black lens in front. Monk tripped a switch, but nothing seemed to happen.

Behind the wheel, Doc drew on special goggles, which were as fat as condensed milk cans. He flipped a tiny switch on the side. The whirring of delicate mechanism came distinctly to the ear. Heart of the device was a picture-forming tube, which transformed an electronic image into visible light by means of a fluorescent screen.

Doc then directed, "Point the black-light apparatus through the windscreen."

Monk did so, then asked, "See anythin'?"

Eyes fixed on the blacktop ahead, Doc nodded.

Stretching ahead, an electric-blue line ran away. It was irregular and as they followed it, it grew thinner and thinner. But the application of the sticky substance had been liberal, and would not run dry any time soon.

The track led them back into the city and to an unexpected but very familiar place. As they rolled into the narrow lanes of Greenwich Village, Monk's simian features screwed up in a grimace and his capacious mouth fell open in surprise.

"Blazes!" he squawled. "Merlin's dump. What gives?"

The taxi was not parked before the unlighted brownstone, but several numbers away. Nevertheless, there it sat, brazen as could be.

"Perhaps it is a trap," suggested Doc.

"I dunno," Monk muttered, peering around.

There was no police guard in front of the home, this time.

"Musta been pulled off the duty to handle the panic that's building," Monk decided.

"Call the others, Monk," Doc ordered.

Monk got on the short-wave set and raised Ham and Long Tom. After a brief conversation, he reported, "They're on their way."

"We will wait for them," said Doc.

"This ain't like you," Monk pointed out. "Usually, you don't hold back none."

"We are up against a foe as diabolic as we have ever encountered," the bronze man said after a protracted silence. "One to whom human life appears to be meaningless."

"I'll tell a man!" Monk exclaimed. "But if they ain't expectin' us, we ought to be able to sneak up on him or her—or it."

"We will take no more chances than necessary," Doc decided. Judging by the chill tone of the bronze man's voice, the apish chemist knew it was pointless to argue.

HAM and Long Tom arrived together. Monk had informed them of the situation by radio. They huddled in an alley across the street.

Doc said, "From the beginning there has been the question of where the master mind behind these depredations has been hiding."

"We know it's not here," Ham asserted.

"Definitely," said Long Tom.

"We will enter the home quietly," stated Doc.

The front door surrendered to the bronze man's lockpick and they eased in, one at a time.

Doc Savage explored every room with his spring-generator flashlight and, satisfied that the brownstone was untenanted, led his men directly to the gloomy cellar region where the dumbwaiter elevator terminated.

"Hitherto," Doc undertoned, "we have assumed that the culprit had escaped via the back door from the cellar. This was certainly the case, in at least one instance."

Doc was exploring the foundation, his eyes in the flash glow alert.

Monk picked up on the bronze man's trend of thought. "I get it, Doc. Maybe there's two ways out of this dump."

Ham Brooks found it first. A catch, disguised as an ornamental bit of gingerbread in the old fireplace mantel. He indicated it silently.

The bronze man examined this and nodded. Doc gave the protruding decoration a twist. There came a distinct *click!*

A section of the deep hearth folded inward, revealing an opening. It was not high. One had to stoop to enter. Doc Savage went first, his flash partially shrouded by his tight-gripping bronze fingers.

The others followed.

They emerged in an adjoining cellar fireplace, to which no light was admitted. The small-paned windows were painted black.

"Tricky," said Monk, looking about.

"Reminds me of home," said Long Tom, who had a similar setup in a former wine cellar uptown, where he conducted his private electrical experiments.

"These old brownstones are built so close together that they share a common chimney," reminded Doc.

They found a set of rickety steps and started to mount the worn treads.

Voices could be heard—one in particular.

A man's voice was saying, "I tell you, I do not know where he is! Confound it, I will not have any further part of this!"

"Who's that?" hissed Ham.

Monk snorted, "Don't you recognize a fellow viper of the law?"

"Hale Harney Galsworth," Doc supplied grimly.

They made their way to the door at the top of the steps, taking care not to step on the wooden stair treads, lest any squeak or squeal.

From the other side of the portal came Galsworth's growing protests.

"This is madness! What can you possibly accomplish?"

A weird voice that was composed more of growl than any human characteristics retorted, "I am going to initiate a reign of reform such as the United States has never before beheld. One that will make the failed experiment that was Prohibition seem paltry by comparison."

"What on earth do you mean?"

"A new civilization can be made, but only from the cinders of the old one," barked the growling one.

From his compartment vest, Doc Savage removed a case containing several pocket grenades the size of robin eggs. He took one in each hand and replaced the container.

Seeing this, the others drew their supermachine pistols, latching the safeties into the off position.

Galsworth's voice complained, "You are the mad Alchemist."

"No, I am the Abolisher of Gold—the one destined to remake the world."

"You sound insane, positively demented," Galsworth persisted.

"For you," growled the other, "the choice is bleak. Join the revolution, or become one of its first victims."

"I do not want any part of this, I tell you!" Galsworth bellowed.

At that exact moment, Doc Savage caved in the door, flinging the tiny grenades in two directions.

The bronze man could judge just so much by voice sounds. He knew that the element of surprise could carry him only so far, as well.

The grenades made noise, and smoke. The smoke uncoiled like a black monster. It swelled into a foul mushroom that pressed against the ceiling.

Before it spread far, Doc saw that attorney Galsworth was tied to a wooden chair with heavy ropes wound about his heaving bulk.

Around him stood men gripping an assortment of guns. Their faces were those of the six missing convicts—minus the one who had perished so horribly.

And standing out from this knot of people hovered a repulsive spider of a person, dressed in robes of royal purple, face framed by the carapace of an enveloping hood topped by a broad-brimmed cavalier's hat.

That face abruptly jerked about.

"Savage!" the figure hissed. "Slay him!"

Guns crashed. Doc veered off to one side. Lead pellets peppered the plaster upon which his fast-moving shadow was rapidly fading.

Monk and the others came boiling out of the cellar, super-machine pistols hooting and emitting stuttering gun flashes.

The room lit up fitfully, outlining many strained faces.

Gunmen began withering. Galsworth screamed in mortal terror. Commotion created additional confusion.

"The ray!" growled the figure in purple. "Activate it!" But in the cloudy confusion, no one seemed to understand the command.

Long Tom suddenly groaned, "My teeth."

The faces of their special wristwatches began glowing with a spectral yellowish light. This had the distinct disadvantage of turning them into excellent targets.

Doc Savage abruptly retreated. In the spreading murk, which was shot by electrical illumination, he found Ham Brooks, who was mindfully hosing the room with mercy bullets.

The dapper lawyer suddenly lost his cane. One moment it was in his free hand, the next it had been snatched as if by some irresistible force.

"Cease firing!" Doc Savage ordered, his voice reverberating with a metallic note. A bronze gong being struck could not have brought forth quicker silence.

The room fell still.

Moving through the roiling smoke, the bronze man held the sword cane high in the air. With his other hand, Doc played the beam of his flash onto the gleaming knob that resembled gold, but was not.

Doc called loudly, "Stop! Unless you wish to die as well!"

A venomous hiss escaped from the boiling pall. A protracted silence followed.

Finally, the growling voice proclaimed, "I am prepared to die for my cause, if necessary."

Doc warned, "Turn off the ray if you have no desire to perish—"

A hum had been building in the room. In the noisy turmoil, it had not been heard. But now it impinged upon the ears.

A switch snapped. The hum died. Simultaneously, the telltale wristwatch faces ceased throwing off glow.

The growling voice reminded, "I can turn it back on at any time."

Doc Savage said, "There is no need for further carnage."

"I will decide that!" the purple one flared.

"What we have is a standoff," Doc pointed out.

"No! I and my men will leave. You may have Galsworth." The harsh voice turned sneering. "Perhaps he can tell you things...."

"But I know nothing of this outrage!" Galsworth protested strenuously.

"Is it a deal?" asked the growling one.

Doc Savage hesitated. In the confusion of smoke and fitful illumination, the bronze man stood rigid, his face a mask of bronze, expressionless as a casting of the metal it resembled. His flake-gold eyes had tiny gales building up in them, as if a metallic storm was about to break loose.

Finally, Doc Savage said, "It is a deal."

Came an answering growl. "Very well. Withdraw to the cellar and wait."

Monk swung over, protested, "But Doc—"

Doc Savage herded his men back into the cellar, displaying an obdurate muscular strength that was impossible to countenance. His men retreated. They had no choice. Even apish Monk lacked the physical power to resist.

Down in the cellar gloom, Monk blurted out, "But that cane ain't gold! We weren't in any danger."

"Earlier, I noticed that Hale Harney Galsworth wore gold cufflinks," Doc said quietly. "He is still wearing them."

"Oh," said Monk. "Then we were almost goners."

Upstairs, low sounds indicated urgent orders were being issued. Feet shuffled. The dragging of heels suggested those who had been felled by mercy bullets were being bodily removed from the premises.

Lastly, hurried feet whetted on the outside stairs.

Long Tom had his gold incisors out of his mouth, and lisped, "Dere dey go!"

The sound of an automobile engine starting, then receding, registered on their keen ears.

"Hey!" Monk exploded. "I think that's Doc's sedan!"

It was. The pilfered New York taxi stood alone when they at last entered the street.

"If dis keeps up," Long Tom complained, "we're going to have to start taking taxicabs everywhere!"

Chapter XVIII

TANGLETALE

THE TIME WAS an hour later. It was one A.M., straight up. Doc Savage had returned to his skyscraper aerie. The night was humidly warm, but the eighty-sixth floor remained comfortably cool, thanks to the modern air-conditioning mechanisms strategically placed throughout.

Attorney Hale Harney Galsworth was seated in one of the comfortable leather chairs arrayed around the vast library room. His large predatory face was suffused with a smoldering crimson, clawed fingers clutching the armrests. He was bellowing.

"I am a member of the New York bar and an officer of the court. You cannot hold me against my will!"

"You are wanted for shooting John Merlin," Ham advised.

"Preposterous! It was an act of self-defense."

"That is for a judge and jury to decide," countered Ham.

"I will take my chances there," snapped the massive lawyer.

"Then there is the matter of the taxi driver who was shot in cold blood at your estate," reminded Ham sharply.

"That was not my doing!" Galsworth insisted. "My kidnappers committed that foul deed."

Doc Savage had been making telephone calls from his reception room desk. Finished with that task, he joined the others arrayed around the perspiring form of lawyer Galsworth.

Doc addressed the man. "Why were you kidnapped, Galsworth?"

"Under advice of counsel, I refuse to reply."

169

"Who is your attorney?" Ham demanded.

"I am representing myself. And I am taking my own advice. I have nothing further to say."

Monk bared his large ape-like teeth in a ferocious grimace. "Doc, how about I lean on him a little?"

"Not yet," returned the bronze man. To Galsworth, Doc said, "Earlier, it was implied that you and John Merlin were enemies. Explain that."

"I have never met John Merlin, and that is the honest truth."

Ham said sharply, "John Merlin is suspected of complicity in the horror bombings that have plagued the city, fellow. I would advise you to come clean."

Galsworth rose from his chair, saying, "I stand on my rights!"

Without making any special effort, Doc Savage pushed him down. A surprised expression struck the three hundred pound barrister. He sat down and stayed that way.

"I am not without resources, Savage," Galsworth warned. "There are laws against holding a man against his will."

Ham interjected, "We have reliable information that Mrs. John Merlin is, or was, a client of yours."

"Your information is in error," Galsworth assured the dapper lawyer. "I have not been retained by her."

Doc asked suddenly, "Do you know Trixie Peters?"

"I refuse to say!"

"Why would A. Alchemist kidnap you?" demanded Doc.

"Again, I refuse to say."

"Are they one and the same?" Doc pressed.

Galsworth made wordless shapes with his mouth, then without uttering a syllable, sealed his pursy lips with finality.

"That refusal is practically an admission in itself," Ham crowed. "Fellow, Doc Savage holds a high police commission. You are obliged to answer any question he puts to you."

Galsworth folded his round arms stubbornly. Clearly, he had made up his legalistic mind to adhere to silence.

"Can I take him to the dungeon now, Doc?" asked Monk impatiently.

Doc Savage maintained no dungeon. But the prospect of physical violence had a marked effect on the large lawyer. He sank in his chair, his loud bellicosity wilting, but remained sullenly silent.

"There will be an inquest into the death of John Merlin," Ham reminded.

Galsworth continued to say nothing. Despite the coolness of the room, his beefy features shone with sweat.

"And the fact that you were wearing a gold stickpin and cuff links suggests that you did not fear the horror bomber," the dapper attorney added meaningly.

At that, Galsworth was roused into a full denial. "No bombings took place on Long Island! You know that as well as I. They have been confined to Manhattan!"

That seemed to settle that point. Galsworth appeared ignorant of the downing of the gold-laden transport plane over New Jersey. Owing to the spread of panic that might ensue, the precise details had been kept out of the newspapers.

"You and S. Charles Amerikanis seem to know one another," Doc pointed out.

"We have had legal correspondence," Galsworth admitted, tight-lipped. "Nothing more."

"Inasmuch as you know many of the suspects in these detonations," Doc Savage informed him, "you are being held in protective custody as a material witness. This is for your own safety."

Galsworth had nothing to say to that last. He was barrister enough to know that he was irresistibly in the bronze man's power, in a legal sense, if in no other sense.

Monk cracked his knuckles loudly. "The dungeon, Doc?"

"We will allow attorney Galsworth time to consider the advantages of a forthcoming attitude," Doc Savage suggested. "Other work needs our attention."

They repaired to the reception room to allow Hale Harney Galsworth time to weigh his future prospects.

DOC SAVAGE employed an organization of private detectives who were immensely loyal to the bronze man. These consisted of former graduates of his so-called "crime college," and who had no memory of the fact that formerly they had been adversaries of the Man of Bronze. Now they worked on his behalf.

Upon his arrival, Doc had set this organization to search for the missing S. Charles Amerikanis. His office and home were under observation. Likewise, a search was underway for Doc's stolen sedan.

Calls had been coming in from these agents. Long Tom fielded them.

"So far, goose eggs," the pallid electrical wizard informed Doc.

But before long, there came a telephonic communication which bore fruit.

"Mr. Mayfair's machine is parked in a conspicuous spot," the detective informed the bronze man.

"Which is?"

"A block from your headquarters," the detective supplied.

"Trap!" Long Tom warned.

"Possibly," agreed Doc. "Do you want to handle it?"

"Do I? Just watch me!"

Turning on his heel, the pallid electrical wizard took his leave.

Doc Savage returned to the library and passed the nervous figure of Hale Harney Galsworth without acknowledging him. Going into the laboratory, he selected a syringe from the medical cabinet.

Holding it prominently, Doc carried the hypodermic back to the library.

Hale Harney Galsworth's glassy orbs seemed to expand in

their sockets as they alighted on the needle in the bronze man's metallic hand.

"What is this?" he cried out.

"You are familiar with truth serum and its properties?"

"I don't give a fig about it!" Galsworth shouted, trying to rise. "I am leaving this place forthwith!"

Ham Brooks unsheathed his sword cane and pointed it at the fat lawyer's face, saying, "Or you can have a dose of this."

Galsworth's eyes fell on the sticky brown substance adhering to the tip of the fine blade. They popped, almost crossing.

"There is no need for coercion," he said, subsiding into the chair. Removing a maroon handkerchief from his breast pocket, he allowed, "I may as well talk freely. I will make more sense that way."

"Quick turnabout," Ham commented tartly.

"I—ah—fear that I have a phobia concerning needles of any sort or size."

Monk scoffed, "Sounds to me kinda like you have a fear of the truth."

"Nevertheless, I feel compelled to speak," the big lawyer uttered.

"Go ahead," invited Doc.

Hale Harney Galsworth promptly got down to brass tacks.

"Very well," he began. "Here are the facts: A week ago, I received a package, along with a letter. The letter contained five thousand dollars as a retainer, the writer explained, in a matter connected with the package. I was instructed not to open the package, and I did not."

"Rather strange," Doc said.

"Very strange," Galsworth admitted. "The next day, I received a telephone call. The person on the wire had a queer voice, a sort of low, unnatural growl. In fact, it was impossible for me to tell if it was a man or a woman; but the speaker had obviously sent the package with the money."

"How do you know that?" Doc interposed.

"The one who telephoned had a list of the serial numbers on the bills, which made up the five thousand," Galsworth recited. "The voice over the telephone instructed me to rent a safety deposit box in the Chemical Trust Bank and place the package in it."

"That's the bank that blew up!" Ham said, waving his blade about excitedly.

Galsworth paused, felt of the bruise on his head, looked at the steel blade, and flinched.

"The voice on the telephone instructed me to call you in to act as administrator of a million-dollar fund," Galsworth continued. "I was given to understand that package contained the necessary papers I was to tender to you. I was further told to telegraph you all once this was accomplished."

Galsworth paused again, eyed them, then explored his bruises.

"I hope you understand everything, now," he concluded.

"Oh, sure," Monk grunted. "Your story tells us why somebody sicced that skulker you slaughtered on you. It explains the crooks camping out in your cellar. It explains why you were kidnapped by that purple spider. And your connections to everyone else involved in this mess. Yeah, it does—*not.*"

Attorney Hale Harney Galsworth looked stunned. "I wondered why the retainer was five thousand. I begin to understand why it was so big. There's something queer behind this."

Doc Savage asked abruptly, "Was there a name signed to that letter you received with the package?"

Galsworth started. "Indeed there was. I forgot that item."

"What was the name?" Doc demanded.

"A. Alchemist."

MONK took that calmly, at first. Then, as its significance sank in, he emitted a startled squawk.

"Doc!" he howled. "That's the mad mystifier!"

"A. Alchemist," Doc Savage repeated slowly. "The signature has since become well known through the newspapers. However, it is not a name, but a title."

"I don't believe this man's story," Ham snapped suddenly. "It sounds like poppycock!"

"I can prove it, gentlemen," asserted Galsworth, eyes shifting between his interrogators.

"Proceed," invited Doc.

Reaching into an inner coat pocket, he said, "Allow me."

Ham brought his snapping blade closer in warning.

Out came a telegram blank of the type available at any telegraphy agency. Galsworth proffered it to Doc Savage, who opened it.

The blank read:

DOC SAVAGE
NEW YORK
HAVE PHILANTHROPIST CLIENT WHO HAS DIED LEAVING NEARLY MILLION DOLLARS STOP HIS WILL REQUESTS THAT YOU TAKE CHARGE OF DIVIDING THIS MONEY AS YOU THINK BEST STOP CAN YOU ACCEPT STOP CAN YOU COME TORONTO AT ONCE TO TAKE CARE OF EMERGENCY ABOUT MILLION STOP ADVISE
HALE HARNEY GALSWORTH

Doc passed the message back.

"Why did you fail to send this?" he inquired.

Galsworth swallowed with difficulty. "I—er—felt uncomfortable about so unorthodox a client, and dallied for a day. Then the horrific detonations started, and I read the name A. Alchemist in the newspapers. I feared that it was the package I placed in the Chemical Trust Bank which had exploded so dreadfully."

"Several packages exploded," Doc pointed out. "And not only yours."

"Blazes!" Monk barked. "I get it now. The plan was to make sure there was enough gold in those safety deposit boxes so that an explosion would definitely result."

"Yes," echoed Ham. "But why that bank, out of all others?"

"That remains to be determined," Doc stated. To Galsworth, he demanded, "Why have you maintained silence to date?"

"For fear of my life," the lawyer said empathically. "You see, after the newspapers published the proclamation by this A. Alchemist, he called me, demanding money. Otherwise, the police would be tipped off that I had been the one to place that damnable package in the Chemical Trust Bank's safety deposit vault."

"Hah!" snorted Monk, "That's a new one. Money being extorted from a shyster attorney, instead of the other way around."

"Did you accede to these demands?" demanded Ham.

Galsworth wetted his lips with a pale tongue. "I am ashamed to say that I did. The extortionist told me to meet him at a specific spot, and to come alone. Which I did."

"Description, please," asked Doc, flake-gold eyes becoming more active.

"I can describe the individual to which I delivered the money that was extorted from me," Galsworth said. "I have a suspicion this creature was A. Alchemist himself."

"Creature?"

"That describes him. He was wearing a medieval garment of purple sackcloth. There was a grotesque hat on his head, and he had long thin arms and legs. A human spider." The big lawyer shuddered at the memory so violently his entire body quaked ponderously.

This revelation caused Monk to have a vivid remembrance of the unhuman shadow they had seen in the brownstone when they rescued lawyer Galsworth.

"Could that have been a normal person wearing an elaborate disguise?" Doc queried.

Galsworth hesitated, then nodded. "It might."

Ham rubbed his chiseled chin thoughtfully. "Some of the pieces of this infernal puzzle are starting to come together," he said thoughtfully.

"We're a long way from havin' a full picture," growled Monk.

"A. Alchemist is the fiend who is behind this," snapped Hale Harney Galsworth. "He has perfected some mysterious, infernal method of doing murder. The victims are found with their heads exploded, or fingers and hands missing. The murder method is quite mysterious and horrible—"

"You can't tell us how bad it is," Monk barked. "We know. What about this extortion?"

"Simple," said Galsworth. "I happen to enjoy wearing gold. Moreover, I am the possessor of more than one gold filling in my teeth. This Alchemist fellow simply convinced me that I would be killed if I did not give money to him, large sums of money. In any case, it was almost two hundred thousand dollars. I suspect that there may be other victims of this brutal extortion."

"Wait a minute!" Ham interjected. "First, he gives you five thousand and then he demands forty times that much. That is not sensible!"

"On the contrary," offered Doc. "It is quite comprehensible. A. Alchemist's plan was to lure me to Toronto in advance of the first detonations, no doubt to keep me out of the way while he or she ran amok. Galsworth's failure to send the telegram foiled that part of the plan."

"I'll buy that, Doc," Ham allowed.

"Me, too," said Monk. "But I still don't savvy the money swap."

Lawyer Galsworth cleared his throat with a deep rumbling before speaking.

"I had the impression in my dealings with this Alchemist person that his plans were not going well," he stated. "Evidently, there was a sudden and dire need of money."

"In other words," suggested Doc, "the funds were needed to

carry forth his campaign, whatever it was."

"Yes. Exactly. I was able to glean an inkling of this creature's stated aims."

"Go on," advised Doc.

"A. Alchemist calls himself a benefactor of humanity," Hale Harney Galsworth explained. "He has appointed himself a one-man committee to see that wealth is redistributed. He is forcing money from the rich, and he undoubtedly selected Doc Savage to see that it was apportioned properly among the poor."

"Well, bless me," Monk grunted.

"You do not know any more?" Doc repeated.

"Exactly," said Galsworth. "I assure you that it is the truth."

WHILE they were digesting that, Long Tom returned from his hunt, the downcast figure of S. Charles Amerikanis propelled before him by the spike-nosed muzzle of a supermachine pistol.

"Nice sleuthing job, you skinny runt," complimented Monk.

"He tried to run a whizzer on me," Long Tom explained, digging the weapon's sharp snout into Amerikanis's ribs. "I gave Monk's flivver the once-over, and found nothing. Then out he popped from the trunk with a gun in his hand. I took it from him and used it to settle his hash a little."

Eying Amerikanis's battered features, Monk said for the unhappy industrialist's benefit, "Don't feel so bad. They say Long Tom can lick his weight in bobcats, wildcats and cougars. You got off easy."

Amerikanis had nothing much to say. His scarecrow shoulders slumped dejectedly. They escorted him to another quadrant of the library, out of hearing of Hale Harney Galsworth.

Doc addressed him, "Is money being extorted from you as well?"

"I haven't given up any yet," Amerikanis said grudgingly.

"But you have received demands?" pressed Doc.

Amerikanis's sulky silence, his lack of denial, comprised all the affirmation they required.

Ham took over the questioning at this point. "Earlier, you warned us not to go to Galsworth, claiming that it was too dangerous. Yet the minute you were at liberty, you went directly there. Explain yourself."

"I had sound reason to suspect that Galsworth was mixed up in Merlin's business—mixed up in an unsavory way. More than that I will not say."

Doc Savage said, "It seems that John Merlin is at the heart of this matter."

"I haven't spoken to Merlin in a damned dog's age," Amerikanis allowed, some of the businessman's polish rubbing off his speech. "I cannot say what got into him."

Doc eyed Amerikanis steadily. "Perhaps you did not wish for us to question Galsworth," he suggested.

S. Charles Amerikanis looked uncomfortable, but offered no further comment.

Ham interposed, "My good fellow, why did you come back here?"

"I figured that it was time to take matters into my own hands," he said sullenly.

"How so?"

"Everyone knows you have a fleet of long-distance planes. It was high time to go hunting for John Merlin's laboratory and get to the bottom of matters in Alaska. I imagined that was your next move and thought I might stow away."

"There are more direct ways of going about that," Ham pointed out.

S. Charles Amerikanis squared his angular jaw. "If you ask me, this is pretty damn direct."

"That reminds me," Monk muttered. "I wonder how Johnny and Renny are coming along in their search for this missing Merlin?"

"We might try to raise them on the big radio later," suggested Doc.

Amerikanis started. His weirdly deep-set eyes widened in their hollow sockets. "What? Hunting Merlin? But he's dead. We all saw the body."

"We sent them to Alaska a day ago," Doc explained.

"Then they are wasting their time. He is dead, I tell you!"

Doc Savage probed the metallurgical industrialist with his compelling eyes. "We have only your word on that. Amerikanis, it is time you told us what is back of all this."

Stubbornness rose in the sunken eyes of the man sometimes called Master Bonesy. From his pocket, Doc Savage removed the needle syringe through which he had compelled Hale Harney Galsworth to speak so freely.

But this had the opposite effect on S. Charles Amerikanis.

Like a scared rabbit, he made a dive for a row of double-sided book cases. Long Tom, lulled by the man's deflated demeanor, was caught flat-footed. He got out a "Hey!" and was forced to hold his fire.

Amerikanis led them on a merry chase. The library was in the nature of a maze. The book cases were tall, large and most boasted glass doors on each side to keep out dust. Since this was a scientific library, it was organized according to the different branches of learning. Each grouping consisted of book cases done in various costly woods—Honduran mahogany, Ceylon ebony, Burmese teak, Malabar ironwood, even lignum vitae from Andros Island. Numerical notations were in the bars and dots grouping which comprised the ancient Mayan number system.

Doc Savage moved to an oak-paneled wall and touched a spot which responded to the warmth of his fingertips. A black electrical panel was thus exposed.

Many were the protective devices installed throughout the headquarters. Doc Savage began pressing studs, locking all doors electrically.

Meanwhile, Monk, Ham and Long Tom were moving among

the book cases and substantial leather reading chairs, whose high backs concealed bullet-stopping armor plate.

It was not an easy hunt. One could not peer through the ponderous rows. And the library was no modest setup, being larger than many public libraries.

There were wheeled ladders which permitted access to the wall shelves that reached the ceiling. Looking like a grotesque baboon, Monk Mayfair clambered up one of these, scouring the layout below with his twinkling eyes.

SUDDENLY, an enclosed book case came crashing down with a jangling of glass.

It nearly flattened Ham Brooks, who recoiled just in time to avoid being crushed under its immense weight. His sword cane, however, was caught, breaking off the chemically-coated tip. The howl of dismay that followed was priceless to Monk's much-scarred ears.

Doc Savage stayed out of the stacks. There were convex mirrors placed at key spots, high up and set in the ceiling. Flake-gold orbs intent, Doc scrutinized these, searching each in turn for some sign of the elusive industrialist.

But the man was evidently crawling along on his belly, because he eluded observation.

That the amazing Man of Bronze had constructed his head-quarters with every conceivable eventuality in mind was demonstrated by what next transpired. Watching the ceiling mirrors as he did so, Doc stabbed selected studs.

Strategically situated book cases suddenly dropped from sight, their tops coming flush with the parquet flooring. It appeared miraculous, but the explanation was simple. These cases sat on scissors jacks. Folding down by hydraulic action, they carried the heavy book cases from sight. The space beneath was untenanted, thanks to the current leasing slump. Doc kept it vacant to prevent enemies from attacking him from below.

These manipulations exposed open spaces and created new

aisles. The orderly arrangement that constituted the vast library was thus transformed into a bewildering, ever-shifting labyrinth. The bronze man hoped to disorient and thus flush out his quarry.

Depressing other studs, Doc dropped additional upright cases while restoring others to their original positions. Yet other book cases pivoted like ponderous doors, snapping together like great blocking jaws.

Monk Mayfair's squeaky voice suddenly exploded the tense silence. He called down from his ladder perch.

"Doc! I see him! Drop C-Sixteen!"

Stabbing a stub so marked, Doc listened for results. Book case C-Sixteen stood on the far side of the library, and not within reflecting range of any ceiling mirror visible from Doc's station.

Monk's excited voice resounded, *"Y-e-oow!* There he goes! Raise E-Four!"

Doc punched the stud that restored the designated book case.

The whetting of running feet mingled in a mad mix of sounds. Doc's men were converging on the spot Monk had called out.

The next thing that happened was that Long Tom emitted a howl of his own, then ripped out a short moaning burst from his supermachine pistol.

After a moment, the puny electrical wizard came reeling out from a lane between two rows of book cases. There was a stricken look in his pale eyes, which grew wide. Abruptly, he collapsed into a thin pile of arms and legs.

"Blazes!" Monk yelled. "Doc! *He's got Long Tom's superfirer!*"

That was obviously the case. Long Tom had been felled by quick-acting mercy bullets.

Doc Savage moved then. He became a great russet animal, prowling through the stacks like a feral hunter, his nostrils dilating. The bronze man's sense of smell was acute enough that he could follow a quarry through scent alone.

"Hold your breaths," Doc rapped in Mayan, the language

they used for secret communication. He began pegging his gas grenades in various directions.

The stuff volatilized in instants, would render a man almost immediately unconscious, but became harmless in short order.

Monk, Ham and Doc all held their breaths. In his chair, Hale Harney Galsworth, noticing their sudden, sharp intake of air, followed suit.

After the required time interval, Doc Savage began breathing again. He resumed his search, then encountered an unpleasant surprise.

Something broke at his feet. The bronze man retreated two steps, suddenly stumbled. Knees growing weak, he began folding on his feet. The expression on his metallic features grew slack.

Too late, Doc realized that one of his own gas grenades had hatched underfoot. Thin-walled glass grapes invariably shattered on contact with solid objects. This one had managed to escape destruction, but was now releasing its invisible odorless contents.

As he lost consciousness, the bronze man realized that Amerikanis had collected it and turned his own weapon against him.

Elsewhere in the library, Monk and Ham joined insensate Long Tom Roberts in unwanted slumber. Feeling it coming on, Monk dropped monkey-like from his high vantage point. He was out cold when he landed.

Only Hale Harney Galsworth, seated far away from the grenade, had escaped its irresistible effects.

Climbing down from the top of the book case designated E-Four, which had unexpectedly lifted him off his feet, temporarily marooning him, S. Charles Amerikanis sought out the immense attorney.

The two regarded one another without words. They seemed to be taking the measure of the other, like a pair of junkyard dogs harboring an old feud.

At last, Galsworth asked, "Truce?"

Amerikanis said, "I will bury the hatchet if you will."

"So long as it is in any back but my own," grunted Galsworth with forced humor.

The two men visibly relaxed. Some of the trepidation oozed out of Amerikanis's hollow, colorless orbs.

"How did you come into possession of that?" Galsworth wondered in a suitably impressed tone of voice. He indicated the curious pistol in the other's thin hand.

"I was lifted off my feet and up into the air by one of those tricky book cases," Amerikanis returned nervously. "I thought I was finished, I did. Then, the slender one came blundering up. He failed to see my hand reach down until I had snatched his own gun away from him."

"With which you gave him a dose of his own medicine, I gather."

Amerikanis nodded. Then he changed the subject.

"I recall that you are quite a sport flyer, Galsworth."

"I am a licensed pilot," Galsworth returned warily.

"Good. I need a man to fly me to Alaska."

"What is in it for me?"

"More money than you can ever imagine. Are you in or out?"

Attorney Galsworth showed his true nature at that point. He hesitated only a fraction of a second.

"In," he said.

"You won't regret this," said Amerikanis. "When this is all over, they will retire the name of Midas from the history books and replace it with Amerikanis."

The other inclined his head in a kind of bow. "And Galsworth, I trust."

They left the eighty-sixth floor suite with subdued haste, claiming Monk Mayfair's machine on the street far below. The sultry night swiftly swallowed them.

Chapter XIX

ABOLISHER OF GOLD

OWING TO HIS remarkable constitution, Doc Savage roused from unwanted unconsciousness well before the others. His golden eyes snapped awake, and he lifted his head.

After-effects of the special gas were virtually nonexistent, so the bronze man was on his feet in instants. He shook his head once as if to clear it, but that might have been a reaction to his utter disgust at being overcome by his own grenade.

Monk, Ham and Long Tom lay sprawled over the floor. Doc went to each of them, to ascertain that they were still among the living. Monk had been snoring bumblebee fashion, and needed no examination.

One by one, they came back to blinking wakefulness—Long Tom last since he had been felled by a more concentrated concoction than the other two. The chemical in Doc's mercy bullets was more potent by far.

After restoring the library to its original condition, Doc Savage repaired to the reception room, to make telephonic calls on the bank of instruments that reposed on the big inlaid desk.

Ham Brooks was the first to poke his disheveled head into the room.

"We were caught with our trousers down," he said sheepishly.

"It was a freak of fate," Doc said. "For some reason, one of the anesthetic balls failed to shatter. Amerikanis rolled it back, holding his breath as he did so."

"There is no sign of Galsworth," Ham reported, features downcast

"They left together," Doc said. "I have the account of the doorman. There is no indication that Galsworth was being forced to go."

"This does not make sense," Ham ruminated. "They were bitter enemies."

"Now they are in common cause," said Doc, a tinge of disconsolation in his vibrant voice. Plainly the bronze man was still rankled by the trend of the evening's events.

"Do not tell me that they absconded with Monk's auto."

Doc nodded. "That is the only apparent good news. It will be easy to trace. I have men working on it now."

But for once the bronze man spoke too optimistically. The missing jalopy proved exceedingly difficult to locate, even with the combined police of greater New York and New Jersey, not to mention the State Police and Doc's platoon of graduate detectives working on the matter.

The morning was well along when solid information reached them. By this time, Monk and Long Tom were on their feet and fighting strenuously.

Normally, these two did not argue, owing to the pale electrical wizard's ferocious temper and Monk's tendency to escalate most altercations into major wars.

"None of this would have happened if you had kept your superfirer in your mitt!" Monk accused.

"Lay off me, you Cro-Magnon," Long Tom uttered darkly. "I am in no mood for your brand of sass. And I didn't see you rush up to save the day."

Doc Savage interrupted with more patience than he felt, saying, "One of our detectives has found Monk's machine."

That quiet statement brought heads swinging around, eyes coloring intently.

"It was found at Roosevelt Field on Long Island," Doc elaborated. "An aircraft registered to Hale Harney Galsworth has taken off from there, ostensibly bound for Vancouver."

"It would be a simple matter to hop over to Alaska from British Columbia," Ham observed. "Do we follow them?"

Doc shook his head. "Matters in Manhattan are far more pressing. I have alerted authorities across the continent and in the Dominion of Canada to be on the lookout for their aircraft."

The trio subsided into dejection. Nothing would have pleased them more than to take off in hot pursuit. But they knew the bronze man was correct in his evaluation of the situation as it pertained to the great city.

This was the morning of the second day after the call for Doc Savage's surrender. It therefore must be obvious to anyone that no surrender was forthcoming.

Worse, they had no clear trail to the whereabouts of the female spider tentatively identified as Trixie Peters, otherwise Mrs. John Merlin.

The morning papers contained a surprise. A shock might be a better way to describe it.

The telephones started ringing along Doc's bank of instruments. Monk and Ham took turns answering them. The calls were from various newspaper reporters. All wanted to know Doc Savage's response to the new demand of the person who had been calling himself A. Alchemist.

"Had been?" Ham asked.

Doc Savage called down to the lobby cigar store and had all the morning editions sent up. After distributing the papers among his men, Doc fell to reading.

This did not improve their breakfast appetites.

The announcement read:

> It has long been held that money is the root of all sin. I declare that this is simply not so. Currency of all kinds is without value, except where it is backed by gold. Gold therefore is the culprit—the true base of all the evils of this existence. For gold begets greed, and out of greed flows all manner of terrible crimes. Murder, theft, and worse.

Know by these presents that I declare gold to be a base metal, and therefore outlawed. It must be abolished, and obliterated. If Manhattan is not cleansed of its ignoble gold by this weekend, I will terrorize again.

Formerly, I have been known as A. Alchemist. That appellation stood for the Anti-Alchemist. Now I will go by the name under which history will record my glorious deeds.

It was signed, *The Abolisher.*

"Abolisher of what?" Monk wanted to know.

Ham snapped, "Of gold, you dope. Don't you see?"

Monk leveled a hairy finger. "Stop ridin' me, you animated writ of habeas pocus. I got me a pounding headache and might take it out on someone like you."

Doc Savage remarked, "This affair has become exceedingly complicated."

"Complicated is right," Long Tom grumbled. "It's worse than a tangled nest of electrical wiring."

Doc addressed Long Tom. "What did you discover about possible locations where this Abolisher and her men have been directing their war on our headquarters?"

"I checked the big skyscrapers," Long Tom said. "Over in the Cloud Tower, someone had been using a newsreel camera to film an arriving transatlantic dirigible. Sounds legitimate. But I'm not sure that was our enemy."

"Why do you say that?" Doc inquired.

"I've been thinking. That rig can't be very powerful if its innards are small enough to be squeezed into a camera case. I doubt it can have any great range."

Doc Savage said, "But we cannot be certain of that."

Long Tom made a sour face. "No. But last night, I came away with a feeling the thing didn't have much power. Maybe the batteries are good for one shot, then they have to be replaced or recharged."

"Makes sense," Monk offered.

"One shot is all that appears necessary to inflict horrific

damage," Ham said bitterly.

"The floor beneath us is empty," the bronze man said. "I have rented it to keep any enemies from using it to stage an attack. And the various alarms and detection devices installed below us show no signs of tampering."

"Well, they could be on any floor under that one," muttered Monk. "That covers maybe a thousand offices. A lot of 'em empty because of the depression."

Long Tom ventured, "They wouldn't need an office. They could set up the ray contrivance in a storage closet or stairwell."

"Or in an elevator," Ham suggested.

"Elevator starters would notice," Monk said contrarily. "And they're all on our payroll."

"I also looked into the autogyro advertising companies," Long Tom added. "But no one rented a gyro for sight-seeing or any such use. Just the usual advertising purposes, which all checked out."

"That doesn't preclude that someone might not have hitched a ride with a pilot," Ham countered.

Suddenly, Doc Savage's eerie trilling issued forth. His flake-gold eyes shot ceilingward.

"The spire," Ham breathed.

As one, they raced for the corridor stairs. Doc handily beat them to the door.

THE eighty-sixth was the top floor of the building, but when the skyscraper had been built just a few short years before, some ambitious soul had capped it with a dirigible mooring mast. This was a hollow spire of an airport, containing a circular staircase for discharging passengers. An enclosed gangplank extending from a stationary airship would deliver passengers to the depot upon mooring. Owing to high winds and the riskiness of docking at the top of a Manhattan skyscraper tethered by a single anchoring cable, only one attempt had ever been made, and it had been pitifully brief. Thereafter, the idea was abandoned as impractical.

But the mooring spire also featured an observation gallery pierced with porthole style windows. It was never opened to the general public. Since it was not normally in use, except for maintenance purposes, furtive admittance could be accomplished by clever and stealthy persons.

They reached the mast, gained entry, and pounded up the stairs to the dome-shaped apex of the cloud-piercing building.

Doc Savage flicked on the lights and they moved about the dusty observation gallery, eyes roving.

A cigarette butt was their only reward. Doc Savage found this on the floor. He picked it up and examined it.

Monk narrowed his piggish eyes at it. "Looks like the same brand you found in Galsworth's basement," he muttered.

Ham scoffed, "It's a common brand."

Doc Savage scrutinized it a moment and said, "The person who smoked this had a habit of biting down on the stem. Notice the distinct teeth indentations? A front tooth has a peculiar chip. One of the convicts who had camped out at Galsworth's basement has been here."

"Right over our heads all that time and we never knew it!" Long Tom complained.

A peculiar expression crossed over the electrical wizard's sour features. "Remember when that tricky Peters woman lammed from our reception room down the elevator, but no one ever saw her leave the building?"

Doc nodded grimly. "It is now clear that she never took the elevator, but slipped out of her shoes and walked barefoot in the confusion created by our smoke-generating device to mount the stairs to the tower, no doubt leaving later—after all expectation of her reappearing had settled down."

"Barefoot?" questioned Ham.

"Conceivably she might have carried a spare pair of shoes in her purse," suggested Doc.

"Maybe it was her that directed the ray on that lump of gold that almost did for us," Long Tom theorized.

"Or a confederate," declared Ham Brooks. "But how was she able to depart the building with so many lobby guards and others looking for her?"

"She is exceedingly clever, and a master at misdirection," Doc pointed out. "She might have donned a gray wig to age her appearance. Her clothing could have been of the reversible type."

"You make her sound like an escape artist!" Ham declared.

Doc Savage said a grim-faced nothing.

Monk made simian faces of cogitation. "Maybe we're looking for two babes, after all—one with purple peepers and the other one silver-eyed."

"But which is which?" Ham wondered.

"We will lock up and watch for their return," said Doc, leading them out of the observation gallery.

When they returned to their headquarters, another surprise was waiting for them.

It was Renny's booming voice, coming over the big all-wave radio receiving set in the laboratory. It made glass beakers on a distant table vibrate in complaint. Renny was the engineer of the group.

"Renny calling Doc Savage. Renny to headquarters. Doc, do you hear me?"

Doc grabbed the mike and snapped a switch.

"Go ahead, Renny."

"We found him—Merlin."

"Are you certain, Renny?"

"As certain as we can be. He's got a shack of a lab out here in the wilderness. Goes by the name of Peter Roff. Short of a photograph to compare with, we think he's our man."

A scholarly voice chimed in, saying, *"An inestimable certitude."*

That was Johnny, otherwise William Harper Littlejohn, noted archeologist and geologist. He loved long word constructions and used them liberally.

Renny asked, *"Doc, what do you want us to do?"*

"Two men are en route to Alaska." Doc Savage then named Amerikanis and Galsworth, giving concise but accurate descriptions of both men. "Endeavor to intercept them. Do not let them near Merlin, if that is he."

"Right, Doc. When should we expect our two friends?"

"Probably not for a day. And we will not be able to join you for at least that long a time."

"Tough. You might miss out on some fun."

Monk snorted, "If you want to see action, Renny, come to New York. The town is hoppin', what I mean."

Doc Savage said, "Renny, stay in contact with headquarters. Keep us informed of events."

"Over and out, Doc," said Renny. The carrier wave returned to its normal protracted hiss.

Monk turned to the bronze man. "What are we going to do next, Doc?"

"Lay a trap."

"The last one didn't go over so hot," the hairy chemist reminded.

"The contrary. The gold was spirited safely out of the city without incident."

Ham inquired, "What kind of a trap?"

"We are facing a clever fiend," Doc Savage said carefully. "We cannot be equally fiendish, so we must be more clever."

And that was all the bronze man would say about it.

A FEW hours later, the mystery was solved when the afternoon newspapers hit the streets.

The headlines screamed:

DOC SAVAGE CLAIMS
MAD ALCHEMIST IDENTIFIED

He is John Merlin, Scientist

The text of the articles all ran essentially the same way: Doc Savage had, through the scientific sleuthing for which he was famed, positively identified electrochemist John Merlin as the author of the recent wave of horror bombings which had brought Manhattan to a virtual standstill.

Doc was quoted as having traced Merlin to a hideout in a wilderness area of Alaska, and had dispatched two of his aides to locate the missing man. Merlin was expected to be apprehended and returned to Manhattan to face justice.

In the matter of his wife, Elvira Merlin, Doc had named her as an accomplice, and had collected proof positive of her complicity in the great scheme.

The proof was the severed finger of the woman, and fingerprints taken from the scenes of her depredations, all of which matched.

Doc Savage made a point of asserting that the evidential digit was in a safe and secure place known only to him.

Reading this, Ham asked, "Where is that finger?"

"Probably in the vault," said Monk, jerking a thumb in the direction of the office safe, which was commodious enough to house a baby elephant in comfort. "Right, Doc?"

The bronze man shook his head slowly. "Pat has it."

Monk exploded, "Pat! Where is she? And how come she hasn't come barging into our business during all this fuss?"

"I sent Pat to Miami," replied Doc. "Where she will be safe."

"You were afraid she might get herself killed," suggested Ham.

"I happen to know that Pat has a back molar filled with gold," returned Doc.

Monk's small eyes began to narrow. "I begin to see this," he said slowly. "You sent Pat south to get her out of harm's way. And to safeguard the evidence too. Pretty slick, Doc."

"The evidence is not so very important—except as a lure to

the person whose finger it formerly was," admitted Doc.

Now it was Ham's turn to look narrow-eyed. "You want the Abolisher to think the incriminating member is in the safe, is that it?"

"Yes. And to try to seize it."

Long Tom removed his superfirer from his underarm holster—he had gotten a new one out of a locked cabinet—and examined the magazine indicator. "Better check our ammo supply before the party starts."

The others fell to following the electrical wizard's example.

Monk happened to notice the golden gleam of his ray-detection wristwatch peeping out from a forest of rusty wrist hair.

"Hey, I just realized—these gimmicks never once worked right!"

"They *did* function," said Doc. "I felt mine heat up back in the brownstone, just before the dial lit up. But they are of insufficient sensitivity to give much warning."

"I can guess why," said Long Tom. "The main reason my teeth react the way they do is that the saliva in my mouth acts as an electrolyte."

Doc nodded somberly. "Also the inside of the mouth is more sensitive than the epidermis. Under stress, a normal person would not notice the metal's reaction against his skin. By the time the dials fully illuminate, death would be upon us."

"Well, if things break right, we won't be needin' them bracelets," said Monk, flexing his hairy arms as if warming up for a fight. "Ain't that right, Habeas?"

The porker had been loafing under a chair. Now he climbed into it and seemed to address the group.

"I will personally bite the ankles of any and all attackers," were the words that seemed to emanate from the porker's open mouth. "Especially lawyers."

"Ventriloquism!" sniffed Ham, lifting his cane as if to brain the shoat.

"You're lucky that pig-sticker didn't blow you to Kingdom Come," said Monk through Habeas Corpus.

Ham went into a stamping rage. "Where's a fry pan?" he howled. "I'm hungry. And only bacon will satisfy my appetite!"

"You might," suggested Doc, "send Habeas Corpus away. It may be too dangerous to bring him along."

Ham made a display of going to the bomb-disposal chute and opening the door.

"Be my guest," he said thinly.

"I got a better idea. I'll call my secretary," said Monk. Going to the phone, he did just that. Words were exchanged and the apish chemist hung up.

NOT twenty minutes later a ravishing blonde put in an appearance. Monk was monitoring a telephoto screen on the reception desk that gave an excellent view of the corridor.

"Here she is," said Monk, rising to open the door.

Monk had long boasted he had the snappiest secretary in New York. The blonde who now entered lived up to that advance reputation. She was striking in all the ways a young woman can be striking. Her fetching frock, athletic form, entrancing features, all achieved feminine perfection.

Her name was Lea Aster. She could have been a Hollywood star, a high-fashion model, or a radio actress. But she had turned down all such offers to remain Monk Mayfair's secretary.

Smiles of greeting were exchanged. Everyone liked Lea.

The snappy young woman placed a leather carrying case on the spacious reception room desk. Grilled windows at either end provided for ventilation.

"In you go, Habeas," invited Monk.

Obediently, the scrawny porker jumped off his comfortable chair and climbed onto another, eventually reaching the top of the desk.

Without any further urging, he stepped into the case and Lea Aster snapped it shut.

"Keep him under wraps until the dust settles," Monk told his secretary.

"Will it ever settle?" asked Lea, growing somber. "It's like a ghost town out there. Fifth Avenue is deserted."

"Don't you worry," Monk beamed. "Doc and me have this about all wrapped up."

Relief lighted her attractive face. And Lea took her departure, Habeas firmly in hand.

"There goes the best secretary a guy could have," boasted Monk.

"Then why don't you marry her?" Ham jibed.

Monk grimaced. "Don't think I ain't asked."

Ham seemed to consider the prospects. "If she turned you down," he mused, "that shows good breeding. Perhaps I should try."

"Listen, you walking clothes tree, you lay off my secretary, see?"

Seeing that he had struck a nerve, Ham sneered back at the red-faced chemist and was about to coin a suitable rejoinder when a sudden sound transfixed them all. It was a woman's startled voice, leaping in anger and fear.

"Corridor!" said Doc.

They raced to the door, squeezed out into the outer hall. The elevator doors were open and there was Lea Aster, pinioned between two rough-looking men.

Their faces were instantly recognizable. They were two of the surviving five convicts who had been sprung from the Tombs. One had an eye that was in the process of closing. No doubt the athletic blonde had gotten in a good sock before being overcome.

"Our boss is lurking around here," barked one.

"Yeah," gritted the other. "Out of sight."

"And she's got that horror ray on her, see?"

"So back off, Savage, or we all die!"

Hairy fists turning to bricks, Monk Mayfair seemed on the verge of charging.

Doc stepped in his path, blocking him.

"No," he said firmly. "Too dangerous."

For a moment, the simian chemist appeared torn by loyalty to his bronze chief and anxiety over the fate of his secretary. He wavered.

Doc captured his gaze, held it with his hypnotic orbs. That did the trick.

Baring his ferocious teeth in suppressed rage, Monk subsided. He squeezed his eyes shut in pain.

"You'll hear from us," said one of the convicts as the door closed on Lea Aster's fear-twisted face.

As Monk watched the elevator indicator reel off the dropping floors, his howl was enough to loosen ceiling tiles.

Doc Savage raced to a telephone. He got hold of the lobby. "There is a kidnapping in progress. Under no circumstances interfere with the persons stepping off the public elevator. To do so would conceivably annihilate anyone caught in the lobby."

"Yes, Mr. Savage," said an emotion-choked voice. "As you say."

Doc Savage had television cameras positioned at strategic locations throughout the giant skyscraper. He activated one now, opening a wall panel which disclosed a frosted glass screen—in reality a closed-circuit television receiver.

Doc snapped it on. A very clear black-and-white image filled the glass.

It showed Lea Aster being hustled off the elevator and through the modernistic lobby. Another transmitted image caught the trio exiting the building by its main entrance. They quickly disappeared from view.

After that, there were no more cameras positioned to capture their movements.

Monk let out another groan. The hairy chemist seemed beside

himself. He stormed about the room in evident pain and frustration. Then he did something uncharacteristic of him.

Bunching his rusty knuckles, Monk hauled off and knocked Ham Brooks into the early evening.

Chapter XX

CONFRONTATION

HAM BROOKS REVIVED, shaking his head groggily. Narrowing eyes veered to a window, saw that the moon had risen. It literally shook, mirage-like, in the atmospheric conditions. The heat of day had obviously not abated.

Carefully, Ham climbed to his feet, checked his clothes and made minor adjustments, as if the state of his raiment was all that concerned him. The fashionable lawyer's pearl-gray hat showed a noticeable dent, so he discarded it in a waste-paper basket.

Reclaiming his sword cane, Ham examined it critically, unjointed the barrel, and checked the blade for damage. Other than the previously broken tip, he saw none.

Doc Savage was present. He was preoccupied with replacing the control board recently shattered by a derringer bullet launched by their distaff Nemesis.

In a voice utterly cool and unconcerned, Ham inquired, "Where is that miserable mistake of nature?"

"Laboratory," supplied Doc.

"Any development of which I must be apprised?"

"None," said Doc.

"Excuse me, then."

Ham Brooks strolled through the vast library as if sauntering through Central Park. He wended his way to the laboratory and before entering, knocked politely.

"Yeah?" came Monk Mayfair's disconsolate voice.

"It is I," returned Ham.

"Go away."

"I wouldn't think of it," said Ham, entering.

Monk Mayfair was the picture of dejection. His neck was never very long, but now his head had sunk into his hunched shoulders so deeply that it was difficult to ascertain that anything stood between them.

His back to the door, the apish chemist was staring at the quaking moon.

"May I inquire," asked Ham in a reasonable tone of voice, "why you struck me?"

Monk muttered, "I had to hit someone. And you were the nearest."

"That is all?"

Monk's voice was thick with emotion, "Yeah. That's the only reason."

Ham frowned. "You have been like a brother to me, Monk."

"Yeah. Same here, pal."

"I understand your grief. I truly do."

"Thanks," Monk muttered.

"And I want you to know that there are no hard feelings."

"Good. Swell."

"After all, you possibly saved my life with that infantile brass-for-gold cane trick you pulled on me."

"Think nothin' of it," Monk mumbled.

"But you must understand that once Miss Aster and Habeas are recovered safely, we have to settle this regrettable matter."

"Sure. Sure. Anything you say."

"I suggest a proper duel."

"Duel?" Monk's voice was dull.

"I will supply the sword canes, of course."

"Whatever you say." Monk was staring out the window as if consumed by overwhelming grief.

"I will take my leave of you now," said Ham in a low voice.

Monk Mayfair replied nothing. He continued to stare out the window, lost in his morose thoughts. His furry fists clenched and unclenched, as if aching to seize and smash something or someone.

A TELEPHONE rang not long after. Doc Savage picked it up.

"Savage speaking."

A growling voice said bitterly, "You are a hard man to kill."

"Your point?" prompted Doc.

"I have the blonde girl here with me. She is in the company of two Tombs escapees who fear for their lives because they know that I am perfectly capable of turning on my abolisher ray and atomizing them both, the girl and the pig with them."

"My earlier offer still stands," interrupted Doc. "We can help you."

"Yes, you can help me. And you will. But not the way you wish to."

Doc said, "We are willing to trade the severed finger for the prisoners."

"I am not interested in that worthless thing!" snapped the voice. "You have something better to trade for them."

"Go on."

"The exact location of John Merlin."

"If you let the others go, we will assist you in finding him," promised Doc.

"Not enough! I need a plane—a large plane capable of flying to Alaska. You have such a ship in your fleet?"

"Yes."

"And I have a pilot. He was one of the men chosen for my grand scheme—which you have continually thwarted." Bitterness tinged the harping voice like dripping venom.

"You will never get away with this," warned Doc.

"I have gotten away with a great deal so far, don't you think?"

Doc was silent a minute. "State your terms."

"Take your airplane into the sky. Tune in to a radio frequency I will name. Then I will instruct you where to land. I will take possession of the ship at that time."

"I assume you want me to come alone."

"Yes…. *No!*" the other shrilled. "You may bring your men. As long as I possess the power of life or death over those under my control, none of you dare thwart me. And I wish to know where you and your men are at all times."

"Very well," acceded Doc. "We will be in the air within an hour."

"This is the point where it is customary to say, no tricks. But I know you are not that foolhardy." The line went dead.

Doc Savage hung up, saying, "The plan worked. The Abolisher is abandoning her Manhattan plans in favor of seeking out John Merlin in Alaska."

Ham frowned. "It sounds like another trap."

"Undoubtedly it is. But our first priority is to safeguard the city and its citizens. That much seems to have been accomplished."

"Sounds too easy," said Long Tom darkly.

"The worst may be ahead of us," agreed Doc. "As long as the Abolisher and her ray contrivance are at liberty, her ability to spread terror and destruction know no bounds."

"So you're certain that we are fighting a woman named Elvira Merlin?" asked Ham pointedly.

"Unquestionably. For she responded in accordance to the motives I have ascribed to Mrs. John Merlin."

"What about the matter of our foe's eye color?" Ham asked. "It has been described as both amethyst and silver. It cannot be both. For that matter, is she a young woman, or a gray-haired crone?"

Doc Savage was thoughtful a moment. "There may be more to those questions than simple disguise," he said at last.

Ham looked interested, but Doc Savage abruptly changed the subject. "We will take to the air at once."

SHORTLY thereafter, the big radio-controlled doors on the Hudson River side of the Hidalgo Trading Company warehouse parted ponderously, and a big bronze plane rolled from the concrete apron under power and slid into the water like an immense duck.

This was a three-engine long-haul flying boat, the latest in the bronze man's fleet. Two motors were embedded in the wings, while a third was mounted on a pylon extending up from the center of the high wing, over the cockpit. It boasted a top airspeed far in advance of any comparable craft and was capable of circling the globe, if necessary.

Doc was at the controls and he jockeyed the plane, motors a-howl, into the wind. The others were at their stations. Long Tom naturally sat in the radio cubicle.

Doc fed the throttles gas and the ultra-modern aircraft started crashing along the surface of the water. He got on step, slamming through two or three wavelets, then took to the air.

The thundering amphibian was a spectacular sight as it arrowed its way south to the Narrows and out in the general direction of the Atlantic Ocean.

In the co-pilot seat beside the bronze man, Monk Mayfair had a question.

"Doc, this is your biggest bus. Why risk losing it to that she-devil?"

"It's likely that we will be directed to alight at a remote locale," Doc explained as he trimmed flaps. "This ship is too big to land most places. Hence, a water landing will be called for, whether our opponent desires it or not."

Monk's spirits seemed to brighten. "Sounds like you got a plan."

Ham said coolly, "Doc always has a plan."

"Yeah, well, so far we ain't been having any special luck,"

Monk said miserably.

No one ventured a further opinion on that score. The homely chemist went to the back of the cabin to sulk.

Doc circled the Atlantic off Long Island for the better part of an hour, Long Tom hunched over the radio set, hands clapped to receiver earphones, listening.

"Nothing yet?" Ham asked out of sheer boredom.

"Did you hear any call coming in?" Long Tom said sourly, taking the headset cans off his ears. "Leave me be."

They flew wide loops for another ten minutes. Then the set crackled to life.

"*This is a message for Doc Savage,*" a growling, possibly female voice announced.

Doc took the microphone and said, "Doc Savage speaking. Go ahead."

"*Here are your instructions. Fly to City Island and then head due northeast for thirty miles. You will see a blue bell buoy. Land. We will meet you there.*"

"Looks like that she-devil was thinkin' along the same lines as you, Doc," Monk ventured.

Doc Savage was silent a long moment. "We have not had much experience dealing with female adversaries," was all he said. It was an admission, as much as anything else, that the metallic giant was experiencing frustration over his inability to fox his persistent foe. Outfoxing others was part of the bronze man's stock in trade. Of late, he seemed always on the defensive.

Doc monitored his instruments as the graceful bronze aircraft droned along at five thousand feet. It was comfortably quiet in the soundproofed cabin. The motor bawl was a constant but blurred vibration of sound.

Soon, they spotted the ocean-going express cruiser driving for the same spot. From this altitude, it looked like a toy of unusually fine workmanship, dragging a lean wake.

"I think that's our opposition," suggested Ham.

"It sure is," put in Long Tom. "Word has come over the commercial radio stations that a cruiser fitting that description has been stolen from City Island Yacht Basin."

Doc tilted the control wheel, and sank the plane lower. The crinkles on the blue ocean below grew into animated corrugations that were never still. The surface reflection of their wings grew steadily.

Monk peered ahead anxiously. "I don't see no blue bell buoy, and we're gettin' mighty close."

The reason for this became evident very soon after.

The express cruiser reached a point and began circling back. The motor was cut; it slid to a soggy stop. An anchor was thrown out, making a tiny splash as seen from above.

They were too high up to see much more than that. Ham got a pair of field glasses from a door pocket, and began scanning the cruiser's deck.

"I spy a person robed in purple," he reported.

Monk all but jumped out of his seat. "Any sign of Lea?"

Ham studied the deck a long time before answering. "Not yet." Then he said, "They're taking a canvas cover off something. I see it now! It's a blue bell buoy. I guess they are taking no chances. They brought their own marker buoy."

Doc Savage took the glass from Ham and studied the scene below.

The ocean was full of swells. Landing would not be tricky—merely routine to an experienced hand.

"It is time to land," he said, returning the binoculars.

They all settled in their seats and Doc dropped the big seaplane toward the ocean's heaving face.

The landing was nearly perfect. They pancaked, slamming across wave tops for over a minute, settled, and Doc cut the four-bladed propellers.

The ship wallowed in the heaving brine. Pressing a dash button, Doc caused a kedge-type sea anchor to be lowered. It found an obstruction on the bottom, took hold, arresting the craft snugly.

Monk opened the door, stuck his head out.

The cruiser was bobbing beside the bell buoy. The crew—which consisted of the few surviving convicts—were fending it off with boat hooks.

"We're here!" Monk boomed in a voice that carried all the force of his barrel chest. "What now?"

"Get ready to jump into the water," a hoarse voice called out.

Monk called back, "Where's my secretary and my pig?"

Out of the cabin came a weird flapping figure in purple.

Chapter XXI

THE TRAP IN A TRAP

THE EMERGING FIGURE proved to be the cloaked and historically hatted apparition they had first encountered in the Greenwich Village brownstone—the strange being who had broken half a dozen hardened criminals out of the Tombs prison and terrorized a city.

A twisted wail emerged from the creature's lips.

"Savage!"

Doc Savage shouldered to the open plane door. "Here."

"These are your instructions. You and your men drop into the water and swim away from the airplane. We will then approach and board it."

"Where are the prisoners?" demanded Doc.

"Out of sight. But safe."

"No deal—until you prove that both are alive."

"You are in no position to bargain," spat back the hooded one.

"That's true, Doc," hissed Ham. "We can't take that chance."

"Neither can we surrender the ship without receiving consideration in return," the bronze man pointed out.

The violet-hued tatterdemalion called out again, "We are wasting time! Do as I say!"

Doc called back, "Produce the girl and the pig if you want possession of this plane."

The costumed leader fell into low converse with assorted

followers. They consulted for several minutes. Not a syllable of their exchange could be made out.

Finally, the purple one called over, "Would the sound of her voice prove to you that she is alive?"

"It would," allowed Doc.

From a fold of the creature's shapeless lavender garment, a pistol was produced. It appeared to be a long-barreled target pistol of small caliber. The apparition aimed the pistol at the blue bell buoy, pulled the trigger once, and sparked a bullet glancing off its painted steel surface.

The buoy rang like a great discordant gong. In the ensuing reverberations, a piercing feminine cry resounded.

Monk howled, "Lea! Doc, that's Lea's voice! They got her trapped in that buoy!"

A piggy squeal followed.

"Habeas as well," said Doc. Lifting his voice, the bronze man called, "I need your word that you will not sink the cruiser after you have transferred to the plane."

The lavender being hesitated. "How do you know that my word is of any value?"

"It is the only coin you possess," the bronze man admitted.

"Very well. I will not sink the boat. You have my word on this."

That seemed to satisfy the bronze man. He told the others, "Follow me."

DOC dropped into the water. All but Ham Brooks followed. The fastidious attorney hesitated. He was dressed in his finest afternoon garb, and was plainly reluctant to immerse himself out of sartorial concerns, if for no other practical reason.

Finally, he slipped into the heaving brine. Ham still retained his ever-present if mangled sword cane. Rarely did it ever leave his manicured hands.

They swam a few hundred yards away from the bobbing plane, waited. Majestic rollers lifted them up as each one passed, depositing them gently back into the trough of the swells as they subsided. Stirring their arms in the water kept them upright in the ever-shifting brine.

The cruiser leapt into roaring life, approached the waiting aircraft with a furious bone of spume in its mouth.

It bumped its fendered prow against the hull. Lines were made fast. Two convicts clambered aboard; they assisted their purple chief into the ship.

The cruiser was unceremoniously pushed off. It drifted away.

Treading water a fair distance from all this, Doc Savage and his men observed operations, knowing that they were vulnerable to being picked off by rifle shots—if the minions of the Abolisher were so inclined.

After a time, the plane's powerful motors were started. The pilot was no novice, but it became clear that the great bronze plane was of a size and type he had never before handled.

"Looks like they're gettin' away with it," Monk growled.

Long Tom looked pained, while Ham struggled to keep his broken blade out of the water. He settled for balancing it across his lean shoulders.

Doc Savage was silent as he watched the takeoff proceedings. He seemed to be waiting for something expected to transpire.

A searing sun beat down upon them mercilessly, adding to their watery discomfit. The vastness of Long Island Sound was an unpleasant spot to find one's self adrift.

The pilot coaxed the throttles and experimented with taxiing about. Awkwardly, by trial and error, the plane canted around toward them.

Then it revved up, all three engines expelling smoke and thunder. Surrounding sea surface rippled and flattened under their synchronized lash.

"They're getting ready to go," Long Tom mumbled.

Unexpectedly, a hatch popped open.

"Savage!" a male voice called out. "Smart work, but no dice.

We're all wearing gas masks."

Frowning, Ham asked, "Doc, what do they mean?"

"I had set a timer on board, hooked up with a canister of our special anesthetic gas. It evidently went off without affecting any of them." The bronze man's voice tone was calm, unconcerned. Nothing remotely smacking of disappointment registered on his metallic features.

The hatch banged shut. Then the pilot gunned all three motors. The amphibian surged ahead, plowing through the swells like a broad-winged behemoth.

"Doc!" cried Ham. "They're going to run us down!"

"Dive!" ordered Doc, setting an example by vanishing from view.

All of Doc's men were expert swimmers. They dropped out of sight and struck off in different directions.

The lumbering amphibian charged through the spot where they had been, barreling along like a metallic monster with furiously foaming teeth, throwing up salt spray in its turbulent wake.

Doc reappeared first. His head broke the surface and almost immediately began shedding water. He watched the amphibian go hurtling past, hull pontoon smashing along the wave tops. It seemed reluctant to leave the water, but finally tore free.

The noise was deafening. Its snarling thunder soon receded, leaving them alone in the shimmering immensity of the Sound.

From the bell buoy, Lea Aster's voice could be heard crying out in confusion. Her hollow words were not distinct enough to be understood.

Monk began swimming toward the buoy. "Hold on, Lea!" he yelled. "I'm comin' to get you!"

His long ape-like arms churned water like a threshing machine. The apish chemist reached the blue buoy in amazing time.

Doc Savage had also leaped into action. He struck out for the express cruiser and reached it first. The bronze man got aboard and discovered everything in working order. He engaged the throttle.

Sending the craft sweeping around, Doc collected Ham and Long Tom, then made for the bobbing buoy. Wake created waves that pushed the sea marker about, causing its bell to clang disconsolately.

Monk was perched atop the swinging hull, making simian faces and looking like a frustrated gorilla in ill-fitting clothes.

"It's bolted together," he complained, as Doc drew near.

"That is preferable to having to employ a cutting torch," the bronze man pointed out.

Doc located a monkey wrench in a deck tool box, heaved it in Monk's direction. The hairy chemist captured it in one powerful paw and fell to working on the big bolts. His burly arms strained, muscles bunching in frightening knots.

Doc Savage's alert eyes went to the departing plane. From a pocket, he silently removed his compact radio receiver. This could be transformed for other uses. Doc manipulated dials, then depressed a button.

Observing him, Long Tom remarked, "An ace up your sleeve?"

"One of several," replied the bronze man.

The bronze-painted seaplane flew onward for a short time, as the pilot sought altitude. Then black smoke began pouring out from various spots in its streamlined structure. Soon, it was a trailing pall.

Ham asked, "Smudge smoke?"

"Combined with a tear gas, as well as another disabling gas that works through the pores," Doc related.

"That means they will have to land!" Ham crowed.

Doc nodded. "Even wearing gas protection, they cannot operate the amphibian for long without being able to see the controls. And it is unlikely that they brought along sufficient oxygen canisters to wear their masks for longer than the regulation period. Too, tear gas cannot be cleared from a confined cabin space without expending considerable time and effort."

The bronze man's words proved prescient. The tri-motored plane began canting wildly, wings flashing in the sun. The pilot fought to keep the ship level. He soon gave it up as a bad job. Altitude was shed. The craft circled cautiously.

It eventually put down amid a mighty pounding of the broad hull against wave caps, but the aircraft was sturdy and could take considerable mishandling.

BY this time, Monk Mayfair had levered the last stubborn bolt off the bell buoy fastening ring and plunged into the squirming swells, where he began struggling to pry off the top. He grunted and groaned like a bull ape, but not much came of his efforts, except rivulets of perspiration.

Doc Savage stepped off the deck and joined him in the swells. Stationing himself on the opposite side, treading water, the bronze man helped heave the top portion of the buoy free. It gave a final groan of protest, then slipped beneath the blue, soon sinking from sight.

Sunlight disclosed the broad bottom portion of the buoy. It was only then that they realized the predicament in which the prisoners lay.

For pretty Lea Aster—Habeas Corpus held tight in her slender arms—was chained to the inner shell of the bell buoy. One wrist was clamped by steel handcuffs. The other cuff was affixed to a single length of stout anchor chain stapled in turn to the steel form—which, no longer sealed airtight, began taking on seawater.

Soon it, too, would repose on the bottom of the drink.

"Blazes!" Monk exploded. "We ain't got much time!"

Doc Savage assessed the situation at a glance. Any effort to climb aboard the half-buoy would tip over the thing with ca-lamitous results. Once it capsized, the anchor chain would drag both prisoners to the bottom, ending all hope of rescue.

Lea Aster looked upward, entrancing features pale with dread. Her well-coiffed blonde locks resembled a wilted flower.

The interior of the buoy had been an oven.

"I can see from your expressions that there is no hope," she said weakly, eyes squeezing closed.

"We make our own hope," Monk returned gamely, grabbing the flange of the buoy with big hairy hands. This caused the shell to tip and take on more water.

"Be careful, Monk," warned Doc. His amazing mind was already calculating possibilities.

Conceivably, he and Monk might snap the handcuff links by main strength. This would require locating a weak link, or other exploitable point. But to maneuver into position to do so would require clambering aboard. As a plan, that was patently disastrous. Once the shell sank, fighting for purchase on the links would be almost impossible in the underwater gloom.

Nor was there sufficient time to work out another stratagem. For rollers were rocking the buoy, causing pails of brine to slop into the shallow shell. Already, a threatening quantity was sloshing about the bottom.

Possibly recognizing the imminence of his peril, Habeas began squealing in concern.

"Perhaps I can hand him up," called Lea Aster. "While there's still time."

But as soon as she attempted the awkward maneuver, the buoy rocked sharply. Water cascaded over both of them. Habeas began squirming in her arms, hooves flailing.

"Doc!" yowled Monk, eyes reflecting anguish. *"Do something!"*

Doc Savage did. It was a calculated risk that he took. But events allowed for no other course of action.

From a pocket, the bronze man withdrew a thing like a black firecracker.

Monk eyed it. "Thermite!" he breathed.

Doc ignited the device. He did this by twisting it. This action caused two separate chambers of volatile ingredients—aluminum powder and iron oxide predominately—to mix. Reaction began.

"Cover your face!" urged Doc, throwing the blazing thing.

The bronze man's aim was perfect. The incandescent chemical torch of a thing landed athwart the staple to which the anchor chain was affixed. There commenced an incredible sputtering. Molten metal began splashing. Habeas became even more agitated. Lea Aster buried her face in her arms and her shoulders shook with emotion.

Monk hastily stripped off his water-soaked jersey and threw this over Lea Aster to protect her from the white-hot spatter.

Doc's voiced crashed out, "Now, Monk!"

Events were happening so fast that at first the burly chemist grunted out a confused, "Huh?" Then he realized Doc's plan.

For the bronze giant knew that the thermite was not only acting on the fat steel staple, but also eating away at the buoy form itself. The stuff was used in welding. It was potent.

Seawater was bubbling and hissing as it entered the scalding hole. The steel shell began sinking, but in a manner than held the buoy stable in the water, with no immediate danger of capsizing.

Doc rapped, "Get ready to grab Habeas, Monk."

As the buoy sank, Lea Aster became cognizant of the fast-rising water. Her eyes flew open, became round with terror. She released the threshing pig, saying not a word. A numb bravery was written on her drawn features.

With alarming speed, the buoy sank to the waterline. The incandescent sizzling of thermite continued.

Monk clutched at the buoy's rim in vain. It got away from him. Suddenly, Habeas was swimming in his direction, ears distended. The apish chemist snatched up the runt pig in hairy arms. Habeas grunted energetically.

Doc Savage gave Monk a hard shove, propelling him away from the sinking shell before it could pull them under.

Then the bronze man plunged into the maelstrom of steaming water created by the bell buoy slipping from sight.

Eyes going wide, Lea Aster held her breath. Her blonde head

vanished from view. She waited for the expected and inevitable demise.

Instead, steel-strong fingers inserted a pill into her mouth. She swallowed it, returned to holding her lungs in suspension.

Doc Savage seized the handcuff chain and began twisting the links. In the fading light, this took some time to accomplish. Cables and thews strained against steel. An eternity seemed to pass. But the bronze man worked as if unconcerned with the danger.

One link parted. Instantly, the anchor chain fell away, staple end still sputtering as the thermite continued melting furiously, unaffected by salt water. It swiftly sank, vanished from view.

They shot free, far below the sunlit surface which seemed to belong to a solar realm that seemed impossibly distant and unreachable.

Feet kicking, powerful arms cradling the exhausted girl, Doc Savage conveyed Lea Aster to open air. Her head broke clear, whereupon she gulped life-giving oxygen greedily.

"I thought my lungs would burst," the blonde gasped out.

"That special pill you swallowed permits the absorption of oxygen in concentrated form," explained Doc. "There was no danger of drowning."

The bronze man neglected to inform her that the tablet was of his own invention, a concentrated chemical concoction that, when mixed with saliva, provided emergency oxygen for a short interval.

Monk Mayfair swam over, towing Habeas by one handy ear.

Floating together, they regarded one another without words. None were necessary. It had been a very near thing.

Between them, Doc and Monk lifted Lea Aster and Habeas Corpus out of the water, handing them off to Ham and Long Tom, who pulled the freed prisoners back on the cruiser's deck. Doc and Monk joined them there, soaked to the skin.

Doc Savage rushed to the controls, got the motor going

again, and sent the express cruiser churning toward the big plane at top speed. Spray pelted them like stinging hail.

"Now we're going to have us a party," Monk said, yanking out his supermachine pistol and unlatching the complicated safety devices which permitted the waterproof weapon to be discharged.

"This affair is far from over yet," warned the bronze man. "The master mind still has possession of the gold-demolishing ray contrivance. We are in a deadly spot if it is turned on."

Chapter XXII

HARRIDAN OF HORROR

UNDER THE SCORCHING summer sun, Doc Savage's face was a mask of metal. As he eased back on the throttle and brought the express cruiser to a slow sliding stop, his flake-gold eyes searched the wallowing amphibian for signs of activity.

The hatch lay open on the big bronze bird. Coils of sepia smoke boiled out of it. Cockpit windows had been cracked open and more of the ebony pall was crawling from those apertures. It looked as if noisome black worms were worrying the helpless craft.

A long time elapsed before the smoke thinned to gray and exhausted itself.

The Doc Savage party prudently remained upwind of it all. Even so, some of the eye-smarting tear gas got into their faces, inhibiting vision.

For a considerable period, nothing stirred within the bronze-skinned seaplane.

"Looks like they can take it," remarked Ham, frowning.

"Everyone on that plane is a hardened killer," Doc Savage reminded.

When the silence had gone on long enough, Doc cupped corded hands to his mouth and called over, "Stand by to be boarded."

"Come no closer," a hoarse and raspy voice replied.

"There is nothing more to discuss," Doc returned. "You cannot take off again without closing all hatches. To do so would invite disaster."

Silence followed. No doubt the situation was being discussed. Some fragmentary yelling came to their ears, but no words that could be deciphered.

"Sounds like they are quarreling among themselves," suggested Ham.

A shot cracked out. After a minute, a body was dumped from the hatch. It was a man. The corpse of one of the convicts, without question.

Lea Aster gave a small cry and turned her pretty face away.

"Cold-blooded murder," Ham breathed.

Long Tom remarked dryly, "I guess the master mind isn't big on dissent."

Monk smacked his lips. "That means we're in for a fight, brothers."

Doc Savage was thoughtful. The body of the dead man was floating face downward in the water. Tidal forces were pushing it away from the amphibian. The bronze man made a megaphone of his cupped hands.

"There is no escape. Surrender is your only alternative. You need not fear reprisals."

Came another shot. This time, it whistled past them.

A metallic flash, Doc pushed Long Tom and Lea Aster to the deck planking. The bronze man had spotted the rifle barrel jutting from the plane door before its dark muzzle blew out flash-fire. Monk grabbed Habeas. Ham Brooks dropped on his nattily-attired stomach.

"Don't come any closer!" the hoarse voice warned.

Doc lifted his crashing voice again. "You need not fear prison. You are obviously not of sound mind. You will be taken to an institution where you will be treated for your mental affliction."

More silence. It grew prolonged. A lone seagull, circling far from land, gave up a raucous cry and wheeled away.

At last, a male voice spoke up, "She says we can surrender."

Doc Savage stood up.

"Slide into the water," he instructed. "We will pick you up."

The remaining convicts did so. Reluctantly, they dropped into the drink and began swimming. One was forced to dog-paddle through a spreading pool of scarlet that marked the spot where his slain comrade floated like a forlorn fragment of flotsam.

"Can we trust them?" asked Ham suspiciously.

"No," said Doc Savage, his eyes alert for treachery.

When the last man was in the water, another rifle shot rang out. It was followed by a dull thud.

The convict nearest the amphibian looked startled. Twisting his head around, he peered through the hatch.

"Shot herself!" he cried out. "Hell's bells! She couldn't take it!"

Lea Aster moaned. "Suicide. How horrible."

Doc Savage could see a purple sleeve lying on the cabin floor, but nothing more.

Ham hissed, "Doc, is that the correct number of convicts in the water?"

"It would seem so."

"They might have collected others," Monk cautioned.

"Right," chimed in Long Tom, knotting his pale fists.

They were all thinking the same thing. Was this another wily trap?

The survivors were swimming toward the cruiser. The expressions on their sweat-soaked faces were ones of utter defeat. They did not look as if they were acting.

"Could be we've wrapped this mess up," Monk started to say.

With his keen vision, Doc Savage was the only one to see the purple sleeve twitch. It was a momentary thing. Corpses often exhibit such fitful animation as life departs their mortal form. Doc tensed, waiting to see if anything else untoward happened.

When something did, it almost caught the big bronze man by surprise. A half second before Long Tom cried out a warning, Doc Savage detected a warm sensation on his skin, just under the electrum wristwatch designed to warn of activation of the gold-obliterating ray.

"Down!" he shouted.

The swimmers were closing in on the cruiser. One man was in the lead. His face was recognizable to any newspaper reader—Jake Means. He reached the stern, lifted a hand up to grasp the Jacob's ladder.

The hand exploded into a moist red puffball!

THERE was hardly any sound. Certainly the man did not cry out. There was no time for that before Jake Means's body disintegrated violently with a sound remindful of a giant expulsion of breath.

Scarlet droplets sprinkled the cruiser deck like a sudden rain.

Other matter also descended, but in such small pieces that they mistook it for precipitation.

In the water, the surviving convicts began splashing and caterwauling like drowning kittens.

They started to turn back, terror etched on their twisted features. They might or might not have understood what was actually happening—particle gold in suspension in their bloodstreams was being violently excited—but they recognized sudden death when they beheld it. They beheld it now.

From the cockpit hatch on the wallowing amphibian, a purple form leapt up, shrieking, an elongated ostrich plume waving from the crown of a flamboyant black hat of a bygone era.

"No! Forward! Go forward! Do my bidding!"

The confused trio thrashed about in the water. They began crying to the heavens for salvation, confessing their myriad sins and praying to their Creator.

For clamped in the purple one's white-gloved hands was the

newsreel camera that was not a camera. Its round lens aperture was being directed toward them.

Doc Savage grabbed for Ham's cane. He lifted it high.

"See if you can hit this!" he shouted, throwing the unsheathed blade.

It left Doc's fingers in a flash. The titanic bronze man's unique combination of great strength, speed and muscular coordination was never more apparent.

The blade hurtled toward the open hatch like a javelin, broken point first. It literally whistled as it split the humid air.

At the last possible moment, it executed a smart somersault.

The round brass head collided with the plumed personage in purple. It knocked the ray weapon from grasping hands. With a weird animal screech, the outrageous apparition splashed into the Atlantic, death device following.

Doc Savage plunged into the ocean after both.

Employing powerful overhand strokes, he swam for the amphibian.

The figure in purple continued thrashing about. Whether it was because he or she could not swim, or for other reasons, was difficult to determine.

Doc knifed through the waves as if born there. He made excellent time. Water seemed as natural an element to this mighty bronze man that he might have been some fantastic denizen of the deep—half-man, half-porpoise.

From beneath the face-enshrouding cavalier hat, the other saw the terrible form of the mighty Nemesis of bronze closing in.

Frantically, clutching hands beat the water frantically for what they sought. Success greeted these wild efforts.

The ray device came up. Evidently its makeshift housing was both waterproof and buoyant, for it had not sunk. Now it pointed squarely at Doc Savage.

"Be careful!" Doc warned. "You could perish yourself."

"No," hissed the other, "you are the one to die!"

The camera lens was directed at a point behind Doc Savage. A switch was thrown—*and a screaming convict became a scarlet fountain in the water!*

An invisible ray swung about, came into contract with the floating corpse of the escapee previously shot dead.

Another gory geyser erupted!

Doc Savage dived under water. More crimson rain pattered the Atlantic's heaving surface under which he had vanished. Tiny pools formed, spread, and overlapped one another.

Explosions were eerie, almost soundless, but they jolted the water with the shock of their force.

More quickly than it seemed possible, the last escaped convict was extinguished—his life callously sacrificed by a fiendish master in an effort to destroy Doc Savage.

The spreading pools of gore produced a predictable result.

THIN triangular blades began cutting the sanguinary ocean surface. Grisly gray fins of marauding hammerhead sharks, attracted by the scent of blood, began circling! The man-eaters snapped at chunks of raw human meat where they discovered any, wolfing them down greedily.

Doc Savage habitually changed the contents of his carry-all vest whenever he entered a new situation. Before leaving his headquarters, the bronze man had stowed several vials of a chemical of his own devising, which had a discouraging effect upon sharks.

Doc began dispersing quantities of this in several directions, but principally upon himself. This would make his muscular form as appetizing to a shark as a rubber boot.

Effects were rapid. The cartilage blades started moving off in frustrated zigzag patterns. One by one, they vanished beneath the surface, where the waters were not chemically fouled.

Before this was accomplished, a voice screamed shrilly.

Looking about, Doc spotted kicking robed-tangled feet in

the lee of the hull superstructure. He arrowed toward them, swimming forcefully, dropping under water as he neared them.

The flapping figure in purple was caught unawares. Doc Savage's great cabled hands seized both ankles and pulled downward.

That was sufficient to disorient his panic-prone opponent.

Doc released both ankles, allowing his prisoner to bob back to the surface. His searching hands sought the ray contrivance that had brought so much violent, unwanted death. It was gone.

Unexpectedly, something flashed silver, and the bronze man felt a sudden sharp pain.

A knife! It had scored a metallic forearm. Salt water touching raw flesh brought stinging pain.

Doc found the wrist back of the knife, twisted, and the blade slipped below the heaving swells.

Then the thing the bronze man wished to avoid happened.

The ray was still operating. Its unseen beam swept the area, inevitably came into contact with one of the minute particles of gold floating in the Atlantic. Results were predictable.

The sea erupted, throwing them up, out of the water! Fish, some already dead from shock, flew up into the air.

Doc slammed back into the ocean, sank a dozen feet, got his bearings. He saw that the violet wraith, limp and clearly stunned, was slipping from sight, drowning.

The bronze man worked down into the deeper depths and reached out. Darkness was clamping over the fading figure. It was growing dim down where sunlight could not penetrate.

It was a near thing, but Doc Savage caught a wrist just before the bedraggled wretch faded from view.

Gathering it up, he kicked free for the surface, broke into open air and administered the proper procedures to counteract water in the lungs.

When he was done, the bronze man saw that he was swimming in a scarlet lake amid the pristine blue of the ocean.

The idling amphibian was settling. Evidently, the multiple eruptions had tossed it about like a duck in a pond. But these gyrations soon subsided. The ungainly flying boat eventually ceased its alarming rocking.

In short order, the express cruiser puttered up to reach him, Long Tom at the wheel.

Monk and Ham reached down and took the limp form in lavender from the bronze man's arms. Then Doc clambered board.

The master mind was laid out on the deck. Doc Savage reached down, removed the glove from the left hand. A maimed ring finger was thus revealed. Then the bronze man shucked off its shroud-like hood. The distinctive black hat had been lost to the waves.

A woman's strong features were exposed. Her tresses were long, stringy and iron gray. Doc seized the hair. It came away. Beneath the wig, lustrous black hair was revealed.

"Trixie Peters!" Long Tom snapped.

"Elvira Merlin," Doc corrected.

"Same difference," muttered Monk.

"Imagine," Lea Aster murmured. "A woman behind the worst series of murders in years."

"Yeah. And we still don't know why," Monk added.

AFTER a while, Elvira Merlin fluttered her eyes open. They were a distinct shade of silver. As they came into focus, purple glints of hate came into both orbs, as if splintered with amethyst. They accumulated in the blazing depths of each iris, finally overwhelming their original hue. This was the secret of her ever-changing eye color. It was some freak of natural pigmentation brought out by extreme emotion.

A moment later, the cloaked woman sat up. She stared fixedly for a moment at the ring of grim faces looking down at her. Her face grew strained.

She stirred, recognized the bronze man. Her voice became

bitter, venomous.

"Bold as brass, aren't you? Why didn't you die?"

"Why did you wish to kill me?" asked the bronze man calmly.

"I can't abide the color of your eyes!" she hissed.

"Good grief!" exclaimed Ham. "The woman is crazy as a loon!"

"Mentally unbalanced," clarified Doc. To the woman, he said, "Your device is lost forever. Your plans have been foiled. You have nothing more to gain and therefore little left to hide. Tell us, why?"

Hanging her head, the cloaked harridan said quietly, "I admit my guilt."

Doc Savage asked suddenly, "You will sign a confession?"

"Yes."

There was silence.

"I am the Abolisher," said Elvira Merlin. "The maimings, the destruction of property, and the extortions from the rich men—"

"Not all of them were rich," interrupted Ham.

"The extortions from the people who had money," insisted Elvira Merlin, "were all my deeds. I was doing them to accomplish what I consider good. I was trying to amass a great fortune, a fortune which was to be given to poor people."

"Your story does not add up," inserted Doc. "Can you explain why the destruction of gold aided that particular scheme?"

"Gold is the basis of money," she spat. "Money is the wellspring of all woe. For my plan to work, the hateful stuff had to be eradicated off the face of the Earth."

"That was not your true motive," Doc said quietly. "It ran much deeper."

The woman came to her feet unaided. She was a pathetic figure, soaked to the skin, her royal purple garment sticking to her shivering limbs. She held her left hand in a tight fist, as if to conceal her disfigured hand. The absent ring finger was an unsettling sight.

Doc Savage continued his questioning.

"Your employer, S. Charles Amerikanis, claimed that you were having difficulties with your husband, the true inventor of the gold-annihilating ray. Yet you went to work for him under another name, and later pointed the finger of suspicion at Amerikanis. Why?"

Elvira Merlin's cold-blued lips thinned to a bloodless line. She said nothing. Gradually, her bile seemed to depart. The amethyst glints on her eyes retreated, and they gradually returned to their normal silvery hue.

Doc Savage pressed, "It is easy to conclude that Amerikanis had something you wanted—something you were trying to frighten him into surrendering. What was it?"

The other compressed her lips. "I have nothing to say."

The bronze man went on. "Your targets were very specific as well. The first was the Kromgold jewelry concern. And your initial attempt failed because you were inexperienced in proper handling of the device. You accidentally severed your own finger, killing two chance passersby in the process. Then you struck at the Chemical Trust Bank, after tricking a patent attorney named Galsworth into storing your gold in its safety deposit vault."

Blazing violet eyes regarded the bronze man steadily. Bloodless lips writhed.

"Allow me to speculate then," continued Doc. "For your first target, you selected one whose name included the word gold. The Chemical Trust Bank bore a name similar to that of your employer's company, Elektro-Alchemical Company. That suggested someone connected with that concern, and antagonistic toward it."

Elvira Merlin shivered in the freshening sea breeze. But she remained silent.

Doc said, "In the beginning, you called yourself A. Alchemist. All this points to a mania surrounding gold. You struck at your husband's employer and at lawyer Galsworth. Why?"

"I despise alchemistry!"

"Another mistake," indicated Doc. "There is no such word. The proper term is alchemy. Yet you used it in the letter accompanying the deadly lump of gold, and again in A. Alchemist's published note, betraying your culpability."

Lea Aster inserted herself at this point.

"Mr. Savage, I believe I understand the significance of the purple robes."

Doc turned, asked, "Yes?"

"As a woman, she would naturally wear clothes that would complement her violet eyes. Furthermore, violet is the opposite hue of gold. She was expressing her distaste for gold by wearing purple."

"Cracked," snorted Monk.

"Crazy as a bedbug," chimed in Long Tom.

Doc Savage held Elvira Merlin's violet orbs with his uncanny golden ones. To most persons, Doc's eyes were compelling to the point of being unnerving. But this woman seemed to shrink from them not because of their strange and eerie hypnotic qualities, but due to their very hue.

Doc asked, "You were on your way to Alaska. Why?"

"To join my husband," admitted the woman.

"From whom you had not heard in a long time. Is that right?"

More silence.

"Would it interest you to know that we are going to Alaska as well?" inquired Doc.

A twitch of emotion tugged at Elvira Merlin's downcast mouth. From stringy hair to soggy feet, she shivered.

"Perhaps you would be willing to tell the whole truth in front of your husband, John?" Doc suggested without malice.

"I cannot resist you," said Elvira Merlin unhappily.

That seemed to settle that.

THEY transferred over to the bobbing amphibian. Doc climbed in first. He claimed a device resembling a chemical fire extin-

guisher and began spraying the interior of the aircraft liberally. He wore a small gas mask as he did so, one which he often
carried which doubled as a diving "lung."

It helped dispel all lingering traces of the tear gas mixture.
Soon, the commodious cabin was safe to inhabit.

Once everyone was on board, Doc maneuvered the powerful
seaplane into the air.

Before long, they were winging their way back to Manhattan,
flying low.

"We will drop you off in the city," Doc informed Lea Aster.

"Thank you, Mr. Savage. But if time is of the essence, I will
be happy to accompany you."

That, too, settled that. Doc pushed the big bird to a higher
altitude, while Ham plotted a course for Alaska. They settled
down for the long flight to the Land of the Midnight Sun.

"I wonder how Renny and Johnny are doing?" Monk mused
at one point.

"Try to raise them," Doc suggested.

Long Tom took the responsibility. He went to the radio
cubby, clamped a headset over his oversized ears and began
fiddling with dials. This produced almost instantaneous results.

The thumping bear-in-a-cave voice of Renny Renwick came
over the air, sounding excited.

*"Holy cow, but we've been hollering into the radio for the last
hour,"* he reported. *"Something strange is going on here."*

Long Tom demanded, "What do you mean, strange?"

"The ground is rumbling. Like an earthquake is about to happen."

Doc came out of his seat, took the microphone.

"Describe the situation, Renny," he said.

*"Johnny and I are camped out near the laboratory, keeping an eye
on things like you said. It's been quiet. No sign yet of the two birds
you mentioned. But the lights are on in the lab. I think Merlin's
working late."*

"Go on," urged Doc.

"For the last hour or two, the mountain has been rumbling."

"Mountain?"

"Mount Grozny, they call it. It's a dormant volcano. Could be it's getting ready to wake up."

Doc Savage looked concerned for a moment. His troubled trilling climbed the scales for some seconds, but he stifled it with an effort of will. "Renny, this is important. Find John Merlin. Take him by force if you have to. But get him and yourselves as far away from that volcano as possible."

"Sure. But it's just rumbling. Don't volcanoes do that from time to—"

Just then an earth-shaking roar transmitted over the ether.

Renny's *"Holy cow!"* was lost in the uproar. It sounded like the end of the world. The echoes of it persisted only a moment. Then they were replaced by the dismal carrier-wave hiss that told all those listening that the big engineer's radio had ceased to operate.

Chapter XXIII

TERROR CRATER

COLONEL JOHN "RENNY" RENWICK dropped the velocity microphone in mid-syllable and hit the hard ground, seeking shelter. He was a muscular mastodon of a man, possessing fists of freakish size. His mournful face reflected his abrupt dismay.

Reverberations of an explosion caused majestic evergreen trees to sway and rustle. A hot wind blew toward him. There was dust, debris, pine needles mixed in with the unpleasant gust.

Nearby, a startled voice exploded, "I'll be superamalgamated!"

That was William Harper "Johnny" Littlejohn, renowned geologist and archeologist. He was a tall skinny beanpole of an individual. When Johnny closed one eye, he resembled a needle. Once he headed the Natural Sciences research department of a prestigious university where academic excellence outweighed all other concerns. Like the other five members of Doc Savage's adventurous band, the bony archeologist had joined cause with the amazing bronze man during the fracas that had been the Great War.

Climbing to his feet, Johnny checked the magnifying glass he wore attached to his lapel like a monocle. It was a relic of the days when he had lost the sight in one eye, owing to an injury received in wartime. Thanks to Doc Savage's surgical wizardry, Johnny no longer needed it, but carried it for its utility.

"Holy cow!" Renny said when he could hear again. He

scrambled to his feet. His long face wore an expression of profound gloom. Normally, this indicated that the big engineer was happy. But now it simply meant that Renny's emotions had been shocked out of him.

In the near distance, the top of Mount Grozny was spouting a species of hellfire. A fiery bubbling danced on the black rim of the crater lip, changing its hard contours.

"A cataclysmic cacophony," Johnny said, which was his way of saying that it was the loudest sound he had ever heard.

"That rockpile sure blew its top," Renny agreed. "Listen, Doc wants us to grab Merlin and get him out of here."

"Indubitably correct," said Johnny. "Let us motivate with alacrity."

They gathered up their things, after ascertaining that the portable short-wave set was on the blink.

"Can you fix it?" Johnny asked Renny.

"Maybe. But let's glom Merlin first."

But John Merlin was nowhere to be found. His lab was a shambles. It lay closer to the volcanic cone than were Johnny and Renny, and upset timber trees had toppled into it.

They poked around the wreckage of the lab. There was no sign of the missing electrochemist. Equipment ranging from shattered glass beakers to twisted electrical coils and capacitors lay strewed amid the ruins.

Johnny discovered blobs of a heavy gray metal mixed in with everything. Hefting one sample, he scored it with a pen knife. It proved soft.

"Lead," Johnny pronounced.

Renny nodded heavily. "Looks like Merlin was experimenting with lead, for some reason."

Johnny examined one blob with his monocle magnifier. "With phantasmagoric consequences," he clipped.

Surveying the shattered surroundings, Renny muttered, "He couldn't have gotten far. Up for a search?"

"Indubitably."

Johnny gave his spring-generator flashlight a revitalizing wind, and together they began prowling the area.

They searched high and low. The air was sulfurous, difficult to inhale and it lacked sufficient oxygen for easy respiration. The going was hard.

AFTER an hour, they decided to split up, Renny ranging farther away from the fiery mount, which spat and splashed lava restlessly.

Ever the geologist, Johnny chose to move closer. It was unlikely that the missing Merlin had gone that way, but the possibility could not be ruled out.

Mount Grozny lay near the edge of the water—a body known as Cook's Inlet. The inlet surface shimmered with reflected fire. Things were happening there.

A superheated incandescent worm of lava was pouring down the mountainside, seeking the shore. Another slopped up and overflowed the crater rim high above. It came sizzling down like a molten chunk of hell, its liquid surface as wrinkled as a serpent easing out of its den.

Fascinated by the awe-inspiring pyrotechnic display, Johnny worked his way around to the far side of the volcano.

He arrived just in time to witness the first groping rope of lava reach the water. A violent hissing ensued. Water boiled, producing billows of steam.

More magma flowed and a second fiery stream wound its searing way into the inlet. Even more scalding steam was produced. Boiled fish began popping to the surface, eyes glazed white.

There was no sign of John Merlin, so Johnny began to retreat inland.

It happened that a splash of lava erupted at that point and landed near him. It sizzled as it struck cool basaltic stone.

Intrigued, the elongated geologist approached the hot splatter of molten rock, for he knew that most lava was just that—ordinary stony matter heated to an incredible degree until it had achieved the consistency of scorching liquid.

Employing his monocle magnifying glass, Johnny carefully studied the bubbling lava. It looked peculiar. He spit upon it. That helped solidify the stuff. Bending down, he began to blow on it, further cooling the eruptive matter.

"Supermalagorgeous," he exclaimed.

Gathering up the stone on which the spatter had cooled, Johnny hightailed it in the direction where Renny Renwick was last seen.

Sweat covered his thin features. But it was not merely the perspiration of exertion in a hot atmosphere, but the sheen of utter excitement.

RENNY RENWICK had better luck. He pushed inland, a looming tower of a man. He soon came upon a man half stumbling through the deciduous pine wilderness.

The man clutched an object in his arm, hugging it as if it were a precious thing. The object appeared to be an electrical device of some new type. The big-fisted engineer recognized that it was built around a powerful transformer.

"Merlin," Renny rumbled.

Gargantuan fists hardening, he picked up his pace.

A strange thing happened. If Renny had not been there to witness it, he would have not credited the story had another given a truthful account.

The fleeing Merlin—if that was indeed he—paused and turned to gape at the furiously erupting volcano, his face twisted in a kind of terror. The man appeared to be in his late thirties. He was tall, athletic looking. Even warped with horror, his features displayed character rather than handsomeness.

Taking a deep breath as if to steel himself, Merlin clutched the device more firmly with one hand. With the other, he performed some quick manipulation, apparently turning a rheostat.

All the while, he kept his fear-stricken eyes on hellish Mount Grozny.

As if in response, the crater picked that exact moment to give forth a tremendous roar. The air shook. The ground underfoot trembled. A blistering, sulfuric breath washed over them. Renny had to brace his columnar legs in order to maintain his upright stance.

In a half-sobbing voice, Merlin exclaimed, "Great mother of men!"

Gathering his bulky device close to him, he fled the scene, Renny in hot pursuit.

Further inland, rough terrain gave way to even rougher forest. Sitka pines and other hardy conifers predominated. Here, Merlin melted into the close-packed growth. After that, tracking him grew more difficult.

Renny Renwick had built bridges and dams all over the world, in some of the more difficult terrain imaginable. His woodcraft therefore was hard to beat.

Moving cautiously, the dour engineer dogged the other's trail.

Up ahead, a startling sound smote his ears. It was the familiar bullfiddle roar of one of Doc's supermachine pistols in operation. The burst was short. But there was no mistaking that series of reports. No other weapon on earth could author it.

"Johnny!" Renny muttered, picking up speed. "He must have swung around to cut Merlin off."

The sound of a body falling was a sullen thing in the forest. But it was unmistakably that which the big engineer detected.

Renny lifted his bull-like voice. "Johnny, where are you? Call out!"

Pine needles actually shook in response. But the precise scholarly tones of William Harper Littlejohn failed to float back to his expectant ears.

Renny tried again. "Where did you go, you walking skeleton?"

If Renny had been apprised more fully of events in New York, he would not have been so reckless in his headlong speed. He charged through the sedge and bracken, more than once almost bouncing off obstructing conifers.

Finally, he came upon a clearing.

John Merlin lay sprawled, his bulky device no longer cradled in his arms. There was no sign of Johnny Littlejohn.

Concern crept into the foghorn-voiced engineer's vocal cords and he called again, "Johnny! Speak up!"

A voice did speak up. But it was not a voice Renny recognized.

"Colonel John Renwick, I presume?" it asked.

THE voice was heavy and came from due east. Renny pivoted.

The man standing there was unfamiliar to him. Renny was an imposing hulk of a man—but this individual outweighed him by a considerable number of pounds. He glowered back.

Renny demanded, "Who are you?"

"That is none of your concern," said the large man firmly.

Reacting to the gruff tone of the man's voice, Renny reached for his own supermachine pistol, snug in its underarm holster.

He never made it. Another voice—this time coming from behind him—said querulously, "Hands up!"

Renny clutched the hard butt of his weapon, briefly wavered over yanking out the superfirer. Then the unmistakable bull-fiddle bellow began ripping out once again.

The big engineer felt a peppering against his back. Impacts were modest stings. Not mortal lead—mercy bullets!

"Holy cow!" Renny whirled, his weapon leaping out. The mercy slugs did not penetrate his bulletproof under-vest. But the next burst caught him in the arms and legs. Eyes closing, Renny fell like a great oak tree toppling.

His superfirer hooted briefly when his finger tightened back on the firing lever. But it did no good. The big-fisted engineer was already out.

S. Charles Amerikanis crept out of the sheltering trees and cast his strangely sunken eyes upon Renny on the ground.

"He'll be out for at least an hour," he informed Hale Harney Galsworth.

Galsworth stopped to pick up the bulky device which he had hidden behind a large rock, after appropriating it from the insensate John Merlin.

"Excellent. By that time we will be back in the air."

"We'd better exercise shank's mare then," Amerikanis said nervously. "That other one can't be too far away."

Galsworth paid that no attention. His deep dark eyes were studying the Merlin device. "Can you operate this thing?" he asked his uneasy partner.

The hollow-faced individual known as Master Bonesy stuffed the compact supermachine pistol into a coat pocket and took the device from his confederate. It was very heavy, and felt as if it were dense with packed electrical components.

"It is much larger and more complex than the other transmutation apparatus." He fiddled with the controls. "This appears to be a switch." He flicked it. Came a low whine. Behind a metal grille, vacuum tubes became visible as they warmed up.

To the south, Mount Grozny gave a mighty cough.

Amerikanis started, the contraption almost spilling from his nervous hands. Galsworth leaped in to help catch it. Between them, they prevented the device from being dashed to pieces on the rocks.

"Be careful!" Galsworth thundered. "We have come a long way for this."

"If it works," Amerikanis muttered darkly. "Merlin might not have finished with it."

"Then he comes with us—a prisoner."

"This is kidnapping," Amerikanis warned, licking his thin paper-dry lips.

"I know full well. I am a lawyer. But the rewards far exceed the risks, in my estimation. If you can manage the device, I will attend to Mr. Merlin."

That proved more trouble than expected. Merlin was far lighter than Galsworth, but he was by no means of welterweight class.

Kneeling down, he took hold.

Hale Harney Galsworth got up with an effort and managed to take ten steps before having to unload his limp burden unceremoniously on a soft spot on the forest floor.

"Perhaps it would be best if we dragged him," he puffed.

The dragging was equally unceremonious. Galsworth bent down and got the helpless scientist by the ankles and pulled him along. It was not easy, but progress was made. As it bumped along, Merlin's scalp left tufts of hair behind.

"I wish we had landed closer," Amerikanis complained.

Galsworth frowned. "That would not do. Seaplanes land in Cook's Inlet often, it appears. But not in this secluded area. It was necessary to avoid alerting anyone."

Amerikanis looked about furtively. "Maybe we had better pipe down. That other Doc Savage aide can't be far off."

"If he is by himself," Galsworth returned evenly, "you may fire when ready."

S. Charles Amerikanis, trudging along with the complicated contrivance, grimaced. "We aren't exactly in a position to defend ourselves if he does. No."

"We will cross that bridge if we happen upon it," said Galsworth, shifting hands. Sweat was beginning to pour from his round face. The air was growing unpleasantly hotter.

THEY worked their way around to the other side of the volcano until they were downwind of the bubbling cone. The air was clearer here.

"If I did not know better," Amerikanis ventured, "I would have thought for a minute there that the volcano reacted to my turning on the transmutation apparatus."

"Why would a volcano behave in such an absurd and unscientific manner?" Galsworth snapped.

"You evidently didn't ever study geology," Amerikanis said sourly.

"I am a patent attorney," Galsworth reminded.

"Most laymen think that lava is molten rock expelled from deep within the earth through volcanic action," Amerikanis explained.

Galsworth eyed him disapprovingly. "Well, isn't it?"

"Much of it. Most. But there are other things mixed in—other elements."

"Such as?"

"Metals. Copper. Tin. Iron. Just about any metal you might name."

Galsworth halted in his elephantine lumbering. He let John Merlin's ankle fall with a distinct jar.

His voice quavered. "*Any* metal, sir?"

"Any metal found in nature," Amerikanis rejoined.

"Including, I take it—gold?"

"Yes. Gold. Certainly. It has happened. But only in modest amounts, often mixed with other molten metals."

Hale Harney Galsworth walked up to S. Charles Amerikanis and took from him the transmutation device. He moved it around in his hands until he discovered the rheostat-type dial that governed its operation.

Galsworth turned this on, then looked to the dark smoldering cone by the bay. He needn't have bothered.

The volcano blew a mighty blast. Fire shot straight up into the sky. Amerikanis was nearly knocked off his feet. He swore vociferously as he climbed back into an upright posture.

Galsworth fared no better. He lost a shoe and had to reclaim it.

The large lawyer shut off the device. He waited. Then he turned it back on again.

When he did so, Mount Grozny bellowed in complaint. More fire rocketed skyward. It made low-hanging clouds flash and smolder redly.

A blast of heat, coming in a fearsome wave, washed over them, wringing the sweat from their pores and drying it in the next moment.

Galsworth and Amerikanis locked gazes. Their eyes were strangely round. Hastily, the big attorney shut down the contraption. The crater seemed to settle down, although fire continually leapt and danced on its rim like a convocation of Luciferian entities.

"We might," said Galsworth after a time, "investigate these lava flows."

Then they did something they never imagined they would have done not two minutes beforehand. They left unconscious John Merlin and his transmutation contrivance behind as if they had not flown clear across the continental United States, dodging Border Patrol airplanes and more, in quest of those selfsame prizes.

Chapter XXIV

SCOUNDRELS TWO

JOHNNY LITTLEJOHN HAD in hand his pocket radio receiver and was energetically trying to contact Renny Renwick.

"Renny," he chanted. "Come in, Renny."

Other than rushing static, the gaunt archeologist harvested exactly nothing.

It was dusk now and Johnny had his spring-generator flashlight out, using its intense white beam to pick his way through the trees of the fragrant boreal forest. Periodically, he gave it a strenuous twist, replenishing it with juice.

Despite a considerable expenditure of time, he did not find the hulking engineer, Renny.

Johnny stood in the middle of the gloomy stand of timber and considered his prospects.

He again examined the chunk of rock in his pocket. It had cooled considerably. "A super-auriferous specimen," he said with not a little trace of wonder in his voice.

The erupting volcano drew his narrow gaze again and again. At a temporary loss for any more fruitful course of action, Johnny hiked back in the general direction of Mount Grozny. The plane lay in that direction, anyway. It was prudent to go toward it.

After a while, he spotted signs of two people walking. Johnny knelt, sprayed illumination. He was unfamiliar with John Merlin's shoe size, of course. While the second set of footprints were large, they did not seem to belong to Renny Renwick. Also they were the imprints of ordinary street shoes, whereas the big-fisted engineer had been wearing rugged hiking boots.

Getting to his feet, Johnny followed the trail. He possessed no reason to think that there was anything dangerous in that.

Night deepened. The ground grew harder, and the bony geologist was once more trudging through the hard cooled lava flows that surrounded the looming basalt cone that was Mount Grozny.

Here on the landward flank, much less lava was flowing. But on the inlet side, steam boiled endlessly. It made the warm night air humid, and oppressive to breathe.

"A hyperbaric asphyxiation," Johnny said to himself. Except when excited, he always spoke thus.

The moisture in the air had collected on the rock-hard lava shelves, and the residue was picked up by the two persons Johnny was trailing. Their footprints were easy to follow by flash ray.

After a time, Johnny came within earshot of them. They were talking in hushed but urgent tones. Johnny drew near and listened.

"If what I suspect is the case," a nervous voice was saying, "this will be worth millions of dollars."

"No," corrected a heavier, more assured voice. "The true amount may be calculated in the *billions.*"

"It is geologically improbable that all of this constitutes gold," continued the first speaker. "There must be other metals mixed in the magma. Copper. Nickel. Probably valueless iron and silica as well."

Johnny's ears perked up, figuratively speaking. These two were speaking his language.

Thinking that he had stumbled across two fellow geologists, Johnny stepped into view.

"Consociative accolades," he greeted.

The pair whirled. Their startled faces were not suspicious in and of themselves. For Johnny had slipped up on them, catching both unaware, and in red-tinted darkness to boot.

"Who are you?" the heavy one demanded.

Johnny did not care for the man's overbearing tone of voice, so he turned cagey.

"My name is Johnson," he said. "Johnny Johnson."

The others did not identify themselves, except to say, "We are vulcanologists." This from the nervous one. It fitted their earlier conversation, so Johnny's suspicions were not unduly aroused.

Coming closer, Johnny splashed his ray around the pair. They winced in the calcium-bright light. "Geology is my trade," he offered.

This seemed to make the pair even more nervous.

The obese one asked suddenly, "What do you make of all this?"

"An unusual pyrotechnic and pyroclastic display," clucked Johnny.

The two men agreed that it was without offering further opinion. Johnny decided to test them.

"Have you yet determined if the lava flow is mafic or basaltic?"

The pair hesitated before answering.

Finally, the large man said, "It appears to be basaltic."

"Yes. Definitely," parroted the other. "Indeed."

"Remarkable," said Johnny, who knew that neither was technically true. That meant that despite their earlier conversation, they were not vulcanologists. They had already agreed between themselves that the molten material flowing down the caldera was metallic, not stony.

In their general appearance, the duo nearly matched the descriptions Doc Savage had given Renny of the pair who had fled New York. Where they did not, could be ascribed to the bad light and some makeshift efforts at disguising themselves. Unfortunately, in the exploding excitement, the big engineer had failed to communicate Doc's descriptions to the elongated archeologist.

Acting as if he were satisfied with their answer, Johnny drifted closer without seeming to make a point of it. He wanted a better look at the suspicious pair.

Abruptly, he stopped dead in his tracks.

FOR his flash beam picked up the familiar grip of one of Doc Savage's supermachine pistols sticking out from the belt of the thinner individual.

The gaunt geologist froze. These weapons were held closely by Doc's group, and were not permitted to fall into the hands of outsiders. Moreover, Doc Savage had refused to allow their implementation by any number of governments for military purposes. The bronze man did not believe in making war, except in self-defense.

There was but one possibility. The weapon was Renny's, and had been seized from the hulking engineer by force. The lanky archeologist had no knowledge of the events which had trans-pired back in New York, wherein Long Tom Roberts had been separated from his superfirer.

Making an elaborate show of staring up at the looming volcano, the gangling geologist surreptitiously reached for his own weapon.

Whipping it into view, he whirled. "Reach for a steam cloud!"

The pair hesitated. Then reluctantly, their hands lifted in unison. Their faces fell in an opposite fashion.

"What—what has come over you, fellow?" blurted the large man.

Johnny ignored him. He pointed the superfirer's snout at the smaller man, the one with the pistol in his belt. "Keep your hands very high. I am going to confiscate that weapon."

The man looked down at his belt. His long face fell further than possible. Evidently, he was only now realizing what had given him away.

The heavy one spoke up. "That is one of Doc Savage's weapons he is holding," he informed his crestfallen companion. "Therefore, he is one of Doc Savage's men."

"Doc Savage loaned this to me," the thin man said hastily. "We are looking for a man on his behalf."

"A lie!" said Johnny, reaching in and harvesting the weapon. He jammed it into his own belt. "Where is Renny?" he demanded.

"Who?" they chorused. They were too pat about it.

"I will ask again," Johnny repeated. "Where is Renny Renwick?"

The fat man eyed the thinner one, gave a resigned shrug. "We might as well tell him. The truth will come out soon enough."

"Very well," sighed the other. "John Merlin kidnapped him. You, of course, know who we mean."

Johnny nodded. His flash ray roved about, making the frowning faces of the others stark in the night.

"Fortunately," said the obese one in a grave tone, "we have something Merlin covets. His scientific device. We can use it to bargain for your friend's life."

Johnny looked interested. "Where is it?"

"We can take you."

Johnny gave this suitable thought. "No tricks."

"We are," said the corpulent one glumly, dropping his hands to turn his trouser pockets inside out, "fresh of out tricks tonight."

At the point of Johnny's superfirer, they marched back inland. Soon, they reached a spot where a bulky contrivance was hidden amid black boulders.

Johnny studied the thing in his flash ray. He was not electrically minded like Long Tom, or a chemist like Monk. So the contraption meant nothing special to him.

"There is a switch," suggested the large individual. "Feel free to turn it on."

"What is it supposed to accomplish?" asked the long-worded archeologist.

"The claim is that it will transmute a base metal into a noble one," said the nervous man, suddenly coming out of his silence.

Curious, Johnny knelt and examined the device carefully. He could make neither heads nor tails of it, so he flicked the switch experimentally.

THE resulting boom blew him off his feet. The volcano had let go. Gory light spread over the landscape. It was entirely unexpected.

In the bedlam, Johnny lost his superfirer.

The other two pounced, hands reaching for both supermachine pistols. Johnny then showed that he could scrap. Making a bony fist, he blackened one eye and barked a shin with a steel-toed boot. This threw the pair into temporary confusion. Johnny scrambled for cover, and unlimbered the captured superfirer, still in his belt.

Aiming by volcano glow, he pulled back on the firing lever. The weapon sawed briefly, then died. Cursing, Johnny checked the magazine indicator. It was empty. He reached into a coat pocket for a spare ammunition drum.

While he was doing so, a hefty rock glanced smartly off his elongated skull and while the bony geologist was not knocked out, all fight was driven from him.

Johnny rolled on the ground, groaning.

The pair fell on him and the mountainous man arrested his squirming by the simple expedient of planting a shod foot in the middle of the skinny archeologist's chest, and rested his considerable bulk upon it.

Johnny found the breath being squeezed out of him. He lay helpless under the pressing weight of three hundred pounds of downward-pressing shoe leather.

"Search him," directed the large one.

The other went through his pockets and got his radio, spare

ammunition drums, and the fragment of volcanic rock.

Judging from their expressions, the fragment of rock proved to be the most interesting to the pair.

"This looks like gold," said the nervous man, now not quite so nervous.

Johnny compressed his thin lips and said nothing.

The huge man had located Johnny's generator flashlight and was shining it into the skinny archeologist's owlishly blinking eyes.

"I wonder…" he said slowly.

"What do you wonder?" gasped Johnny between wheezes.

"I wonder if you overheard our conversation earlier."

Johnny did not validate that inquiry. He was too busy panting for air when the heavy foot lifted off his chicken-bone sternum, as it did occasionally.

"Answer me!" snarled the heavy man, pressing down so hard that Johnny's lathy ribs crackled audibly.

"I have been—aware—of the true nature—of the lava flows— before I encountered either of you," Johnny finally gasped out.

"In that case," affirmed the fat one, "it would be better if you stopped breathing here and now."

Johnny felt one of the supermachine pistol muzzles digging at his shaggy head.

He did not flinch. Johnny knew that the weapon was charged with mercy bullets, not mortal lead. After a minute's reflection, he reconsidered that thought. They had confiscated his spare ammunition drums. One, Johnny recalled, was charged with penetration slugs.

Johnny's thin lips grew thinner. He waited, unable to rise or resist.

The nervous one interrupted. "I am not comfortable with murder," he told his corpulent accomplice.

"Billions of dollars are at stake. Perhaps it is time you considered that."

"All the gold in the world cannot ransom a man from Death Row," the other pointed out, rather reasonably.

"You have a point," said the colossal one.

"I am glad you are being sensible," said the second man, visibly relieved.

"Besides, Doc Savage employs ammunition that does not kill a man, only renders him temporarily stupefied. This will not harm him permanently."

So saying, the big man aimed the remarkable weapon squarely at the center of the gaunt geologist's wide forehead.

"I will have you know," Johnny said coldly, "that even now Doc Savage is on his way to Alaska."

"That is very good information to have," remarked the big man, calmly changing ammunition drums. "Thank you."

After he had clipped the other drum into place before the trigger guard, he aimed again.

The weapon discharged once, and Johnny Littlejohn's upraised head snapped back.

A single hole appeared and began leaking scarlet. Not much. Bullets to the brain do not produce significant blood.

S. Charles Amerikanis cried out, "You killed him!"

Coolly, Hale Harney Galsworth ventured, "I would bash out my own dear grandmother's precious brains to get my hands on a billion dollars in pure gold."

He said it as if he meant every word, too.

Chapter XXV

MERLIN

IT WAS LONG after midnight when Renny Renwick bestirred himself.

Sunset had come finally. This was the time of year, well past the summer solstice, where the nights were short—only a few hours in duration. But darkness had at last clamped down and would hold sway until the early part of morning. Except for the lateness of its arrival, a normal—if abbreviated—evening lay ahead.

Renny sat up, studied the night sky and tried to figure out where he was by the constellations. It was a full minute before his brain began working properly and his mental machinery reminded him that he had been in Alaska for more than a day.

The gloomy-faced engineer patted himself, discovered that he still had his wallet and several personal items. But no trace of his supermachine pistol could he discover. His pocket radio transceiver was smashed, probably when he fell on it.

Likewise, John Merlin was nowhere to be found. Renny could discern no evidence of him, nor any sign of the direction in which he had gone. It was too dark.

"Holy cow!" he roared. "Is my face red!"

Climbing to his feet, Renny struck out in the only logical direction—back to the camp where he had left the big radio. Johnny should be there by now. No doubt, Renny reasoned, the skinny archeologist had failed to find him in the forest at night, and gone back to camp.

It was one of the contingency plans Doc Savage's men had in circumstances where they had become separated—to rendezvous at a common point.

Confident that he would come upon his friend before long, Renny worked his way out of the forested area and sought camp.

The cone of Mount Grozny was venting fire and evil black smoke. It made the midnight sky a fitful Hades. Difficult to imagine it had been so quiescent scant hours before.

From time to time, malodorous smoke got into his lungs and Renny fell into a fit of coughing. The coughing was explosive enough to set nearby branches quivering and frighten night-roosting birds from their perches.

Reaching the camp, Renny found no sign of Johnny Littlejohn. His long face grew even longer, if that was possible.

After tinkering with it, Renny tuned his radio to the frequency of the small portable set.

"Johnny. Can you hear me?"

A shocking voice answered after a while.

It said, *"He cannot hear you. For he is beyond hearing."*

Renny bellowed, "Who is this? Where's Johnny?"

"Dead. As you will be very soon."

The voice sounded like the colossal personage Renny had encountered previously.

Renny demanded again, "Stop horsing around. Who is this?"

But the radio went silent.

Shocked by what he had heard, Renny began a search of the surrounding terrain.

He was on edge by the time he saw a shadowy figure creeping through the trees, for his searching had naturally brought him back into the forest.

Renny dared not use his flash. He relied instead on moonlight, which was not plentiful. He crept forward.

The skulker melted into the trees. Renny backtracked and attempted to circle around, in an effort to head off the other party.

He did a good job of it. But the lurker had evidently caught sight of him because that individual had shifted in his course and took up a position of ambush. His silhouette possessed a familiar thinness.

As Renny passed through a copse of aspen, a rock fell out of a branch overhead and struck him with sufficient force that the towering engineer crashed to the forest floor, stunned.

A figure dropped after the rock, landing beside him.

Renny twisted his giant body as he fell, managing to hit on his side. By that time, his head had cleared from the unexpected blow out of the darkness. He hooked an arm upward, snared a human neck, held and clubbed with a fist that was a quart or so of knuckles.

"*Ho-o-o-o!*" hooted the assailant in agony.

"Johnny!" Renny exploded, recognizing the voice.

"*Renny!*"

THE bony archeologist looked foolish in the moonlight. He helped Renny to his feet.

"Man, you're sure a disaster to take hold of in the dark," Johnny said sheepishly, completely forgetting his big words.

Renny demanded, "What was the idea of landing on me like that, you long bag of bones?"

"An unfortunate eventuality," Johnny told him, recovering sufficient poise to summon up his vocabulary. "I was endeavoring to follow two assailants I chanced to encounter."

"A human hippopotamus and a skinny bird?" asked Renny.

"The same. I heard you come along and thought you were one of them, so I belted you one. I am contrite."

Renny heaved erect and the apologetic Johnny backed a pace uneasily. Renny listened until he could feel the effort deep in his ears, but heard nothing. Nor did he see anything, either, except the volcanic glow in the near distance.

"I had John Merlin, but lost him," Renny supplied. "His device too."

"I encountered the infernal contraption," Johnny said rue-fully.

"Infernal?"

"It appeared to have a singular effect on the volcanic cone."

Renny looked interested. "You might elaborate," he sug-gested.

"It ignited an eruption," said Johnny, as if expecting a snort of disbelief issue from the mournful-faced engineer.

Instead of derision, Renny demanded, "Why would it do that?"

Johnny said, "I was bringing you proof of a remarkable discovery, but I encountered misfortune, and lost it, along with my superfirer."

Renny grew glum of mien. "Me, too," he admitted.

"We are without resources until Doc Savage arrives," Johnny reminded.

"That doesn't mean we're helpless," Renny pointed out, block-ing his formidable fists until the knuckles stood out like white stones. The big engineer suddenly noticed that Johnny had been through a lot. There was a wound in the center of his forehead and he looked as though he had gotten too close to the vol-cano's smothering heat.

Renny asked, "Hurt bad?"

"Hell, yes!" returned Johnny, lapsing into uncharacteristic profanity. "A mercy bullet split my forehead. You?"

The hulking engineer examined his burned hands and felt his rough, blistered face. Lying unconscious had allowed steam from the volcano to wash over him with much the same effect as a sauna bath.

Renny complained, "I'm all ready to be served on a bun with mustard." He spoke hoarsely, having a little trouble with his humor.

"You look positively superamalgamated," Johnny agreed.

"Man, this is a pickle we're in," Renny grunted, looking about. "We're in the middle of nowhere and John Merlin has spung disappeared."

"Let's look around some more," Johnny suggested. "Do you have your flashlight?"

Renny checked his person, shook his long face gloomily in the negative.

Having no light, they worked among the boulders, searching for some familiar landmark by which to judge their position. They had supplies in their plane, but it was anchored far from here, out of concern for the secrecy of their mission.

To pass the time, Renny asked a question. "What was that discovery you mentioned a while back?"

"The volcano is reacting to John Merlin's device for a significant reason."

"Which is?"

"Unless I am very much mistaken, there were subterranean deposits of raw gold deep within the cone," explained the skinny archeologist.

"Were?"

Johnny levered a emaciated arm in the direction of the faraway glow.

"Ore has been pouring out all night," he enlightened.

It was a long minute before the significance of Johnny's assertion sank in.

Renny asked, "You saying that all that lava is molten gold?"

"Not entirely. No doubt other matter is mixed in with the magma, but I discovered some ejecta ore that appears to be pure gold. Regrettably, it fell into the hands of our mysterious adversaries."

Renny regarded the looming cone with worried eyes. "That means we're looking at the most valuable mountain in the entire world."

"Possibly that is an understatement," Johnny remarked.

"How could it be an understatement?"

"The way the lava keeps pouring out," Johnny said flatly, "it may be the most valuable anything in the world."

Renny grunted. "Well, they can rename it Mount Midas if they want."

"Or Mount Terror," rejoined Johnny. But he refused to elaborate on why he had put it that way. But the gangling archeologist was plainly worried about something.

THEY found John Merlin quite by accident.

Literally, they stumbled upon him.

Renny and Johnny were prowling along, exercising cautious stealth, when abruptly, the urgent peas-in-a shell whirring sound of a sidewinder's tail rattle arrested their progress. They began backing away, only the suddenly too-loud squeaking of their boots betraying their retreat.

Picking a good spot, they hunkered down and waited for the disturbed rattlesnake to settle down, or better yet, slither off. Big-fisted Renny entertained himself by saying unflattering things about sidewinders in a loud earnest whisper. He didn't like rattlesnakes, and particularly sidewinders which came out of their holes at night, and could crawl in all directions and still watch a given point.

"Blamed sidewinders can crawl forward, backward, port and starboard," muttered Renny, "and still keep looking at you."

After a time, Johnny said, "I just remembered something. Rattlesnakes aren't native to Alaska."

Renny reddened. "Shucks, I knew that. I just plumb forgot."

They got to their feet, felt around in the brush until the unnerving rattle sounded anew. One of the long-faced engineer's mammoth hands seized the source of the sound.

"I'll be durned," said Renny, holding up a small metal box that had been suspended by strings. He opened it to reveal a handful of lead ball bearings. When disturbed, the box produced the unpleasant noise.

"A rudimentary prowler alarm," breathed Johnny.

Renny nodded. "That means he's close by."

He was. Johnny literally tripped over his recumbent form, and made a scarecrow pile of bones beside their quarry. He unfolded himself while Renny laughed like a contented bear in a cave.

"Big night for red faces," he rumbled.

Evidently, the missing man had been wandering about the forest, in a daze and, nearing exhaustion, simply lay down under a sheltering spruce and fell asleep. His sleep was so deep the rattler contraption had failed to rouse him.

They shook him awake.

John Merlin sat upright, fright on his face, terror in his intelligent eyes. He took in the dark visages of Johnny and Renny, both rather grim, then his gaze veered to the volcano boiling beyond them.

"I have failed," he said thinly. Then his shoulders began shaking. "I sought the secret of the alchemists and all I accomplished was utter destruction."

Renny grunted, "You may have accomplished more than you thought."

"Yes," added Johnny. "It appears that you discovered the most valuable vein of mineral gold on earth."

Merlin blinked. He shook his head foggily. "Am I dreaming?" he asked.

Renny reached down and pinched him on the shoulder. Wincing, Merlin caught at the painful spot. Renny's finger and thumb could bend sturdy nails.

"That convince you?" asked the big-fisted engineer.

It apparently did. There was no more argument.

"Who are you two?" asked Merlin.

"Doc Savage's men," supplied Renny. "He sent us here to fetch you."

"What interest would Doc Savage have in me?"

Johnny offered, "That is as yet unclear. But conceivably it has something to do with the unfathomable detonations that have been deviling Manhattan."

"Detonations?" Merlin looked flustered.

"All hell has been breaking loose." Renny cocked a huge thumb in the direction of Mount Grozny. "Looks to me like it's spread clear to Alaska."

John Merlin was struggling with wakefulness. Otherwise, he might have assembled what he was being told into a coherent question. But he did not.

Renny helped him to his feet.

"Where is my—um—device?" Merlin asked at last. "Do either of you have it?"

"No, the other two glommed onto it," Renny informed him.

Merlin looked blank. "What other two?"

"The two Doc warned us about."

Beyond their range of sight, a new voice broke in.

"I believe the big fellow is referring to us."

Renny and Johnny reacted as they were trained to do. Their hands leapt for their underarm holsters. Fingers grasped air instead of steel.

Consternation tugged their expressions downward. They realized that their own weapons were pointed at them.

A pregnant silence followed. It was John Merlin who broke it. "Mr. Amerikanis! What are you doing out here?"

"Becoming wealthy," advised S. Charles Amerikanis.

"Very, very wealthy," added Hale Harney Galsworth.

John Merlin seemed to have trouble processing his perceptions. His thin mouth made silent shapes. His eyes slowly protruded from their sockets. He did not appear to know who Hale Harney Galsworth was.

"Since you all seem to have survived somehow," Galsworth said slowly, "perhaps you can be turned to good use."

"What do you mean—use?" Merlin demanded thickly.

"Doc Savage is due here, sooner or later. No doubt he will arrive in a plane large enough to carry his usual complement of men and equipment."

"Yes. A plane far larger that the one we came in," said Amerikanis, warming to the subject.

"One suitable for carrying back to the States more slag gold than King Croesus ever imagined in his most avaricious dreams," added Galsworth.

"Holy cow!" thumped Renny. "If you think you can take Doc Savage, you're dreaming."

"Or in for a nightmare," added Johnny thinly.

Waggling his superfirer at all three men, Hale Harney Galsworth ground out, "We have not done so badly thus far. Now march, you helpless hostages."

Renny took the lead. Blocking his gigantic fists, he shot a scornful look at the smug pair. "Better mugs than you have bucked Doc Savage and rued the day."

A rumbling laugh issued deep from within Hale Harney Galsworth's commodious belly. "History," he drawled, "is written every day."

Chapter XXVI

REVELATIONS

DOC SAVAGE RAN his amphibian full throttle most of the way to Alaska. When refueling became necessary, they did so in Seattle, the bronze man reasoning that a stopover would allow for a quick meal and enable them to complete the last leg of the grueling journey and arrive relatively refreshed.

Taking off again, Doc flew the Seattle to Seward steamer route. Navigating therefore required little effort, since they remained within sight of shore much of the way. From five thousand feet the numerous islands looked like uncut emeralds marked round with lines of angry surf.

Worry rode the faces of Doc's men. They had not been able to raise Renny or Johnny since the loud explosion that terminated their last communication.

"What the devil could have happened?" Ham asked no one in particular.

"Anything," said Long Tom, looking downcast.

Their prisoner had not contributed much. Elvira Merlin passed most of the trip as if uninterested in anything other than reaching their destination. Her eyes had retreated to the silver-gray coloring that characterized them when the woman was in a subdued frame of mind. She had restored her glove, thereby masking the grisly sight of her maimed hand.

Doc Savage attempted to draw her into conversation numerous times, but without success. Lea Aster, who had assumed responsibility for the prisoner and her needs, fared no better.

Monk took a stab at it once they were back in the air. The hairy chemist went aft to spell his pretty secretary, who was only too glad to swap the dreariness of the back of the plane for a cockpit view of the northern skies.

"What I've found out just about clears the whole thing up," Monk declared when he ambled forward again. "Turns out she talks in her sleep, and I got an earful just by askin' the right questions."

"Suppose you quit bragging and give us the story," Ham suggested bitingly.

Monk complied. "The way I figger it," he was saying, "Mrs. Merlin got upset that her husband was plannin' to desert her to work in Alaska. She stole his device and hid out with it, thinkin' that would stop him. But it didn't. He lit out anyway because he was plannin' on building a better one. Then she got herself a job at Amerikanis's works, hopin' to get a line on him. But Master Bonesy was a cagey old goat, and wouldn't give up a thing."

"Sounds thin," Ham sniffed.

Monk ignored the dapper lawyer. "Then she hits on another scheme. She decided to go on a rampage with the gold-destroying dingus, figurin' word would reach her husband in Alaska and he'd come tearin' back to look into it. But he didn't, on account of he was way out in the wilderness, away from radio and newspapers."

"What about the idea of building up a fortune to be administered to charity?" asked Ham.

Monk grinned. "A fake. She had cracked up mentally, and that was just a story chargin' around in her addled skull—a way of gettin' Doc out of the picture so she could go to town with that terror-ray gimmick."

It did sound as if Monk had unearthed the solution to the major part of the mystery. This disgusted Ham, and he withdrew to the rear of the plane to fume in sulky silence.

Fumbling among the packing cases back there, he made a

discovery.

"Great Scott!" Ham squawked and suddenly gave a violent jump.

Monk whirled. Almost at the same instant, something struck his legs, all but upsetting him.

From among the equipment cases and other stowage rolled one of Ham's spare sword canes.

Monk picked it up, examined it critically. "Looks like genuine gold to me. Good thing that devil ray didn't touch it, or we'd be needin' a new plane."

"Give me that, you insect!" snapped Ham, lunging forward to claim his stick. "I must have left one of my spares on board and forgotten to retrieve it."

From the pilot seat, the voice of Doc Savage warned, "Ham, be careful with that."

The dapper lawyer raised a supercilious eyebrow. "The device is destroyed, is it not?"

"Do not forget that Merlin was working on another."

Ham frowned. Reluctantly, he returned the cane to the rear of the plane, saying, "Keep firmly in mind that I have challenged you to a duel, you simian monstrosity."

Monk glowered. "When that time comes, I won't need no pig sticker." He blew on his rusty knuckles, one set at a time, by way of illustrating his point.

In the back, Ham subsided. "At least that dratted pig is asleep."

"Don't be so sure of that," Monk said airily. "I thought I saw him chewin' on one of your spare shoes a minute ago."

Which sent the dapper lawyer to poking his nose into every nook and compartment in the big amphibian. At the end of a full twenty minutes, he was satisfied that the hairy Monk had been merely pulling his leg. There were no chewed shoes on board.

Monk whistled a cheerful tune calculated to arouse Ham's

deeper suspicions. The sartorially-resplendent barrister chose to ignore the musical taunt.

At Ketchikan, the bronze man turned due west, departing the shoreline to volley across the Gulf of Alaska on a direct heading to their destination.

DOC SAVAGE picked up the haze-wrapped bluish blur that was the rocky, forbidding coast of lower Alaska. It materialized under the drawn-up landing wheels of the amphibian with a suddenness that was magical.

There was practically no beach. Instead, the water ended in tumbled masses of boulders, back of which was a fringe of scrawny pine and cedar, laced together with a tangled carpet of green briars that covered everything. The whole place looked ominous, barren.

"Looks bally cold," Ham observed.

"After sufferin' through all that blisterin' heat back home," Monk remarked, "I'll take it. Even my toenails are sunburned."

"Let that teach you to not to go barefoot like your baboon ancestors," sniffed Ham.

Doc calculated wind direction from the spindrift blown from the wave tips. There was brisk breeze. He leveled out, worked his feet on the rudder bar to fishtail from side to side and lose flying speed, then set the lumbering amphibian onto the churning surface of Cook's Inlet.

"Will you look at that!" Long Tom breathed.

Mount Grozny reared up, looking like a fortified outpost of the lower regions. The rim of the crater was a devil's cauldron of flaring fluid. Lava was pouring into the inlet, setting up a great bubbling steaming broth.

"Mount Grozny," Doc offered. "So named during the Russian period of Alaska's history. The word means fearsome, or terrible."

Monk said, "Looks like it's been spillin' lava ever since we lost contact with Renny. That's a lot of hot rock. I wouldn't be surprised to see imps out of the hot place paradin' around down there."

Doc Savage took the field glasses from the apish chemist and studied the searing fingers of molten lava forming new land bridges at the watery volcano base.

He studied for a long time, then surrendered the binoculars without comment.

Fifteen minutes later, Doc had brought the amphibian to a rest at water's edge, a safe distance from the erupting crater. A sea anchor was dropped and, once the huge flying boat was secured, the main cabin door was flung open and the group—all but Lea Aster, Elvira Merlin and Habeas the pig, who remained in the cabin—disembarked, wading the short distance ashore.

They behaved the way men behave when they are tired from traveling, but somewhat excited, too. They stretched and stamped and there was some horseplay—a sparring match between two of the aides, Monk and Long Tom, with much jumping around.

During the playful boxing, a supermachine pistol was brandished. Monk was the brandisher. Plainly the hairy chemist was spoiling for a fight.

"Be careful where you point that thing, you trigger-happy ape," Ham complained.

Monk holstered the unusually-shaped pistol and said, "I was just thinkin'. This is the first time anyone ever made off with one of our superfirers."

"Remind me again, will you?" Long Tom said sourly. "I keep forgetting."

"Bet you I can outdraw either of those two bozos in a fair fight," said Monk. The apish chemist had grown up in Oklahoma when it was still wild, and could back up his fast-draw boast with bullets.

Ham inserted, "At least they got away with only one drum of ammo—and that was mercy slugs. They can't do a lot of damage."

That seemed to mollify the puny electrical wizard, forestalling one of his infamous outbursts of temper.

While they were thus entertaining themselves, Doc Savage was unpacking a collapsible rubber raft, which inflated pneumatically. This he dropped into the water, then eased on board.

Doc called over, "Monk, bring your equipment case."

"Sure, Doc. But ain't we goin' to look for Johnny and Renny first?"

"That will be Ham and Long Tom's job, once we return. Follow me."

The bronze man had brought along an equipment case of his own, and they set out in the direction of the smoldering volcanic cone. Doc propelled it along, employing a telescoping paddle.

"Looks like a choice parcel of Hell on earth," Monk muttered as they drew near.

The water was hot—scalding. The bronze man made no effort to leave the raft. Experimentally, Monk brushed the tips of two fingers against the steaming surface and withdrew them with alacrity. He had to suck on those fingers until they ceased stinging.

Doc took from his case a simple tool—a ladle of some stony material. With this he began scooping samples from the water. These were black clinkers, such as might have been ejected by the volcano. Some still smoked angrily.

Kneeling, Doc began to work on these. First, he immersed them in water to further cool them. With a tool, he began scraping the soot off the surface of each clinker. A warm yellow color showed through.

Monk whistled. "Is that what I think it is?"

"Unquestionably," said Doc.

"I've heard of gold being mixed in with molten rock before, but these babies look like the pure stuff."

"We will soon find out." Doc performed certain tests, during which a vial of *aqua regina* was brought into play. It easily pitted the yellow ore.

When the bronze man was done, Monk Mayfair said, "Are you thinkin' what I'm thinkin', Doc?"

"It cannot be a coincidence."

"Yeah, I guess Merlin got his new gold-transmuter workin' all right. Except it ain't operatin' the way he wanted—any more than the old one did."

"Doubtless." Doc studied the lava flow. It crawled down the shoreward slope of the caldera, oozing along like fiery fingers and overflowing into the inlet. It was red hot—even white hot in spots. This made it impossible to tell from the color of the incandescent stuff how much consisted of gold in a molten state.

Monk seemed to read the bronze man's thoughts. "If these clinkers are any proof, there's millions of dollars' worth of raw gold percolatin' out of that black cone. All waitin' to be scooped up."

Doc nodded. "That is what concerns me."

Monk's homely features gathered up in pleasant wrinkles. "Yeah? How so?"

But the bronze man, characteristically, did not reply.

"We had best return to the plane," he said at last. "No one is in a position to harvest this wealth under such circumstances."

Doc sculled the little boat back to the big amphibian.

HAM BROOKS was leaning out the aircraft's hatch when they hove back in sight. "No word from Renny or Johnny," he reported. He looked uneasy.

They took on passengers and made for land.

Doc and his men assembled on the rugged shoreline, amid the rough brush and the horsetails. The wind off the inlet water was sluggish and sweltering.

"What now, Doc?" wondered homely Monk.

"We will endeavor to locate the aircraft of lawyer Galsworth."

"Wouldn't we have spotted it from the air?" asked Long Tom.

Doc shook his head slowly. "Not if it is camouflaged. Inasmuch as we are seeking a seaplane, it would be smart to search along the coastline first."

Doc Savage scanned the rugged coast in both directions, saw something that intrigued him, and led the way.

The bronze man's skill in observation proved accurate. The elusive seaplane was tucked into a little cove. A lean-to shelter had been made out of brush and rude saplings, mostly paper birch and evergreen boughs which had a fresh crisp color as if they had been recently cut.

It was rudimentary, and would not conceal the plane from the ground, for all the engineering had gone into making certain that nothing could be discerned from the air.

Doc Savage climbed onto the wing and began opening the engine cowls. In short order, he had removed certain engine parts—distributor caps and spark plugs—and carried them down, cradled in his metallic arms.

These he cached a fair distance from the aircraft.

Monk grinned from ear to rear. "One thing's for sure—they're not goin' anywhere any time soon. Not without that stuff."

Returning to their own craft, Doc sought out Elvira Merlin, the erstwhile Trixie Peters. She had not stirred from her seat since her long nap.

"We cannot leave you alone," he explained patiently. "You will have to accompany us."

The raven-haired murderess of many said nothing to that.

"It may be dangerous," Doc advised.

Again, there was no meaningful reply. The silver-eyed woman avoided Doc's steady frank gaze. Her attitude reminded one of a wounded animal.

"There is an excellent chance we will learn your husband's fate," Doc told her.

That statement snapped her chin up. Her oddly-colored eyes

focused.

"Fate?" Her voice quivered.

"We have known for some time that the purple-robed man who was slain at the home of Hale Harney Galsworth was not your husband," Doc revealed. "That was a ruse to throw suspicion off John Merlin and yourself in a single subterfuge. One that S. Charles Amerikanis played along with, because he feared the discovery of Merlin's device."

"How did you know?" sneered Elvira Merlin.

"Confirmation came from police fingerprint records," explained Doc. "The dead man was a convicted criminal. No doubt a confederate of the escapees from the Tombs, tricked into becoming a victim."

Mrs. John Merlin dragged her silvery eyes away from Doc's probing flake-metal gaze.

"What about John?" she asked.

"Nothing has been heard of your husband in some weeks," Doc related. "And the blast from the volcano has flattened a few trees. If his laboratory was situated close to the crater wall, he may have been injured, or worse."

The woman licked quivering lips nervously.

Doc pressed, "May we anticipate no further trouble from you?"

Elvira Merlin nodded somberly. All the ire and fight seemed to have oozed out of her, like poison from a wound.

Doc Savage said, "Miss Aster will take charge of you."

They set off, began hiking inland.

Day was getting along. The party trudged over brambles and ledge-like stony outcroppings so black it might have been carved into blocks and used as flagstones on the floor of Hades itself.

No fauna did they spy until the little party was more than a mile inland, then a small animal scooted along in their path, almost too fast to be identified, and disappeared from sight.

"Fox," said Doc.

Monk chortled, "Ham will be glad to know it ain't a—!" Then the hairy chemist was too busy dodging a lusty whack of Ham's sword cane to add the word "pig."

But for all their seeming indifference, these men were deeply aware of their danger. Too, there was the sobering thought of Renny and Johnny's possible fate.

Abruptly, Monk eyed Ham and barked, "Hey! You brought your sword cane, after all. Didn't Doc say—"

Ham raised the stick, showing that the gold knob had been removed. Black electrical tape had been wound around the top of the shaft to create a makeshift handle. "I left it back in the plane, just in case."

Monk shrugged apish, sloping shoulders. The group pressed on.

Chapter XXVII

ABJECT SURRENDER

THEY STUMBLED UPON the ruined laboratory shack of John Merlin later in the day. Stumbled might not be the correct word. For over a mile before they came upon it, Doc Savage began sampling the foul air like a bloodhound on a scent.

"Volcano gettin' ready to blow again?" asked Monk, noticing the frequent dilations of the bronze man's sensitive nostrils.

Doc Savage shook his head slowly. But he changed course with a firm decisiveness.

Using his well-schooled olfactory organs, the bronze man led them to the lab. As it came into view, pungent metallic odors touched their nostrils.

With his cane, Ham poked about at the shambles that was the place.

"You scented spilled chemicals, didn't you, Doc?" he queried.

The bronze man said, "Yes." He began rooting through the wreckage as well.

Amid the shambles lay examples of lead that looked un-natural. Doc picked up one and examined it at length, turning it in one metallic hand. The golden flakes in his eyes grew brisker in their ceaseless motion.

Long Tom observed, "Looks like a blob of hot lead that was thrown into cold water."

Doc shook his head. "Immersion would not produce such fantastic results."

It was true. The lead specimen bore a marked resemblance to certain natural crystals that grow in subterranean depths, whose shoots and spars reach out in all directions. At the same time, there was an unreal quality—as if the metal had frozen in mid-eruption.

"Guess Merlin was gettin' someplace with his experiments," Monk muttered.

"But not very far," Ham sniffed. "That stuff still looks like lead."

Doc found nothing else noteworthy, except to say, "If anything untoward befell Merlin, it did not happen here. See? Tracks lead away."

The earth here was spongy to an unbelievable degree. It felt like treading on a rattan mat suspended over an unguessable space. This made walking an unsettling activity.

Doc directed his question to Elvira Merlin. "How much did your husband weigh?"

Mrs. Merlin hesitated, as if contemplating defiance, then said sullenly, "One hundred and sixty pounds."

Doc said, "It is difficult to judge in this terrain, but the imprint of Merlin's shoes indicates that he was carrying something heavy."

Doc Savage began following the tracks.

To the south, Mount Grozny was quiescent. Only a red glare reflecting off low-hanging storm clouds, and the after-smell of sulfurous odors, warned them that it was not dormant.

TWO hours of walking and searching produced little in the way of result. From time to time, Long Tom or one of the others tried to contact Johnny and Renny with their pocket radios. But nothing resulted from their efforts and, in order to conserve the precious battery supplies of the small devices, they ceased trying.

Before dark, Doc Savage made a significant discovery that only further depressed their hopes.

Among the birches, he came upon Renny's flashlight. They knew it was Renny's because the big engineer's granite fists were so strong that sometimes his gripping fingers and thumb deformed the metal of the flashlight case. This one had held such dents.

"Johnny never mangled his flash like that," Monk confirmed.

It was sharp-eyed Ham who made the next discovery.

"Look, fellows!" he hissed.

Coming up from the ground where he had knelt, Ham offered his palm. In it was cupped a handful of the small brass cartridge casings that invariably spewed from the ejector mechanism whenever one of Doc's intricate supermachine pistols discharged.

Doc took in the ground at a golden glance. "There was a fight here."

"But with who?" Long Tom wondered. "With Merlin, Amerikanis or Galsworth?"

No one knew. Doc, examining the ground, found a profusion of trampled-over footprints and ventured only, "Several men struggled here. But Johnny Littlejohn was not one of them."

They found a smear of blood on a rock. Not much, but enough to etch alarm on their faces.

"It's a cinch they couldn't have gotten very far in this wilderness," Monk decided. "Not with their seaplane still anchored back in that cove."

Ham asked, "Would it be better to split up?"

Doc Savage shook his head in the negative. "Too dangerous. Do not forget that Amerikanis escaped with one of our superfirers."

"Don't rub it in," groaned Long Tom. "I haven't lived it down yet."

Ham remarked, "Maybe that wasn't Long Tom's superfirer that discharged, Doc. It's equipped with so many safety devices, it might take weeks to figure them all out."

Doc said, "Amerikanis understands metal fabrication. On

the long flight here, if he exercised patience, he could have defeated every locking device."

Doc led them further inland, following trail signs so slight that none of the others could detect anything. The ground held traces of mica. It was an old cowboy trick to watch for bright specks of disturbed mica. Doc tracked these.

In the end, Fate handed them a surprise.

Doc Savage and his party did not find their quarry. Their quarry found them.

Out from behind a grotesque outcropping of basaltic black rock, stepped S. Charles Amerikanis and Hale Harney Galsworth. They held their hands very high in the air and wore the expression of worried and defeated men.

"We heard your voices talking," volunteered Amerikanis. "Yes."

"And we decided to offer ourselves in surrender," added Galsworth. "May we advance?"

"Carefully," Doc Savage advised.

Both men emerged into clear sight. Superfirer muzzles snapped in their direction, covering them thoroughly.

"Trap!" warned Monk.

"Trick!" echoed Ham.

"Not at all," returned Hale Harney Galsworth solemnly. "And to prove our honest intentions, you will find your machine pistol on a rock just a few yards behind us."

Long Tom rushed past the two nervous men and after a very short time, came back with a superfirer, saying, "He wasn't lying." The electrical wizard extracted the drum and announced for all to hear, "Empty!"

"We—ah—expended all of our ammunition in testing the gun," Amerikanis explained, eyes retreating into their too-deep sockets.

To which Galsworth added, "We had no idea it emitted bullets as rapidly as it did. It was a rather frightening experience to operate one."

"That'll teach you to steal property you ain't got the brains to understand," snorted Monk.

The two men looked suitably chastised. Then Galsworth said, "We have some dire news."

"Go on," invited Doc Savage.

"I am afraid that poor John Merlin has perished," said Amerikanis. "Unfortunate. Yes, it is."

A LOW moan came from the purple-shrouded form of Elvira Merlin. Evidently, the pair had not noticed her, hanging back with blonde Lea Aster.

The woman wilted on her feet, caught herself, then steadied a trembling arm against a birch bole until she had regained her equilibrium.

"Is that—?" asked Amerikanis.

"—the she-spider herself?" concluded Galsworth.

"Yes," said Doc Savage. "The master mind behind the so-called miracle bombings in New York."

"It doesn't take a lot of masterminding to see that she's headed for the electric chair, or the gallows, now that you captured her," Galsworth pronounced.

"That remains to be seen," said Doc Savage. Addressing the pair, he asked, "Merlin's original apparatus has been lost. But he was working on a second, more potent one. Where is it?"

"Merlin never completed it," insisted Amerikanis.

"Yes," affirmed Galsworth. "He confided that much before he died."

"How did he die?" asked Ham suspiciously.

Galsworth replied levelly, "When the volcano exploded, it rained fire and ash all over the area, as you can see. A hot rock expelled from the crater did him in. He was quite mangled when we happened upon him. He did not die right way, I fear. He was able to gasp out explanations. Hence our information."

"We came all this way for nothing," added Amerikanis, wringing his thin hands. "Unfortunate, yes. But the matter now appears to be settled."

The bronze man studied the pair carefully.

"You might," invited Doc, "explain your strange behavior through all of this affair."

"The explanation has to be credited to an old and understandable motive," admitted Hale Harney Galsworth. "Namely, greed."

Amerikanis chimed in. "Yes, we have been greedy, Mr. Savage. You see, when these terrible bombings began, I recognized that they might have been the work of Merlin's device. I feared that blame would attach itself to myself and my company, Elektro-Alchemical. I did not want John Merlin implicated, lest my investment in his research go up in smoke."

"For my part," inserted Galsworth, "I was a victim caught in a war between a man and his wife."

By this time, the two prisoners had dropped their hands to the level of their clavicles. This was natural, since it is nearly impossible to keep one's arms comfortably erected for long periods of time.

Galsworth was saying, "I formally represented Amerikanis's company in their patent affairs. And I was also Mrs. Merlin's legal counsel. This presented no problem as long as they were in unanimity. No. But once they fell in conflict, I was caught in the middle."

"You are taking a long time to get to your point," snapped Ham.

Doc Savage had long ago developed vision which missed little of what went on around him. He saw something now. He whirled, his bronze hand whipped out. He got his fingers closed over the wrinkled wrist of Skelton Charles Amerikanis.

Master Bonesy had been drawing a small-calibre automatic surreptitiously from within his shirt. It fell to the ground.

Amerikanis howled in anguish at the pressure of Doc Savage's iron grip.

"No more moves of that sort," the bronze man warned.

Amerikanis pointed to the unsteady form of Elvira Merlin.

"Killing is too good for her," he gritted. "She's a murderer. She's such a damn cold-blooded killer that I think the courts will declare her crazy. She'll get off. They'll send her to the booby hatch."

"That," Doc Savage said, "is where she is going."

Both conspirators registered astonishment. Amerikanis looked aghast. Galsworth waved his ponderous arms angrily.

"This virago is a fell murderer!" he bellowed. "She has slaughtered dozens of people, maimed several others and dragged Amerikanis and myself into the muck and mire of utter ruin. We would never have behaved as we did if she had not entered into a murder spree that—"

Doc Savage interrupted. "Galsworth," he said. "You are a rather good actor. But not nearly as good a liar. Your story about John Merlin, for example. You claimed that he perished in a cloud of ash, but Mount Grozny is not emitting any such clouds. That is one of the suspicious things about its behavior. In fact, no residue of pumice is present in the vicinity of the eruption."

Galsworth spun, gasped. He made a move to flee, but the bronze man lunged, grasped his arm, stayed him.

The large lawyer struggled for several minutes in the unbreakable clutch of the metallic giant. Realization seemed to come to Galsworth. He struggled violently. But he was helpless in the grip of the other, and, after a moment he gave up all thoughts of accomplishing his escape by violence.

"Contain yourself," said Doc, releasing the man.

"Yeah," said Monk. "We've got you red-handed. Don't try to give us a stall!"

"I assure you gentlemen," said Hale Harney Galsworth, "that I am on the up and up, even if my nervous friend here has gotten trigger happy under the stress and strain of latter events."

Doc Savage said, "We know about the gold."

The effect upon the two men was electric.

"Gold?" They uttered the word almost in perfect unison, their voices blending in an unmusical manner.

Doc advised, "The recent volcanic activity is not a natural one. Further, it has caused molten metals rather than basaltic lava to extrude from the crater."

The two men stood in the gathering gloom like light-struck owls. They did not blink for the longest interval. Their feet began shifting aimlessly.

"Chief among these elements is molten gold," Doc Savage explained. "It is not unheard-of, but never before witnessed to this degree."

Still nothing from the two startled men. Their wide eyes were rather stark.

"Since the chief product of the eruption—the main magma metal—has proven to be gold," concluded Doc, "it stands to reason that a second transmutation device triggered the eruption. Where is it?"

S. Charles Amerikanis and Hale Harney Galsworth licked fear-dried lips, hung their heads, looked down at their leaden feet and performed other shufflings indicative of guilt and shame.

"I told you that he could not be fooled!" Amerikanis hurled to Galsworth.

"I feared that you were correct, but we had to take the chance. Too much was at stake." Galsworth shifted his frank gaze to Doc Savage and said, "Very well. I know when I am beaten. We will take you to the place where we cached the contrivance."

Ham Brooks raised his sword cane like a military saber, gave it a flourish that made the fine blade sing, pointed the tip in no direction in particular, then commanded, "March!"

They marched.

Chapter XXVIII

THE MOUNTAIN OF MENACE

THE MARCH LED in the direction of smoldering Mount Grozny, frowning over the tree-shattered terrain like a black portent of doom. It seemed to have settled down some, although its leaping glare continued to threaten the low-hanging cloud scud.

"It is not far," promised Hale Harney Galsworth.

"Yes. Not far," added S. Charles Amerikanis.

Ham warned, "Do not try any tricks, either of you."

"We are," the corpulent lawyer affirmed, "two very chastened men."

Doc Savage walked immediately behind the trio, with Monk and Long Tom beside him. At the rear, Lea Aster escorted Elvira Merlin, looking forlorn in her plum-hued robes and single protecting glove. Her raven tresses hung low in defeat, downcast chin bumping her collarbone.

Long Tom was exchanging low words with Doc Savage.

"If what you suspected is true, Doc, then the improved gadget created by that man Merlin has the same flaw as the original."

Doc nodded. "Yes. I imagine it is an electro-sonic vibratory device which affects the molecular construction of gold alone, interrupting the inter-molecular path of the composite electrons so that gold molecules disintegrate with all the characteristics of a violent explosion."

"Then why is the blasted stuff still pourin' out to beat the band?" muttered Monk.

Doc said, "From past observation, it appears that the more pure the gold ore, the more completely it vaporizes. Electrum, for example, being an alloy, is merely excited, but does not detonate. No doubt the present flows consist of a mixture of ores, copper making red gold, platinum producing white gold, and the like. Where the gold ran pure, those subterranean veins detonated, unleashing a flood of mingled ores from the magma chamber, which were made molten by the terrific violence of the explosion."

Long Tom felt of his teeth. "I wonder if the new device affects electrum?" He pulled on one sail-like ear worriedly.

"We will be certain not to experiment with the device until we are back in the States," Doc assured him.

Just to be safe, Long Tom removed his front teeth, wrapped them in a clean handkerchief, and looked around for some safe place to store them.

Ultimately, he decided to stuff the bundle in his back pocket, where it could be removed simply by pulling on the handkerchief knot.

They came at last to an outcropping of jumbled rock. This stood on the inland side of the volcano, where the lava did not intrude.

Amerikanis and Galsworth drew to a halt. They had been silent a long time. Now Galsworth spoke.

"The diabolical device—and I rue the day I ever heard about it—lies over there," he said, pointing a thick finger.

Doc Savage approached the place with care evident in the motion of his metallic form. He seemed to flow to the spot as if he were a bronzed finger of molten lava himself.

The bronze man found what he sought atop a fang of stone.

The invention was larger than the one he had a glimpse of back in New York. It was designed along the lines of an inverted bowl housing an electrical transformer. Copper coils jutted out. There were other metallic protrusions. A dry cell battery was evident.

Doc Savage studied it intently without picking it up. On one side was a black Bakelite panel with indicators and a rheostat dial, but the bronze man kept his hands far from it.

"It does not appear to be booby-trapped," he pronounced at last.

"Dreadful thought," said Galsworth.

"Horrid," agreed Amerikanis. "We would not be so foolish."

Bending, Doc Savage grasped the device firmly and lifted it. His flake-gold eyes were whirling as they roved the mechanism, noting wiring and other visible connections.

Curious, Long Tom and Monk approached.

"This is not a ray contrivance," Long Tom judged. "There is no nozzle or parabolic reflector."

Doc nodded in agreement. "It is more in the nature of an oscillator, which generates a field of electrical force. All chemical gold that lies within range when the device is in operation acquires an explosive potential."

Monk spoke up. "Better be careful, Doc. We're right at the edge of that crater. One wrong move and we all go whango!"

"We will convey this mechanism back to our plane as the first order of business," Doc decided.

"What about Renny and Johnny?" asked Ham, who had custody of the two new prisoners.

The immaculate attorney could not help but turn his head as he asked the question that was his undoing.

Both Amerikanis and Galsworth had taken up positions near a particularly grotesque outcropping. They had set their backs to it, expressions placid.

As with one mind, both men reached behind themselves and discovered objects previously concealed amid the rocks.

Their hands snaked out, and the muzzles of two of Doc Savage's supermachine pistols abruptly menaced the group.

Ham Brooks was the first to realize their danger. He reacted with the lightning speed for which he was known. He attempted to part his walking stick and whip out the keen blade of Damascus steel. The only result was that he stood there looking foolish. Lacking the knobby gold head to grasp properly, he failed to separate the two parts.

"Now it is your turn to reach for the clouds," grunted Hale Harney Galsworth.

Amerikanis sneered, "And don't think that there isn't solid lead in these drums. We made sure of that before we planted them here."

Everyone reluctantly obeyed. Except Doc Savage, who was holding the device and therefore in an awkward position.

Amerikanis waggled the muzzle of his superfirer toward the bronze giant.

"Savage, put that thing down very slowly."

His expression unreadable, Doc complied. Under the circumstances, there was nothing else he could do.

After he had set down the device, Doc erected both hands.

"Where are Renny Renwick and Johnny Littlejohn?" he asked. "Those are obviously their weapons."

A female voice spoke up. "And where is my husband?" This was Elvira Merlin, who suddenly roused to life, her eyes full of silver sparks.

"All are exactly where we placed them," Galsworth replied.

"Which is?" asked Doc.

"You carry a lot of fancy gadgets on you, Savage," said Amerikanis. "Anything like a pair of field glasses?"

Doc nodded.

"Then take it out and look to the volcano's summit."

Carefully, Doc removed from his equipment vest a complex device consisting of a slim black tube and attached arrangement of lenses. This he converted into a pocket telescope by manipulating its component parts.

The bronze man carefully trained it on the smoky summit.

THREE figures were silhouetted against the hellish backglow. Doc Savage could make out Renny's towering form and Johnny's skeletal profile. The third man was undoubtedly John Merlin, as indicated by his hapless condition.

"If you want nothing to happen to them, you will do as we say," warned Galsworth.

"Yes," echoed Amerikanis. "Exactly what we say."

Jabbing his gun muzzle, Master Bonesy shifted them over to one side, and went to the device.

"If I turn this on for just one second," he announced, "all three of them will be blown to atoms."

"Atomized," clarified Long Tom.

"Call it what you will," said Galsworth, grim of voice and mien. "But that devilish device and these clever guns give us the upper hand."

"For now," agreed Doc.

"Forever!" snapped Galsworth. "Let us get down to brass tacks."

"Yes, brass tacks, exactly," said Amerikanis.

Galsworth continued, "We will all walk over to the opposite side of the volcanic cone. Each of you will begin harvesting the gold flows, and these will be carried to your plane for transport."

"You cannot get away with this," warned Lea Aster, fists tightening.

"We *are* getting away with it," taunted Galsworth. "For we have the upper hand, as I have already indicated."

"At present," said the calm and steady voice of Doc Savage, "we will do as you say. For Renny and Johnny's sake."

That seemed to settle it.

Galsworth took the second supermachine pistol from his confederate and held both muzzles on the group while Amerikanis went among them, relieving them of their superfirers. He harvested quite a collection when he was done, which included Ham's useless sword cane.

When the two men joined one another, they were bristling with weapons.

Doc Savage carried no weapon in the conventional sense, so they made him remove his outer clothes, including his gadget vest. Sewn into hidden pockets of his coat sleeves were some of the glass anesthetic balls he habitually carried. In closed confines, he could have broken one or more of these, thereby overcoming his opponents. But here in the open air, with a wind blowing capriciously, the bronze man realized he stood little chance of success.

After the pile was complete, Doc Savage stood attired only in the black silk swimming trunks which he wore in lieu of underwear.

Stripped, Doc's great bronze body was an awesome sight. It was easy to see where his Herculean strength came from. There seemed to be no flesh on his body—nothing but cables and cords and bars of tendons like piano-wire steel, with the whole lacquered over in dull bronze.

Sight of the bronze man's graven muscles seemed to send a chill over the two criminals. They all but blanched.

"No wonder you don't pack a gun," Galsworth grunted.

"You are a dangerous one without any weapon, yes," Amerikanis added soberly. He indicated Monk Mayfair, and said, "You appear to have burly arms. You will carry the device."

Monk picked up the transmuter-oscillator and set it on one simian shoulder.

Galsworth pointed the way forward and ordered, "March!" There was immense satisfaction in his *basso profundo* voice.

The prisoners moved as a group. In subdued silence, they trudged along over rude rock.

The way was long, and hard. They skirted a caldera where one side of the cone where a magma chamber had collapsed inward. At times, shifting winds brought sulfurous smoke down from the summit, bringing forth spasms of hacking and coughing.

Even Galsworth and Amerikanis could not escape the noxious stuff.

In time, they worked their way down to the rocky shore, where the still surface of Cook's Inlet mirrored the threatening red sky. It no longer steamed.

LONG tubes of lava had crept into the water of the inlet and cooled. From the outside, they were the color of sooty coal. But when scuffed, shoe tips brought out golden gleams.

"If a fraction of this is virgin gold," proclaimed Hale Harney Galsworth, "we will be very, very wealthy men."

"There is only one problem," Doc Savage pointed out.

"What is that?" asked Galsworth suspiciously.

"There may be too much gold."

"How could there be too much gold?" snapped Amerikanis.

"Just that," replied Doc.

A peevish expression twisted Amerikanis's morbidly skull-eyed face. "You are trying to confuse and confound us."

Galsworth said suddenly, "I have heard that Doc Savage does not lie. Out with it, then."

Doc Savage said, "A little reflection on basic economics might be advisable here. As everyone knows, the price of gold depends almost entirely on its scarcity. The quantity of that element that has so far flowed out of Mount Grozny suggests a great reservoir of gold yet untapped. So much, that if all of it is mined and placed on the world market, it will certainly drive down the prevailing price and further depress the world economy."

"Ridiculous!" Galsworth bellowed.

"He has a point," Amerikanis admitted. "This may only be the beginning of the outflow of underground gold."

"Exactly," said Doc. "The center of the earth is believed to consist of molten matter. No one knows what that magma consists of. What if the greater portion of that is metal? Specifically gold in liquescent form."

The two men blinked like befuddled owls as this information sank in.

"Most of the world's currencies are backed by deposits of gold," continued Doc, "and are valued according to the prevailing price of that metal. Should that price collapse, so too will national currencies, with the net result that the present business depression might continue for a generation, or longer."

The pair exchanged uneasy glances.

At last, Hale Harney Galsworth spoke. "It does not matter. We will harvest what we can. The rest can boil and bubble at the center of the earth for all eternity. And none will be the wiser."

"So much for lectures," seconded Amerikanis.

Doc Savage spoke up. "The work will go more efficiently if Renny and Johnny are allowed to pitch in."

"Not a chance," snarled Amerikanis. "They are our guarantee against revolt."

"Not much of a guarantee," Doc Savage said, "since at this proximity to the volcano, you dare not turn on the Merlin invention without risking your own lives."

Hale Harney Galsworth pondered this assertion for over a minute. "He makes sense," Galsworth said at last.

"That will give us three more prisoners to control," Amerikanis protested. "It's too dangerous, I tell you."

Galsworth considered conditions for a time. He took from a pocket a blue silk handkerchief and used it to swab sweat from his heavy features. Finally, he issued curt orders. "Savage, you bring them down. All three."

Doc Savage proceeded to demonstrate another aspect of his remarkable physical prowess.

Barefoot, he scaled the cone, finding purchase where none seemed possible, working around obstructions. So careful was he that, although there was considerable loose volcanic debris lodged in cracks and nooks, the bronze man managed to dislodge only the smallest stone—none of which contributed to forming a landslide.

"Doesn't he ever make a mistake?" Galsworth ruminated aloud.

"Not often," Ham Brooks remarked.

They were already working to break some of the lava tubes into sections for easy transport. But it proved not to be easy. Gold is very heavy even in modest proportions, and the tubes were of substantial size.

The labor proved arduous. They had only the tools scrounged from Merlin's wrecked laboratory.

Doc Savage came down by a different route than he had ascended, owing to the fact that he had to carry a man slung over his huge shoulder, and needed to tread carefully.

Renny and Johnny came down under their own power, looking as if they had spent a weekend in the outskirts of Hades. Soot plastered their faces. Their eyebrows had been singed off. They peered through heat-pinched eyes.

Doc Savage laid his burden on the ground, not far from where Elvira Merlin had sat silently up until now. Through the operation, she had not contributed, owing to her emotional state. No one had thought it worth the effort to persuade her otherwise.

Her silvery eyes fell upon the soot-smeared face of her husband with its shut eyelids and slack lines. With a horrid shriek, Elvira shot to her feet.

"No! No, John!"

Features twisting, she lunged for the oscillator.

Doc Savage shifted on his bare feet, intercepted her with his powerful arms.

"Do you wish to kill us?" he asked sharply.

Elvira Merlin floundered helplessly in Doc's unyielding grip. "I don't want to live without John. Let me go, you golden-eyed devil!"

She twisted and squirmed in his arms so violently that Doc

Savage was obliged to take action. Seizing her neck in one hand, he applied steady pressure on certain nerve centers.

With a sigh, all animation draining from her frantic limbs, Elvira Merlin collapsed into his cabled arms.

Doc set her down beside the limp form of her husband.

"What did you do to her?" Galsworth asked, licking his thick lips nervously.

Doc Savage did not reply to that. Instead, he addressed Lea Aster.

"When she wakes up, explain to her that her husband is not dead, only unconscious."

"Enough of this!" Amerikanis ordered harshly. "Get back to work!"

DOC SAVAGE picked up an axe and began chipping at a finger of volcanic gold with arms that reminded everyone of the legendary steel driver, John Henry. He was like a machine, tireless, unflinching, seeming to have no need of rest or respite.

This display of animal vitality did little to reassure S. Charles Amerikanis and Hale Harney Galsworth that they had the situation fully under their control.

After an hour or so of hard work, Doc Savage halted his relentless exertion. The sudden cessation of his machine-like activity caused all eyes to fall upon the bronze man, as they do when a powerful engine suddenly ceases to operate.

"What is wrong?" Galsworth demanded.

"Someone will have to bring the amphibian to this place," the bronze man replied in a reasonable tone. "Transporting all this gold on foot would take days."

"I will do it," Galsworth volunteered.

"Wait a minute!" Amerikanis bleated anxiously. "You can't leave me here with eight prisoners."

"Well, you cannot fly a plane, now can you?" returned the prodigious attorney.

"You know I can't," Amerikanis flung back.

The pair looked at one another in confusion. Mutual mistrust plucked at their expressions.

Doc Savage said, "There is only one way to resolve this. I will fetch the plane."

Amerikanis and Galsworth looked equally stricken by that simple suggestion.

"It is the only sensible solution," Ham Brooks pointed out.

"Yeah," added Monk. "Doc won't try any funnybiz because he wouldn't stand for any of us gettin' hurt."

Long Tom offered, "And Doc can reach the plane faster than any of us."

Amerikanis and Galsworth conferred in hushed tones for several moments. At length, the large lawyer directed, "Go ahead. I won't warn you of the consequences of treachery. You already know what they would be."

Doc Savage had been standing ankle deep in water. It had simmered down in the intervening hours. Now the inlet was only as hot as a piping bowl of broth.

Suddenly, he was no longer there. A splash came. But there was no sign of the amazing bronze man.

Eyes scoured the water and after a while they could see a bronze-haired head, barely visible, slicing through the water with the speed of a shark.

Doc Savage was taking the fastest route back to his anchored flying boat. By swimming.

Hale Harney Galsworth had to clear his throat three times before he could get the words out. Then he bellowed, "Back to work! All of you! You know what will happen if he doesn't come back."

But everyone understood that Doc Savage would return.

Chapter XXIX

MEMORIES

DOC SAVAGE SWAM with the supple ease and agility of some fabulous merman of the deep. Some part of the time, he was underwater, holding his breath and seeming to have no need to come up for air. The explanation was simple. As a youth, the bronze man had learned the art of holding one's breath for a considerable period from the masters of the art—the pearl divers of the South Seas.

By some unerring instinct, he found his way to the anchored amphibian.

Doc climbed aboard, paused to let moisture run off his sinewy limbs and sought out Habeas Corpus. The shoat looked hungry, so Doc gave him an apple—which was greedily devoured. Habeas loved apples.

There was a second apple, a small one, and Doc slipped this into the waistband of his swim trunks. From an equipment case, the bronze man brought forth a bottle of some yellowish fluid and lathered it atop the scrawny pig's back.

The shoat seemed to enjoy the libation immensely. He trotted around in happy circles, presenting both flanks to Doc's ministrations.

Doc made no other preparations. He climbed into the control bucket and began warming the three massive engines. They coughed into life, blue smoke gushing forth from the cowl bayonets.

When he had all three running smoothly, Doc pressed a

button, reeling the winch anchor back into its nose compartment.

The huge flying boat began drifting from shore. A freshening wind caught it, making it spin lazily. Doc gunned the engines and began taxiing back to the infernal spot where his friends labored in the shadow of terrible Mount Grozny.

The big plane was not easy to maneuver, but as he approached the correct spot, Doc brought it to a smooth gliding halt. After it wallowed for a while in place, the kedge anchor paid out again and the ship was thus made fast, only yards from land.

Gathering Habeas up in his arms, Doc Savage stepped out. He waded for shore, holding Habeas Corpus high over his head to show that he was unarmed.

When Doc's feet touched the obsidian-like outcroppings, Habeas was deposited on land. He went bounding for his master.

"Habeas!" Monk howled.

The shoat leaped into Monk's hairy arms and they enjoyed a reunion that consisted of the hairy chemist tickling the porker's skinny ribs and taking him by one gigantic ear, swinging him around. The pig enjoyed this roughhouse exercise immensely.

"Habeas, you smell like you need a bath!" Monk complained, dropping the scrawny shoat at last.

"Why did you bring that animal!" demanded Hale Harney Galsworth of Doc Savage when the bronze man was back on shore.

"It was reasonable to assume that you intend to maroon us here, so you can safely fly off with your cargo," replied Doc. "Habeas is a valuable pet."

Galsworth made a harrumph of a sound in his thick throat.

Beside him, S. Charles Amerikanis said thoughtfully, "That pig looks edible."

Which comment brought a fresh howl from Monk Mayfair.

"You so much as take the curl out of that hog's tail and I'll—"

Galsworth directed his rapidfirer at the simian chemist's ample midsection.

"You'll eat a lead lunch without having to open that big gullet of yours," he warned.

Monk subsided. But a fighting gleam lurked in his deep-set eyes.

Doc Savage picked up the scrawny porker and handed him to Ham Brooks.

"Hold Habeas for a moment," he requested.

The formerly elegant barrister accepted the shoat, then evidently thought better of it.

"I am not consorting with that porcine monstrosity!"

Ham promptly handed Habeas over to Long Tom, who tucked the pig under one arm, although he did not look pleased with the responsibility.

"That's enough!" Galsworth reprimanded. "Start lugging that gold on board. Snappy!"

THEY returned to work. By this time, John Merlin had come back to his senses. He looked dazed. Peering about, the disheveled electrochemist noticed his wife, lying unconscious on the ground, and gave a jump.

"Trixie!"

Ham exploded, "That's really her name!"

"Her stage name," Merlin admitted. "She was Trixie Peters when I first met her. She was working as a magician's assistant in those days, for a man who was a clever escape artist."

"Don't that beat all," mumbled Monk.

Long Tom said sourly, "Explains her slippery ways."

"Get moving!" Amerikanis insisted.

They began picking up the gold. It had been reduced to broken fragments, some too heavy for one man, although Doc Savage managed several of these unwieldy chunks. Monk and Renny toted one between them, every visible muscle creaking in complaint during the combined effort.

Setting an example, Doc placed his burdens on his shoulders. Some he balanced on his head. That made it easier to bear the heavy matter. The others followed suit, doing the best they could. Even the two women, Lea Aster and Elvira Merlin, gathered up some of the heat-scorched golden stuff. Mrs. Merlin had been brought back to sensibility by the bronze giant's chiropractic manipulations.

Doc supervised the stacking of the gold throughout the cabin, saying, "If the weight is not distributed evenly, the ship will not get off the water. Worse, it may tumble off a wing and crash, should any cargo shift suddenly."

Neither Galsworth nor Amerikanis appreciated the bronze man's taking charge as if he was not a prisoner.

"Who does he think he is!" Amerikanis snapped.

"The big fellow seems to know what he's doing," said Galsworth, who had a pilot's understanding of how dangerous the takeoff would be.

At last, the final loose portion of hardened molten gold was loaded on board. Galsworth and Amerikanis looked supremely satisfied.

"You will have trouble getting her off," Doc warned. "The ship is dangerously overburdened."

"You let us worry about that!" snarled Amerikanis.

"Yes," drawled Galsworth, waggling his supermachine pistol in warning. "That is our concern, and ours alone."

They began backing to the amphibian, superfirer muzzles trained on the prisoners. When they reached the water, Galsworth instructed, "Please fold your hands atop your heads. All of you."

"Marooning us here is not wise," Doc Savage cautioned.

Galsworth sneered, "By the time you reach some outpost, we'll be in a certain South American country where no one will question our rather lavish holdings."

"Yes, and don't try to find us, either," spat Amerikanis.

Ham Brooks whispered, "They're not going to maroon us."

"Not likely," Long Tom undertoned.

"Yeah," Monk agreed. "That's blood in their greedy eyes. They're goin' to stage a kill party."

"You men will know what to do," Doc said without moving his lips. He did not speak English, but the Mayan tongue, which they all understood.

Amerikanis and Galsworth began wading backwards so as not to lose their ability to cover the prisoners. It was awkward going. The sea floor was rough and littered with unexpected stones. Amerikanis had trouble keeping his feet. But lumbering Hale Harney Galsworth proved as sure-footed as an elephant, and covered the group whenever his partner struggled with his footing. He cradled the gold-exciting apparatus in the crook of one thick arm.

At length, they backed to the open amphibian hatch.

"I'll go in first," Galsworth said, turning to clamber in through the gaping aperture.

Amerikanis waited anxiously, colorless eyes darting this way and that. The rigors of the expedition had plainly worn on his nerves. His gun hand trembled visibly.

"They are going to get away with it," moaned Lea Aster. "Isn't there anything that can be done?"

Doc Savage stood as rigid as a statue of actual bronze. The tensity of his giant body suggested impending action. His eyes were very active, almost weirdly so.

Again he spoke in Mayan, his lips not seeming to move. "Everyone understand what needs to be done?"

Faintly imperceptible nods came.

With a show of nonchalance, Long Tom released Habeas Corpus.

The pig slid from the puny electrical wizard's arms. His unexpected action elicited a nervous response from S. Charles Amerikanis. He swiveled the muzzle of his superfirer in the shoat's direction.

While he was thus diverted, Doc Savage carefully dropped a hand and removed the small apple from his waistband. This, he pegged at the porker. It bounced and began skipping down a lava slope.

Habeas squealed happily. The apple continued rolling and bounding toward the water, the trotting pig in eager pursuit, his ears fanning out like wings.

Amerikanis bleated, "What—" He took square aim at the long-legged shoat, and began to depress the firing lever.

A shot rang out—another!

For once, Doc Savage was caught off-guard. His golden eyes veered toward the source of the gunshots.

There on the ground lay Elvira Merlin, a tiny derringer in her hand, both barrels smoking. No one had seen her pluck it out of her luxurious tangle of hair, where it had been secured by a rubber band.

SEVERAL things happened in rapid succession.

S. Charles Amerikanis dropped his superfirer and collapsed into the water, sunken eyes ghastly with a shocked surprise. The center of his chest was a spreading lake of scarlet.

Habeas Corpus bounded into the same stretch of surf. Instantly, a surge of billowing black exhalation rose up around him. The pig began squealing and thrashing about in consternation. More black smoke arose, uncoiling like a terrible sea serpent coming to life.

Doc, Monk, Ham and Long Tom dived for the water. They plunged in, arms foremost. The moment their hands came in contact with seawater, coal-hued billows began boiling up around them. Faster than it seemed possible, the entire shoreline was enveloped in a smudge of ebony smoke.

It became impossible to pick out targets in the billowing blackness.

The three engines were turning now, and the backwash churned. But not sufficiently to dampen the writhing serpents of smoke that were coming from the chemical preparation smeared on the hands of Doc and his three men. Not to mention Habeas the pig, from whose bristled hide they had acquired the noxious substance.

Jumping in, Lea Aster wrested the derringer out of Elvira Merlin's good hand. The silver-eyed woman made a move to fight back, hands turning to claws.

The snappy blonde secretary showed that she had not forgotten the cruel death trap from which she had been rescued.

Lea became red, then stepped forward suddenly and swung her right hand at the woman's fierce face. Elvira Merlin ducked, but Lea's left hand, sweeping up in expectation of just that, delivered a resounding slap. The raven-haired woman cried out and sat down heavily.

"You can dish it out," Lea told her, spanking imaginary dust off her hands. "But taking it is another matter entirely."

With a cry of outrage, John Merlin attempted to intervene. Long-limbed Johnny tripped him. He fell. Renny sat on his back and held him down.

Doc Savage had not remained idle. He plunged out into the inlet, making for the amphibian hatch. It was still open.

Visible in the cockpit, Hale Harney Galsworth gunned the throttles and the giant amphibian lunged, tearing out a section of nose where the anchor chain was wrenched free. He had not known how to raise it.

No human body, indeed, no living thing—although they do say a tiny fly in Africa can travel in excess of seven hundred miles an hour—can successfully cope with high-speed machinery in contest.

As part of his daily routine of exercises, Doc Savage had spent a stunning number of hours in the water. Naturally, since practice does indeed make perfect, he was good.

His swimming skills proved sufficient to the emergency. The bronze man reached the open hatch just as the vibrating ship charged forward.

Grasping the door frame, Doc pulled himself up, but was hampered by the chemicals smeared on his hands, which were still emitting a blinding exhalation.

Doc stuck his bronze head in. Galsworth wrestled around in the control bucket, trained the superfirer at him. The little pistol sawed long and loudly, muzzle sparking.

Doc was forced to jump back. Firm bronze fingers clung to the hatch edges. He tried entering again, crouched there.

"Galsworth!" Doc rapped out. "Do not turn on the device."

The gun hooted anew. The bullets were mercies. But that did not matter now. Doc was unprotected from the potent shells. He was forced to twist away to evade a pencil-thin parade of pellets. His steel-strong fingers clung as if welded.

The bronze man was shouting above the propeller din. "Do you hear? Your plan is clear, Galsworth. To turn on the device will mean your destruction!"

Hale Harney Galsworth emptied the supermachine pistol and picked up another. Doc evaded the stream of slugs easily. They splattered harmlessly on bulkhead walls.

The thundering plane came up on step. Doc could feel the high wing grabbing air and begin to lift the fuselage. His perch was growing precarious. Soon, they would be airborne.

Having no choice in the matter, Doc flung himself out of the hatch.

He entered the water cleanly, submerged. Before long, his bronze head popped up again.

The huge flying boat lurched into the air, and went hammering away. Turning, Doc struck back to shore, his expression grim.

When he emerged, his hair seemed only slightly wet. Soon, it was dry, its water-repelling qualities coming to the fore.

The others had dragged the battered body of Skelton Charles Amerikanis onto a lava outcropping. The industrialist was coughing erratically. Blood spattered his grimacing lips.

"We're doomed," he hacked.

Doc addressed him. "The plan was to turn the transmuter on full power and blow up the volcano once and for all, wasn't it?"

Amerikanis nodded, pain-curled lips turning crimson. "That way—we'd seal all the rest of the gold inside. Our share—safe—"

"Blazes!" exploded Monk. "Won't all that gold on board blow up too?"

"No," croaked Amerikanis. "It is a super-amalagam—of metals and stone. Like electrum, it may react but not—detonate. We discussed this."

All eyes went to Doc Savage expectantly.

"The odds are in Galsworth's favor that the magma gold is of insufficient purity to become so unstable as to react with violence," said Doc. "Not so any pure veins still lying deep within the volcano. Their explosive potential cannot be reliably measured."

A kind of death rattle sounded in Amerikanis's throat. "I have calculated—that there is still sufficient—gold underground to turn Mount Grozny into a—a modern Vesuvius."

With that, Master Bonesy rolled his hollow orbs up in his head and expired. Eyes closing, his funereal face almost immediately took on the fixed semblance of a skull.

Craning his bullet head about, apish jaw sagging, Monk Mayfair watched as the droning amphibian reached an altitude of about one thousand feet and dipped one wing.

"Uh-oh," he muttered. "Looks like he's comin' around."

Lea Aster had overheard everything. Her face was drawn. "Are-are we—" She could not get out the word.

Monk put a protective arm around her. "No use in runnin'. We wouldn't get far."

Doc Savage went to John Merlin, pulled him back on his feet. "Your device. What range has it?"

Merlin was still dazed. He was staring uncomprehendingly at the spidery ruin that was his spouse's left hand. Doc repeated the question.

At last he spoke, "A few miles." His face was ashen.

Long Tom growled, "Once he spins that rheostat, we're in for a hot time. And I mean literally."

Long Tom's words sounded funny and he realized he was without his front teeth. Reaching into his back pocket, he yanked out the handkerchief, unknotted it, and extracted his two gold incisors.

Resolutely, he thumbed them into his mouth. "Might as well go out with all of my choppers," he said in a resigned tone.

They waited. There was nothing else to do. Doc Savage had herded them into the water until they were all standing at the depth of their clavicles. The smoke-producing chemical had given out by now.

Closing in, the roar of the mighty amphibian became an urgent sound.

"He's linin' up on the crater," Monk warned.

Long Tom announced, "My teeth are startin' to sting."

"Get set to immerse yourselves," Doc said. His eyes were on the aircraft expectantly, the golden flakes in them stirred up to the force of a gale.

"He's almost three miles out now," Ham breathed.

Long Tom reached for his mouth, suddenly realizing something that he had overlooked—that he never did learn whether his electrum teeth were proof against the improved transmuter.

The electrical wizard never got them out in time.

WITHOUT warning, the tail of the amphibian blew apart. The craft had been swinging around in its ominous approach. It lurched, broke in two, and began falling.

"I'll be superamalgamated!" Johnny exclaimed, eyes widening.

"What the heck happened!" Monk exploded.

Doc Savage directed his gaze toward Ham Brooks. "Where did you leave the gold knob of your sword cane?"

"In the tail section," said the dapper lawyer. His voice was thin.

"I did not have time to look for it," Doc Savage explained. "Otherwise this outcome might have been different."

In silence, they watched as the pieces of the aircraft showered down to splash into the open waters of the inlet. When the last of it—a wing—knifed from sight, they began breathing once more.

Ham Brooks wore an expression of great anguish. "It was all—my fault," he said thickly.

"Holy cow," Renny told him. "You saved all our lives."

"Actually," Doc Savage corrected, "Monk did."

Homely Monk blinked. "Huh! Me?"

"If you had not replaced Ham's gold-headed cane with one of brass, this affair might have turned out very differently," explained the bronze giant.

The apish chemist grinned from ear to ear. He turned to Ham Brooks, beaming. "Any time you want that duel, you animated clothesrack, just say the word."

But for once, the dapper lawyer was struck speechless.

Clearly, there would be no duel.

THEY trudged back to dry land to take stock of the situation. Doc Savage approached John and Elvira Merlin. "There are some aspects of this affair that are still unclear," he began.

"You might say," John Merlin began, "this was all Hale Galsworth's fault."

"How so?" asked Ham.

"Unbeknownst to me, Galsworth was Mr. Amerinkanis' attorney," Merlin explained. "Through this work, he learned of my first gold transmutation device, which Mr. Amerikanis sought to patent. Behind his back, Galsworth began writing me letters, advising me upon my rights to the metal transmuter. It was Galsworth's view that the device belonged to me, even though I created it during my employ at Elektro-Alchemical Company. He urged me to take out a patent in my own name, but I refused."

"Rightfully, it was a joint patent," stated Doc.

"Exactly. Galsworth asked for a hefty percentage of the proceeds in return for cutting Electro-Alchemical out of the deal. Knowing that my wife and I were at odds, he approached her, offering to represent Elvira during any divorce proceeding, hoping to acquire an interest in my oscillator by that subterfuge."

"A blatant conflict of interest," snapped an outraged Ham.

"I told you he was no good," Monk put in. "Lawyers! They're a curse upon the world."

John Merlin continued, "So I fired off a note to Galsworth, telling him if he did not cease badgering me, I would report his disloyalty to Mr. Amerikanis. Later, Galsworth discovered that Elvira wanted no part of any divorce. Instead, she desperately sought to locate my whereabouts. Galsworth was stymied. No doubt he then began working on Mr. Amerikanis, hoping to convince him to cut me out of the picture."

Doc nodded. "Only the fact that the device had not yet been perfected, and consequently could not be registered with the patent office, foiled his scheming."

"I wish I had never embarked upon this mad quest," John Merlin concluded. "I have lost my wife, my job—everything I held dear." The expression on his regular, heat-blistered features suggested unalloyed misery.

No one disputed the unhappy scientist's sentiments.

There was some dissension over the disposition of Elvira Merlin, however.

Doc Savage explained to John Merlin the nature of his strange institution in upstate New York, where evildoers were rehabilitated, and his intent to consign the disturbed woman for treatment there.

"Aren't the authorities seeking Elvira for the New York terror bombings?" Merlin wondered.

"It will be explained to them that your wife perished in

Alaska," explained the bronze man. "Given that she will cease to be Elvira Merlin after going through rehabilitation, that story will be factually correct, even if not literally true."

Predictably, Ham the lawyer raised an objection.

"But Doc, she is guilty of capital murder many times over. Is that appropriate, given the magnitude of her crimes?"

"As much as I hate to agree with this overdressed mouthpiece," Monk muttered, "Ham has a point. Will justice be served by lettin' her off the hook?"

Long Tom added, "These two make half sense. Maybe this is one time we hand an enemy over for legal prosecution."

Renny and Johnny looked over to Elvira Merlin, lying supine on the rocky ground. They offered no opinion, but looked troubled of mien.

The bronze man was thoughtful for a time. "Her crimes were motivated by mental illness," Doc said at last. "Would justice be served by electrocuting her? Would the death house cure her? If she is executed, will the dead be restored to life, or the maimed made whole?"

No one thought that would be the case. An abashed silence reigned. No further objections were registered. As always, the wisdom of their bronze chief was difficult to deny.

John Merlin continued worriedly. "Will Elvira know me when she is cured?"

"All memories of her past will be expunged," Doc informed him.

"I bear some responsibility for all this mayhem," the metallurgist admitted slowly. "It was my invention that killed. My neglect of my wife that contributed to her emotional breakdown, caused her to steal my troublesome device. I don't want those memories. I can't bear them."

Doc Savage said, "We can put you through a limited course, and insure that you will again find happiness together as husband and wife, with a fresh start in life."

So that was that.

THEY reached the personal seaplane of the late Hale Harney Galsworth later that day. Doc excavated the engine parts he had buried as a precaution and replaced them. When he fired up the motors, they sang satisfactorily.

It was a tight fit, but they all got aboard. Doc Savage dared not take off with so many excess passengers, but he taxied the craft down the inlet to the spot where Renny's floatplane had been secured. There, some of them transferred over. The two aircraft lumbered into the sky and began the long flight home.

Ham was seated beside Doc Savage in the cockpit. "What about the gold magma that is still bubbling down inside that volcano?"

"Only a natural eruption can release it now," the bronze man imparted. "That might happen in ten years, or a hundred. Mount Grozny lies in a remote location. Only by chance will anyone discover that some of the remaining lava is not hardened rock and iron ore. If they ever do."

"That settles that."

"Not quite," said Doc, suddenly turning uncomfortable.

Monk scratched his head. "What's left? I can't think of nothin' we forgot."

"Pat," said Doc.

"What about her?"

"Knowing my cousin, she will have opened that package entrusted to her by now." Concern touched the lineaments of his metallic countenance.

"But you told her not to," said Ham.

"Exactly," said Doc.

"Let me handle this." Monk got on the cabin radio and dialed around until he located the wavelength the bronze man and his aides habitually used.

"Monk calling Pat. Come in, Pat Savage."

Pat must have been waiting by the radio receiver, because her musical voice came over the air almost immediately. But it was not so musical now.

"*Monk, where is that sneaky cousin of mine?*" she demanded.

"Right here. Want to talk to him?"

"*You bet I do!*"

Doc Savage reluctantly accepted the microphone. "Hello, Pat."

"*Don't you hello me, you bronze-plated prevaricator. I opened that package.*"

"You had strict instructions not to," Doc reminded.

"*Well, I did anyway. And I discovered a human finger. I almost fainted.*"

"I cannot imagine you ever fainting," Doc told her.

"*I will never trust you again,*" flared Pat. "*You tricked me into leaving town!*"

Doc Savage sighed. "That package was in truth evidence in an important criminal matter."

"*So what do I do with it?*"

"Burn it," said Doc. "The case is closed forever."

"*Hah!*" Pat jeered. "*I knew it. It was all a hoax. You probably cut the finger off some poor woman's cadaver just to frighten me.*"

"Pat!" said Doc, shocked.

Carrier hiss filled the cabin for a long time. At length, Pat Savage's voice calmed down to its normal timbre. Curiosity tinged it. "*So what did I miss?*"

"Not very much," offered Doc.

"*I want the truth! Monk!*"

Monk inserted, "We almost got blown sky high by a volcano, and for a while there we were hip deep in more gold that you could ever spend."

"*Gold? I hope you're bringing me a whopping sample.*"

"Sorry, Pat," said Monk. "It got blowed up by accident."

"*In that case,*" gritted Pat Savage, "*you boys owe me an adventure. And I aim to collect it next time.*"

But Pat Savage was destined never to collect on that adventure. Before long, a new menace would seize Doc Savage and his band of adventurers.

Out of the Orient, it would come, a fabulous prize over which men fought and died. *The Infernal Buddha!* Like nothing ever before seen, it would grip the world in a vise of terror unimaginable.

Wearing a visage of incalculable evil, it was destined to tower over all. Nothing less than the future of the planet lay in the balance. For the more *The Infernal Buddha* exerted its vile influence, the mightier it grew.

But none of them suspected that yet. Most of all Pat, who through no fault of her own would miss out on the whole incredible thing.

"You might just get your wish after all," the homely chemist informed her.

"What makes you say that?"

"I just noticed somethin'. Doc almost smiled."

"Somebody snap a picture!" whooped Pat. *"This I must see!"*

About the Author
LESTER DENT

LESTER DENT (1904-1959) has been called the Father of the Modern Superhero, and with good reason. As the co-creator of the immortal Doc Savage, Dent laid the foundation for generations of superheroes to come. Superman owes much of his mythos, as well as his Fortress of Solitude, to the Man of Bronze. Batman borrowed his scientific training and utility belt. The format of the Doc Savage series was a major inspiration for Stan Lee and Jack Kirby's long-running Fantastic Four. The creators of landmark series ranging from *The Man from U.N.C.L.E.* to The Destroyer have acknowledged the Doc Savage influence.

One can trace the roots of heroes as diverse as *The X-Men's* Beast and Buckaroo Banzai back to the pages of *Doc Savage Magazine.* The unemotional scientific reserve and Vulcan nerve pinch that make *Star Trek's* Mr. Spock such a memorable character were borrowed from Doc. And James Bond's world-famous gadgets owe more to the inventive genius of "Kenneth Robeson" than they do to author Ian Fleming.

Of course, the Man of Bronze was not created in a vacuum, but was a combination of great heroes who had come before, both real and imaginary.

A real-life American hero of the Spanish-American War, soldier, diplomat, engineer and author Colonel Richard Henry Savage, served as the initial inspiration.

In developing Doc, Lester Dent once admitted, "I looked at

what people had gone for already, so I took Sherlock Holmes with his deductive ability, Tarzan of the Apes with his towering physique, Craig Kennedy with his scientific knowledge, and Abraham Lincoln with his Christliness. Then I rolled 'em all into one to get—Doc Savage."

As for Dent himself, he grew up in Missouri, Wyoming and Oklahoma, an only child in the final days of the old pioneer West. Pulp magazines were his main source of boyhood entertainment, and it was while working as a telegraph operator in 1928 that he decided to become an adventure pulp writer.

Street & Smith published Lester's first story in 1929. Doc Savage came along in 1933. Over a thirty year career, Dent wrote for magazines ranging from *The Shadow* to *The Saturday Evening Post*, becoming one of the most popular and successful writers of the pulp era. Beyond Doc Savage, Dent's other characters include Genius Jones, the Blond Adder, the Cowled Nemesis, the Crime Spectacularist, Click Rush, the Gadget Man and *Black Mask* detective Oscar Sail, who reads like a prototype for both John D. MacDonald's Travis McGee and *Miami Vice*.

photo ©2011 Will Murray

Sixty years after *Doc Savage* magazine ceased publication and over fifty years after Lester Dent's untimely passing, both continue to entertain audiences in classic reprints and all-new adventures. The greatest pulp hero of the 20th century is alive and well in the 21st!

About the Author
WILL MURRAY

WILL MURRAY (1953-) is the author or co-author of over fifty novels, few of which have appeared under his own byline.

With Warren Murphy and/or Richard Sapir, he contributed some forty exciting entries on the long-running paperback series, The Destroyer, starring Remo Williams and Chiun, the Master of Sinanju. Collaborating posthumously with Lester Dent, Murray has so far produced nine Doc Savage adventures, with several more in various stages of completion. All appeared under the pen name of Kenneth Robeson.

Solitary Will Murray novels include *The Executioner: Red Horse* and *Mars Attacks: War Dogs of the Golden Horde*, which appeared under the anagrammatic byline of Ray W. Murill. *Nick Fury, Agent of S.H.I.E.L.D.: Empyre* is so far the only novel to bear the prolific author's undisguised byline.

Murray's short stories have ranged from the Lovecraftian classic, "The Sothis Radiant," to numerous novelettes starring iconic heroes as diverse as Superman, Batman, Wonder Woman, Spider-Man, Ant-Man, the Hulk, the Green Hornet, The Avenger, Honey West, Sherlock Holmes, the Phantom, Sky Captain, The Night Hawk, and others.

Will Murray fiction can be found in anthologies such as *The UFO Files, Future Crime, 100 Wicked Little Witch Stories, 100 Creepy Little Creature Stories, 100 Vicious Little Vampire Stories, 100 Clever Little Cat Capers, The Mammoth Book of Perfect Crimes and Impossible Mysteries, The Mammoth Book of Roaring Twenties Whodunnits, Horrors! 365 Scary Stories, The Cthulhu Cycle, Disciples of Cthulhu II, Cthulhu's Reign, Dead But Dreaming II, Horror for the Holidays* and *Spicy Zeppelin Stories.*

His non-fiction can be found in Jim Beard's *Gotham City 14 Miles,* S.T. Joshi's *An Epicure in the Terrible, Dissecting Cthulhu: Essays on The Cthulhu Mythos, Dark Forbidden Things, The Best of Blood 'n' Thunder, Bloody Best of Fangoria,* and *Writings in Bronze,* a massive collection of his Doc Savage essays recently released from Altus Press.

The list of scholarly journals, fanzines, booklets and similar periodicals on popular culture to which Murray has contributed are too numerous to list, but they run the gamut from *Alter Ego* to *Xenophile.*

Murray has contributed entries to the encyclopedias *St. James Crime and Mystery Writers, St. James Science Fiction Writers, Contemporary Authors, Cult Magazines: A to Z,* and *The Dictionary of Literary Biography.*

In 1985, Murray adapted *The Thousand-Headed Man* for *The Adventures of Doc Savage* radio program originally airing over National Public Radio. For Marvel Comics, he scripted their adaptation of The Destroyer in several incarnations, wrote several Marvel Masterworks introductions, and, with artist Steve Ditko, created the immortal Squirrel Girl.

For over 25 years, Murray wrote for *Starlog* magazine, for which he interviewed countless celebrities and covered Hollywood films like *Total Recall* and *Watchman* on locations from Vancouver to Prague.

Over the last six years, Murray has served as consulting editor on Sanctum Books' successful series of reprints of Street & Smith's classic pulp superheroes, Doc Savage, The Shadow, The Avenger and The Whisperer.

He also serves as series producer for Radioarchives.com's "Will Murray's Pulp Classics" line of audiobooks. Radioarchives. com is also releasing Murray's original seven Bantam Books Doc Savage novels as audiobooks. *Python Isle, White Eyes* and *The Jade Orge* have already been released.

A prolific producer of scholarly introductions, Murray has penned prefaces for popular pulp presses such as Altus Press, Black Coat Press, Black Dog Books, Off-Trail Publications and others.

In 1979, Will Murray was presented the Lamont Award (named after The Shadow's alias of Lamont Cranston) for his contributions to pulp fiction research. Twenty years later, he earned the Comic Book Marketplace Award for research excellence in that field.

He counts himself lucky to have known Mrs. Lester Dent, Doc Savage editor John L. Nanovic, Lester Dent ghostwriter Ryerson Johnson, and The Shadow's Walter B. Gibson—all of whom were instrumental in helping him become the Kenneth Robeson of his generation.

Forty years after he read his first Doc Savage novel, Will Murray is still fascinated by the Man of Bronze, and is not ashamed to name Lester Dent as his favorite writer.

About the Artist

JOE DeVITO

OVER THE PAST thirty years Joe DeVito has illustrated, sculpted and designed hundreds of book and magazine covers, posters, trading cards, collectibles, toys and just about everything else in a variety of genres. He is especially known for classic depictions in both painting and sculpture of many of Pop Culture's most recognizable icons. These include King Kong, Tarzan, and superheroes such as Superman, Batman, Wonder Woman, Spider-Man, and *MAD* magazine's Alfred E. Neuman (a superhero to some). He sculpted the award trophy for the highly influential art annual *Spectrum*, and his poster painting has become their logo.

Deeply rooted in the fine arts, he has sculpted two monumental statues of the Madonna and Child, one of which is placed in Domus Pacis at the Our Lady of Fatima Shrine, in Portugal. The other resides at the World Apostolate of Fatima Shrine in Washington, New Jersey, where several of his original oil paintings hang in the shrine's gallery. Joe has also restored historic icons, such as the Odessa Madonna, now in Kazan, Russia.

An avid writer, Joe has co-authored (with Brad Strickland) and illustrated two novels. The first is *KONG: King of Skull Island* (DH Press, 2004). The second book, *Merian C. Cooper's KING KONG,* was published by St. Martin's Griffin, in 2005. He has also written many essays and articles including "Do Android Artists Paint in Oils When They Dream?" for *Pixel or*

Paint: The Digital Divide in Illustration Art. He has recently finished the screenplay for his "faction" world of truly epic proportions tentatively titled *The Primordials.*

DeVito's present endeavors include the continuing painting of covers for *The Wild Adventures of Doc Savage* written by Will Murray, participating in the development of *KONG: King of Skull Island* as a movie, the upcoming release of *KONG: King of Skull Island* in Kindle, iBook and cutting edge app formats through his new, jointly owned company, Copyright 1957, LLC, sculpting the official centennial anniversary statue of Tarzan for the Edgar Rice Burroughs Estate, as well as ongoing painting and sculpting of fine art commissions and lecturing.

photo ©2011 Joe DeVito

www.jdevito.com
www.kongskullisland.com

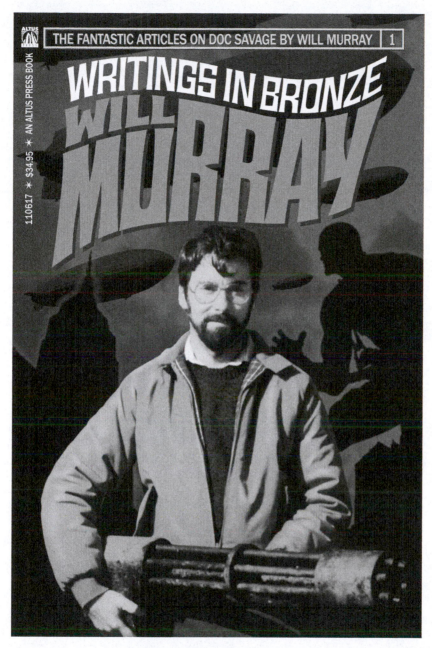

For 40 years, pulp historian Will Murray has been writing about Doc Savage and Lester Dent in the pages of many fanzines. Long out of print and very tough to find, the best of these articles have been updated and collected in this new book. Includes over 450 pages of Doc info, spread across over 50 articles.

Available for order from
www.altuspress.com

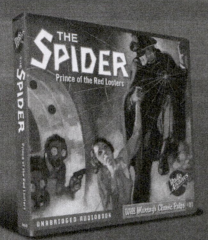